GW00359691

# Travel Page

Every publication from Rippple Books has this special page to document where the book travels, who has it and when.

# The
# Bicycle Teacher

## Campbell Jefferys

Rippple
Books

Copyright © 2005, 2013 Campbell Jefferys
All rights reserved

The right of Campbell Jefferys to be identified as the Author of the Work has been asserted in accordance with the Copyright, Designs and Patents Act 1988.

First published in 2005 by Janus Publishing Company Ltd.
This edition published in 2013 by Rippple Books

Cover design: www.simoneflorell.de
Layout: Susanne Hock

This publication may only be reproduced, stored or transmitted, in any form, or by any means, with prior permission in writing from the publisher or, in accordance with the provisions of the Copyright Act 1956 (amended).

This book is sold subject to the conditions that it shall not, by way of trade or otherwise, be lent, re-sold, hired out, or otherwise circulated without the publisher's prior consent in any form of binding or cover other than that which it is published and without a similar condition including this condition being imposed on the subsequent purchaser.

All the characters in this book, except for real people referred to in historical contexts, are fictional. Any reference to people living or dead is purely coincidental.

Rippple Books
Rippple Media
Postfach 304263
20325 Hamburg
Germany
www.rippplemedia.com

A CIP catalogue record for this book is available from the British Library.

ISBN: 978-3-9814585-8-9

# Wall

I thought it would be straight. But it curves, turning sharply left or right in some places, defying logic. It rises high, solid concrete blocks with round concrete piping on top. The graffiti covering it is a disguise, a camouflage attempting to blend the wall into the city landscape. It is not an act of protest or defiance. If anything, the spray paint acknowledges the long term existence of the wall; just another place to declare undying love, or to announce to the world that you were here on such and such a day. I always wondered what drove people to scribble their names on walls and buildings. To make it their own? Achieve some kind of immortality by leaving a mark on a structure that will outlive them? Or simply to say to the world that they have no respect for the structure they carve their initials on? We have been doing it for thousands of years. There is nothing new about graffiti.

On Niederkirchner Strasse, high up on the wall, out of reach of graffiti artists and future wall hackers, and partly hidden by trees, my name is scribbled in black pen: Michael Smith, 12/6/81.

That was my first visit to West Berlin, the first time I saw the wall. It did not match the image I'd had in my head. For some reason, I'd imagined a head high wall, which people could lean on with one arm and talk to a person on the other side, or get themselves a box or a small ladder and pop over and see someone; like the asbestos fences between the houses in Perth where I grew up. The fence marked only the line where one property stopped and another began, but it was always the case that you could jump over that fence. Games of backyard cricket or football had each of us popping over at some point to retrieve a ball.

In Berlin, the wall was high and marked an unbreachable border. It divided the city, a clean cut right through the heart of what was once the centre of Europe; a city that marched the world into death twice in twenty-five years, and then became the focal point of the Cold War. The wall marked the line between East and West, where one ideology competed with another in a pointless battle of propaganda and innuendo to prove one was evil and the other good, depending on who you chose to believe, on which system you were born into.

But the border was not to be crossed. The divide between East and West Berlin was a constant, solid fortification. And people did not want it breached in fear of another war. This time a more dangerous war, a nuclear war that would have no survivors: no one to pick up the pieces of shattered lives, and no groups of embattled women to band together to salvage bricks like they did after the Second World War. This war would have no winner, and so the wall remained untouched and unquestioned. It made the world secure.

It amazed me the close proximity in which people lived to the wall in West Berlin. It stood almost four metres high, but also protruded another two metres at the bottom because the concrete slabs were L shaped. The border ran at the point the L began, leaving a two metre no man's land in front of the wall. It meant that vandals were crossing the border when they wrote their graffiti. There were special gates which the Grenzpolizei, the East German Border Police known as Grepos, would use to appear magically from the other side. They would detain anyone defacing the wall, and paint whitewash over certain politically damning graffiti. This daily life could be witnessed from hundreds of apartment windows that looked down on the wall and the death strip beyond. The wall ran along the footpath on some streets, metres from office buildings and apartment houses. People walked past it every day, parked their cars against it, could wave from their windows to Grepos sitting in observation towers. Everyone lived with it. In only twenty years, the wall had become part of the West Berlin cityscape; an unquestionable, unremarkable structure people accepted with the daily routine of their lives. Those born after 1960 knew nothing else. For them, the wall was normal. Twenty years after was when I first saw the wall, but it had been accepted and ignored long before I came. I would learn that Berliners are no strangers to changing landscape and ideology. Even the street names have changed according to whatever political persuasion is dominating, to whatever ruler is worshipped.

That first time in West Berlin, I learned more about a country, a history and a people than I ever could have learned in school. To be there, to see modern history, to pass the huts at Checkpoint Charlie, to wait under intense scrutiny in the immigration office, and to get that first glimpse of East Berlin, the city I would one day call my home and put all my hopes and dreams into only to have them left unfulfilled. In East Berlin, some buildings were like skeletons, fenced up with broken windows, and with old red brick signifying another era. There were ghostly underground train stations where the train did not stop, where Grepos stood bored, looking at advertisements from 1961. I witnessed the West Berliners living with division, accustomed to a state of potential emergency: drinking beer in the shadow of a concrete monolith, unable to visit grandma for a spot of tea and a slice of cake on a Sunday afternoon, or lay flowers on the grave of a fallen relative, buried on the wrong side of the wall. These first images portrayed to me a people of amazing resilience; a people who have lived through destruction and war, rape and pillaging, and a final and total division that ran through the very fabric of everyone's lives. Theirs was a unique spirit, a spirit that had survived so much it had an arrogance, that they too would survive this division, and one day Berlin and Germany would become whole again. But no one thought it would happen so soon or in the manner in which it did.

In East Berlin, the wall was grey, dull and uniform, like the outer shell of a concrete bunker. Children didn't kick soccer balls against it like in West Berlin, graffiti wasn't splattered on its monotone whitewash, nor did people seek to lend their name to history by signing it. Jokes were not made at its expense. A very different wall was experienced in East Berlin. They didn't look at the reverse side of the West Berlin wall. Rather, they looked at the back up wall. Beyond it lay a thirty metre stretch of no man's land replete with observation towers, perimeter fence, razed grass, patrol road, guard dogs and numerous Grepos. To attempt to breach the wall meant possible death, and East Berliners learned not to pity those who were caught trying to cross; the risk was clear. They never spoke of the wall, never looked at it, never ventured in its direction. The wall was always patrolled by suspicious Grepos and Vopos, the Volkspolizei, and they demanded your documents and wanted to know what business you had being so close to the wall. The Ossis learned to live with it, but in a contrasting way to the West Berliners. They knew the wall was to keep them in, and it was best not to think about it.

Conversely, the wall for the East Germans was unifying. The physical presence of a divide from the rest of Germany and the western world united them in their own cause. Their sense of community was their greatest strength, the fact that theirs was an inclusive society that had no non-physical walls. People were not divided by wealth, competition or jealousy, by family standing and breeding, by the type of car they drove and where they ate brunch on Sundays. This made it, for me, the perfect society. It was a revelation that people could be so bound to each other, so helpful and, in many ways, completely inter-dependent. They could not exist without each other. The construction of the wall stopped the loss of manpower to the west which had drained the population for fifteen years after the war. A cultural programme open to all gave them a sense of identity, success in economy a reason to believe in the ideology. Everyone could be educated, could work, could see a doctor, and eat three meals a day. Nobody was left out. There was a place for everyone, and something for everyone to do.

On my first day in East Berlin, I completely forgot about the wall. In West Berlin, I felt all the time that the wall was there, lingering, creeping further onto the territory, showing its graffitied face, its consequence, daring you to defy it. The wall was always there in West Berlin. They joked about it, threw things at it, and didn't realise that it was a metaphor for their lives; that capitalism is a world of walls. Society is divided by status and intellect, power and privilege, those who are allowed to come in, and those who must stay out. Most of society is like a giant sports club, with high walls, locked gates and over-scrutinised membership applications, and they create for their members a world within a world where the riffraff are kept out and all of society's derelicts can be forgotten. The capitalist society is not inclusive. It's an endless competition of getting and using, of success and failure, of inner walls and social division; an elbow society where those with nothing to offer are left in the cold and scoffed at by the successful ones who must support them with welfare.

West Berlin interviewed me. Everyone I met, saw and made eye contact with attempted to put me in a box, to place me with others of my ilk, with a barrier to keep me out if I didn't fit their requirements. My education, my hairstyle, my brand of shoes and my smell were all taken into account. What was my profession? Which soccer team did I support? What music did I like? Everything was under scrutiny to discern whether I could belong to the society or not, and from which parts I could be excluded.

East Berlin welcomed me. Nothing was called into question. There, history was left to the propaganda pages of books and not debated or discussed. This influenced how the people dealt with each other. All had an active role in society and had the opportunity to become more than they were. All shared practically the same existence. Help was always at hand, doors always open. People shared what little they had, and helped a family put on a tremendous welcome dinner for me when not all ingredients could be found. And East Berlin was home to the most beautiful girl in the world.

Looking at the wall from east or west didn't offer an immediate sense of how the situation really was. It was most visible from the air. Flying over the city, the divide was clear. It was like a fat snake sleeping in the centre of the city, twisting and turning, curving and bending, from north to south, east to west, rarely straight. Observations towers could be seen at perfectly distanced intervals, and small specks of Grepos walked the patrol road in groups of three. The wasteland between east and west was a wide expanse of nothing, a massive stake driven between the houses and buildings. From the air, you could see both sides of the picture. A stalemate. Posperity and growth taking different courses on both sides. In East Berlin, the time moved slowly, for time was a commodity they had, and growth came with increased production levels and not with individual accomplishment. In West Berlin, time was not to be wasted, for if you dawdled, someone would beat you to the prize you sought for yourself. Time was money, and the capitalists waited for no one.

From the plane, I looked upon West Berlin with scorn, the mirror of my own society, the one I was never included in, never understood, and fought always to leave behind; the society I had no chance in. The people would exclude me until I died, buried in a cheap grave in the poor part of town.

Everyone deserves at least the chance to prove their worth, if not to society but to themselves. Communism gave me that chance.

# Perth

The buildings rise high to the sky, reaching and stretching in a competition of glass, steel and concrete. The sun shimmers on the countless glass windows, casting disconnected rays of light on the gridlocked downtown streets. The river meanders through this scene, bordered by parklands and fields. Boats sail and water skiers jump and splash. The river is wide, and takes its course twenty-five kilometres west to the coast. To sail this stretch is to see a peaceful beauty unknown in such a big city, and to look upon mansion after mansion, each larger and more extravagant than the last, built upon the hills and cliffs that the river carved over thousands of years. Dolphins are known to swim up the river to feed on baitfish. To sit on the river's banks or to cruise the waters is to leave the world behind. The competition, greed, crime, lies and traffic jams can all be forgotten with one look over the wide expanse of blue-brown water; the only sound being the lapping of small waves on the shore, or the consistent rumble of an engine comfortably working downstream.

The river narrows at the coastline, allowing the beaches to dominate. The white sand stretches far to the north, as fine as icing sugar. On hot days it stings the feet, a reminder that even paradise has its occasional drawbacks. The water flows up from the south, from the icy depths of Antarctica, and is clean and cold; deep blue at a distance, but turquoise green in the shallow waters. Sand whiting nibble at your feet when you stand in the shallows, and the occasional dorsal fin pops up not far from shore. The beaches are rarely crowded, and can offer a scene of new bikinis, territorial surfers, families with everything inflatable, or the quieter places where people roast themselves while reading books and newspapers, stubbing out their cigarettes in the sand.

The beach suburbs are the ideal place to live, especially in summer when the hot days are tempered only by the afternoon breezes that come rolling off the ocean. No threat of bushfires here either. But more than that, it's the quality of life. The streets are clean, and the houses stand in dignified rows with well-kept front gardens and double garages. The trees are tall, relics from a forgotten time, before the hand of man cut some of their branches to make way for power lines and street lights. There are swanky cul-de-sacs, private communities with surrounding walls, expensive restaurants and outdoor cafes. Security cars patrol the streets at night to keep those unwanted at bay, but crime is still high, and the residents always complain that something must be done. There are private schools for the children; they wear ties and knee socks, and have the opportunity to become doctors and lawyers. Their lives are already lived for them, and they won't have to struggle. There are golf courses, playing fields, small cinemas, lush parks, and of course, the beach. The suburbs sprawl in an urban paradise from the coast east to downtown. Everyone lives in a house, drives a new car, has a handsome dog, and their children have all the chances in the world.

East of downtown, the divide between rich and poor is clearer. The streets are wide and dirty. There are strip malls here, petrol stations, discount department stores, bowling alleys, factories, depots and warehouses. It's dry, decrepit, run down. The schools are single weatherboard buildings; freezers in winter, saunas in summer. There are narrow streets parents warn you to avoid, and welfare-funded Aboriginal slums. There are rusted gates and asbestos fences. Old cars spew out dark exhaust, with a grizzled father behind the wheel, a mother as faded as the car's paintwork next to him, and the small, scraggly heads of their restless children in the back. There are topless bars, withered sports fields, stray dogs, kids roaming the neighbourhood looking for adventure, and unemployed youths drinking cheap spirits under the shade of skeletal trees. Lost hopes, forgotten dreams, reality, bitterness, the past always better than the future.

People say Cannington marks the border, others claim it's Victoria Park. We lived further east, in Maddington. This was the only world I knew in the sixties and seventies. But once or twice a summer, my parents would pack the car to take us for a day at the beach. We never went to the really nice beaches; we visited the same beaches as other people from the eastern suburbs. We sat next to and played with carbon copies of ourselves: the fathers potbellied and sitting on their eskies; the women scrawny, dried up and beaten; and us kids thin, raucous, and hopeful, young enough to not yet be burdened by reality. To get to the beach we would drive along tree-lined streets, past big houses, some with two storeys, and see the lush green parks and beautiful people. It was another world. How happy they must all have been. But they recognised we were outsiders, and looked down their noses at us. As I grew older, I dreaded the trips to the beach. I did not want to be subjected to ridicule and scorn. I preferred to

7

stay in Maddington, with its familiar pot-holed streets, single brick houses, run-down schools and all the shops with iron security bars for windows. But as a child, I dreamed one day I would move to the coast and make it. Maddington had few with such ambitions. Many had accepted their role in life, that opportunities were limited and it was best to aspire to the things that everyone else aspired to: learn a trade, get married young, enjoy barbecues and drinking, work hard to pay the bills, and bring the next generation into the world to continue the cycle. So many had given up. They had found their place in society, to be the mechanics, the fitters, the plumbers and the factory workers, nothing more. Society needed these people, and the eastern suburbs of Perth brought more of them into the world to don overalls, pick up spanners, and earn $6 an hour.

As a child growing up in the sheltered world of Maddington, I had little concept of rich and poor. All my friends lived much like I did. There were no rich kids at school to remind us our clothes were second-hand, that our shoes had no brands, and our hair was cut by our mothers. It was like living in a bubble.

Dad was a bricklayer. I remember being on sites with him when I was four or five, because mum worked at the local supermarket and someone had to look after me until my older sister came home from school. The hardhat was too big for my head and the other men laughed. I liked that. They had a camaraderie and spirit I enjoyed. They were all big burly men, cut from the same mould as my dad: round barrel chests, hairy shoulders, bushy moustaches, and with the same dirty sweat-stained blue singlets and grey shorts. I would sit in the wheelbarrow, on top of a big pile of bricks, and dad would wheel me around. The days were long and hot, the blue sky never threatened by clouds. I marvelled at the planes that flew overhead, landing and taking off from the nearby airport.

"Where's that one goin, dad?" I would always ask, straining my neck to look up.

"Faraway lands, Mick," he would say, looking up from his work only briefly. "Places where they drive on the other side of the street, speak different languages."

When I was fifteen, dad had a double hernia operation that left him unable to do heavy labour. Mum was forced to go full time at the supermarket when dad's compensation ran out. He could no longer work at the one skill he had and needed to be retrained. But he would not succumb to this, nor would he work at a desk. He took his welfare money, unemployed on the wrong side of forty, drank, and became bitter. His hair fell out and he put on weight. He became a pathetic creature, casting grey shadows on me just as I was starting my own life. We fought a lot; shouts and insults, but never physical. He threatened, but found hitting my mother easier; he knew she would never hit back. Dad envied my youth, vitality and hope. I began to loathe him. He was one of the unemployed masses they complained about on television, the people politicians claimed were milking the country; the paternal rich supporting the criminal, wasteful, lazy poor, who simply took their welfare money and then pissed it all away.

The divide between the haves and have-nots became clearer as I grew older. Venturing into the city taught me everything I needed to know about society. We made trouble with our tight black jeans, AC/DC shirts, and large boisterous groups. People feared us, scoffed at us, talked behind their hands, and wished we'd all go back to our place in the eastern suburbs where we belonged. They would wall us in if they had the chance. It wasn't fair. We hadn't asked where we would be born. Why did they hate us and fear us so much? I wondered if my friends were as sensitive to this as I was. They all seemed to like being feared, that people got out of their way when they walked down the fashionable streets of the city. The power of the group strengthened them; to walk alone was very different.

As I grew older, I crossed the river more and more, just to see the other side and maybe make sense of it all. I learned that I had to dress differently or I would stand out and become the target for scolding stares and private conversations. Every shop window advertised articles of great price and temptation. There were shops here you would never find in Maddington: high price clothes, expensive jewellery, antique books, and big department stores where nothing was on sale and everyone else could afford the prices. They dressed well, looked healthy, ate expensive food, lived in houses sheltered by trees, walked their dogs at sunset in the parks, and locked their doors and windows so people like me wouldn't climb in and steal their televisions.

It was an exclusive world, one designed to keep those from the eastern suburbs out. The rich made the decisions for society, ran the government, controlled the businesses; we cleaned their toilets and tuned their cars. One born in the east had little chance to attend university or become a person of standing or wealth. The best he could do was learn a trade and make some money for the family he was sure to start. This was a society with walls. The working class held the power of number, but didn't have the education and experience to wield it. They would always be subject to the rich.

Dad eventually got work as a taxi driver, only because the unemployment office threatened to cut off his welfare; he had never looked for jobs. He hated it, sitting in the car all day, chauffeuring suits and ties around the city, from offices to meetings to golf courses. Those who could afford a taxi never went near the east. He drove through affluent suburbs and grew more bitter by the day, returning to the flat expanse of Maddington to drink the night away in solemn silence in front of the television. No one reached out to him during the week. On the weekend, he sometimes turned back the clock and became a shred of the man he once was. On Saturday afternoons, we went to local football games. We knew people there and it was comforting to be surrounded by those like us. Dad looked forward to every footy season. As I grew older, it was one of the few things we had in common, but we eventually found a way to fight about that, too.

Narelle married out of our situation. She was a secretary and met a man from England at her office. I never liked him, but soon they were wed and left to live in England. We got long letters from her, detailing life in London, with its winding, medieval streets and fast pace. She talked about Paris and Spain and Venice, all of it just on her doorstep. She liked it there and said we should visit, me especially. By this time I was working as a mechanic. I saved money in the hope I may have enough to travel to London. But I couldn't imagine being whisked away to the other side of the world in a plane. That was something other people did: rich people. Still, I held fast to the dream. It motivated me as I sweated and struggled at the Ford dealership.

I always felt most sorry for mum. She seemed to be a person stuck in the wrong place and the wrong time. I remember as a child how beautiful she was, and in the early days, dad would always say so, romantic within the confines of his own home, away from the boys. Things were good then. Narelle inherited her beauty, but not the distant look of her eyes. Mum always looked like she was somewhere else in her head, as if her mind and her body where listening to different songs. But she was not scatterbrained or stupid. She was the most intelligent person I knew growing up. She read books from authors I couldn't pronounce, and used words I didn't know. Maddington was the one place where mum didn't belong. She looked out of place in the supermarket, a rose standing in a cornfield. I loved her beauty, her spirit, and the fact that while she clearly wanted more from life, she never complained about what she had. She loved my father. Perhaps she knew things about him that I didn't, saw in him qualities I never could; knew a different man from a different time and held fast to that image. When dad was unemployed, I had sometimes wished that she would leave him, take me with her, and we would start a new life. But she would never do that. She helped him into bed when he was drunk, and consoled him when all seemed lost. My father knew he would be nothing without her.

Such strange memories does a person cling to, moving pictures of the past mixed with dream and fantasy. Those images that over the years blend into a confusion of times and places, real and unreal, of wishes left unfulfilled, and hopes forgotten. In the struggle to succeed in life, to work and have a car, and one day a house and family, how much is pushed aside, left by the side of the road on life's journey? Ideas we held fast to our hearts as children when we drifted off to sleep at night; thoughts that came in the darkness of what would add up to a better life. A house on the coast, a new car in the garage, a chance to go to university, not having to wait hours to see a doctor, tree-lined streets, and new things all the time. New products and clothes, technological gadgets and wizardry you only saw advertised on television. These were all the things others had and what we could never have. But you hang onto the dream of having that too, until the cycle of life takes you away into a battle for survival: paying that next electricity bill, fighting hard to save money for a down-payment on a single brick home, and having enough to put the kids through school until they were old enough to fend for themselves.

This was what I was destined for. I would have mum's faraway look for the rest of my life if I chose to succumb to the situation I had been born into. One day, I would be old and bitter, resentful of the bounding youth around me, lashing out with drunken insults at whoever was in my circle.

I used to think that when I was forced into the world, another boy was born at exactly the same time. This boy lived a life completely opposite to mine, that by chance he had got the life that I was meant to have. And yet, I knew this boy didn't appreciate his situation, living out by the beach. He took it for granted and never thought for a second that he could have been me: uneducated, fenced in, chance-less, hungry and poor.

I deserved more. I saved money, took a chance, and left to visit the sister I had once adored.

# London

Nothing is how you expect it to be. As a kid, I'd dreamed that the flying boxes in the sky would be small carriers of paradise, like a cruise liner sailing the clouds. In reality, they are cramped, suffocating prisons where the people are nothing less than cattle. Before landing, the plane veered around to straighten for the runway. On its tilting side, I had my first feeling of panic, as I realised we were very high up; the city lay miles beneath and the smallest error would kill us all. There would be no way to survive. I gripped the armrest, felt nausea spin the airline food, but kept looking out the window, the way a person does when driving past a car crash. Death is gripping.

Narelle's stomach showed the slight bulge of the pregnancy she had failed to mention in her letters. She looked so much like our mother, except that her brown eyes were solid and clear. Her hair had been cut short, but was still bleached blonde. She wore a dark pleated skirt with a wool pullover even though it was June and summer in this part of the world. Apart from her bright face and welcoming smile, she looked nothing like the sister I remembered. She looked old, grey and wrinkled.

She hugged me, crying, and I felt the soft bulge of her stomach, like a pillow stuffed underneath her pullover. Tears streamed down her cheeks, a flood that made me feel uncomfortable. It was good to see her, but I didn't feel that emotional. And there were so many people watching our reunion.

"You're pregnant."

She nodded, biting her lower lip in an old gesture of anxiety. She wiped her tears away with a white tissue.

"Look at you," she said, voice dry from crying. "You're all grown up."

She tousled my hair like when I was a boy, when the six years between us had seemed then like an eternity. But she had to reach up to do it this time.

"You missed the worst parts," I said, smiling. "My face covered in pimples, arms too skinny, chicken legs, voice like a broken speaker."

She laughed, too loudly, as if she'd forgotten how to and now tried too hard to make it work again. "Well, I can't see that now."

"You're lucky," I croaked, mimicking the way my voice had sounded when it had broken.

We took the train to London. I'd never been on a train before. People spoke with strange accents, and I noticed Narelle had a different voice as well, picking up a twang from her adopted home. The train flew past suburbs with thin houses and straggly trees. The sky was overcast and so were the people. Grey hung over them like heavy blankets, pushing their shoulders forward and their heads down. On the train, they buried their faces behind newspapers and books to avoid the faces of others. The men wore suits and ties, had shiny shoes, shaved closely, and looked very depressed. Narelle's face had something of that grey pallor, an unnatural turning down at the corners of the mouth acquired from living a dour life. A smile still made her face come alive, like it always had, but the light was fading.

"How's dad?" she asked tentatively.

Dad hadn't liked her husband from the beginning, and resented the fact the Pommy bastard had taken his baby girl away to the land of the enemy. She also knew about my recent troubles with the old man. I had hit him a few weeks ago, when we had argued about me spending so much money on a flight when I could spend that money on house repairs. That old chestnut of having financed my childhood – food, clothing, shelter, school, the basics – was wheeled out again. We yelled and screamed. He threatened, and I swung; old anger that manifested itself in a hard right that caught him on the side of his jaw. Without saying a word, he picked himself up and crawled off to the pub. We hadn't spoken since.

"Yeah, alright," I said without conviction. It was shameful, but I hoped he wasn't long for the world. The best way to solve our differences was for him to die and take it all to his grave. "He's a taxi driver now, you know." She nodded. "But he don't like it so much."

"He doesn't like it."

"What? Oh, right. No, he doesn't like it. I guess he was born a bricklayer. He wasn't hot about me coming here either. Jealous, I guess."

Yeah, jealousy, that was it. I had the courage to do it and he didn't. The familiar confines of the local pub were safer than flying to the other side of the world, getting drunk easier than trying for a better life.

"And mum?"

"Yeah, getting by. Still slavin' away. The supermarket changed hands. She gets paid a little more."

"That's nice." My sister stared at the floor, looking as if she had other things to say but couldn't find the words. One hand cradled her stomach; it looked bigger sitting down.

"What about Ashley?" I asked. "You said in your letters he was becoming something of a big shot."

Her face didn't brighten as I expected it would. She had adored Ashley when they were in Perth, and I hated it because she no longer gave me the attention I was used to. Ashley monopolised her.

"He's a big shot alright," she mumbled. Her bottom lip quivered. She bit hard on it and looked out the window.

"Everything alright, Narelle?" I asked. She didn't respond, so I let it go.

We had once shared so much. She had told me of boyfriends and experiences, of feelings towards our parents, of how shitty it was growing up in Maddington, how life should have been more than it was. I was too young to realise this beautiful girl had felt so trapped. In a different situation, she might have been a model or a movie star. Instead, she left school at fifteen and became an office girl. Just another secretary. And it was only because she was pretty that she had got that job.

She turned her heavy eyes on me and smiled. Her cheeks dimpled, and I recognised the sister I had grown up with, peered in the steamy bathroom window at.

"I'm glad you're here, Michael," she said, using my full name as always. It always made me feel older than I was. She had never called me Mick like dad did, or Mike as mum did. "It's been too long."

The train started to run underground. With no more scenery to look at, we stared at the floor. I followed my sister out at Russell Square station. We emerged from the underground cavern in the heart of the city. The streets were narrow, the footpaths also. It did not seem possible for two cars to drive without side-swiping each other, the same with people on the sidewalks. A light drizzle was falling. Everyone had an umbrella. They jostled and hurried along the crowded footpaths, all with an arrogance of purpose, most hurrying simply for the sake of hurrying. Narelle walked smartly, turning around to see if I was still behind her. I couldn't keep up, bag or no bag. It seemed everyone was running. Cars flew past, taxis roared, and the air was thick with the smell of exhaust. People ducked between speeding cars to cross the road as if dodging bullets, but with a sense of tired routine. The buildings were low and old, with balconies and decorated facades of stone and metal. Everything seemed so old, as if the buildings and streets had yet to catch up with the modern world. Each corner housed a small bar, with names like The Stone Turkey and The Blacksmith's Brew, and seemed like medieval ale houses and not corner locals. They had thick wooden doors and beer signs I didn't recognise. Through the window I could see men leaning stoutly on the bar, throwing back beer with the professional detachment of morning drinkers.

People knocked me, shoved me, brushed my shoulders, hit my bag and kept on walking, not breaking stride, no apologies. Nobody gave way. People walked with their elbows out from their body, giving them a little bit more personal space and the opportunity to shove someone who got in their way.

I was glad when Narelle led us off this main street. The car fumes made me nauseous. She waited for me to catch up and we walked side by side down the cobblestone street at a more leisurely pace.

"Shit," I said. "What a scene. I thought London would be slow and boring. You know, horses and carts, and tally-ho, and all that."

"I hate that street, but there is no other way to go. The best you can do is stick your head down and plough through like everybody else."

I laughed, but my sister didn't. There was resentment in her voice. Things hadn't gone as she had thought they would. Her letters had sometimes hinted at an underlying frustration, and she wasn't so good at crossing things out; you could still see what she had written, negative things. We walked in silence, turning down another side street called Short Green. I laughed at the street name.

"All the streets are like that," my sister explained. "Everyone'd be lost without one of these." She produced a book from her handbag. *London A-Z*. "Don't worry. We've got a spare you can use. It's a bit old but so are the streets. And I have to work tomorrow, so I can't take you around."

The door to her building was almost three metres high. It lent to visions of an enormous hall beyond, built of large stone blocks with candles for lighting, swords and shields on the walls, roasted pigs with apples in their mouths, and goblets overflowing with wine. But inside, the staircase was old and decaying. The stairs creaked and groaned as we climbed the floors. The banister swung loosely and was no good for helping you up. Narelle unlocked the two locks of a thick door, and led me into her apartment.

Was Ashley such a failure that this apartment was the best he could afford? But they both worked. Perhaps they were saving money to buy a house. The door opened into a small hallway with five doors. The ceiling was low and the hall felt cramped; too many doors and too much stuff. A mirror hung on the wall between two of the doors and had you staring at yourself as you entered. It revealed to me a face of dumbfounded shock that was my own. I couldn't show this face to my sister.

"It's not much," she said, as if she'd prepared this justification long before or said it often, "but it's not so easy to find apartments in the centre of London. The rents are incredible. And some have only coal for heating." She laughed a little, as if this life were not a serious one, that time was only being marked until the real life could begin, whatever that was.

Two of the doors were closed. I guessed one to be a bedroom and the other looked like a bathroom. On that door was a picture of a soccer player in action. He had long curly hair, thin arms, practically no chest, and looked like he would fall over in a strong wind. A hero of Ashley's perhaps. They looked similar. Perhaps white chicken legs were a national trait.

I could see through another door into what was the living room. A low sofa was pointed in the direction of the television set I couldn't see but knew was there. The last door led to the kitchen. It was the size of a toilet.

"You can sleep in here," Narelle said, leading me into the room next to the bathroom. It was very small. A mattress stood upright against the wall. A low bookcase was tilted against the wall and was full of sporting books and magazines. A small desk had a covered typewriter on it, and on the wall hung a red jersey with unidentifiable black signatures all over it.

"We've got some extra blankets," she added, pulling the mattress down and flopping it on the floor. "It gets pretty cold at night. There's no heater in this room."

"That's okay. I've got my sleeping bag as well."

I put my bag against the wall and we lapsed into silence, unsure what to say to each other. Mum had told me once that if you couldn't compliment someone honestly, it was better to say nothing. The

17

apartment was awful. The white walls had faded and were stained to a putrid yellow. There was a lingering smell of dank cigarette smoke, which was terrible because I'd promised myself to use this trip to give up smoking. The grey carpet was worn and thin, with the odd burn mark and life-long stain. Everything felt old and used, and this dog box was hard to come by, one people had to fight for. No wonder Narelle was grey and frustrated.

"Some tea?" she asked from the doorway, her back turned to me, seeming to want to be out of the room. It was very much a man's room.

"Sure. But maybe I could take a shower first," I said, uncomfortable with having to ask my sister for a shower. "I need to wash away the flight."

She smiled, opened the door to the bathroom, and turned the water on.

"You need to let it run for a bit to get hot," she explained. "Need a towel?"

"Nah, thanks. I got one."

"I would think with a bag that big you might have three towels," she said, smiling that cheeky smile I remembered.

The tepid water met my fatigue with a rush, and suddenly I only wanted to sleep. The excitement of seeing Narelle and being in London couldn't sustain me. Out of the shower, Narelle gave me sheets and blankets and I laid down on the pillow with wet hair.

A vivid dream had me back on the plane. The language spoken around me was familiar but foreign. I couldn't understand anyone. I asked the stewardess where we were going but she shook her head, unable to speak English. But I felt relaxed and comfortable. I didn't know my destination but was somewhat content to go there. My sister was waiting at the airport. I could see her from a distance, but she had long blonde hair, naturally blonde, and wore pants, and turned out not to be my sister at all, but a pretty, smiling young girl who hugged me and kissed me and cried. Her face was out of focus and I couldn't make it clear to identify who this stranger was. Short words and sentences came out of her mouth in English, but with an accent. She had long hair that tumbled all about her and a tremendous figure, with large round breasts and wide shoulders. She stood upright with purpose, confidence and strength. I knew her, but I couldn't place from where. She picked up one of my bags, took my hand and led me out into bright, warm sunlight.

I woke with the feeling someone was squeezing my hand. Narelle sat on the floor next to the mattress smiling. I came out of sleep slowly, with a kind of fatigue I had never experienced before.

"What were you dreamin' about?" she asked. "You had the biggest grin on your face."

"Oh, you know, girls and cars, what all men dream about."

"That must've been some car." She got to her feet, dragging me up by the hand. "Come on. You've got to get up now or you won't sleep later."

"But it's so comfortable," I whined.

"You haven't changed at all," she said smiling, letting my hand go so I flopped back down on the bed with a thud. "Come and have some tea."

"Yes, mum."

We sat on the low sofa staring at the blank television screen. This room was different to the others. It was bigger with large windows that let in the grey afternoon light. It was a pleasant room, and the sofa, though old, was comfortable. Posters adorned the walls, pictures of aliens and spaceships, and rock bands I knew only by name. Behind the sofa was a small dining table with two chairs. Everything felt cheap and used, but there was comfort in old things.

"Feel up to having a walk around?" Narelle asked. "We could wander down to Covent Garden and see some of the sights."

"Sounds good." I paused. "But I think you should tell me a little more about what's going on. What's with the baby? And work? And life here? And why do you look so miserable?"

My sister stared at me. Her eyes were clear and sad.

"Come on," she said, getting up. "We can talk on the way. Have you got a raincoat? It always rains here."

The three-metre high door closed by itself behind us. Narelle popped open her small umbrella and I pulled the hood of my raincoat over my head. It was only drizzle, slightly stronger than in the morning, but it was very wet, and it quickly found its way through my coat, down my neck, and into my shoes. The sky was the colour of cold dishwashing water. Narelle seemed unfazed by the weather, but every now and then she shook the water from her umbrella vigorously, taking no care not to spray it on passers-by.

We walked down crowded streets to the Covent Garden district, peered in shop windows and took refuge under awnings and roofs when the drizzle worked itself into rain. The streets were narrow, and twisted and turned in a maze that confused me. I lost all sense of direction, but enjoyed the walk nonetheless. I kept thinking how far removed I was from Maddington, how far away that world was, and how long ago it seemed. The struggles of the people there meant absolutely nothing to the people here. They had their own problems to deal with. But there was something impersonal about London. They walked with their heads down, immersed in their own worlds, shrouded by their own cares. The sky hung heavy on their shoulders like a burden. At least the poor folks of Maddington had a sense of community. They didn't have much, but shared what they had. The people in London were just like the people living in the west of Perth; concerned only with their own successes and tribulations. The neighbour could push his own car if it ran out of petrol. Nobody gave way on the streets of Covent Garden. People would literally run into each other because they didn't have the decency to display even the most limited of manners.

I quickly learned that in London everything is for sale, at prices I could never afford. The Australian money seemed worthless against the pound. Even buying a drink was a financial decision.

"Thirsty?" my sister asked. Her maternal nature would never cease. She acted sometimes like my aunt or godmother.

I looked at the drink prices at the corner store we were standing in front of. I converted roughly and lost my thirst.

"Come on," she said. "I'm buying."

Reluctantly, I asked for a coke. It tasted like an ordinary coke. The price did not make it better or worse. The product was the same.

"Why is everything so expensive?" I asked, as we continued our meandering down the wet cobblestone streets.

"I tell you, it took me ages to get used to it," she said, as if she still wasn't really used to it. "But it's relative. People make more. But to come here as a tourist breaks the bank."

"So, do you make a lot of money where you work?"

"Polite people normally don't ask such questions," she said, mimicking an English accent. "It's not Brrrrritish."

I laughed. She hadn't changed as much as I had first thought. Perhaps my arrival had taken her back to things she had forgotten.

"Like I said," she continued, "it's relative. But the problem isn't the prices, it's the quality. I mean, take the apartment. We pay a fortune for that place. Dad was only a brickie, but at least we lived in a big house."

"I guess we didn't really appreciate it so much."

"Well, I do, now."

"Do you miss it?"

She laughed. "Maddington? No way. But I miss the life. I was somebody there. Here, I'm no one. You're no one. Ashley's no one. Nobody cares about anyone else. At least in Maddington the people cared a bit about each other."

"But you only ever wanted to get out. Are you saying you want to go back?"

"I don't know." A red double-decker bus roaring past made her stop. "It's just that....I mean, look at this. It's raining in summer. Can you imagine what the winter's like?"

"Shit."

"Exactly. So dark and miserable."

"But what about Ashley and being in Europe. You wrote that there's so much to do here. France, Spain, Italy."

"All Ashley cares about is his bloody football. So we don't go to Paris for the weekend like he said we would, because every weekend there's fifty football games. We went to Spain last summer, but it was a package holiday so we sat on the beach with thousands of other Poms."

Poor Narelle. It sounded like all she wanted was to leave all this ugliness behind. But wasn't returning to Maddington taking a huge step back? And she was now pregnant. She couldn't simply walk away from everything.

"Is Ashley no good to you?"

"No, he's fine." She paused. "It's just…things haven't really turned out the way I expected. Take my advice, don't expect too much from things in life, that way you won't be so let down."

We walked in silence back to Short Green. Something told me that as homesick as Narelle was, she was planning to stay right here in London, have the baby, and continue with Ashley. It was depressing to see my sister, who once dreamed of so much more, resigned to a fate.

***

I first met Ashley Pritchard when Narelle invited him to a barbecue at our house. He wore khaki shorts and a red soccer jersey, but what I remember most vividly were the skinny white legs that stuck out of the bottom of his shorts. They were also covered with long, black hairs. No sport, no sun. His accent also made an impression on me. It made him sound superior, more educated and intelligent. Dad and I stood by the barbecue, two combatants banded together by a loathing of a common enemy. It was bad timing for Ashley because the Australia and England cricket teams were fighting it out that summer for the Ashes. Dad loved his cricket and hated it when the English won. But Ashley seemed nice enough if not for his pompous accent. As we got to know him further, it was clear he wasn't rich, nor was he that intelligent. He wasn't so different to us, and this helped him enter the realm of our family. He also lived in Victoria Park, meaning he wasn't so far removed from our suburb and culture.

As mum said, "He was nice."

Nothing spectacular, just nice, good for Narelle. He'd look after her, mum said, but in the end, took her away.

The door closed with a slam.

"Is 'e 'ere?" he called out from the hall, before bursting into the living room. He wore a long beige coat that was dark at the shoulders and in splotches down the front from the rain. He shrugged it off to reveal a blue suit. He looked classy and professional, but had a bulging belly that rivalled his wife's. His round, pudgy white face was covered in dark stubble, and his cheeks were pink from the walk. He really was no athlete.

I stood to take his hand.

"How was ya flight?" he asked smiling, full of humour and joviality. He draped his jacket over one of the dining chairs and loosened his tie. "It's a killa, innit?"

I didn't remember his accent being so strong. It took me a few seconds to decipher what he had said.

"Yeah, bloody long. I felt like a cow in a road train."

He laughed, too loudly, and with too much shaking of his head and shoulders, as if he wanted to show to the world what a jolly fellow he was and what a great laugh life was. Captain Hilarity.

"Ya want a beer?"

"Sure."

"Naz?"

My sister shook her head. She seemed a little embarrassed by Ashley's manner and behaviour. He filled the living room, making it feel cramped and claustrophobic. When he left for the kitchen, the room felt strangely empty and peaceful, but he was soon back, and squeezed himself into the sofa between me and Narelle.

"Cheers," he said, clinking my can. "Welcome to merry old England."

He sighed with satisfaction after a long, loud mouthful.

"Hard day?" asked Narelle.

"Bloody Jones 'ad 'is end up all day," Ashley said loudly. "Gave us all the shits. The work'll get done if he gives us a chance. We're not machines."

"Where do you work?" I asked.

Ashley gave Narelle a quick glance and a frown as if to say that this information should surely be common knowledge in our family. It had slipped my mind.

"The Marks and Sparks o'er near the Circus," he said proudly. I had no idea what he was talking about, but nodded as if I did. I didn't want this Brit to think I was stupid.

"Narelle took me around Covent Garden this afternoon," I said, trying to sound like I knew London already. "It was pretty nice."

"Lovely part a London," Ashley said, again with pride, as if the suburb were his own. "Lots of ripping bars that we should make a point a visiting. But maybe not till the weekend."

"Alright." I only hoped Narelle would come too. I didn't want to be alone with Ashley, nor did I want to meet any of his friends: more white legs with black hairs, pink, jowly faces, canned laughter and unintelligible accents.

"How about some tea, love," he said to Narelle. "Something warm and 'earty."

Narelle lifted herself from the low sofa and went into the kitchen. Ashley didn't move, and stayed wedged against me as if Narelle was still sitting next to him. I pushed harder against the arm of the sofa for some more room, but our shoulders still rubbed. I could feel his hip. It felt unnecessarily pointy.

"Christ, you've grown," he said emphatically. "I remember you as a scrawny kid trying to look cool with a fag in 'is mouth." He laughed and his whole body snickered along with it.

I was starting to hate him all over again, but for different reasons. I wanted to say that I remembered him for his hairy white legs, but thought it best to be polite. I noticed a shade of white creeping out from under the hem of his trousers, a few black hairs flattened by the sock.

"I've given up the smokes," I said quietly.

"Good on ya. I wish I could, but it gives me a reason to pop outta

23

the office every hour for a quick one. Ha-ha." He gave me an elbow in the ribs, but he sat too close and didn't have the berth to get a wind up so the elbow felt like nothing. But I could feel its point, more than normal like the hip. "Of course, Naz 'ad to stop causa the baby." As if reminded, he produced a packet from his shirt pocket and lit up. The windows were open, but the smoke lingered around his head.

"Congratulations," I offered meekly. For some reason, Ashley made me feel shy and inferior. I wondered if he made everyone feel this way, and if they hated him for it just like I did. He dominated, took all the attention, filled all the available space. But it wasn't his charisma or presence; he was just annoying.

"Tah. Yep, he's gonna be a right football star, that lad. I'll get 'im going early." He spoke loudly and Narelle was sure to hear from the kitchen. She had said nothing to me about the baby. Who knew what was going on in her head?

We ate dinner with the television on. A show reviewed the weekend's soccer matches. Ashley made comments contrary to that of the experts and drank more beer. Narelle sat next to him, plied him with drink, and said nothing, but Ashley talked to her the whole time. Narelle tried to talk to me, about home and friends and family, but Ashley told us to be quiet. Bored, and feeling more and more like an intruder, I explained I was tired from the flight and excused myself.

In my room, I lay in half light. It was just after nine, but still daylight outside. With the door closed, I could still hear Ashley, scoffing and boisterous, words for anyone in earshot. His voice was like an engine long out of tune, and it sent me to sleep grinding my teeth.

\*\*\*

I woke late with heavy eyes and a dry mouth, as if I'd spent the night cleaning out old ashtrays with my tongue. For a minute, I lay on my back trying to remember where I was: mattress on the floor, smoke-stained walls, sky the colour of dust, soccer jersey on the wall, Ashley, London. I left the warm cocoon of my sleeping bag and staggered into the shower. I stood naked for five minutes while the water turned from cold to lukewarm. All around the bathroom, a light brown grime stood out against the white fixture of taps, tiles and drains. Even the water was old and used. I washed myself with the brown water and felt no cleaner or refreshed than before.

24

A key lay on the kitchen counter on top of a note.

"Front door and the door downstairs. Back around six. The map is on the bookshelf somewhere. Help yourself to everything. Have a great day. Love N."

I found the map, located Short Green, and over tea and toast, plotted a course that would take me to the main sights I'd read about back in Perth. The museums didn't interest me, but I wanted to see Buckingham Palace and Big Ben, and just walk around. The city didn't look so big on the map.

As I ventured around London, I began to realise the city defied all logic. Streets went around in circles, one straight road had several different names, narrow lanes led to unmarked dead ends, and you could walk for hours thinking you were going north only to discover you were heading south. And it was ugly. Apart from the famous buildings which received the most attention and care, the city was decrepit, run down and crowded. Endless cars and buses spewed exhaust into an already thick haze. I couldn't walk down Oxford Street without gasping, and was forced to seek refuge in a nearby park. No trees lined the streets. It was a jungle of concrete and stone, and I thought the whole of England would be the same. No wonder they had jumped on ships and ventured overseas to find better lands.

The week passed like that. I saw Ashley and Narelle in the evenings, and that was too much of one and not enough of the other. I spent the days walking around different parts of London, leaving the apartment hopeful I would stumble onto something great, but always coming back disappointed and depressed. There was so much greed and competition. People jostled in lines at the supermarket, shoved each other to be the first on the bus, and gave way to no granny or mother and child. And everyone seemed so rich and important, even Ashley with his blue suits and loud voice. I was dreading the weekend. I did not want to go to bars with him. He'd even talked about taking me to a soccer match. Could I really handle three more weeks of this? It was not turning out as I had thought it would.

***

I was standing in a bookshop, out of the rain, killing time reading magazines that I couldn't afford to buy. In the process of returning one and retrieving another, the *London A-Z* fell out of my raincoat pocket.

"Hey," a voice said behind me, "you don't want to lose this."

I turned to see a short, young guy with a blue cap on his head that said Yankees. He had a stubby nose, pale eyes and the beginnings of a beard that grew only in patches. He smiled as he handed me my book.

"You an AC/DC fan?" he asked, peering at the magazine I had picked off the rack. He had an accent like the people from American television shows.

"I can't believe that they're popular here," I said. "No bands from Australia make it overseas."

"Man, they're huge in the States," he said emphatically. "You ever see them live?"

"Couldn't sleep for three days after," I laughed, remembering one of the greatest nights of my life.

The American laughed as well, and stuck out his hand. "Jason."

"Michael."

"Nice to meet you, man. Where're you from?"

"Australia," I said, but I left off the Aus, so it sounded like Stralia.

"Man, I can't wait to get down there. Maybe next summer." He paused while I put the magazine back on the shelf. "What you doing here in London?"

"Visiting my sister. You?"

"Just bumming around," he said loudly. "I only got here two days ago. I don't like London so much. I'm going tomorrow to West Germany."

He made it sound like this faraway land was just around the corner. He talked with so much experience and confidence, it empowered me to do the same, or at least to copy him.

"Yeah, I don't like London either."

"You want to grab a beer or something?"

"Sure."

I followed Jason into a bar he knew. The Hare and Rabbit. The beer seemed cheap. I forgot about converting the prices and drank away, trying to be as relaxed as he was. By our third Guinness, we had agreed to take the ferry together.

# Hamburg

The North Sea was wind-swept and choppy. The ferry rode the undulations well, balanced by the weight of cars and buses on the lower decks. I wasn't seasick, but Jason was. He laughed as he vomited over the railing, as if this was just another travelling experience. The sea below was light brown and looked like a river after an enormous mudslide had washed into it. It was dirty and uninviting. Even the Swan River in Perth was cleaner than this.

The ship hugged the coastline. Houses and villages dotted the coast. But it was not like the west coast of Australia. The sea met the land here with no display of might or force. The beaches were flat, peppered only by the occasional cliff. No giant rocks sprang out of the ground to meet oncoming waves in a union of splash and spray. It was all very peaceful and timid. In the distance I could see the masts of small sailing ships swaying with the ebb and flow of the tide.

"Man," Jason wheezed, lifting his pale face from the railing and swaying a little, "I'm never having an English breakfast again as long as I live."

"So, you're not a sailor's son."

"I'm not even the son of a sailor's accountant." He let out a crazy laugh, turned pale, and heaved himself back over the railing.

It was warm enough to stay on the railing, and Jason seemed to prefer the fresh air and privacy. But the wind was biting and sometimes swirled around and blew from the east and met us with a slap in the face. So much for summer.

The ship veered right and we headed inland up a wide channel. It narrowed quickly until it was clear we had left the sea behind and were on a river. The tops of buildings from small villages appeared beyond the shoreline, each with an old church spire dominating. Enormous cargo ships came from the other direction; piled high with coloured containers sporting names like Maersk and Sealines. Jason recovered as the ferry evened out on the flat waters of the River Elbe. As we drew nearer to Hamburg, the wide expanse of the harbour came into view. The right side of the river was given over to loading docks, each with two or three cranes reaching high above the docks they sat on. Other passengers joined us on the railing to take in the scene.

Boats sounded, smaller ferries puttered around, and plucky tug boats worked diligently and patiently to move the big liners into position. The cranes were like dinosaur skeletons up close, the people sitting inside them as small as ants. We passed the headland and the skyline came into view. But there were no skyscrapers or tall buildings; church spires and domes were the sole owners of the sky here. It gave the city an air of peace and tranquillity, as if it were only an expanded version of the villages we had seen earlier. Quiet, rural and provincial.

We docked at Landungsbrücken, Jason resisting the temptation to kiss the dirty, bird-shit covered pier. His short, squat legs looked unsure on land, as if they'd only just got used to being on the boat.

"Come on," he said with confidence, pushing his way through the crowd. Everyone was eager to be off the boat: some unsteady on land, others rushing into the arms of friends and relatives, and a few not knowing which direction to take and so standing in everyone's way. "Follow me."

He led me up a steep hill. As we rose higher, I kept stopping to take in the view of the harbour stretched out below and to catch my breath. Jason waited at the top, looking over the harbour like a king surveying his domain.

"Best hostel in Europe," he exclaimed proudly. "What a view."

I dropped my bag and stood next to him, my breath loud and heavy. From the top of the hill we could see west down the river we had come. The sun was slowly heading towards the horizon in a haze of orange and pink. The days were so long here. Towards the centre, the harbour was a maze of canals and docks, with a large brick structure beyond.

"That's the Speicherstadt," Jason said, following my gaze. "It was once a customs free zone. We'll take a look there tomorrow. The buildings are really cool and the smell of coffee is overwhelming."

I was glad Jason was with me. I would never have done this trip alone. And boy was it good to be out of London. Narelle hadn't liked it when I'd said I was leaving for a few weeks, but seemed to understand. It was clear to her I didn't like Ashley. She felt ashamed. Reality can be more striking when reflected through the eyes of an outsider.

We checked into the hostel and found our beds, in separate rooms. Each room had two bunk beds. In my room, three beds were taken, but the occupants were elsewhere. It hit me then that I was in West Germany. I had just paid in German Marks, and now found myself grappling with foreign bed sheets that had a different system to the ones back home; the pillow case closed with buttons.

Jason stuck his head through the open door. "Not bad, eh? Come on, I'm starving. I'll take you to where the action is."

It was late in the evening, but daylight remained and made you lose all sense of time. We walked down a wide street, past a large brewery, which was fittingly one of the first German buildings I saw up close.

"That's the cheap beer," Jason informed me. "But even that's better than anything in the States."

Past the brewery, the neighbourhood was dirty and run down. Beer cans littered the streets and the footpath was covered with broken glass and cigarette butts. We turned right onto David Strasse, passing a corner bar with two scantily clad girls standing in the doorway. They were tall with long legs and broad shoulders and could well have been men. Their faces were heavily painted with striking colours that didn't fail to hide the dark rings under their eyes. One said something in German. Jason shook his head and then gave me a wink.

"Even the hookers are beautiful," he said smiling. "What a country."

We continued along the ugly street. Girls wearing almost nothing walked the footpaths. Large men lurked in the shadows, immersed in the smoke from their cigars. Rag wearing people with dirty faces huddled in the doorways of decaying buildings and whispered for small change, and it was hard not to stare at them as we passed. Jason looked straight ahead; I copied him. Nothing was clean, and it was a stark contrast to where we had started outside the hostel, where there wasn't a speck of paper in sight.

Jason pointed in the direction of a sealed street. "That's Herbert Strasse," he said. "The hookers sit in shop windows. Only men can walk down there."

I gave it a quick glance. The front looked like a construction site. A man walked on the opposite side of the street, glanced quickly up to see if anyone was watching him, then crossed the street and ducked between the barriers. At the same time, two burly men emerged, talking loudly with beer cans in their hands.

On the next corner was a large building with Polizei written in green and white lights. It was vaguely reassuring that there was a police presence in this dangerous neighbourhood.

The street sign said Reeperbahn. I remembered this street and its reputation from a Beatles biography I'd once read. I stopped at the corner and looked down the street. The word sex was lit in neon, hanging from almost every building, accompanied by words like Live and Show and Kino. In front of each sex theatre stood a man, sometimes two, handing out cards and talking to the large groups of men that passed, trying to entice them inside with promises of beautiful girls and raunchy dances. Snack shops and bars were crowded between these theatres and advertised things like Bratwurst, Currywurst, Pommes Frites and Holsten. Cars cruised past with the windows down and stereos thumping. The street throbbed with a heartbeat of decadence and filth.

Jason started to walk away. He turned and shouted, "Come on. There's nothing to be scared of." He laughed a little at me and I didn't like him for it. I took off after him, walked with confidence, determined not to let this foreign country intimidate me.

We stopped outside a shop that advertised Döner, and ordered from a window open to the street. Jason ordered two and paid for both.

"You can buy me a beer later," he said, handing me what looked like some kind of sandwich. The bread was shaped like a triangle and was filled with meat, tomatoes, onions, lettuce, and red cabbage.

"Alright."

"Not bad, eh?" Jason said, white sauce at the corners of his mouth.

We ate and walked. When finished, we were cornered by two large guys and bullied into a strip joint. We protested quietly, but the men didn't understand English, and forced us inside. It was dark and practically empty. We turned to go back outside, but the two men stood in front of the door, gesturing for us to sit down. Jason, looking timid, led us to a table in front of a T-shaped stage. There was no cover charge, but the drink prices were outrageous.

"Let's have a beer," Jason stuttered.

A naked waitress took our orders. She had small limp breasts and was very thin. Her arms were skin and bone, dirty around the elbows with bruises and markings. Two beers in long, thin glasses landed on our table. Almost immediately, music started and a young girl, who could not have been more than sixteen, came out and gyrated all over the stage. She looked lost and uncomfortable, and her body held the purity of youth that made her look completely out of place against the backdrop of deep red curtains and flashing lights. Two more beers appeared on our table while she was dancing. I glanced at Jason who looked steadfastly at the girl. The look on his face was not of pleasure, but a grimace. We drank in silence and then another girl came out, younger and more out of place and awkward than the last. During her dance, men come out of nowhere and filled the tables, whistling and jeering in a universal language. I shrank in my seat.

***

I woke the next morning to the sound of the three others hauling themselves out of bed. The one part of my throbbing brain that was still functioning managed to process that breakfast was only until nine o'clock. I heaved myself up and struggled downstairs. Jason, his Yankees baseball cap firmly on his head and shadowing his bleary eyes, raised a hand. I took my tray over and sat next to him, my chair scraping on the floor in the process and making him grimace.

"Mornin'," he said flatly.

"Yeah, morning. Do I look as bad as you?"

"Fortunately, it's not a competition," Jason said, managing a weak laugh.

I poked at my rolls with no appetite. My head felt like it was filled with concrete and a little man inside was trying to split it with a jackhammer. I sipped my tea gingerly, filled two rolls with cheese, wrapped them in a napkin and put them in my pocket for later.

"That's a bright idea," Jason said, watching me. He did the same with some dark bread.

Noise enveloped me: scraping chairs, trays slamming on tables, loud conversations, thumping footsteps, and all the while, the little man inside my head hammered away. Even Jason's whisper sounded like a shout. At one point, a coffee cup was knocked from an adjacent table and it was as if grenade had exploded next to my ear.

"I think we should head outdoors," Jason said.

I nodded. My whole body felt the balance shift.

"But let me take a shower first," I said. "Maybe things will become a bit clearer." I stood up and started walking away.

"Hey, Mike," Jason called out. "You've got to put your tray back on the rack." As I walked back and picked up the tray, he added, "Those are the rules."

"Well, we can't have chaos," I said sarcastically, my dislike of being told what to do so clear that I startled myself as well as Jason. "Back

31

in fifteen," I said, managing a smile that pulled tight all the muscles in my neck.

If there is anything with stronger healing powers than a hot shower, I haven't found it. Even in the middle of a sweltering Perth summer, a hot shower is the one thing that will freshen you up. I stood under the burning water in the Hamburg hostel, closed my eyes, and let the water run into my mouth and ears without flinching. It trickled down my back and fell warm to my feet. Droplets of spray dampened the whitewashed walls of the cubicle, and steam rose like smoke from a bush fire. It cleared my head and the night unfolded before my eyes.

Under the flashing lights and red bulbs we watched girl after girl attempt to arouse us with supple bends and pouting lips. They had beautiful bodies, but the awkwardness of movement that comes with gangly youth. They were not sexual or desirable creatures. They were simply naked girls, attempting to garner interest with their nudity. And the men around us, old, haggard and pathetic, cheered for more and shouted obscenities. I remembered finishing my second beer feeling light-headed, confused as to why I felt like that after such a small amount of beer. It was stronger than anything in Australia, but didn't taste like it.

I stood in the shower and grimaced as the previous evening ran like a movie inside my head. I was watching myself in the strip club, going from silent observer to shouter like the others, making rude gestures to the girls and laughing loudly with Jason. More beers appeared; we never had to order. Some other Americans heard Jason's accent and sat down at our table. Their behaviour was obscene, but the alcohol made them funny. I saw Jason and I stumbling out arm in arm as daylight broke very early, as if night had never fallen.

I shook my head, but the images stayed with me. Not even the hot water could wash them away.

Outside, I found Jason sitting at a picnic table, taking in the view with vacant eyes. The sun was bright and high, and hurt my eyes. The glistening river reminded me of Perth. Suddenly, I felt desperately homesick. I missed my friends and the familiar confines of Maddington. I was in a city I knew absolutely nothing about, where on my first night I'd got completely drunk in a strip club. I felt young and stupid, angry that I'd made the trip and left everything that was safe and comfortable behind.

"My wallet's empty," I said, startling Jason. "We get robbed last night?"

He quickly composed himself and forced a smile. "Practically, and you owe me twenty Marks as well. It was lucky I had extra otherwise we could've been in a lot of trouble. Money is everything here."

"I'll cash a cheque later."

He waved me off as if it was nothing, but I could see in his eyes he wanted the money. It was a wall between us. He wasn't rich, but I was sure his family financed his travels. Being an only child has its benefits. Jason was in the lucky position to have enough money not to care about it, and to wonder why others did. We had a lot in common, but this one difference kept us worlds apart.

We left it at that and didn't speak about the previous night. For some reason, I blamed Jason for it all. Making it his fault meant I didn't have to deal with my own lack of forthrightness. I didn't want to admit to being a sheep. But the fact that my wallet was empty and I was down twenty Marks meant I'd spent almost fifty Marks in one evening. I couldn't throw money around like that. It was easy for Jason to shrug it off. I kept thinking about all the necessary things that money could have bought. I had to be more careful. Running out of money scared me.

We walked down the hill to the river, but without the zest and energy of new friendship and adventure that we'd climbed it with yesterday. Jason was quiet, speaking only to point out special places that he knew or to comment again on what a lovely day it was. I was starting to wonder why I'd followed this guy to West Germany. London may have been shitty, but at least my sister was there. If I split with Jason, I would be alone without a clue as to what to do next. The best thing was to stick it out with him and hope things might improve.

After a walk around the Speicherstadt, with its old, red brick warehouses, cobblestone streets and overpowering smell of coffee, Jason took his leave. He said he was tired and was going back to the hostel for a sleep.

"How do I find the hostel?" I called out after him.

"Just follow the water to Landungsbrücken, then walk up the hill."

I watched him walk away, uncertain if I should follow him or not. It felt good to be alone. I was sick of his arrogance and superiority. He made me feel small and stupid. Dad used to say, "The people who had bricks only ever wanted more of them, while the people who had none knew how to build their houses without them." I missed the old man then, and I wished it was fifteen years ago and I was sitting on top of a pile of bricks watching the planes fly over, half-listening to my father breaking life down to a philosophy of bricklaying and dreaming of faraway countries. He hated people with money, saying everyone had more than they really needed.

I began walking towards the church spires, to what I thought was downtown. I bought a cheap map from a corner shop and considered buying a phrase book, but didn't think I would be in West Germany that long.

The centre was a mix of old and new buildings, the old ones with artistic facades and statues. By accident, I stumbled onto the Rathausmarkt, a large square shadowed by an enormous sandstone building that looked like a castle. It was adorned with statues, each intricately carved, and green spires. It was like a castle from a fairy tale. I wondered if Rathaus meant house of rats. But the building was too grand to be given such a title. I sat on some concrete steps and took in the structure. It had a large, arched doorway which could once have been a drawbridge, if ever there had been a moat. Above this was a balcony where a King and Queen may have waved to a crowd, made speeches, told lies, or called a people to battle. Every tower and every statue, leant itself to fantasy, to images of knights with long swords and heavy armour, of buxom maidens with pale skin and rosy cheeks, of bearded and noble kings, and of rat infested dungeons and torture chambers.

"Excuse me," I said to a couple next to me. "I can't speak German."

"Dat is okay," said the man proudly. He had a large, horsey face and spoke with grunts. "I speak English."

"Great. Can you tell me what this building is?" I asked pointing.

"It is the Rathaus," he said, looking up at it. "Zumthink like a city hall."

I thanked him and walked away, not wishing to engage in conversation. The fact that it was a government building removed much of its mystique and fantasy. I crossed the square and stood on a bridge. To my right was a large expanse of water. I headed for it.

It was Sunday, but the streets were crowded. Families strolled together, enjoying the sun. Kids ran and chased each other, their German a high pitched squeal. Couples walked hand in hand. An old man with a dirty beard stood turning the handle of a large box, filling the air with classical music. People put money in a hat that lay

34

on the ground in front of him. He looked poor but dignified. Everyone was well-dressed. The men wore mostly pants and dress shirts, with jackets or pullovers slung over their arms or shoulders. The women were pretty and tall. Their blonde hair seemed different to that of Australian women, because it didn't come out of a bottle. It shone in the sun, turning another shade of gold in the process. Everyone looked happy and carefree, and had a self-assuredness and honesty I admired.

I found my way to the edge of a large lake and stood against the railing. I could see a bridge in the distance and more water stretching behind it. Water shot up from a fountain in the centre of the lake, and the light breeze blew cold droplets of spray on me. Red and white ferryboats docked and departed. A large group of old people boarded one, and I followed it with my eyes as it went under the bridge and out onto the larger lake beyond. Brick buildings five or six stories high made a ring around the inner lake. Trees grew between the path next to the lake and the road. It was easy to forget you were standing in the centre of a large city. It made London look like a garbage dump.

I followed the water, past the waiting ferryboats, to where the shadows offered relief from the sun. From the opposite direction came people with ice cream, some eating from paper cups, others with cones. It was blood to a starving shark.

I found the ice cream stand and stood in a long line that moved quickly. Kids left their parents to look at the ice cream on offer and came back shouting words like Schokolade, Vanille and Banane. This reassured me that I could order without making a complete fool of myself. The girl in front of me ordered quickly. She had long hair that couldn't decide if it was brown or blonde. It smelled of apples, and tumbled in long waves onto her shoulders and down her back, unkempt yet stylish. She wore a tight white shirt over a cotton dress that stopped just above her knees. Her legs were the colour of very milky coffee, with strong calves tapering only slightly to rather thick ankles. There was some confusion as she counted small money. I saw her hold up a twenty Mark note and assumed this was all she had. I reached into my pocket and tapped her on the shoulder. She turned around with annoyance, and I saw that her shirt had Daytona Beach written on it in red letters It accentuated the size of her round breasts. I opened my hand and offered her my change, a collection of brown and silver coins I still had to look closely at to identify. My hand shook slightly.

"What do you need?" I asked, forgetting where I was. I stared at her light blue eyes, which rippled like water, and then at the scar line through her left eyebrow.

She was taken aback by my English, but recovered and asked softly, "Five?"

I located the coin and gave it to her. She smiled. Her cheeks dimpled. The wind blew a strand of hair in front of her eyes and she brushed it away subconsciously.

"Danke," she murmured, then turned, paid and slipped away.

A voice spoke and I guessed the ice cream man was talking to me. I ordered Schokolade, held up one finger, paid and quickly moved away, emboldened by my ability to make myself understood. I looked around for the girl, but the ice cream stand was crowded. People sat by the water's edge on white plastic chairs around white plastic tables. The girl was gone. I moved past the tables and leaned against the railing, looking out over the shimmering expanse of water and the beautiful buildings surrounding it.

I ate my ice cream by the water.

"Where do you come from?"

I turned to see the girl standing next to me, her eyebrows raised awaiting a response. She faced the sun and her eyes seemed to change to an aqua blue in the light. She was young, but had a mature air, as if she had already seen so much.

"Australia," I croaked.

"Wow," she exclaimed, smiling again. Who knew my nationality would be such a turn on? "And you come all the way just to see Hamburg? Oh, I'm sorry. My English is so bad." She giggled.

Her voice had a sound that was somehow familiar, as if my brain was already keyed into her tone and had heard her laugh before. All her words were clear and echoed inside my head.

"You're English is great. I'm sorry I don't speak German. My sister lives in London," I stammered. "But then I met an American and he convinced me to come here."

She repeated her wow from before and we lapsed into silence. I was never very good at talking to girls. I always second-guessed what I wanted to say and then the moment passed and I'd said nothing, but wasn't convincing enough to be the strong, silent type. It was a game I didn't understand.

"Nice day," was the best I could come up with. I had to say something or she might have walked away.

"Yes. Is it not beautiful?" she said, smiling and turning her gaze onto the water. The wind blew her hair back from her face and revealed a profile with a small, pointed nose and a rounded chin. The scar through her eyebrow was sexy and I stared at it, until I saw the corners of her eyes and she smiled, knowing I was staring at her. I turned to the water.

"So, are you from Hamburg?"

"No," she said, still looking over the water. "I'm not a Hamburger."

I laughed, but it wasn't meant as a joke. I collected myself and pressed on. "Where are you from?"

She seemed reluctant to answer, sucking in one cheek and chewing on it, moving her lower jaw slightly from side to side; a masculine gesture.

"I'm from East Berlin," she said finally, with a certain amount of pride.

I knew little about East and West Germany except that they were countries that existed on a map in mum's old atlas. We didn't learn much European history in school, except about Hitler and how bad Germans were, and I wasn't about to mention that. But the fact she had said East Berlin implied that there was perhaps a West Berlin and that they were not the same. I didn't know what to say.

"That's East Germany," she added softly, as if guessing I was ignorant but not wanting to insult me.

"Right," I said, trying to sound informed. "My name's Michael."

"Kathrin." It sounded like Cat-rin. She turned to face me and thrust out her hand. It was small but strong; she shook hands like a man, looking me square in the eyes. I liked her confidence.

I plucked up my courage. Butterflies fought for freedom in my stomach, and I tasted acidic chocolate ice cream at the base of my throat. "What are you doing now?" I asked. "Would you like to take a walk around the lake?"

She raised her scarred eyebrow. If she said no, it would take all my effort not to plunge into the water below. She looked at the clock on the Rathaus tower.

"I have to be back by six," she said, with some hesitation. I recognised a safety net, but didn't care. "It's my Great Aunt's birthday tomorrow and we must make the party." I began to shrink, readying myself to leap over the railing and end it all. "She lives in Winterhude, so we can walk along the lake in that direction."

She started walking before I had processed the information. She went five metres and turned as I rushed to catch up. I asked her if it was her first time in Hamburg and she explained the last time she was here was for her Great Aunt's sixty-fifth birthday. But what about Christmas?

"It is not so easy to get the permission," she explained, and left it at that. I didn't press.

We crossed a long bridge and took in the view of the city, with the Rathaus tall and golden, and the fountain casting a haze of spray in front of it. It was beautiful, the girl was beautiful. And how far away were the pot-holed streets of Maddington with its low, beaten houses and disappointed people.

Kathrin had small feet and walked quickly with short steps. I tried to slow her down by pointing at buildings and asking questions. Who knew how far this Winterhude place was? I wanted this walk to last as long as it could.

All Kathrin wanted to know about was Australia. She asked questions about kangaroos and did they really hop around and put their babies in pouches? And where did the Aborigines live? Did we have television? Was it always so hot? She knew some things from school, but almost everything I said lit her eyes up with delight. I described dangerous spiders, deadly snakes, bushes with sharp needles that gripped your clothes and weeds that grew on the ground and flowered small prickles you had to pull out of your shoes and feet. My normal world sounded incredibly exotic and far removed from her own. I loved it when my simple words astonished her.

We followed the lake for about an hour. We crossed bridges, stopped to take in the view of downtown and marvel at how far we had walked. We dodged hundreds of people on bicycles, and swapped stories. You could have shot me and stuck me in the ground I was so happy. All the years spent getting to this point felt like wasted time, that time had only begun when she had taken the five cents from my hand.

At a bridge called Fernsichtbrücke, we turned right and left the lake. Apartment blocks stood side by side in long lines down both sides of the streets. There were no gardens or individual houses; just long brick structures, all inhabited. The doors were close to the street and cars were parked inches from each other in a long straight line. Kathrin stopped in front of one building that looked just like the rest.

"This is the house," she said. Since leaving the lake, she had slowed her walk to a crawl. "Thank you for the nice walk."

"My pleasure," I said. It was the end. The sun had shined on me for a couple of hours and that was all anyone from Maddington would ever get. We shook hands, hers much weaker than before, and as she made her way up the stairs, I turned to go.

"Um, Michael," she called from the doorway. Cars probably rumbled past, horns might have sounded, gears could have grinded, perhaps ten cars piled up, because I heard none of it. I stared into her eyes and hoped I wouldn't melt into the pavement. "Do you like to come to the party tomorrow?"

"Yeah, absolutely." I thought my voice might explode into song. "I mean, that sounds great. Is it okay with your family?"

"Sure." She smiled brightly, showing small, thin teeth, the front two of which crossed over each other. I had only just noticed it. "Be here at five. The name on the bell is Horstmeyer. Number twenty-six," she added, pointing at the number above her head.

"Okay. Do I need to bring anything?" Boy, I must've come across as one anxious idiot.

"No."

"Five o'clock. Forestyer."

She laughed loudly. "No, Horstmeyer."

"Sorry. Horstmeyer."

"Perfect. See you tomorrow."

"Wild Horstmeyers couldn't keep me away."

She turned and obviously didn't get my stupid joke, but smiled and waved before closing the door behind her. I started down the street, almost at a run; I may well have skipped. But then I stopped at the next intersection and had absolutely no idea where I was.

Eventually, I found water, but it looked more like a river or a canal; not the lake of before. The map showed that Kathrin and I had walked clear of it. Panic seized me as my mind filled with visions of aimless walking, nobody able to speak English, and then me dying under a bridge having walked in circles for three weeks without food or water. A voice from behind revived me.

"I'm sorry?"

"Ah, you are English," said the small, middle-aged man. He was short and squat, a large object crammed into small packaging, but had friendly eyes and an open face. "You look a little lost. Can I help?"

I showed him my map and pointed to where I wanted to go.

"It would be more easy if you take the train." He spoke each word carefully, pronouncing every letter and syllable.

The train sounded intimidating. I said I wanted to walk. If I could just find the lake again, I would be all right.

"Well, then you best follow the Alster." I raised my eyebrows at him. "That is this lake," he said, pointing at the part of it that was on the map.

"Great. How do I get there?"

He gave me directions, said it wasn't far and sent me on my way.

During the course of the evening, I would ask for further directions and encounter more nice people that put to bed everything I'd been told about Germans being unfriendly. One guy even walked with me for a while along the Alster. He had a large Dalmatian and threw a tennis ball ahead of us that the dog would tear off after and return with. He spoke good English and was a student at the local university.

The sun was setting over the river when I finally made it back to the hostel. I bought a döner and ate it sitting on the dock at Landungsbrücken watching the sun set. Kathrin took up all my thoughts. I couldn't believe she was interested in me; I was never such a success with girls that they just started talking to me and then asked me to parties. That only happens in the movies, or to guys with fast cars and money. I decided not to get my hopes up, so then I wouldn't be disappointed when nothing happened. But it was such a negative way to approach life, like what Narelle had said about expecting too much. What is life without dreams and fantasy? Life would only get better if we imagined it could.

I dragged myself wearily up the hill, wanting only a hot shower and a bed. I looked for Jason but couldn't find him. Maybe he was out on the town again. I collapsed into bed, stared briefly at the ceiling, and replayed the day. I had to see Kathrin again. It was like we had already known each other for years. At times, we had walked along the water in comfortable silence. She wasn't going to run away if I stopped talking, and I didn't feel I had to impress her. There was a comfort and security with her, a familiarity beyond that of fast friendship or lust.

***

40

I woke early and thumped downstairs hungry for breakfast. I couldn't see Jason, so I took my tray outside and sat at one of the picnic tables that looked out over the harbour. The morning was warm, but the sky was grey and threatening. Some people followed my lead and sat at my table and the two others. We swapped backgrounds and nationalities. They were from all over the world, with different coloured skins and strange noses. Some had big eyes like night animals and others had beady eyes too close together; some with big lips and others with very thin lips. For the first time in my life I had an awareness of the size and scope of the world and the people in it. I felt very small and inconsequential. Maddington was a minuscule shell on an enormous beach.

But there was no sign of Jason. At the reception desk, I paid for another night and asked after him.

"He left yesterday," said the attendant flatly.

I thanked him, then went back upstairs and lay on my bed. I was angry. That lousy, arrogant American had dragged me over to this foreign country only to abandon me without a word, not even a goodbye. What was I supposed to do now? After Jason had left me yesterday, I had ventured out into the wilds of Hamburg alone and survived. Not only that, I'd met a fantastic girl and had a wonderful afternoon with her. That would never have happened if I'd been with Jason. Maybe I was better off.

I jumped from the bed. Five o'clock could not come fast enough.

I strolled downtown and killed time looking in the stores along Mönckeberg Strasse. The streets were crowded with people making their way to work. They wore fashionable, expensive clothing and walked with purpose; not with the beaten routine of Londoners, who had long ago given up. The people here seemed to approach each day as a new start. I liked the way they carried themselves; there didn't seem to be any bullshit. What you saw was what you got. Faces were hard set, but could soften just as quickly into a smile, then harden again. Eyes were clear, sharp and quick-moving. In the German people, I saw a character far removed from the Australian people. We thought of ourselves as relaxed, easy-going, laugh-at-your-troubles, lend-your-mate-a-hand people. But I'd never been able to identify with that stereotype. All through childhood I was restless and impatient, always wanting more than I had, prepared to make great sacrifices to escape my situation. And I was honest about it, saying to my sister that we deserved more, announcing to my mother when I was very young that

I thought she was a queen. I could not lie to cover things up. If asked a direct question, I would answer it honestly. Dad had told me long ago that lying was for the weak. But everyone lied. The cheque's in the mail. I'll finish it tomorrow. You're my best mate, Mike. It was this dark side of the Australian character that stuck with me: the secret lives, the behind-the-back slandering, the proclaiming of mateship only to turn your back when the mate really needed you. Promises unkept, resolutions forgotten, lives destroyed by loss of work, people shattered by regrets and lost opportunities, and a clear divide between rich and poor that was never called into question. People knew their roles and stuck to them.

In the Germans, with their clear eyes and purposeful stride, I saw a character of resilience and commitment. I'm sure they broke promises and had secret lives, but there was honesty in the way they didn't play games. Yesterday, Kathrin hadn't toyed with me the way an Australian girl would have, playing an endless game of courtship and seduction while trying not to be too keen. She hadn't wasted time or messed around talking in circles. She liked me, spoke to me, looked me in the eye and invited me to a party without a single hesitation as to what the world might say about her.

Back home, I had never understood the game.

All I wanted was honesty, for people to be themselves and be comfortable with it. One day with Kathrin had put to rest many of my childhood confusions; it wasn't me after all.

It rained heavily just after lunch and I sought refuge in a nearby mall. I sat in a café, had an expensive cup of tea and read an English paper. It had no news about Australia, and I wondered what incredible changes could have taken place in the last seven days. I laughed. I'd only been away one week, but it felt like a month. Travelling prolonged the time. Every day was a full day. There were no appointments, no routine, no hauling myself out of bed to slave away in a stinking hot workshop. I sipped my tea, trying to forget how much it cost and felt glad that I'd left everything behind and come to Europe. My confidence was growing.

The rain had become drizzle when I emerged from the mall, but the clouds were moving quickly, exposing patches of blue sky. I decided to explore more of the city and, at the same time, walk in the direction of Winterhude. I still had plenty of time, but was too excited to concentrate on other things.

I skirted the main train station, navigating with my map, which was already starting to whither and tear, to the St Georg district. On the other side of the railroad tracks, the city changed dramatically. The streets were dirty and littered with broken glass and empty beer cans. A large group of homeless men stood around the entrance of the train station. They drank beer from cans, pissed against the wall when it pleased them, talked and laughed raucously, and attempted to con passers-by out of their small change with desperate pleading. People walked through the group with their heads down, ignoring the poor rabble, and ducked quickly down the stairs to catch trains. The scene was not unlike the area around the Reeperbahn. Here too there were sex shops and strip joints, and people slept in doorways while others rummaged through rubbish bins for beer bottles, discarded food and half smoked cigarettes. The buildings had long ago been left to decay: paint peeled, iron balcony railings had rusted orange and large pieces of concrete flaked off and left grey gaps in the faded paint work. It was amazing that only five hundred metres away there was a rich shopping stretch where everything was overpriced and everyone could afford to pay it. It was just like in Perth.

If only a balance could be found, where everybody had a reasonably equal share, then all could enjoy the benefits of life. The situation here was one of resentment. The poor hated the rich for being rich, and vice versa. There was food and shelter enough for all, but it was monopolised by those who made the prices and could afford them, excluding the undesirables and unworthy in the process. I walked fast down a street full of strip joints, avoiding all contact with the men standing outside them. This horrible area gave way to a street lined with Turkish shops. All kinds of fruits and vegetables were piled outside, and men called out their prices in German and Arabic. I turned left and walked along a wide street which had a hospital on one side and a swimming hall on the other. At the Alster Lake, the sun came out and I took my shirt off and lay on the slightly damp grass. I closed my eyes, daydreaming about Kathrin, and checking my watch every five minutes. The time passed slowly, before I let go to my visions and forgot all about time.

So much so that I fell asleep, and when I woke up I had to run to Winterhude to make it by five.

I got to the building and pressed the Horstmeyer bell, but it made no sound. A buzzing noise came from the door. I pushed it open.

Slowly, with my stomach doing back-flips, I began climbing the stairs. An old woman peered out of the doorway at the top of the first floor and smiled at me. She turned and said something in German to the people inside the apartment and I heard loud laughter. I felt my face flush, my ears burning. The old woman, presumably the birthday girl, came out of the apartment and stood at the top of the stairs. From my view, she looked tall and imposing. Her arms were folded and she stared down her nose at me, scrutinising my every feature and movement. I looked at my feet as I stumbled up the remaining stairs. With one step left, we were at eye level. Her grey eyes held me frozen and my mouth seemed unable to open or form words.

"Zo, you are Kathrin's new friend," she said harshly, her English broken, accent thick. "But she said you have two heads."

She screwed up her old face with confusion, but her look suddenly turned friendly and she burst out laughing. A man's laugh, deep-throated, and her thin shoulders bounced with each chuckle. Two other women, one middle-aged and the other as old as the great aunt, stood in the doorway and also laughed at me. My humiliation was their joke. They spoke to each other in German, laughed and pointed at me. I wanted to turn and run down the stairs. I didn't need this. Kathrin pushed through the doorway and stood next to the great aunt. She wore a yellow cotton dress covered with orange and red flowers and would have brought summer to an Arctic winter. She wore a matching yellow hair clip that pulled her wild tresses away from her face. My jaw hit the last step.

She smiled, showing me her crossed over front teeth that made my knees weak. "Aren't you popular?" she teased, before turning to the old woman next to her. "Come on, Tante, you had your fun."

Tante was beaming. I was her greatest comedic moment.

"I thought you don't can come," Kathrin said, shaking my hand and pulling me up the last step. I now stood a head above the old woman and felt tall and gangly, taking up more space than necessary. I just wanted to hide from them all. But their eyes were friendly; there was no malice. The joke was some kind of initiation, and I felt I had passed.

"Nothing could have kept me away," I said, smiling through my embarrassment.

"This is Gertrude," said Kathrin. "But we call her Gertie."

"Happy birthday, Gertrude," I said, shaking her small and withered hand, which clutched mine with surprising strength. "I hope you have many more."

Gertie turned to Kathrin and received a translation. But Kathrin kept talking, looking and pointing at me, and smiling. Gertie said something, then Kathrin spoke again and I felt like part of the wallpaper. I took a step backwards towards the door of another apartment, insecure and stupid. Then Gertie looked at me, said something that sounded a little like wonderful, and ducked inside the apartment. Kathrin smiled at me; everything seemed to disappear. It seemed hours passed before the plucky old woman returned with keys and a small toolbox. She bounced down the stairs, defying her age.

"Come on," Kathrin said, grabbing my hand. "This is your chance to become more popular."

Gertie walked with quick short steps similar to Kathrin; both had very small feet. We stopped at a green sedan that looked a bit like a Ford Cortina, except it was called a Grenada. It was then I guessed that Kathrin had told Gertie I was a mechanic. I thought I'd heard that word. But I knew nothing about European cars. I didn't want to damage it. I held my hands up and pleaded for mercy. But Gertie grabbed my hand and led me to the driver's side door.

"She says it does not work," said Kathrin, who seemed to enjoy playing translator. "And that you can make it work."

Gertie smiled hopefully and handed me the keys. It was my first time sitting in a left-hand drive car. Everything felt backward. I found the ignition, jammed in the key with shaking hands, and felt their eyes and expectation. The engine turned over but wouldn't ignite. I tried it only once, not wanting to drain the battery, found the right lever and popped the bonnet. The engine was not unlike a Cortina's and I quickly located the source of the problem.

"See, now there's your worry," I said, speaking to the engine, like I always did. "Your main pump is all blocked up."

I removed the line, put it to my mouth, enjoying its familiar smell but not its taste, and blew into it hard. I felt the pressure in my head, which was surely turning an embarrassing dark red, but kept blowing until the blockage came out the other end. I helped it out with my fingers. Gertie and Kathrin watched closely, but I felt comfortable because this was my world. I laboured over reconnecting the line to be sure there would be no leaks and to prolong my success, before getting behind the wheel. I pumped the accelerator and gave it a try.

The engine sputtered and then roared to life. Gertie clapped and spoke words of praise I didn't understand. I tinkered a little more with the engine: lowered the idle, tightened a few loose screws, oiled the fan belt; made it sound better. Gertie was greatly impressed.

I gave the keys back to her. "Nice car. Steering wheel's on the wrong side though."

"What was the problem?" asked a rather astonished Kathrin.

"Oh, just a blocked fuel line," I said confidently. "Tell Gertie she shouldn't run the car down to empty all the time. Small pieces can get stuck in the line."

Kathrin seemed to understand and translated. Gertie listened closely. They exchanged some more sentences and I had the strange feeling they were talking about me. Both kept looking at me out of the corners of their eyes. It was uncomfortable. I didn't like them speaking about me as if I wasn't there, and felt like an idiot because I couldn't speak any German. We never learned languages at school, because there was no need. When would a small boy from Maddington ever need to speak a foreign language?

Upstairs, I closed the apartment door behind me and remained there as Gertie explained the car was working again. The women clapped and cheered. I hunched in the doorway and, smiling, modestly raised a hand. Gertie came over to me, took me by the hand and led me into her small apartment, which wasn't decorated in any way for a party. The ceiling was low and at six feet, I felt like a giant. The two women who had laughed at me from the doorway stood in front of me.

"This is Hilde, my sister," Gertie said. Hilde was also small, with thin, narrow shoulders and wisps of white hair parted viciously down the middle and pulled back from her face in a tight bun. Her face was lined and she wore almost no make-up. Her high cheekbones and dark blue eyes were a window to the past, when she was perhaps a young girl of great beauty.

"Nice to see you," she said, shaking my hand and laughing at her own voice speaking English. "Oh, I speak not English since school." And the two old women laughed together.

"I am Monica," the middle aged woman said, extending her hand. She was a handsome woman, short, with a thin waist and wild hair slightly thinner than Kathrin's. All four women were cut from the same mould. But Monica's eyes were harder and her mouth more

46

firmly set. A smile turned her face into a road map. "I am de mother von Kathrin," she added.

Monica wasn't as warm to me as the two old women were. There was suspicion in her look, like I was a criminal who had tried to reform himself, but was still considered a criminal. I think she wanted to intimidate me and she did. Something told me I would never get to Kathrin without getting past her first.

"My mother does not speak very good English," Kathrin said softly in my ear. Her breath was hot and tickled my ears. They seemed to reach off my head and meet her breath half way. Monica shot a glance at her daughter. Kathrin fell back and I felt uncomfortable encircled by these four women, who were present, past and future versions of each other.

I was rescued by a young man who came out of the kitchen to introduce himself.

"Hi. My name's Thomas," he said confidently, but giving my hand a limp shake. "Kathrin's brother."

He was my age and height and together we seemed to tower over the women. He had dark skin, the same aqua eyes as Kathrin, though they seemed softer, almost weaker, and he had a moustache that was a shade darker blonde than his hair. He was handsome, muscular and confident, as if he knew that he would reach all the goals he set for himself.

"I hear you did wonders with Gertie's old shitbox," he said quickly, not wanting her to understand. His good English relaxed me. I had thought language would be a barrier.

Gertie heard her name and fired rapid German at Thomas. He laughed, saved face with some witty remark that made all the women laugh, then led me into the kitchen. Kathrin followed us, but Monica called after her. Kathrin smiled, telling me with her eyes that I was handling myself very well. There was something in our ability to communicate that made me feel like we were an old couple.

Thomas put a cold beer in my hand. "Welcome to Germany," he said, clinking his bottle against mine. "Kathrin said you only got here a few days ago."

The kitchen was small, with room enough for both of us, but Thomas stood very close to me, making me lean back and take small steps away from him to maintain a space I considered comfortable. But he would simply come closer again. During the conversation, we would turn together in a slow circle as I stepped to the side and he followed, as if we were slow dancing to an even slower song. His breath smelled like cigarettes, and it made me want one to help me relax.

"That's right. Took the ferry from London on Saturday," I said, leaning back from him, and trying to sip my beer without hitting him in the face with my arm.

"London's a great town," he said emphatically. He spoke with a slight British accent when he said this and continued to do so, as if only just remembering how. "I don't go there enough."

I nodded, not wanting to say I thought it was the biggest shit hole in the world.

"Well, Hamburg is pretty nice," I said, taking a small step to the side.

Thomas matched me; our shoulders touched.

"Ach, I don't like the people here," Thomas said, trying to keep his friendly tone. "They think they're so superior."

"Are they nicer in East Berlin?"

He laughed loudly, then gave me a condescending look. "The people in East Berlin know nothing," he said. "They are sheep. They follow whatever master leads them around. Dumb Ossis."

I sipped my beer and looked at the floor. It was a dark yellow laminate. The pattern was still visible near the walls, but had worn away in the middle.

The kitchen was well organised, with labelled jars and containers sitting on a shelf below a cupboard. In an incredible feat of engineering, given the size of the kitchen, a fridge, washing machine, and oven stood side by side along one wall. In front of the window was a small table with one wooden chair.

"But don't tell Kathrin I said that," he said, giving me a thin smile. He liked the fact that within five minutes, we already shared a secret; the way children do in a playground when they become friends.

I wondered why Thomas was so ashamed and critical of his home. From his clothes and manner, I assumed his was not a poor family. But it's always those who have everything that are in the position to be critical of everyone else. Like a rich man saying money means nothing to him.

"I won't."

"Come on," Thomas said, turning to leave the kitchen, satisfied we had shared some kind of intimacy, "let's sit in the living room. This is too small."

As he walked away, the space around me became free and it was as liberating as being let out of solitary confinement. Thomas took away my personal space and made me appreciate it more by giving it back.

The living room wasn't much bigger than the kitchen. An old sofa was positioned under the only window. In front of it was a small coffee table. Next to the sofa was a matching armchair. I quickly sat down in it, thinking that if I sat on the sofa, Thomas might sit on me. A full bookcase was against a wall and next to this was a large shelf with a television and photographs on it. I recognised Kathrin as a blonde, freckle-faced six year-old in a bridesmaid dress, her smile showing gaps in her teeth. There were pictures of Monica in various stages of womanhood, Thomas in a blue and white striped jersey, and a black and white photo of a young man standing tall in an army uniform adorned with Swastikas. But he did not look like the evil Nazis from the films. His smile gave him away, as if the uniform was an outfit for a fancy dress party. He could have been Gertie's husband or brother. The uniform was probably the last clothes he wore. Thomas saw me looking.

"She should take that photo down," he said harshly. "That time has to be forgotten."

I offered a vague agreement, unsure how to word my feelings.

Thomas leaned forward and sat on the edge of the sofa to allow more intimacy. "Tell me," he whispered, "what do you learn about that?"

I didn't want to say the wrong thing. "Not much," I said honestly. "I left school when I was fifteen. I didn't like it so much."

"Me, too. School was boring." Thomas moved deeper into the sofa and drank his beer thoughtfully. "I met an Australian once," he went on. "He worked at my uncle's bank and used to come to dinner at our house sometimes. He was a really boring guy. Couldn't answer any of my questions about Australia."

"Where was he from?"

Thomas frowned. "Can't remember."

"Probably from Sydney or Melbourne," I said. "They're pretty up themselves."

"No," Thomas said, shaking his head. "He was from some weird place. He kept talking about the view of the river from his office."

"Sounds like Perth," I said softly.

"That's it. Perth," Thomas said, pointing a finger at me. "Said it was always hot, but he lived by the beach."

I knew this man. He had a name like Brockman, or Dwyer, or Smythe, and had a large house a few streets from the beach. In the driveway sat a new car, washed and waxed every Sunday by his private school son. The lawn was cut low and was a lush green because it was watered every day in summer despite the water restrictions. The garden was well cared for; the housewife had plenty of free time to look after her precious roses. The front door had two locks and a security screen in front. As a teenager, my friends and I had driven past these houses at night, looking for the ones with older style windows, which could be opened by pushing carefully in the right place, and other houses where we guessed the people were away on holiday. But the people were onto us, and replaced their windows. Security screens increased along with their fear, and police patrolled the streets more. I never felt any remorse or guilt stealing from these people. They had enough. As an old friend used to rationalise it, "Call it wealth redistribution."

"Where are you from again?" he asked.

"Perth."

"Really? So, you also live by the beach."

"Not quite."

"Ah, you're from the outback," he said knowingly.

"I guess you could say that. The outback from Perth."

A look of confusion swept his face. He wrinkled his nose; the lifting nostrils made him look like a sun-tanned pig, especially with his wispy moustache. A strange woman entered the room and spoke to him. She was in her late thirties and did not look like the others. She was taller, her hair darker and her face rounder and paler. Grey eyes looked out at the world with sadness. Her pink lips were thin and grim.

"I'm Antje," she said, after finishing her conversation with Thomas. "Monica's sister." No handshake, no smile.

She left as abruptly as she had entered. Thomas looked at me, read my thoughts. "I know. She doesn't looking much like my mother. Different fathers," he said, and left it at that.

We drank in silence. I could hear the sound of cars below. The odd horn honked, and that reassuring sound of a city, a siren, wailed somewhere in the distance.

"So, what's your plan for Germany?" Thomas asked, trying to be friendly again, somewhat uncomfortable with silence.

"No plan," I said. "But I have to be back in London in two weeks to fly home.

He leaned forward again, resting his beer bottle on his knee. "And what about Kathrin?" he asked softly.

"Well," I began carefully, "she's a really nice girl. But we only met yesterday."

"She likes you," he whispered confidentially, his eyes bright and wide. He even wiggled his eyebrows.

"That's only because I fixed Gertie's shitbox."

He laughed, falling back against the sofa so his feet kicked in the air a little. It was an exaggerated, over the top gesture. And his girlish giggling made me wince slightly. Kathrin entered the room just as Thomas had regained his composure.

"We are ready," she announced. Thomas drained his beer and I did the same.

We gathered in the hall. Make-up had been applied, hair done up more elaborately, dresses changed and jewellery adorned. I felt somewhat under-dressed in my faded jeans and plain white t-shirt. Gertie led us downstairs. The older women climbed into the Grenada, while Kathrin and Thomas led me to a dark blue BMW. Gertie lurched her green Ford out onto the road and we followed behind, Thomas driving. The BMW purred like a cat warming itself in front of a fire; it had a musical, hypnotic sound. Sitting in the passenger seat, I felt completely disoriented and when Thomas made a late turn, I reached out for a steering wheel that wasn't there and pressed my foot against the peddle-less floor.

Thomas kept his distance and giggled as Gertie veered from lane to lane. Kathrin said something to him in German and he stopped laughing.

I looked out the window at the suburbs of Hamburg. The houses were for the most part identical; brick structures about five stories high with the same square-shaped windows perfectly distanced apart. They were uniform but nice. Trees lined the streets and it seemed every second or third corner had a small park, or an old church. The blue sky showed no sign of the rain that had dampened the afternoon. We drove in sunshine alongside a canal and then through a large park. There were joggers of all shapes and sizes, with dogs to match. Cyclists cruised along, either with the determination of a worker wanting to be home or with the relaxed ease of someone with the evening free. It was only six o'clock, but with the sun high and warm, it felt like two in the afternoon.

We parked behind the Grenada on the side of a wide street. The younger women were helping the older two out of the car. There was much talking and laughter. They gave the impression of people who hadn't seen each other for a long time.

"Nice car," I said, walking between Thomas and Kathrin.

"Thanks," said Thomas, like it meant nothing to him. "It really goes on the Autobahn."

As we walked, it took me a minute to realise Kathrin and I were holding hands, as if it were completely natural. I clutched her hand with shock. She squeezed mine back and looked at me softly, saying with her eyes it was okay, normal almost.

Gertie and Hilde walked arm in arm through a gate and down a narrow path. We walked past low, one-room houses that had gardens and plastic sun chairs in front. Each had a gate and shared fences. I saw one old man taking in the evening sun naked, his dark body withered and leathery, like an old beachcomber.

"The Dachas here are wonderful," Kathrin said to me. "We have one, but it's not so nice like this."

I guessed she was talking about the garden houses and the small plots of land. Having never lived in an apartment, I couldn't fully understand why people would want a small weekend house, or simply to have a garden. It was a completely different kind of living to what I was used to.

The restaurant was like an old hunting lodge, all wood with a grand entrance and high ceilings. Colourful streamers hung from the walls, balloons were taped to wooden beams and a long table was covered with a purple tablecloth. Gertie entered the room and was greeted with cheers and clapping, followed by a song, which I guessed was the German version of *Happy Birthday*. I mouthed along, trying not to look out of place. I could hear Kathrin singing loudly next to me, clapping time like the others. It was a very warm atmosphere.

A man handed us beers. He was a cousin, Kathrin said, and I forgot his name as soon as I was told it. He was tall and beefy, with a large, jowly face, and was pulled away by two short and beefy boys before we had finished the introduction. The beer spilled from his glass as the boys tugged his free arm.

"Prosit," Kathrin said, as we clinked glasses. She looked older than yesterday, without her innocence; as comfortable and secure with her family and relatives as I had been under the bonnet of the Grenada. I hoped she wouldn't leave me in favour of talking to her relatives. I felt the eyes of everyone in the room, the only stranger.

Gertie and Hilde circled the room like aged princesses, still arm-in-arm, and greeting everyone with hugs and kisses. They stopped to talk with two other old ladies. They chatted and laughed, and looked at me and pointed. I smiled.

Kathrin took me around the room in a rush of introductions. She pronounced my name Mick-hail. I didn't remember a single name, nor the family connections. I couldn't say who was a cousin, who was a niece or a nephew, who had just got married, or whose husband was recovering from a heart attack and couldn't be excited or drink any alcohol. But every face smiled at me. I shook every hand. They introduced themselves proudly in English, and never had I felt more welcome in a room full of strangers. Kathrin was somewhat shy with most of them. She asked about health situations, children, and so on, but few questions were asked of her. I suddenly realised I didn't know what Kathrin did for work. In fact, she was as much a stranger to me as all the others. The room was stuffy and warm, and it was my second beer on an empty stomach. I felt the blood rush from my face; my heart started to pump madly, panicked by the anxiety of collapsing in a crowded room. I felt my hand being shaken, my head nodding, my mouth moving as words came out. "Nice to meet you." "Yes, that's right, Perth, the west coast." "No, the other side of the country." One face blended into another in a whirlwind of names, occupations, blonde hair and cigarette-stained teeth. I could feel myself drifting out of my body, the way I used to as a boy, in that short time between closing the eyes and falling asleep; I thought everyone could do it. I looked down on the scene from above. The people crowded around me. Children giggled at the funny way I spoke. Old ladies laughed and pointed, talking behind their hands. Kathrin stood next to me. It looked as if her holding my hand was keeping me from falling. I could see the muscles of her thin forearm flexing, her mouth working frantically as she moved from German to English and back to German. Subconsciously, I put the cold beer to my lips and its sensation brought me back to my body. Kathrin led me towards the back of the room, where large windows looked out over a train station and a thick forest beyond it. I fell into a chair next to Thomas. I felt Kathrin let go of my hand. It was wet with perspiration and I wiped it on my jeans.

"Get all that?" Thomas said laughing, moving closer to me, his chair scraping along the wooden floor.

Seated, I had my bearings again.

"None of it," I said, raising my beer glass to him. "Except this. Prosit."

Thomas laughed and hit his glass hard against mine. "Wunderbar."

Gertie sat at the head of a long table, her eyes wide and bright. Her friends and relatives sat close together down both sides of the table. There was much talking and laughing. Everyone smoked, the air fast becoming so thick with smoke that all the windows had to be opened. The fresh air and Kathrin's return renewed my strength. I drained my beer and another one appeared. Salad and bread were served followed by a main course of some kind of dark meat.

"It's Hirsch," Kathrin said to me. "Gertie's, how do you say, favourite?"

"Is that from the cow?" I asked.

The table fell silent as Thomas asked if anyone knew the English word for Hirsch. A child got down on his hands and knees and did an impression of the animal using two forks for horns. Everyone laughed. A man in a suit with his tie loosened, yelled out Bambi.

"Ah, deer," I said to everyone, and they all cheered and repeated the new word. "Tastes like kangaroo," I added. More laughter from those who understood and late laughs from those who got translations.

Kathrin spoke into my ear. "Do you really eat Kangaroo?"

"Of course, but they're mostly made into dog food."

"But they're so cute."

"So is Bambi," I said, putting a forkful into my mouth and chewing happily. Kathrin laughed and lightly slapped my thigh, before translating the joke for Gertie and Hilde who promptly laughed with mouthfuls of food, small bits of meat stuck between their teeth. The joke went around the room, each group laughing in turn and clapping in my direction. I raised my almost empty beer glass to them.

The time passed quickly. A cake was brought out. It was covered in candles, but not enough to be seventy. Gertie made a speech, then we ate the cake with coffee and liqueurs.

"I have an idea," Thomas said. He downed another of the sweet liqueur they called Schnapps and was slurring his words. He had a

54

small dollop of cream on his chin he was completely oblivious to. "Why don't you come with me back to West Berlin. You could stay with me and visit Kathrin."

"That sounds great," I said. "But why can't I stay with Kathrin and her family?"

Thomas frowned. "You can't stay in East Berlin."

The beer had loosened my tongue. I thought Thomas was trying to protect his little sister. "And why not?"

Thomas's eyes went from foggy to clear in two seconds. "You don't know why?"

I shook my head and he couldn't believe it.

"I don't know where to begin," he said, sitting up straight in his chair. He looked around to see if anyone was listening, then past me to be sure Kathrin was talking to a girl across the table from her. "Well, Kathrin and our parents live in East Berlin."

I nodded.

"And that's East Germany."

I nodded again and he smiled, thankful that I was with him so far.

"And that's a communist country."

"So?"

"So, you just can't walk into a communist country," he exclaimed, trying to keep his voice down. "For the same reason they can't just walk out. The borders are secure and heavily guarded."

"How does that affect me?" Pictures I'd seen on the news of soldiers, the Russian enemy, the Red Threat, the Cold War, tanks and other modern war devices, came into my head in disconnected visions. What would the evil communists do to me?

"Well, I have to apply for a visa and then I can go there for the day," Thomas explained. "It's like buying a ticket for a really boring Disneyland."

I wondered if Thomas was playing me for a fool. He sounded serious, but who could tell.

"So, I'll do that then," I said, wanting only to see Kathrin again.

"No, you can get in with just a passport," he said smiling. "We're driving back tomorrow, but I think it's better you come with me. I don't want to give my mother any trouble at the border. It's hard enough for them to leave the country just for two days. Can't have them bringing back a Westerner."

I had so many questions, I didn't know which to ask first. Thomas and I agreed to meet at Gertie's apartment at noon the next day. Kathrin started to talk to me again and the questions I wanted to ask moved to the back of my mind.

The party was soon over. Families left early to take their tired kids home to bed. Tomorrow was a school day as well as a work day. I said goodbye to faces I remembered, but whose names I had forgotten. Kathrin drove the BMW, dropping Thomas at Gertie's apartment before driving me to the hostel. She did not know the way and simply followed the signs with boats on them, or others that said Hafen.

At Landungsbrücken, she parked the car and turned off the engine.

"Thanks for a really nice evening, Kathrin," I said.

She stared down at her hands. Her face was sad and she chewed her cheek, this time to stop herself from crying. I reached over and put my hand under her chin, turning her face to mine. A tear trickled down her checked and into her mouth. The next one ran onto my thumb. I put it in my mouth and tasted its saltiness. Kathrin followed my thumb and our lips met. Hers were soft and warm, her tongue hard and moist. She kissed softly at first and then more aggressively, pulling me by the neck toward her in what felt like frustration, not passion. I gently removed her hand.

"I'm going with Thomas to West Berlin tomorrow," I said softly, as tears dripped from her face and onto her yellow dress, making round dark patches where they landed.

She smiled, her face brightening, and we kissed deeply. There was more time. Frustration was replaced by passion.

"I have to go," she said reluctantly. "Thomas will panic if I take too long."

I closed the door and watched the back of the BMW disappear into the night. A chilly wind blew off the Elbe, finding its way up my shirt as I staggered up the hill to the hostel. A drunk was sleeping on a bench. I tripped over his leg. He jumped awake and started shouting. I ran the rest of the way.

# West Berlin

Thomas said, on our way out of Hamburg, that it should be easy to cross the border, if we had luck. There were sometimes long delays, he explained, when they shuffled your passport back and forth only to make you, and everyone else behind, wait.

An observation tower looked down on the border crossing. After waiting about half an hour, a young guard with a green saucer helmet waved us forward and took our passports. He didn't greet us nor engage Thomas in small talk. His face was pale, set off by the red marks of youth made redder by being picked at and squeezed. A large rifle was slung over his shoulder and he had a utility belt that would have made Batman jealous. His uniform looked like it had been made by his mother for a fancy dress party. He took our passports into the office building. Thomas laughed as he strode away.

"What's so funny?" I said nervously; whatever we were doing, it was wrong.

"Saxon accent," he said. "Always makes me laugh. When you learn German, you'll understand."

I thought it strange he said when and not if. But my thoughts were interrupted as a new man marched toward us. He also wore a military uniform but with a collar and tie that lent him superiority to the saucer-helmeted private. He had a stringy moustache that seemed to start from deep within his nose. He leaned down to Thomas's open window, but did not attempt to touch the car. He looked directly at me, accusingly and interrogatively, like a school principal awaiting a child's confession.

"You the Australian?" he barked.

I nodded.

"Your business in West Berlin?"

"You don't have to answer that," Thomas said to me, but the man put him into place with harsh German. Thomas looked at his hands. Suddenly, he seemed so young.

"I'm just going to stay for a couple of days with him," I stammered, thinking honesty was the safest route.

"Will you visit Berlin, capital of DDR?" His English was halting, and he spat his words, with small droplets of spit collecting in the strands of his moustache.

"He means East Berlin," Thomas said softly. The man looked at him sharply.

"Yes, I think so," I said, a little too over-eager.

"Good," the man said, trying to force a smile that ended up looking like a grimace. "Is more beautiful than Berlin West."

He handed Thomas back our passports. Inside mine was an envelope. The man leaned closer to the window. He breathed old cigarette smoke into the car. "Please, post that for me in Berlin West," he said softly, in a voice completely different than before. I nodded. He smiled for real this time, friendly and warm, revealing a face that gave children birthday presents and told bedtime stories. But he moved back from the car quickly.

"Remember, stay on Autobahn," he ordered. He straightened his jacket and signalled for us to drive on with an outstretched arm.

Thomas shook his head. "Man, I think you have angels watching over you."

"Why?"

"I've never had it so easy crossing that checkpoint. They normally check the whole car, look under it with mirrors and empty the boot."

"What do I do with this envelope?"

"Put a stamp on it and post it. Trust me, he just did us a huge favour. Sometimes they make you pay tolls or for mysterious road repairs, even though the government pays all that to them in one hit." Thomas laughed. "I hope you have the same effect at the West Berlin checkpoint. They can be real Nazis there."

We drove for the next hour with the radio filling the silence. Thomas sang along tunelessly to English songs, clueless to how bad he sounded. Moreover, he was proud he knew the words, and when to ooooh and when to aaaaah.

Four lanes of road stretched into the distance. Trucks and slow passenger cars kept to the right, and the left lane was reserved solely for passing. There was no speeding. Old cars like cardboard boxes on wheels puttered along, dark smoke belching from the exhaust pipes. Thomas drove impatiently, speeding up to pass only to catch himself and slow down again. Before crossing the border, he had driven like a maniac, so fast that I'd had to look out the side window and not at the road ahead. But once in East Germany, he slowed down. They had strict speed limits, he said, expensive fines, and police at every turn off. Other cars were just as impatient, like riders holding their horses at a trot when they wanted to gallop.

The land was flat, with brown fields and small forests. Bored cows shared the fields with large pieces of rusted farming machinery. Sometimes a small group of deer raised their heads to watch the passing cars with curiosity. It was my first time seeing deer; I thought they would be bigger with large horns like in the Christmas movies, but they were small and wiry, like fat dingoes. I saw no houses and only the odd building in the distance. Signs pointed to towns, but there was no advertising of sights of interest or landmarks or fun parks. If not for the cows, you would think you were driving through an unpopulated area.

"Why were there so many guys with guns at the border?" I asked.

Thomas leaned forward and switched off the radio. He smiled at me. "You see, the East German government is very scared that all their loyal comrades will leave if the border is open, but they say they are protecting everyone from Fascist-Imperialist aggression, the West."

I nodded, not really understanding.

"The life's really not so good in East Germany. It's boring and a lot of them want out. They have no, how do you call it, spontaneity?"

On saying this, he pulled out into the left lane and floored the BMW. It lurched forward as if it had been waiting for this moment. Six cars flew past in a flash, and just as abruptly, we pulled out of the lane and resumed the same speed as before. It felt like we were walking.

"That's why they built the wall in Berlin," Thomas continued. "To keep them in. You'll see. It's like a big prison." He laughed. "I'm sorry. It's just amazing to meet someone who knows nothing about this. I can't wait to show you around."

"But don't you have to work or something," I said. "I mean, what do you do?"

"I'm a student."

"What are you studying?"

"Wirtschaft, um, like Finance or Banking."

"Economics?"

"Yes, that's it."

"Thomas, I know this may sound like a stupid question, but why do you live in West Berlin. I mean, did you move there for university or something?"

"I lived in West Berlin almost my whole life. It's an interesting story. I'm surprised Kathrin didn't tell you."

"She didn't tell me anything really, except that she was from East Berlin."

"Well, when the border closed, I was just a baby. My mother and father got married the year before and lived in Prenzlauer Berg, in the east, where father was an engineer. Antje still lived with my grandmother in Schoeneberg, in the west. When the border closed, my mother couldn't visit them like before. She didn't like East Berlin so much, but she loved my father and wanted to be with him. The wall then was only a string of barbed wire." He paused. "The day after the border closed my mother met my grandmother at the border and passed me over it. My grandmother told me the story when I was older. She said a guard came running over when it happened, but he was too late. Once I was in the west, he couldn't touch me, but he pulled my mother back. I grew up in the apartment of my grandmother."

"And you didn't see your mother or father or Kathrin?"

"Sometimes, but it wasn't like we could see each other whenever we wanted."

Nothing was clear. How could it be that a city was divided by a wall and nobody could cross it? I wasn't able to picture it in my head.

"So, how come Kathrin and Monica were in Hamburg?"

"Well, they can apply for special visas if there is an important family event."

"Okay, but why wasn't your father there?"

"A married couple aren't allowed to leave together," Thomas said flatly. "The government is afraid they won't return."

I stared at the road, speechless. Thomas turned the radio back on, but didn't sing like before.

He saw the confusion on my face. "Don't worry, it makes no sense to me either, and not really to anybody else, but we all live with it."

"When was the wall built?"

"August thirteen, 1961."

I laughed.

"What's so funny?"

"That's my birthday."

\*\*\*

When you approach Perth from any direction, the skyline is visible from at least twenty kilometres away. There's always that moment that

60

signals journey's end when you crest a hill or round a corner and the tall buildings can be seen through the haze. It's then you begin to pass through the outer suburbs and new areas under development. After driving along flat, dry highways, the skyline and houses make you sigh with relief that the boring trip is almost over.

As you approach West Berlin, there is no glimpse of skyline, nor a skirting through newly developed suburbs. The first clue that you're close is when the checkpoint comes into view, or you hit a line of stopped cars so long that you can't even see the observation towers.

"I'm glad it's not weekend," Thomas said, as we pulled to a halt behind about a dozen cars. He stopped the engine, leaving the gear in neutral. As the cars in front slowly moved forward, he would open his door and give the car a slight push with one foot, so as not to start the engine again. I assisted.

We passed through the checkpoint without hassle and drove along a wide, tree-lined street called Heer Strasse towards the centre. Soon, there were concrete houses and buildings, lush parks and playing fields. We turned right onto a narrow street and passed several high rise apartment blocks. They looked like the kinds you saw in Victoria Park, just on the eastside of the river in Perth, where the eastern suburbs began and got poorer and uglier the further east you went. We crested a hill and a large concrete structure came into view. It was like a modern colosseum, high and round and grey.

"That's the Olympic Stadium," Thomas explained. "The one Hitler built for the Olympics in 1936."

Apart from its history, it was an unimpressive structure: concrete, lifeless and dull, as if it had been built in a rush and time hadn't been taken to make it beautiful, or to take into account the surrounding forest. The concrete edifice looked completely out of place against a backdrop of high trees.

"What is it used for now?" I asked, wondering if Hitler's colosseum had been abandoned and forgotten as Thomas wanted the era to be.

"Football games," he said flatly, showing no interest for the sport. "And sometimes concerts, but really, the place has a terrible atmosphere because of its leprosy."

"Leprosy?"

"You know, because of the history."

"Oh, you mean legacy."

"Sorry, legacy. What's leprosy?"

"A disease when all your fingers and toes fall off."

He laughed, a high pitched squeal that made me cringe. He breathed in his giggles, the way small boys and girls do when they learn about sex.

"Almost," he said.

We drove away from the stadium and back to the tree-lined Heer Strasse. It was early evening and the streets were full: Mercedes, BMWs, VWs, the odd Porsche. Seldom was there an old car puttering along. The cars were new, well-designed and took off fast when the light turned from red to amber to green. If the car in front didn't accelerate immediately, horns were honked in an abusive, impatient way. Thomas did this subconsciously. I assumed it was the German way.

A tall column was visible in the distance. Behind that was a taller column, some kind of tower, grey, and shaped like an enormous lollypop. We drove towards the first column, through an enormous old gate, under a railway bridge and through a large park, before stopping at the traffic lights underneath it. I leaned forward. Perched on top was a golden woman with a staff in one hand and a laurel in the other. She had golden wings, and seemed to be taking a step forward, as if any moment she would fly off the column.

"That's the Golden Angel," Thomas said, looking not at the column but at the red traffic light, one hand on the gear stick, the other gripping the steering wheel, ready to drag race. "The victory column," he added.

I wondered why the German people had a column commemorating victory when they had lost both wars. Had the victors erected it to serve as some kind of memorial to stop the Germans from starting another war? The angel was beautiful, and I kept trying to get a look at it until Thomas tore off from the traffic lights. It grew smaller with distance, clouded by the haze of car fumes.

We continued through the park. Joggers were pulled along by dogs, while cyclists negotiated strollers and walkers, and peddled on with determination. The sky had turned overcast, with dark clouds jostling for position to rain on stranded individuals. The cyclists seem to sense this and peddled with vigour, glancing at the sky once or twice to predict how much longer they had before the heavens opened.

"That's Brandenburg Gate," Thomas said, pointing his finger at a large Roman looking structure ahead of us. It had tall columns and a person standing in some kind of chariot on top. Two red flags were in front while a black, red, and gold flag was on top. Up close, the gate was dirty and ruined, as if at any moment it might collapse. A low barrier kept us from driving any further. A sign in front said "You are leaving the British Sector" and was written in other languages as well. Two people stood on a wooden observation platform taking photographs of whatever was on the other side; three young children chased each other around the bottom of it, playing a game only they knew the rules of. Thomas quickly turned the car around and drove back down the road we came. He slowed as we passed two green tanks. A large bronze statue rose above the tanks, surrounded by a half circle of columns and walls. Two blank-faced soldiers stood at the entrance.

"What's that?" I asked. The statue was a soldier.

"The Russian War Memorial," he said coldly. "Whatever you do, don't mention it to Hilde or Antje."

"Why not?"

He turned his eyes on me; they were ice blue. "Because Antje's father was a Russian soldier. This is a memorial to all the women that were raped when Berlin fell."

He put the car into gear and we took off.

We drove in silence, Thomas breaking the lull with short explanations of other places and buildings. West Berlin was a prosperous city. There were many restaurants and bars, and high rise buildings adorned with names like Commerzbank and Allianz, and recognisable logos like the Mercedes star. Windows were shiny, the streets orderly and clean. There were people everywhere: cramming the sidewalks, hopping on and off buses, jumping in and out of cars, and disappearing into the underground train stations. It was a hive of activity, a community thrust together by political geography, and dealing with their strange existence by losing themselves in the regularities of routine. The looks on their faces didn't show that armies were gathering in their midst, or that the Cold War was being waged on their doorstep. They went about their business like people in any city, occupied by the never ending process of getting and spending. I watched the strange buildings rush past the window; some were old with grand statues and beautifully carved facades, while others were concrete edifices seemingly dropped from the sky and wedged between older buildings, out of place and ugly. The streets were wide and full of cars. Thomas circled a church with a large square in front of it three times before finding a parking place. He

63

walked briskly across the square with short, jumpy strides. He was tall, but had small feet like Kathrin and looked a little unbalanced, as if he would topple over if he took too big a stride. Some children roller skated on the square; others held dogs on leashes, waiting for them to finish shitting on the concrete before walking away from the steaming pile, left for someone to tread in.

"You're in luck," Thomas said, unlocking the door to his building. It was grey, the concrete unpainted. Each apartment had a balcony that looked down on the square. It was how I'd imagined London would be. "Hans went to America last week for the summer. You can sleep in his room."

"Great," I said, trying to sound enthusiastic. But my head was full of all the images I'd seen: the border guards and checkpoints, the barrier in front of Brandenburg Gate, the war relics, and what Thomas had said about his grandmother being raped by a Russian soldier, maybe by more than one. Something told me each person in West Berlin could tell a story like that, of lives ruined by war, and families divided by walls and guns. But what was most telling, was how the life continued here as if nothing had happened, as if there had been no Hitler, no loss of a generation, and no political split. The people had learned to live with it, and hoped that, by ignoring the past, they could somehow erase it.

Thomas lived on the fourth floor. The door had only one lock, and as he turned it, it was opened from the other side.

A bald, middle-aged man smiled and said something to Thomas in a soft, feminine voice. He had a silver hoop earring through his right ear and wore tight blue jeans with a pink tank top tucked in.

"Joachim, this is Michael," Thomas said in English, once we were inside the apartment. He pronounced his name Yo-ah-kim. I shook his limp hand; he did not grip mine at all. It was like shaking hands with an empty glove.

"Oh, you're an Englishman," Joachim squealed excitedly. "Wonderful. I can train my English."

"He's from Australia," Thomas said proudly.

Joachim put a hand to his cheek in disbelief. "How exotic," he exclaimed. "A real man. Well, come in, come in. Want some coffee or tea?" He turned to me and lowered his voice. "You want a beer, right?"

His attempt to be masculine was comical. I felt uncomfortable, not sure how to stand, what to say, or where to look. Thomas led me to a bedroom. I put my bag in there, then followed him to the living room. It was a bright room with two sofas, a television and a large hi-fi with records stacked on shelves next to it. The floor was wooden and the faint smell of lemon scented cleaner rose from it. I sat on the sofa next to a glass door that was open to the balcony. The sound of traffic and the unintelligible hum of many people talking rose from below. Sometimes, the noise died down and you could hear the clickity-clack of a woman's heels.

Joachim brought three bottles of beer in with him, each with a wedge of lemon stuck in the top. Thomas jumped up and put a record on. I recognised the opening of Queen's *Night at the Opera*.

"Great album," I said. "I'll drink to that. Prosit."

Thomas and Joachim both clinked my bottle softly. The beer was sour with the taste of lemon, but for some reason, it worked.

"So," Joachim began, "tell me everything. Where did you find this handsome young man?"

"Kathrin found him," Thomas said. "And then brought him to Gertie's party."

Joachim stared at me. His green eyes were wide. His smile made crow's feet at the corners of his eyes and pulled the tendons of his neck tight. With his wrinkled bald head, he was ugly when he smiled, and reminded me of some teachers I had known. A smile made them look more devious and cunning.

"So, your little sister got her hands on him first," he said, trying to sound charming. "Wasn't she lucky?"

"I'd say I was more lucky," I said. Joachim laughed shrilly. I wondered if Thomas had picked up his laugh from Joachim. But more, I wondered why Thomas lived with him.

"He was lucky at the checkpoint, as well," Thomas said. "We got through in ten minutes. It was a record."

"Ten minutes? Did they not check your, um, Kofferraum?"

"No. The guard gave Michael a letter to post and that was that."

Joachim smiled at me, as if I had some remarkable gift at having sunshine on me while everyone else had rain.

"I once had to wait three hours," he whined. "Because I had some design and fashion magazines with me. They thought I was going to throw them out the window on the Autobahn." Thomas and Joachim laughed together. With one's inhaled giggles and the other's squeal, they sounded like girls in the playground. I drank my beer and tried to smile. I felt awkward, out of place, masculine.

"What do you think of West Berlin?" Joachim asked.

I considered my answer for a second, looking thoughtfully at the floor, uncertain whether to air my true feelings or hold my tongue.

"It's really nice," I began. "Thomas showed me some interesting things on the way in. And I like this square," I added, pointing to the balcony. "That's the way I thought London would look."

"Thank you," Joachim said, taking what I said as a compliment. It made me assume this was his apartment and had been for a long time. It gave the impression of furniture unmoved, an atmosphere unchanged, the same smells. Thomas must be only a roommate. He may not be gay after all. I relaxed.

"Saw you the wall?" Joachim asked.

"I think so." I turned to Thomas for confirmation.

"At Brandenburg Gate," he said. "But it doesn't look like that everywhere," he said to me. "I'll take to you to meet Gaby later. She lives right next to it."

"Okay." With luck Gaby would be his girlfriend and everything could return to normal.

"I'll telephone her and tell her we're coming." Thomas got up and left the room. I looked at the floor, unsure what to say to Joachim.

"Zo, will you see Kathrin in East Berlin?" he asked.

"I hope so." Reminded of how much I missed her, I wanted more than anything to be back with her.

"I wish you luck at the border," Joachim said. "Sometimes it's not so easy to get permission, and you must wait a long time."

"Thomas mentioned that."

"Well, I'm not an expert. I never go to East Berlin. It's so horrible and ugly, and they are all so grey and depressed. And you must now change twenty-five Mark for their worthless currency, and pay for the visa." He scrunched up his nose and shook his bald head at the absurdity of his world, that everything had been made difficult to offset his need to not waste time.

"Well, maybe I'll get lucky," I said, as Thomas re-entered the room and sat down next to me.

"It's all set," he said smiling. "Gaby invited us for dinner. We can go after we finish this beer."

\*\*\*

66

We drove alongside a canal that had a railway line above it. Familiar things like petrol stations, libraries and fast-food restaurants made me feel more comfortable in this foreign city. There were brands I could cling to: Shell, McDonalds, BP, Coca-Cola. Home didn't seem so far away.

Gaby lived in a decrepit neighbourhood compared to the structured beauty of Winterfeldtplatz where Thomas lived. He called this area Kreuzberg. The building was old, but run down and in need of renovation. The streets were dirty and littered with broken glass and scrunched up beer cans. But more startling was the high wall that ran alongside her narrow street. We parked against the wall and walked down the street. Thomas was right; the wall here was unlike that at Brandenburg Gate. It was high, a good four meters, with round piping on top, and covered with graffiti. Colourful shapes and names flew off the wall in a vigour of creativity. One area had been whitewashed recently. Near the ground, the paint had run from being laid on too thick in a rushed job. The graffiti underneath was still visible but not clear. The wall ran along the pavement further down the road, bending to the left at the end in a well-formed arc. Behind us, it took a right angle at the corner and continued parallel with another narrow street, its structure uniform. Standing next to it, it seemed ridiculously high, but I'd also thought that of another wall, one protecting the playing fields of a private school in Perth; some friends and I had wanted to play football on the perfect field, but couldn't find a way over. That wall was about as high as this one, but was made of brick, not concrete. The Berlin Wall's height made it seem comical, especially here where it was so close to the pavement and houses, like some kind of stupid practical joke. Even though it was concrete, it seemed not to be so strong, like it could have been made out of foam; a theatrical set.

"Bet you never saw anything like that," Thomas said, with a hint of pride, the way an Australian might point out the Sydney Opera House or a kangaroo.

"Actually, it reminds me at lot of Perth," I said. "I mean, it's just a wall right, and there could be a factory on the other side, or a private school."

Thomas looked a little shocked. The wall hadn't affected me like he had thought it would. "But there is no factory," he exclaimed. "There's another country over there."

He was offended. I was supposed to look at the wall with awe, the way other tourists probably did. But I had grown up with walls; so many places attempted to keep people like me out with walls and fences. The idea of being excluded wasn't new, and seeing a high wall not so startling.

"Well," I said flatly, "I guess they have their reasons. You don't build a wall for nothing."

Thomas laughed sarcastically. "You wait. You will see it when you go there. My family lives three streets away," he said, pointing at the wall, "and I can never see them when I want." It meant that Kathrin was maybe two hundred metres from where we stood, but we couldn't see or speak to her. Thomas nodded at my acceptance. "Now do you understand? People go to the factory to work and leave at the end of the day. These people can't leave. They're stuck where they are. Believe me, we are on the right side of the wall here. We can go and visit and come back, and I'm glad we can only go for the day. Longer than that and I get too depressed."

Thomas's words were stirring, peppered with emotion and feeling, but I resolved not to be influenced by him. I would pass my own judgement after I had seen East Berlin. If Kathrin lived there, that bright, smart, beautiful girl, it couldn't have been as bad as Thomas said. I looked up at the wall, at the piping that was dull grey against the blue sky. When a cloud passed over, the colours blended and only the graffiti gave the wall away.

Gaby lived on the third floor. The building, old and decaying on the outside, was in better shape inside. The stairs were solid wood and curved around in a spiral, like in a castle tower. Windows looked down onto a small courtyard littered with bicycles and plastic sun chairs. A dog was sprawled on the high grass, making the most of the last ray of afternoon sunlight that found its way into the courtyard.

They kissed cheeks in the European fashion, suggesting more friendship than intimacy. Gaby was a tall woman, as tall as Thomas even with flat shoes, and around thirty. It struck me immediately that everything about her was pointy. She had angular features, thin arms and legs; pointy knees stuck out the bottom of her dress, and sharp elbows protruded from the rolled up sleeves of her pullover. Her cheekbones were high, but too far around the side of her face to be considered attractive. Teeth slightly bucktoothed, nose pointed, chin pointed, even ears pointed. They only thing that flowed was her blonde hair, which fell in waves to her shoulders, and which she pushed back with pointy fingers when it fell in her face. Her hair lent some softness to the harsh structure of her body. It could simply have been the hair of a normal person, but against the backdrop of her angularity, it seemed all the more soft and luxurious.

Gaby shook my hand firmly when we were introduced. She spoke English confidently, explaining she needed it for her work as a secretary for an international company, whose name she didn't give. The apartment was large, with wall-to-wall carpet and high ceilings. The lights were so high they felt like streetlights. Our voices echoed. It was a two room flat; the living room led to the bedroom. It wasn't possible for two people to live there separately without one having to always walk through the other's room.

"Come and look at this." Thomas stood in front of the living room window.

We looked down on the wall. It didn't seem as high as it did from the street. Behind it was a large area of cleared land. But there were no people kicking footballs around or letting anxious dogs off leashes. The area was barren and razed, and you knew that buildings had once stood there; the vacant area didn't fit the city landscape. There was a narrow road a few metres behind the wall, which would be lit at night by the large lights that were about twenty metres apart along the road. Behind this was a wire mesh fence, the kind companies have around their warehouses, and beyond that another wall. I followed Thomas's pointing finger to the large observation tower looming high over the razed area. It was tall and square, with windows just below the top. The sun was shining on the windows, preventing us from seeing in. The roof had a handrail, meaning it doubled as a viewing platform. I thought I could see some kind of searchlight on top, but wasn't sure. It may also have been a gun.

"We'll have another look later," Thomas said. "When they have a light on, you can see the guards inside and even wave to them."

He said this like we were going to see a reclusive animal at the zoo; it comes out of hiding so all the tourists can photograph it. Thomas left me and joined Gaby in the kitchen. I stayed watching the scene, looking past the barren strip to the apartment blocks beyond. Kathrin lived in one of them. I searched the windows for signs of life. I saw some people were relaxing on balconies, talking or reading. It looked quiet and peaceful over there. I was distracted by three guards coming into view. They walked along the narrow patrol road and were carbon

69

copies of the young guard at the border near Hamburg: saucer helmets, big guns slung over their shoulders, jackets pulled tight with belts. One guard walked behind the other two. He looked up at buildings on the western side as he passed them. Our eyes met. I resisted the urge to wave or shout. His stride was purposeful, strengthened by the gun on his shoulder. His face was pale and placid, but grew harder as he stared at me. Was it envy or hate? He didn't break stride or turn his head to maintain eye contact. He looked at the next building, hoping to catch another with his icy stare of contempt.

Thomas handed me a bottle of beer. No lemons this time. He followed my stare to the three guards.

"One reads the regulations, one witnesses them read, and the third keeps an eye on those two dangerous intellectuals," he said laughing.

"Can we see Kathrin's apartment?" I asked.

Thomas smiled. "You really want to see her again. No, we can't. It's behind that big one over there." He pointed with his beer.

"She's a really nice girl."

"Who is?" Gaby said, falling onto a low sofa. She crossed her legs, her pointy knees like twin mountain peaks.

Thomas said something in German and Gaby laughed loudly.

"You're doomed," she said, recovering herself. "Stay away from the Ossis. They're all looking for a way out."

Later, we ate pasta with a bland tomato sauce. Gaby didn't seem at home in the kitchen and ate quickly, throwing food into her mouth like pumping petrol in a car. She talked about her trip to Australia and made jokes about the wall. She didn't seem to take it seriously, yet she woke up every morning looking at it. I got tired of this attitude and asked her bluntly why she lived so close to it.

"The rent is very cheap," she said. "And look at the apartment. You can't find places like this in West Berlin. And it's better than looking at offices or a factory."

The words were old, like she'd said them a thousand times before, her force of conviction the result of repetition. I didn't like Gaby. She was too uptight and edgy. She cleared the dishes away in a flurry and left them in the sink. Her movements were quick and awkward; she had no grace. I was glad she wasn't Thomas's girlfriend.

We took fresh beers into the living room. Gaby and Thomas sat on the couch talking German while I stood at the window. Night was falling, and the area behind the wall was brightly lit by the high searchlights. There was a single light on in the observation tower. The heads of two men were visible. They wore no helmets. Both were smoking. They looked bored. But the area was so quiet. Gaby's street had few cars, and in a big city, the absence of roaring engines and honking horns resulted in an eerie silence. It made you listen harder for sounds in the dark. On the other side of the wall it looked even quieter. The voices of the patrol guards carried through the night, bored murmurs breaking the silence. I thought I heard the word football.

I turned to Gaby and Thomas, and waited for a break in their conversation. "Is it always so quiet here?"

"Isn't it wonderful?" Gaby exclaimed. "Some of my friends live on main roads and I don't know how they sleep it's so loud."

I wanted to say that the silence was restricting and suffocating, like in a cemetery or a hospital. It made you scared to move, to make any sound. And you sat in fear, breathing shallowly because if you breathed normally, it sounded like the wheezing and sucking of an industrial vacuum cleaner.

Two young kids were spraying fresh graffiti on the whitewashed wall as we walked to the car. They wrote their street names in wild letters with symbols and signs so people could recognise it on other places around the city. But the whitewash wasn't dry enough; the spray paint mixed with the white and dripped down the wall pink and purple.

At the corner, I stopped and looked down the street. The wall was dark, immersed in shadow and looming. How out of place it looked, as if it had fallen from the sky by accident and this was where it had landed, and was why it curved and turned. But in the last twenty years, it had become as much a part of the city landscape as any other structure. Thomas knew no Berlin without the wall. He was only twenty, and lucky, he said, that he had been passed over to the better side. It was no wonder the West Berliners talked so much about the wall; they lived with it in their faces. It cast shadows on gardens that needed sun, cut off streets, made you take long detours, and was an omnipresent reminder of the way of things; that you couldn't visit your cousins, or chase up old school friends. Thomas said the East German government built the wall to keep its citizens in like prisoners, but it seemed to me that the West Berliners were the prisoners. The wall kept them inside their area, restricted their movements, and invaded their lives. The city was an island, isolated by concrete instead of water.

Hans's bed was soft and short, like a bed for a child. My feet hung over the edge and I felt the blood being cut off. With the window open, I could hear the familiar sounds of city life that were absent at Gaby's apartment. It was comforting noise. Rain had started to fall as we drove home, and now I heard the panicked voices of those rushing home through the rain without umbrellas or rain jackets. What is it about rain that makes people energetic and anxious? It's like a barrier to all the things that had been planned and were then cancelled because of bad weather. Looking out the window at a wall of water falling from the sky, children know they can't go outside, the postman knows he'll get wet, and the family's day at the park is ruined. The wall of water stops them from going outside, and they become prisoners.

I like rain. I like the way it creates a little bit of chaos, that well-organised events can be completely ruined by the power of nature. I like it when man is reduced by nature. I like the smell of rain and the sound of it hitting an old iron roof, like the one on our first house in Maddington. The sound was loud, but rhythmic and soothing. Rain could wash away yesterday's dirt and give you a fresh start. And it was an equaliser. All people, rich or poor, were reduced to the same drenched state when caught in the rain. It also brought strangers together, huddled under shelter and exchanging comments and jokes, waiting for the rain to stop. These people could come from all walks of life and be equal standing there. Rain ruined expensive suits, made makeup run, drenched important documents, flattened well-styled hair. Rain was liberating: kids darted from their parents to take running jumps into puddles, footballers took long slides in wet grass and gave up trying to keep their jerseys clean, and sometimes people just stood in the rain, accepting they were completely wet and relishing it, letting the water splatter on their faces and drip into their mouths.

The rain fell in fat drops onto the street below. It ran down the window and sometimes when the wind changed direction, a few drops hit me lying on the bed. It was cold and ticklish. I let the water run between my legs or down the side of my stomach. I closed my eyes. Being hit by raindrops didn't wake me as I slept.

Kathrin was in my dreams. We lay on a beach. The sun was high and warm, but not scolding like it was in Perth, and a light breeze blew swiftly enough to stop your sweat from forming into large enough droplets that would trickle down your sides. The water was flat and dark blue. Boats cruised along in no hurry. I guessed it was a weekend. Kathrin was naked. Her young body glistened in the sun. She lay on her back with a hat covering her eyes. As I took in her rounded form, I became aware of my own nakedness, and a wave of self-consciousness passed through me. Kathrin raised her head and said something in German. I heard my own voice reply, sounds and words that almost shocked me awake. She laughed, leaned over to kiss me, but I pulled her on top. Her body was warm and covered with small white circles of dried salt. We were alone on the beach. The sun was directly behind Kathrin, putting her face in the shadows. I was aware I was dreaming, but the sensations were strong enough to maintain the dream. I could smell her sweat and taste the dried salt on her mouth. But then her face changed to that of my mother, who looked at me with curiosity, as if she didn't understand what I was doing. I tried to explain to her, but only German words came out. She didn't understand, turned angry and slapped me in the face.

I woke with a start. I rolled over, but the images of the dream were too fresh in my head and I couldn't go back to sleep for some time. I felt alone. The sound of the rain comforted me.

# East Berlin

We sat in the car like two spies on a morning stakeout. Thomas sipped coffee from a paper cup. He looked towards Checkpoint Charlie, and down the road past the barriers to East Berlin.

"Don't take anything to read," Thomas warned again. "Not even a newspaper. Or any more money than you need."

"I have only thirty Marks like you said."

"Makes it easier." He sighed. "It's actually quite good. There won't be a long line. Not as many people go over now they increased the money exchange."

A large sign informed that you were leaving the American Sector, in three other languages as well. It looked old and out of date, a relic from a past era, dented and dirty, as if kids threw rocks at it every day. A small, low white hut stood in front of a red and white striped barrier, like the ones at railway crossings. The American flag was limp in the breezeless morning. Sandbags were stacked shoulder high in front of the hut.

"I'd come with you, but I only get thirty days a year," Thomas explained. "I have to use them for special times. And I have university today."

"Will they be able to speak English?"

He nodded. "I think so. A lot of foreigners go through this checkpoint. They also get all the tourist buses."

"That's comforting."

"I'll meet you here at ten."

"Okay."

I got out of the car and slammed the door; nerves manifesting themselves in uncontrolled energy. I didn't look back at Thomas for moral support. I walked slowly towards the white hut. The windows were eye level; two young soldiers looked at me and smiled, pointing in the direction I had to go. They said something to each other, but I couldn't understand it. They laughed. There was an arrogance about them I didn't like; a tilt of the head, something in their eyes and manner that lent them a kind of self-enforced superiority. They were Americans, and just like Jason. The time I'd spent with him in Hamburg felt like years ago.

I crossed a wide white line painted on the road. On either side of the street, the white line ran to where the wall met the street. It seemed a long way to the next white hut. I took short steps, wondering what I was getting myself into. I was just a poor kid from Perth. I knew nothing about politics, had no experience with crossing borders and spoke no German except the one sentence Thomas had written on a piece of paper for me: "Sprechen Sie Englisch?"

A large tourist bus came from behind me and I stepped out of its way. The familiar smell of burning diesel filled my nostrils and made me drowsy. It stopped at the white hut, the barrier was raised and the bus pulled into a big car park next to another bus.

I walked towards the hut. Two soldiers turned to me and eyed me suspiciously. Both wore saucer helmets, had clean shaven faces and smoked stubby cigarettes. I held up my passport as Thomas had instructed. The older guard pointed to a large building on the left side of the road. I walked towards it.

I didn't want to be late. Kathrin and I had arranged in Hamburg to meet at the corner of Friedrich Strasse and Unter den Linden at nine. It was half past eight when I entered the building. I joined the back of a line of impatient, nervous people, mostly middle-aged businessmen. They shuffled their feet, moved their weight from one leg to the other, checked their watches and whispered fast words that betrayed their anxiety. The narrow corridor was dimly lit, with mirrors on the ceilings. You had the feeling dozens of eyes were watching, waiting. The line moved slowly, the time creeping closer to nine. The couple in front of me were Americans. They spoke loudly, complaining about the waiting time. The man was large and quite ridiculously wore a yellow cowboy hat with a denim jacket and denim jeans. The woman had the same denim uniform, but didn't hide her dyed red hair under a hat. They looked comical, their voices an annoying whine.

The guard was in a small room positioned above the people. You had to strain your neck to see his head. He had a large, round face and drooping, tired eyes. He looked like a failed farmer who had come to the city to start life again, but always dreamed of the land and wanted to get back to the farm. He took the passports from the American couple; they exaggeratedly expressed annoyance as they were led to another room to have their bags checked. A glimmer of a smile crossed the guard's face.

I slid my passport into the slot with the five Marks. The guard stared at the photo briefly, then at me for what seemed like a long time. I tried to look innocent, but his eyes searched my face for any discrepancy that would give him the pleasure of denying me entry. He looked back at the photo and then again at me. It was horrible being stared at like that. I wanted to shrink to the floor, to have the glare of spotlights taken off me. And it felt like he wasn't the only one staring at me, judging me.

"Why you go to Berlin?" he growled finally. His voice was hoarse from the dry air inside the box, or maybe from saying so little.

"I want to see the city and visit the museums," I said. It was what Thomas had told me to say. He had said East Berlin had famous museums. I didn't want to lie, but Thomas had been adamant that I shouldn't mention Kathrin or her family. It would only get them in trouble, and make it harder for them to leave for the next important occasion.

"Have you camera?"

"No, sir." It was the first time in my life I'd said sir. The word sounded strange, like it was only used in movies and sounded artificial in real life.

"Newspapers, books, journals?" he pressed, his voice becoming smoother with talking.

"No. Nothing."

He looked at me suspiciously. I carried no bag, and I knew too much for a first-time tourist. I wanted to explain, but Thomas had told me not to give any free information, only to answer their questions.

The grate slid open and I took my passport out. "You must change twenty-five D-Mark." He pointed down the corridor.

"Danke," I said, trying to sound friendly. Manners were out of place here; the word bounced off the walls and into everyone's surprised ears, before the silence resumed as the next person was scrutinised.

"You can take not money out of DDR," the next guard said harshly, handing over flimsy, crumpled bills totalling twenty-five. They looked and felt worthless, like the withered bills from an old monopoly set.

Outside, the sunlight hurt my eyes. Was it really so dark in the immigration building? I walked along the side of the road quickly. Buses were lined up, waiting to pass the final hut. I looked behind me. The American flag was blowing in the breeze now, but seemed far in the distance. At the last white hut, I showed the fresh stamp in my passport. The young guard smiled.

"Have a good day," he said.

I smiled back at him. The pressure lifted. "Danke. You too."

I left my fears behind and walked quickly down Friedrich Strasse. The street was lined with shops, but I didn't stop to look in their windows. Crossing the border hadn't been so bad. Thomas made it out to be some kind of torture. My watch said quarter past nine.

From a distance, I saw Kathrin standing at the corner. She saw me and started walking. Her worried look turned to one of happiness. Her breasts moved up and down as she strode over, walking quickly, but awkwardly, as if she was keeping herself from running. I noticed she was slightly knock-kneed. Despite the brisk morning, she wore a blue skirt that stopped at the knees and a darker blue pullover that hugged the contours of her upper body. I knew then I would have waited days at the border, subjected myself to all manner of searches and interrogations, just to have this one moment with her. Instead of wrapping her arms around me like I thought she would, she took me by the hand and led me behind a building. There, her mouth dissolved into mine and her arms held me tight. Two tears left the corners of each of her aqua eyes, which were startling against the blue of her pullover.

"I thought you have problems," she stammered. Her cheeks were red from the cold wind, but her smile was radiant. Her crossed over teeth made me melt. "At the border, you know."

"No. No problems." We kissed again. I felt her soft breasts against my chest and her strong arms holding my neck tight. Passion was building from within me. But it wasn't driven by lust or desire; to sleep together just seemed like the next logical thing, as if both of us had waited our whole lives for this time, and knew beforehand exactly how it was going to be.

We held hands and walked through the city, down streets I'd never seen before, past buildings I took no notice of. I saw only Kathrin and could find no room in my thoughts for anything else. We swapped details of our respective journeys. I told her about the guard's letter, how I'd posted it and how I'd wanted very badly to read it.

"You will have no problem finding work here," she said laughing. I didn't understand the joke but laughed anyway.

The apartment building was old, shadowed by the new high rise blocks around it. They reached high to the sky white, uniform and modern. Kathrin's building was like Gaby's. Paint peeled on the outside, and there were some round markings and holes, but the inside was wonderful. The street was called Alte Jakob Strasse.

"We all work together to keep it in good condition," Kathrin said, as I admired the solid wooden staircase.

I liked the idea of this small community helping each other. It reminded me of how dad and his mates had helped each other build their houses on Sunday afternoons. They drank, laughed, laid brick and had a barbecue in the evening. Us kids would help out and the women would come with food and more beer.

I wanted to tell Kathrin this, tell her everything about my life, and how it all had seemed like wasted time until I'd met her. But I said nothing as she led me through her parents' apartment and into her room. She had posters on the wall of the Rolling Stones, and advertisements for jeans and other clothes cut from magazines. It struck me then that Kathrin was just a girl, younger than Thomas, and I knew nothing about her.

We sat down on her single bed. I felt nervous, but strangely comfortable and content. I'd been in this situation with other girls before only to end up kissing once or twice and have it stop at that. But Kathrin played no games. And there was more here than just a kiss at a party with a girl who looked better in the dark.

She took off her pullover. She wore no bra. The mid-morning sun came through the windows and shone on her naked chest, golden like the angel atop the victory column in West Berlin. She took my hand, put it to her breast, pressed it and smiled. Her nipple went firm under my palm.

We fell back on the bed and discovered each other's body without rushing. I had to be out of East Berlin by midnight, but felt like I had my whole life to press myself against this girl. She rose and fell like an animal let out of its cage, without the inhibitions and restraints of the few women I had known; they thought of sex as something to give a man and not something to enjoy. I lost myself in Kathrin's rhythmic abandon, emboldened by her animal grunts and powerful thrusts. I became the animal, a raging monster intent on taking her to another realm of ecstasy, and in the process taking myself beyond the limits of physical pleasure I'd previously known.

In the calming aftermath, we drank sweet Margon Cola from fat bottles and said nothing, each of us trying to make sense of what was happening. A scratched Beatles record played softly. Kathrin would reach out with her leg and kick the turntable anytime it got stuck.

"Kathrin," I said finally. "I know this might sound like a strange question, but I don't even know what you do. I mean, I know now you live at home, but do you go to university or school or anything like that."

A tired, warm smile crossed her face, and she lay her head down on my chest. "My mother wants me to be a teacher, like her," she began. "My father wants me to be an engineer, like he is."

"And what do you want to be?"

She raised her head, her aqua eyes gleaming. "I want to be with you."

"I'm here," I said. "And I want to be with you as well. But it's not so easy."

"I know," she said, sighing. "I don't want to leave my home."

I'd expected her to say the opposite. Gaby had warned that all Ossis were trying to find a way out. I'd thought Kathrin might only want me as a way to escape, and maybe find her way to Australia. Gaby made my homeland out to be the greatest place in the world, that it was everyone's dream to live there. But she didn't know the Australia I knew.

"I would never ask you to do that," I said.

"You could come here," she said hopefully, sitting up. "I know what Thomas says, but he's wrong. The life here is much better than in West Germany. The people here help each other, and care."

"I know what you mean. It's everyone for himself in Perth. The rich get richer and the poor have another toilet to clean."

"It's not like that here," Kathrin said, propping herself up on her elbow. "There are no poor people. Everyone has what they need. Everyone works."

"Come on, Kathrin. There are poor people and unemployed everywhere. It's a fact of life."

"Not here. The government takes care of everyone. It is a worker's republic."

"Sounds like paradise," I said.

"Well, it may not be paradise, but it's fair."

I propped myself up on an elbow and faced her, a mirror image of her own position. "I'm from a poor family," I said. "I had to work a long time to save for this trip. I never had the chance to go university. We never had much growing up, but the people in my area had each other and that was something. And now, I'm just a mechanic."

"That is a good job here," Kathrin said. "You can make D-Mark on the weekend."

She was selling me her country and I was listening. I wanted to be with her, whatever the consequences. Would it be so hard to move here for a year or two just to see if it works? Did Kathrin want to marry me? Did I want to marry her?

She took the cola bottle from my hand, placed it on the floor and climbed on top of me. We kissed gently, and she murmured as she felt my dick throb against her stomach.

"As long as you're here, Kathrin," I said, "this is paradise for me."

We made love again, fast, with an urgency, as if each thrust was like an intake of oxygen, a necessary part of living. Kathrin peaked several times and I knew each time because her hand would squeeze my neck hard, her fingernails digging in as the pleasure thumped through her body like waves slamming on the shore.

But we did not linger in bed this time.

"Come on," she said, playfully pulling my limp body off the bed. "My mother is home soon. I don't want her to see you like this."

I remembered Monica's warmth, or lack of it, from the party. I wasn't looking forward to seeing her again. The job of teacher fit.

Kathrin wore a bra this time. It was plain, white, cheap and looked like a million dollars on her. I felt weak pulling on my jeans; the last ounce of strength had been sucked from my body. We stumbled into the afternoon light. The sun was hidden behind dark clouds that looked just like the ones that had rolled in the day before. The air smelt of rain, but I didn't care. I walked on the clouds, my feet hardly touching the pavement. In East Berlin, I had been transformed into a new person: confident, intelligent, experienced, desirable, passionate. I had just slept with a girl from East Germany. My friends in Maddington would never believe it.

We followed a canal, walking towards tall buildings I guessed were part of the centre of East Berlin. A large tower rose high to the sky. It was grey and thin, round and wide at the top, with viewing windows; the same tower I'd seen when Thomas and I had driven into West Berlin. Kathrin called it the Television Tower. From the top you could see the whole of Berlin, she said, East and West. We could go up there on the weekend when there was more time.

"Why not tomorrow?" I asked.

"I have to learn," she said. "And I have my youth meeting tomorrow night. It is better you come back at the weekend. Twenty-five D-Mark is a lot of money."

"Are you learning to be an engineer or a teacher?" I asked, trying not to sound rejected.

"I learn to be a secretary," she said flatly. "It's because both my parents went to university and have good jobs. The system gives the children of workers first chance to go to university."

This communism thing was sounding better by the minute. In such a system, my sister and I could have gone to university, while the private school kids would become the mechanics and the bricklayers.

"I think it's good that the poorer people get the chance to go to university," I said.

"Yes." But she said nothing more and I guessed that she was unhappy about being denied a better education.

We left the canal and walked along a wide street towards a building with brown, tinted windows. It turned out to be a long building, seemingly made entirely of glass. Kathrin called it the Palace of the Republic. It had only recently been built. She sometimes went with friends to the disco there. Jealousy rippled through my body as I imagined her dancing with boys, flirting, the centre of attention and the most desirable girl in the disco.

We stopped in front of the steps. A large church was on the other side of the street further down and beyond that stood an old building with large columns in front.

"This is the symbol of the DDR," Kathrin said, pointing at a round sign above the doorway. "The compass, the hammer, and the circle of, what do you call it, to make bread?"

"Wheat."

"Right, and this is because the state is run by workers and farmers. The Soviets have the hammer and...Sichel, you know, to cut the wheat."

"A sickle."

"The leaders are workers and farmers and they make decisions on behalf of the people. The state owns and controls everything."

We walked towards the church, then turned right on another big street.

"What do you mean the state controls everything?"

Kathrin gave me a condescending look, as if reproaching me for knowing so little. "Nothing is private," she explained. "That way, everyone gets an equal share of everything."

"I can't believe that. My parents only ever speak about how the government in Australia takes more money from the people who have less, in order to keep them poor. I don't understand how it works here. Are you saying the government makes sure that each person has enough to live? Nobody lives on the street, or shares a house with another family, or that kids aren't forced to leave school to work?"

"That's capitalism," Kathrin said with spite. "It's only a good system for those with money. They have more products and more freedom to travel, but they do not have equality even though they say they do. You should come to one of our youth meetings."

We walked through a small park and stopped in front of a bronze statue of one man standing and another sitting. They had their backs to the Palace of the Republic.

"Are these the founders of East Germany?" I asked.

"You don't know Marx and Engels?" Kathrin exclaimed incredulously.

"I know the Marx Brothers, but he doesn't look like one."

"They are the fathers of socialism. It is because of them that we live in this society today. The world would be nothing without them."

I felt stupid, uneducated, inferior, immature. Kathrin knew everything, had all the answers, and spoke them confidently, unaware how small she made me feel. Compared to me, she'd had it easy. Both parents were educated and had good jobs. She lived in a big apartment and never had to worry about money. Her parents did not live in fear of losing their jobs, or of being forced onto welfare by redundancies.

The centre of East Berlin was a wide expanse of concrete. As we walked towards the base of the television tower, we passed a large red building. Kathrin called it the Rathaus. I gave her the translation I'd learned in Hamburg.

"Very good," she said smiling, and then kissed me warmly. She seemed to be unaware of how stupid she had made me feel at the Marx and Engels statue. "You learn fast. I think my mother wants to teach you German. She's a good teacher."

I grimaced slightly. "Sounds good."

The centre was peppered with trees, statues and fountains. People walked casually. They didn't rush the way West Berliners did. They took their time, stopped to talk with others or to relax on a bench and watch the scene. I became aware of how slowly the city moved. The few cars in the centre chugged along and there was no obnoxious honking of horns. The pace was completely different to West Berlin. It was like walking through the main square of a small farming village on a Sunday, and not a bustling capital. Businessmen wore dull grey suits and carried briefcases. A few had their jackets slung over their arms, getting hot walking in the summer afternoon. It was neither sunny nor hot, but warm enough to make you sweat if you moved fast enough. But most moved slowly and kept their jackets on.

Kathrin slipped her hand into mine as if she'd be doing it all her life. "Isn't it beautiful?" she asked.

I recalled Perth with its lush green parks close to the wide river downtown. The tall skyscrapers jostling for position and glistening in the sun. The mad rush to get into the city in the morning and to get out in the evening. The money, the greed, the division, the exclusion.

I looked across the wide concrete expanse of East Berlin. The city hall deep red and beautiful, like a burning afternoon sun setting on the square. The Neptune fountain spurting water while small children splashed in the shallows. The television tower, that giant grey lollypop, high and mighty above it all. The green spires of churches an historical contrast to the modern buildings and shops. And the people, dressed similarly, greeting each other, friendly and warm, not pushing or shoving, and not divided by clothes or wealth; workers and farmers all in it together.

"Yes," I said, kissing my new girlfriend on the forehead. "It is."

We walked past the tower, onto another wide expanse called Alexanderplatz. Kathrin showed me the world clock. It gave us the time in Perth and reminded me how far away that world was, and that soon I would return there, leaving Kathrin behind. The distance was so far. There could be no weekend visits. If I wanted to be with her, it had to be here. And looking at the faces of the people, the calmness, the equality, the patience, the acceptance, I felt like one of them, that these were my people. They did not wear expensive clothes or drive BMWs. They were simple people living simple lives. Everyone had a chance. Everyone was included.

"Come on," Kathrin said, pulling me by the hand. "We have to spend your money. You can't take it back."

"I'll buy you whatever you want," I said.

I felt reckless, free, uninhibited; a new person in a new place. A beautiful girl held my hand, and we walked through the centre of a world I never thought could exist. We entered a large store called

Zentrum. It sold all manner of goods. Some were piled high in simple displays, while other spaces were empty because the goods had sold out earlier. The signs still remained which gave hope to the idea that a worker might bring out more. The simplest things cost almost nothing: beer, wine, basic clothing, necessary things for the house. But then a television would be an enormous price. Twenty-five Marks, at first, seemed like nothing, but with Kathrin's help, we spent all the money and came out with full boxes.

"That was fun," I said, carrying a heavy box with both arms. Shopping had always been a painful process for me, where you had basic needs, but could never seem to fulfil them with the money you had. Even the simplest t-shirt was expensive. But Kathrin had shown me how to make it work, that while some products were expensive, the things you needed for life were incredibly cheap. Television was a luxury you could live without. They were expensive in Australia as well, but so were the basic things. Here, a person could walk into a shop with twenty-five Marks and buy everything he needed for the week.

"We were lucky," Kathrin said, breathing hard because of the heavy box she carried. I had offered to take the heaviest stuff, but she had firmly refused; she wanted to carry the same amount as me.

I thought of my mother, earning a lower wage than a man for doing the same work, but expected to work harder to prove her worth. Kathrin showed the kind of power that would have women in Australia scratching their heads. I liked the fact she thought herself equal to me. I had never liked the gender situation in Australia, the way the women were so dependent on men and never attempted to change their roles. The men drove the cars; the women sat in the passenger seats and said nothing.

Kathrin led us downstairs to the underground train. I had no money left, so she bought two tickets. They cost twenty pfennig. We sat down on the train with the large boxes on our knees. We looked comical, with only our heads visible. People smiled at us. We smiled back. Kathrin engaged in conversation with some of them, and everyone around us was listening and laughing. Nobody felt shy about talking to strangers, sharing a joke or offering to help. I liked the friendliness, and the lack of impersonality. Here was a real community.

We got out of the train and walked to the apartment. I had five hours left and wondered what the rest of the day would bring. I smiled. The sun burst through the gaps of dark clouds and the streets glistened. It had rained here, but not at Alexanderplatz. It felt like the sun was shining on me, and I could feel its warmth, its caress, urging me to stay here longer, where the sun shone on me in the same way it did on everyone else.

Kathrin slipped off her wet shoes, put them on top of her box, and walked up the stairs barefoot. I followed, slipping a little in my socks as I negotiated the stairs with the heavy box in my arms. Kathrin rang the bell and Monica opened the door.

"We come with gifts," Kathrin shouted. Monica took the box from her daughter and carried it easily. I followed her into the kitchen and put the box on the floor.

"Nice to see you again, Monica," I said, offering her my hand. She smiled meekly and shook my hand. Her hand was firm but greasy, as if she'd just covered it with cream. Her face also was shiny with some kind of lotion, and she had put it on too thick, leaving white areas at the top of her forehead, around her nostrils, and on her ears. She spoke to Kathrin in German. Her tone was playful; she could not suppress her delight. I heard my name, the German Mikhail that my ears were used to hearing. I guessed Kathrin explained how we had spent my money, the money I couldn't take back with me.

"Thank you," Monica said, turning to me. It was genuine, but not overly warm. It wasn't that Monica didn't like me. I think she considered me some kind of threat.

A large man entered the kitchen and I turned to look at him. He was tall, with a heavy chest that you could see was hairy because his shirt was open at the top. The shirt was tight and was made looser by undoing the top four buttons. It made him look like a retired boxer, but he didn't have a boxer's face. His nose was long and straight, and on it sat a pair of thick-rimmed glasses. His hair was brown, greying at the temples and starting to thin, but only recently. His hair made him look youthful, but his long dangling ears and thick glasses made him look like the old man he was.

He threw out a calloused hand with dirty fingernails. On the side of the hand was a large bandage, but he didn't grimace when I pressed it to shake his hand. For an engineer, he had the hands of a worker, like how I remembered my father's hands to be.

"I am Heinrich König," he said, at once proud of his English, but somewhat embarrassed using it in front of his family. "Zo, you are the great mechanic."

He smiled in a warm, friendly way. His teeth were more cream than white and didn't suit him; too wide to be normal teeth and too big for his mouth. False teeth.

"Not yet a great mechanic," I said, "but getting there." I looked at Kathrin, who was smiling in a daddy's-little-girl way, and realised I'd been trapped again. "Are you having some trouble with your car?"

A look of confusion crossed his face, a deep furrow like a valley between two mountains formed between his bushy eyebrows. I had spoken too fast.

"Your car," I tried again, but slower. "Everything okay?"

"No problem," he said. "I have friend, doctor, I must help. You come?"

I looked at Kathrin. Her eyes urged me to go with him.

"Of course," I said, nodding.

"Good," he said, and left the kitchen.

"He has problems with his heart," Kathrin whispered in my ear. Her breath was hot and tickled my ears, and reminded me how she had grunted in my ear only a few hours earlier. I wanted to drag her into her bedroom and throw her down on her single bed. "The doctor helped him a few weeks ago," she continued, "got him some tablets that are not so easy to get. He wants to give the doctor something back."

"Okay."

She looked at me hopefully. "You understand?"

I nodded. She kissed me shyly on the cheek. Monica was putting products away, thumping large cabbages and cauliflowers on the counter, and heaving out big bags of potatoes and long loaves of dark bread, making sure we were aware of her presence.

Heinrich returned slinging a key ring around a mangled finger. He wore a jacket as tight as his shirt, and I didn't think he was able to zip it up without ripping it at the back. He said something to Monica. His voice was deep and slow. He didn't rush his words and spoke to his wife with respect.

"Come on, mechanic," he said to me. "We work."

We climbed into a small, pale blue car with only two doors. Trabant was written on the side in fancy lettering that didn't suit the simple car. Thomas had passed cars like these on the Autobahn. It didn't look like anything I had ever seen before. It looked cheap and slow, with tail fin lights like cars from the sixties. The car was so narrow our shoulders were almost touching, and Heinrich's knees were wedged under the steering wheel. He rocked the car back and forth and the engine ignited with a dull roar. The wind was behind us; faint, black smoke drifted past the windows.

Heinrich said nothing. The engine was loud and I think he felt self-conscious speaking English over the noise. He wanted to appear strong and powerful. He had no problem hitting me with his elbow every time he changed gear. The Trabant had a column shift.

We drove slowly along wide streets, past high buildings that weren't tall enough to be skyscrapers, but were still impressive. Everything looked new and modern, as if every building had a fresh coat of paint. West Berlin had struck me as drab and grey, the only colours coming from advertisements and company logos. We passed a large square that had three beautiful historic buildings; two were churches and the one in the middle looked like some kind of theatre. Heinrich called it Platz der Akadamie. I marvelled at the age of the buildings. You didn't see such things in Australia. There, a fifty year-old building was considered an historical landmark.

I recognised the corner where I had met Kathrin. It seemed like years ago. Brandenburg Gate was visible in the distance. There were guards with green saucer helmets and guns on their backs. Their shoulders were hunched in postures of boredom and they attempted to engage the people walking past in conversation. I felt sorry for them; such an unexciting job. We turned right at the last intersection before the gate. We crossed a bridge. To the left was a large grey-brown building with turrets like a castle. But Heinrich increased his speed, downhill, and the castle disappeared behind some other buildings.

The road was wide and a little bumpy. We passed a series of red buildings covered with green vines. Heinrich made a fast u-turn and parked in front of one of the red buildings. The car shuddered to a halt, seemingly sighing with relief.

"Stay here," he said, before hauling himself out of the car. It rocked from side to side with the change in weight. He lumbered towards the entrance. The building was called Charité, and from the comings and goings of people dressed in white, and others with casts on their arms or legs, or with crutches and limps, I guessed it to be a hospital. If it had had a wall, it would have looked more like a mental institution. The dark red bricks gave it a restrictive feel.

"Doctor go home," Heinrich said, falling into the car. "But he not far."

We drove past decaying apartment buildings, most with simple shops on the ground floors. They looked the same as where Kathrin lived. I wondered if they were as immaculate inside, or decrepit as the outside suggested. Most buildings still showed the scars of war, with large pock marks and scattered bullet holes dimpling the front walls, making them look like large, square, grey golf balls. There were more hills in this part of the city. The Trabant chugged uphill reluctantly, with Heinrich urging the car on like a jockey whipping a tired horse. Trams ran along the main streets loud and dominant. When they stopped to drop off and pick up, all the cars had to wait behind.

Heinrich parked on a hill in front of a scarred building. A train line went down the middle of the street, over ground like the one last night in West Berlin. This time, I got out with Heinrich and followed him to the front door. It was high, the woodwork intricately carved and decorated, like the door to a palace.

"Doctor come down," Heinrich said, after ringing the bell. He pushed his glasses higher up on his nose. They had slipped while he was driving because the roads were bumpy and potholed.

A tall, thin man opened the door and descended the three steps to where we stood. He shook Heinrich's hand, and spoke in a nasal whine that, even if I knew the language, would find difficult to understand. His shoulders were very square, as if he hadn't taken the coat hanger out of his shirt. He turned to me and shook my hand.

"Nice to meet you, Michael," he said. His English was surprising clear and his voice soft, as if this was his natural language. "Heinrich says you are a mechanic."

"That's right, doctor. Are you having trouble with your car?"

The doctor smiled. "It's a funny thing. I drive for ten minutes and the car becomes so hot. And I must keep putting water in the...I don't know how you call it, the water box?"

"The radiator," I said. "Why don't you take it to the workshop?"

The doctor frowned. "That is not so easy. The workshops are always full."

"Where is your car?"

The doctor led me down a narrow alley and behind his building. There were five Trabants like Heinrich's, but in brown and beige as well as pale blue, and one yellow, boxy sedan. The doctor opened the door to this one and popped the bonnet. Heinrich appeared with a toolbox in his hand and joined me under the bonnet.

An engine is an engine. As cars go, the basic components are always the same, as are their deficiencies. First, I inspected the radiator for leaks. I felt its heat against my hands and face but saw no sign of leakage. This left the hoses and clips.

"Doctor, can you start the engine, please?"

The engine was loud and rusty. The dry fan belt squealed and water flew out of a hose that connected to the back of the engine.

"Na ja," Heinrich said, smiling at me.

"Okay, doctor. That's enough."

I looked at the hose. It came off the joint easily, water coming out of the hose and the joint. I pocketed the rusty clip. The end of the hose was frayed and worn, split on one side. But it couldn't be cut to the end of the split because it would then be too short.

"You wouldn't have another hose, would you, doctor?" I asked.

Heinrich laughed. The doctor smiled. He had a soft face with glassy eyes, and didn't seem to be a man of great humour. He held his hands open and shrugged.

I paused. "Okay, do you have a washing machine, or a dishwasher in your apartment."

"I have a washing machine," he said proudly.

"May I see it?"

Heinrich stayed by the car. I took two screwdrivers and a knife from the toolbox. It was a long shot, but maybe I would get lucky.

The doctor's apartment was on the first floor. For a doctor, he lived somewhat modestly. The furniture was old, and the laminated floor was worn and lifting at the corners. The washing machine was in the bathroom. Painted over mould was visible on the ceiling above the shower. The smell of someone recently using the toilet lingered in the air. The doctor wasn't embarrassed.

The washing machine hose was coiled at the bottom, too long for the short distance from machine to tap. I smiled, disconnected the hose from the tap, cut off a suitable length, then reconnected it. I could feel the doctor's anxiety, but felt confident.

"That should do," I said, holding up the piece of hose. On one side, it had a thin film of dust.

Outside, Heinrich was leaning against a car, not the doctor's, smoking a cigarette. He saw the hose and said something in German.

The doctor explained how I'd procured it. By the time he was finished, I'd connected it.

The three of us crowded over the engine, inspecting the hose.

"Tomorrow morning, fill the radiator and let the engine run for about five minutes," I said to the doctor. "The hose will need to loosen up a bit. And you might need to tighten the clips a little."

The doctor nodded. "It is okay?"

"Sure. We do it all the time back home. Spare parts are expensive. To buy the same hose for a car is twice the price as for a washing machine, but it's the same hose."

I closed the bonnet, picked up the toolbox and led the two men down the narrow alley to Heinrich's car. The doctor shook my hand and spoke to Heinrich in German. I guessed that the two men had an understanding that would benefit them both. Heinrich slapped me on the shoulder and we drove back to apartment. I felt important and useful; confidence pumped through my veins.

At the apartment, dinner was waiting. The table was set on the balcony with large plates and open bottles of the red wine we'd bought from the Zentrum. Large dishes of potatoes and creamy cauliflower were next to the centrepiece of a tray of sausages. They were long and thick with dark lines from the grill. Heinrich was in excellent spirits. He told his wife and daughter how I'd fixed the doctor's car. We toasted glasses and Monica laughed. I knew then her worried demeanour was for her husband, that his heart might give up any day. I helped the doctor, who would help Heinrich, and this relieved her. I relaxed, feeling comfortable in my surroundings. Once again, my mechanical abilities had helped me gain acceptance.

The evening was fine and clear. The balcony faced south and we got enough of the evening sun to keep us from reaching for pullovers or jackets. The sausages were heavy, and with the wine and the potatoes, I felt like an overfed cow, satisfied and sleepy. I was happy just to sit there next to Kathrin, hold her hand under the table, look out over the small park below and let them talk in German. I felt neither excluded from the conversation nor ignored. I watched the expressions on their faces, listened to the tone of their voices and tried to guess what they were talking about. Body language was universal. I heard Thomas's name and a girl's name, Christine, and wondered who she was and what connection she had to Thomas. Hopefully, she was his girlfriend.

The hour grew late and I had to return to the checkpoint. Heinrich shook my hand in the doorway and thanked me for my help. He was drunk and the alcohol gave him more confidence with his English. He made terrible mistakes and laughed heartily at them. Monica also shook my hand, thanked me for the food and asked if I was warm enough.

"I'm okay. Thank you for the wonderful dinner."

"Come weekend," Heinrich slurred. "We make big party."

Kathrin walked with me towards the checkpoint. It wasn't far, but I was tired and sleepy and wanted to lie down under a tree with this girl in my arms. We held hands and walked with uneven, crooked steps, intoxicated by alcohol and love. Before Friedrich Strasse, we stopped and kissed. Her breath smelt of red wine and mustard, and her tongue was lazy and slow. But the feelings were strong and leaving her hard. The weekend seemed years away.

"I can't wait for Saturday," Kathrin said, her arms tight around my waist.

"Me either. Should I bring anything?"

"No. We spend the twenty-five Mark again."

"Alright."

We kissed again and I had to unhook her arms so I could go. It was almost ten and I didn't want to keep Thomas waiting.

"Thanks for the great day," I said.

"We meet us at the corner like before, okay?"

I nodded and turned to go.

"Don't run," she called out.

I waved to her before walking towards the checkpoint. I turned to look back, but she had already disappeared around the first corner.

Charlie was brightly lit, the white huts gleaming like beacons in a foggy sea. Up close, the hum of the lights was loud and droning. I stumbled under the first barrier and lurched towards the immigration building. I felt drunker than before, in love and happy about it. With no alcohol in my veins, I still would have staggered along. A short stocky guard eyed me suspiciously and turned me around, pushing my face to the wall. He frisked me and found nothing. Disappointed, he let me go. I smiled and wished him a good evening, before staggering out of the building as if in a dream. I waved to the arrogant American soldiers sitting in the white hut on the west side of the white line. They laughed and swapped jokes, relieving their boredom with suppositions of my day in the east. Who cared what they thought. They were part of a different world.

It felt like I was crossing into West Berlin as a visitor, and not returning to the place I was staying.

The BMW was parked under a street light in front of the Haus Am Checkpoint Charlie. I got in.

"You're late," Thomas said in a tired voice. He closed the file that was open on his lap and threw it on the back seat.

"I got searched at the border."

"Everything okay?"

I looked at him. He was sad and worried. He had so many things to think about: how to pay the rent, could he afford to buy an expensive pair of fashionable jeans, how much money was he going to make when he finished university. It was all so pointless. I didn't want to be part of this capitalism thing anymore. Paradise lay a hundred metres away, and in my drunk state, high on loving someone and knowing that you are loved, I wanted only to get back to East Berlin. It was human there. I was someone.

"Never better," I said.

"Depressing place, is it not?" Thomas asked as we drove towards his apartment.

I looked out the window at the crowded streets and the grey, lifeless buildings. Cars pushed and shoved and honked their horns and the drivers hated each other. Cyclists hated the drivers. Pedestrians hated the red lights. Commuters hated the crowded buses and trains. People ploughed head down into the world, obsessed by their own plight and worries, and hurrying simply for hurrying's sake.

"Yep. It sure is."

We lapsed into silence. Thomas didn't ask any questions and I didn't want to tell him my true feelings. He wouldn't understand. He was destined for a life of desire: the next new BMW, the bigger house, the larger TV, the higher salary, and so on until he died. It was a miserable struggle. All I wanted was to be satisfied and set, to have the necessary things for life. I didn't need a new car, or a fancy television. But more than anything, I wanted to be a part of the big picture. In Perth, I was no one. My children would have no chance to become anything more than plumbers or bricklayers or cleaners. The people in Maddington were stuck. No, they were kept there by the system. The workers held the power, but were unable to wield it because the rich kept them uneducated and poor. It was the same in West Berlin.

But not in East Berlin.

"Are you going back?" Thomas asked as we walked from his car to the apartment. He had been forced to park three streets away.

"Yep, on the weekend."

"You can't stay the night there, you know."

"I'll go for the day again."

On Winterfeldtplatz, an old man with dirty clothes and ragged hair wheeled his full shopping trolley to the bottom of the church steps. He became lost in shadow, but I saw his outline as he prepared his bed for the night. I heard him groan in the darkness as he lay down. Was he once a successful lawyer, or a rich businessman society had chewed up and spat out? Capitalism was about extremes. If you were born into a good position, or worked towards it, life was good. If you were at the other end of the spectrum, life was cruel and hard. Why did people put up with it? The complete lack of humanity and community?

Joachim was still awake when we returned. He had coffee ready for us and we sat on the balcony drinking it, talking loudly over the sounds of cars and people.

"Zo," he said, "how was it on the other side of the wall? Not so nice as here, I'm sure."

It was then I realised that I hadn't thought about or seen the wall the whole day, nor had anyone mentioned it or made jokes about it. East Germans had accepted it as part of their lives, like any new structure, and didn't feel the need to constantly refer to it. In West Berlin, it was the opposite.

"Well, it was very nice seeing Kathrin again," I offered, sure that Joachim would fail to understand my feelings. I had sobered up quickly, absorbed by the fast pace of the city: the collective desire to get things done, drive cars fast, walk quickly and leave the weak behind.

"I think our young man is in love," Joachim said, with a familiarity I didn't like.

Thomas smiled into his cup of coffee, but remained distant and aloof. He seemed tired and took his leave early, leaving me with Joachim on the balcony.

"He has love problems as well," Joachim said.

I thought of the girl named Christine and the German conversation over dinner: the worried tones, the concerned faces. I didn't know what to say so said nothing, and drank my coffee quickly.

"Thanks for the cuppa," I said, standing up. "Good night."

I felt Joachim's eyes as I walked through the living room, but didn't look back to see if he was watching me. I closed the door to Hans's room and fell quickly to sleep. A long dreamless sleep.

In the morning, I woke fresh and new. Life was different.

***

I wasted two days in West Berlin, walking around and seeing the sights. I wrote my name on the wall. It was an interesting city, both old and new, rebuilt and renovated, and rich. The whole place reeked of money. People didn't hide their wallets or protect their money; they threw it around like old tissues. The streets were full of Mercedes and BMWs. People spent money wildly on the Kurfürstendamm, buying things they didn't need, updated versions of products they already had. It was all so wasteful.

On Friday night, we went to dinner at Hilde's apartment. Antje was there with her husband Thorsten. They had no children. Antje acted like a mother towards Thomas. I assumed she had probably raised him while Hilde worked. There was nothing spectacular about Thorsten except that he was from Frankfurt. He was lured to West Berlin by higher salaries and lower taxes. The government tried to encourage people to move to West Berlin, he said. Living within the wall was hard; a lot of people couldn't handle it and left. But Thomas whispered to me that Thorsten had actually come to avoid national army service, as West Berliners were exempt.

Thorsten was normal height, with blue eyes and blonde hair that had long ago started to thin. He combed it over to one side so that half his head was bald. He wore thin-rimmed spectacles which made him look intelligent, but also lent him an air of superiority. He held his chin high and looked down at people.

I didn't like Thorsten. He was a banker who worked ten hours a day and drove a Mercedes and could only talk about money and interest rates and taxes, and how the poor people bled the economy dry. Hilde gave Thorsten the biggest slice of meat and always served him first.

The apartment was located in an attractive area called Charlottenburg. The street was narrow and so full of parked cars that only one direction of traffic was possible. Two cars coming from

94

different directions were forced to stop and decide who would reverse back to the start and let the other through. This had happened to Thomas when he had failed to find a parking place and was forced to continue to the end. Another car turned into the street and stopped in front of us. Thomas flashed his lights and leaned out the window shouting German. The stand-off lasted about twenty seconds before the other car reluctantly began to reverse. Thomas followed barely a metre from the car.

Hilde's apartment was cluttered like her sister's in Hamburg; too many things in such a small space, the collected artefacts of a long life. It had the musty smell of windows unopened, dust under furniture never swept up and rugs never beaten. I said very little during the dinner, the conversation being mostly in German, and spoke only to answer the questions asked of me. I didn't want to be rude, but could think only of the next day.

Thorsten did all the talking. After an hour, I stopped listening to him, my ears only tuning in to sentences in English when I knew I had to be alert. Thomas was going to be just like Thorsten, and I wondered if that was what he wanted, or if he was just following him because he paid all the bills. Thomas had no part-time job. Thorsten's role, and position, in this family was clear. It was as if I had been picked up and dropped in a house in the western suburbs of Perth.

\*\*\*

I woke to the sound of rain. The sky was dull grey, like a dying man's face, but I jumped out of bed with energy and vigour. Using Thomas's instructions, I negotiated the expensive underground train – I thought it would be only twenty pfennig like in East Berlin – and got out at Koch Strasse in front of Checkpoint Charlie.

The American flag was limp and wet, listless in the damp, still morning. Rain patted the roof of the white hut. In it sat two blank-faced Americans, different from before but the same. I recognised the wideness and clarity of the eyes – arrogant, innocent, ignorant – and that half-smile, half-frown smirk that showed they were representatives of the world's most powerful country and should be respected and feared accordingly. But there was something fake about the look, as if these military men had learned it in school, told by their superiors that this was the look they wanted to present to the world. Underneath that put on face, they were helpless creatures like any others, products of their society. Like Jason, they had learned arrogance, been taught to believe that their country was the world's dominant power, on the side of good, its citizens the world's best. If I'd grown up in America, I would have worn such a face. Society would have taught me how to look. But just like Jason, I would have been human under my disguise.

Confidently, I marched towards the immigration building. There were half a dozen tourist buses crammed in the parking lot. Faces filled the windows, peering down at me as I crossed the lot, watching me like an animal in a zoo.

I joined the back of a long line, much longer than on Wednesday. I had thought this might be the case and had budgeted an extra half an hour. I didn't want to keep Kathrin waiting. I hoped she would lead me back to her bedroom again, and I would follow behind like a trained dog. Anything to lie with her once more. The line moved slowly. People spoke in whispers, turning their heads occasionally to see if anyone was watching or listening. The air was thick with anxiety.

A short man with stumpy legs was being checked at the front of the line. The guard had asked him to take off his hat and he held it gingerly with both hands, his bald head glistening with sweat under the lights. I stood three places behind him. Suddenly, there was a great commotion. Two large men in plain brown suits were pushing towards the front. The short man started to panic. His eyes bulged and he looked around for a way out and, when there wasn't one visible, at the faces of the others in line, pleading for help; that there were twenty of us and only two of them. We did nothing but watch. The first policemen threw him against the wall while the other undid the man's belt and pulled down his pants. He wore pantyhose stuffed with magazines. Through the nylon, I saw titles like *Bravo* and *Stern*. They looked like ordinary magazines; one had John Travolta on the cover. The policemen cut the hose with switchblade knives and the magazines spilled onto the floor; famous faces, toothy smiles. The man pleaded in German, but the policemen ignored him, talking only with each other. They scooped up the magazines and led the man away in handcuffs. He tripped over his pants, which still hung open around his ankles. The two men practically carried him. The next in line was called towards the booth and the routine continued.

Kathrin waited at the same corner as before, leaning against an office building, trying to get some shelter from the drizzle. Clouds still hung low and grey, and the ends of my sneakers were damp enough that I could feel moisture in my socks. I felt myself rushing towards her, moving subconsciously between pedestrians and shoppers, my stomach bustling with nerves and desire. We slammed into each other like two racing cars, with a force of impact that left the two cars smashed together as one. Like yesterday, she took me off the street to kiss me. She looked stunning in tight blue jeans and a knitted pullover, like a girl straight off the farm and into a Hollywood movie. Strands of wet hair clung to her face. She tucked them behind her ears, but they fell forward again. There was something incredibly pure and simple about her beauty. She didn't try, wore no makeup, had plain clothes, and I was sure she was also breathtaking at the first light of day. She had no regard for her looks, as if she didn't consider herself that pretty. I couldn't take my eyes from her. Every movement, every word, every gesture drew me closer, and I wanted to hold her so close to me that we would cease to be two separate people, that by force of physical contact I could lose myself in her.

We left Friederich Strasse and headed for her apartment. I told her about the dinner at Hilde's, how I didn't like Thorsten or West Berlin. This made her curious.

"Well, I guess it's because it's not so different from where I come from," I explained. "All the people think about is money. And if you don't have it, you're nothing and you've got no chance. Thorsten's the best example of it. I mean, he seems like a nice guy, but there's more to life than money."

"I only met him once," Kathrin said flatly. "But I was a young. It was their wedding. We went for the day."

"I think that West Berlin is full of people like me," I continued, feeling an anger burning inside. "People who really have no chances in life except for the lowest things. How does the son of a plumber become the leader of the country?"

"It happens here," she said.

"All they do over there is make money and spend it. They waste it on things they don't need, things they already have. A TV for the kitchen when there's already one in every other room."

"I don't like television so much," Kathrin said. She seemed to be enjoying my outburst, as if she had been expecting it, and felt verified hearing it.

We turned onto Alte Jakob Strasse. Other people walking past greeted us; some even used Kathrin's name. They carried bags for shopping, wore simple hats to keep the rain from their faces and smiled warmly, their eyes open and keen, their steps patient and unhurried.

Kathrin rang the doorbell and then sat down on the top step, tucking her knees under her chin. I sat next to her. She reached an arm around me and pulled me closer, as if that was where I was supposed to sit. I looked down the street and saw the grey curve of the wall cutting off the street. Green specks of Grepos strolled around listless and bored. One of them had a dog on a leash and was having trouble controlling it, to the amusement of the others.

"Kathrin, I know this sounds crazy," I said, avoiding her eyes. The fear of rejection never goes away. "But I want to ask you something. And you have to tell me honestly what you think."

She nodded, her aqua eyes brightening in expectation.

"What I want to say is that..."

The door opened behind us. Heinrich put down a box full of food and bottles to shake my hand and slapped my shoulder heartily. A cigarette came crookedly out of his mouth and he was in excellent spirits, as if he had drunk a bottle of vodka for breakfast.

"Michael, my son," he said. "Good you here. We make trip today. Ah, my English is better on weekend."

He laughed loudly. Kathrin laughed too, and picked up her father's box. The bottles clinked against each other. Monica appeared in the doorway carrying a canvas bag. She swapped it to her left hand to shake mine. This morning, I could see the aged beauty that was still youthful in Kathrin. The daughter would grow up to look just like the mother and that was okay with me.

"Good morning," I said, unsure what I could say given Monica's limited English. "How are you?"

"Na gut," Monica said, smiling. I noticed she had crossed over front teeth like Kathrin, although more yellow with age and passive smoking.

"Come," Heinrich said, puffing smoke out the side of his mouth. "We start."

We piled into the pale blue Trabant, Kathrin and I with our knees under our chins in the back.

"Ah," Heinrich said as the engine roared to life. "Trabi know when it weekend."

We all laughed as the car lurched forward. Monica and Heinrich talked over the sound of the engine. Kathrin and I sat close together, because there wasn't enough room to do otherwise. Monica didn't seem to care. I wondered if I had been the topic of discussion the past two days; that I was just a visitor and would leave Kathrin's life as quickly as I had entered it. So, there was no reason to be worried about her. She was young. Let her have a fling.

"What did you want to say?" Kathrin asked me.

"I'll tell you later," I said. The moment had been lost. It's never easy laying your heart on the line, and I wasn't going to do it in this noisy lawnmower in front of the girl's parents.

We drove out of East Berlin. The sun was still blocked by clouds so I didn't know in which direction we went. Soon, the wide streets jammed with apartment buildings gave way to open fields and forests. Out of the city, the clouds cleared and the sun shone brightly on the fields. Cows huddled under trees to sleep in the shade. Grass glistened with morning rain; a farmer walked through it and got his boots wet. Everything looked fresh and new. The sun was already high and I had the feeling we were going north. The main road was populated by steady lines of Trabants, and other cars similar to the doctor's, with the odd Beetle burping along. There was no competition or passing; the cars struggled to reach a decent speed. It looked like a convoy of tortoises, each intent only on getting to the destination. Time wasn't a factor.

We pulled off the highway and followed a narrow bumpy road towards a village called Altenhof. I presumed this was our destination, for I hadn't been told where we going or why, but we drove through this small town, Heinrich puffing his cigarette in rhythm with the car's puttering engine.

A left turn took us down a narrow road. There were puddles from the morning rain. The trees were high, the path encased by shadow, with no chance for the sun to dry out the puddles. The Trabant bumped and creaked, threatening with each hole to pop its rivets and fall into a million pieces. But the buggy held together and we emerged through the forest and parked at the edge of a large lake. The small beach was deserted.

Heinrich jumped out of the car like a child, urging us to follow him into the water. He was half way there, with his shirt off, by the time Kathrin and I had got ourselves out of the back. Heinrich threw off his pants and started walking into the water naked, his arse white and sagging. His legs were skinny and dark, and with his wide chest, he looked like a hairy beach ball on stilts. Monica slowly took off her clothes. She carefully peeled off each layer, folded it neatly, and placed it on the bonnet of the Trabi. Her body had a feminine roundness that beautiful women were lucky to hang onto in middle age. Heinrich kicked water at her before she dunked herself and started a smooth breaststroke further out.

"Come," Heinrich shouted. The water was shallow and he stood, urging us in. The hair on his chest started from his tackle and went over his shoulders like a thick rug. The water was cold and his member had retreated. I tried not to stare.

All of sudden, Kathrin whipped off her pullover, threw off her jeans and ran for the water. Her nakedness was startling, her body round and firm. She got to the edge and ran back to me, her breasts bouncing and swinging. She helped me out of my shirt.

"Come on," she whispered. "Don't be shy."

The excitement of seeing Kathrin completely naked was too much. I had to get into the water quick where the coldness might stave off embarrassment. Swimming nude with the girlfriend's parents. It was all so crazy. Kathrin giggled when she saw my burgeoning prick.

"Later," she said, grabbing my hand. We hit the water together with a loud splash. Heinrich clapped. Monica, who was now almost to the middle of the lake, turned around and waved. The three of us started to swim towards her, talking all the way. Heinrich swam on his back, his round chest rising in and out of the water. His cigarette was wet and clung to his lips. We got half way before he realised it was there and spat it out.

The water was dark green and cold. When we reached Monica, she was having a conversation with people in a rowboat. They were two men, both holding beer cans, and I saw one lean over the side and jokingly offer to help her into the boat, but she declined with a laugh. Heinrich, swimming on his back, saw none of this. The two men saw us coming and rowed away.

We treaded water in a circle. Monica said something in German, Heinrich responded, and all three laughed. I felt a little left out when they spoke their language, like an intruder in their small and secure world. The lake seemed deserted, apart from a few boats and a scattering of people at what looked like the main beach. It felt like I was treading water in the middle of the Indian Ocean, alone, with no land in sight, unsure in which direction to start, convinced no matter where I headed, I wouldn't make it.

"Come on," Kathrin said, snapping me out of my daydreams. "Race you to the other side."

She launched into a powerful freestyle, her kick splashing green water high into the air.

"Go, son," Heinrich urged. "Kathrin good swimmer. Win for the men."

I took off after her, my arms languid and slow. I hadn't swum like this since school, when I had been the reluctant star of a few swimming carnivals. But I fell into a good rhythm, relaxed into the water, and climbed the ladder like my swim teacher had taught me, reaching out far and stroking smoothly. Near the other side, I was at her feet. The bubbles from her kick tickled my face. I pulled up alongside her just as my hand hit sand. It was no longer deep enough for me to swim, but Kathrin's arms were shorter and she continued right to the end, flattening out into a breaststroke, before sitting in the shallows. I dog-paddled up next to her. We sat in the shadows made by the tall trees that hung over the water, and looked out over the lake trying to catch our breath.

"You win," I said. "You're a good swimmer, but you also had a head start."

She splashed water into my face. "You were too slow," she said. "But you also swim good, but you come from Australia."

"Hey, I live miles from the beach, and hardly ever go swimming anymore."

She smiled. "Then, you must come here to swim."

She stood up. I tried not to stare at her. Water dripped off her naked body, sliding around her curves, and chilling her in the shadows. I had known this body, explored its caverns and canyons, yet it still felt new and foreign to me.

"It's cold here," she said.

"Shall we swim back?" I looked out over the lake. Monica and Heinrich were nowhere to be seen; the other side of the lake looked miles away.

Kathrin walked out of the water. She turned and gestured for me to follow. We came to a small grassy area between two trees where the sun was shining through. I could feel my nakedness, but it was

101

comfortable being that way with Kathrin. The grass was warm against my back as she laid me down on it. She climbed on top of me and we made love quickly. The sun was behind her head, and as she rose and fell with each movement, the sun either shone in my eyes or was shadowed by her.

This was my new life: lazy summer days, swimming naked with a beautiful girl, and having sex with her in a forest. Was I dreaming? Was it possible that a poor kid from Perth could have such a life? It was all so exotic and exciting, beyond anything I'd ever imagined. Even dreams never went so far.

We lay panting on the grass, shifting slightly to gain the last rays of sun shining through the trees. We were the only people on the whole planet. Naked and in love. Now is the time, I thought.

"Kathrin," I breathed, "I've never met anyone like you. I mean, I know really nothing about you, but feel like I've known you all my life."

She snuggled up against my chest and caressed my stomach. Her wet hair still smelled of apples.

"And I also want to say that I've never felt so happy in a place. With you, in East Berlin, with your family. It's like I was born in the wrong country."

She sat up, stroked my cheek. Her eyes gleamed. She began to cry. "You must not say it," she said. "I know you must go."

"No, that's not it. I want to stay. I want to live here, with you."

The smile left her face and she looked away, through the trees and over the water to where we had started our swim. Here it comes. I felt the anxiety swell in me like a bubble trapped in my throat.

"It's not so easy," Kathrin said. "It is wonderful you want to come here, and I want to be with you. But it is not so easy."

"Why? I could work as a mechanic, we could live together, see what happens. I want to try. I can't let you, let this, go."

Kathrin stood up. Her knobbly knees were stained green from the grass. She looked so young then, just a girl. I grabbed her hand, stopping her from walking away. Her turning around blocked the sun from my eyes.

"Kathrin, I love you."

The words didn't have the effect I thought they would. She smiled, and I knew she loved me and thought it wonderful that we had found each other, but was pragmatic at the same time. Our lives were fraught with difficulties; barriers I didn't know about or understand. Could I just leave Australia forever to live in East Germany, in a communist country? Give up everything for a girl I'd just met? The communists had always been the enemy. The system was evil and oppressive. But that was propaganda. They didn't know how the life was here, better than anything I'd seen in Australia or England. It was like the rich criticising the poor. They only viewed them from afar, from their own point of view, with their own reference points. They didn't understand that the poor were people too, most of the time with more heart, courage and spirit. The rich never saw this; they saw only our poor clothes, the money we took from the government, our lack of class, manners and education, our collective worthlessness. We weren't like them and for that reason, we had to be kept separate. And they only saw the armies of the communists, and feared them because they had the courage to reject everything American. This was capitalism versus communism. Greed versus sharing. Individualism over community. I knew what I wanted. I had no chance in capitalism. Communism gave me hope, that people could work together for a common goal, help each other and be kind. The system was fair. Women were equal, everyone had a job and an apartment, and food was cheap. Everything was within my reach. There were no barriers to restrict my life here. I had the chance to be so much more. And I would do it with this beautiful girl who had opened my eyes to all of it.

"Come on," she said sadly. "Let's swim back."

The water was cold and we swam a slow breaststroke in silence. The sun was high, the sky a grey blue like a dolphin's skin. I wouldn't let Kathrin's pragmatism dampen my enthusiasm. I wanted life here and would do everything I could to get it.

Monica waited at the water's edge. She had a towel around her waist and a plain white shirt thrown hastily over the top. She handed us towels as we got out and said something to Kathrin. Her smile was warm and relaxed, her manner slow and easy. She was a different woman here, as if the teacher and housewife persona was just a costume she wore during the week. Out here, by the lake, she came alive. Heinrich lay naked in the sun, spread-eagled on a towel too small for him, his round chest inflating and deflating like a seething bull's, a loud snore emanating from his throat. Kathrin wrapped the towel around her waist and copied her mother by throwing a shirt over her top. The towel was not long enough to reach around my waist and I had to hold it together with my fingers. I couldn't lie naked in the sun like Heinrich. Instead, I sat on the edge of the towel, and let the other half cover my tackle. Kathrin sat next to me and handed me a plastic cup that was warm and smelled of coffee. It wasn't as good as what Thomas had, but it was coffee nonetheless, and it warmed me up inside. I leaned back on my elbows and let the sun warm my chest. The coffee reminded me of my empty stomach. I could see some kind of potato salad on the other side of Heinrich but didn't want to ask.

Monica sat next to Kathrin. The three of us looked out over the lake while Heinrich snored. I felt strangely content, as if a great decision had been deliberated over for years and was finally made. I knew what I wanted to do, and now just had to figure out how to do it.

Mother and daughter spoke quietly together. I didn't listen. I stared at the water. I had to tell myself that when they spoke German, they weren't always speaking about me. I concentrated instead on life in East Germany and how it would be. Mechanics seemed to be in short supply. Maybe I could start my own shop, save up enough money to buy a big house for Kathrin and me. Maybe live somewhere out here, near a lake. It didn't seem so far from the city. It would be possible to drive there to work every day. I had to learn the language. Perhaps Monica would teach me, and Kathrin would help too, and it wouldn't be so hard if I was living here and surrounded by the language, forced to speak it. But what about my home, my friends and family? Narelle was already living in London. How would my parents feel if I announced I was going to live in communist East Germany? If I explained how the life was here, they might want to come as well. Life had suddenly swung from the childhood idea of survival to the other end of the spectrum, where anything was possible. Life had no limits here.

"What do you smile for?" Kathrin asked, handing me a plate of food.

"Just dreaming," I said. "Thanks."

I ate it in three minutes. After, we took a walk. Monica called after Kathrin and I wondered if we had to be back at a certain time. It sounded like that kind of an order.

We followed a narrow path that sometimes forced us to walk single file. I picked small flowers and handed them to Kathrin. Never had I been so romantic. This was East Germany; I could act however I wanted. There was nobody here who could remind me of all the mistakes I had made, or call up the past to hurt and embarrass me.

I pulled Kathrin close and kissed her when I felt like it, but she grew more reluctant and started to withdraw.

We sat on a bench. It looked completely out of place next to the water and surrounded by old trees. It was dirty and we wiped it with our hands before sitting down. Old lovers had pledged their feelings with names circled in hearts and others simply declared that they had been there on a certain date, alone. I put my arm around Kathrin. She looked steadfastly at the lake. I wanted to ask her why she thought everything was too difficult, why she seemed to be giving up on us when we'd barely started. But I left it. We sat in silence and then walked back. The time on the grass felt like years ago. I felt old and weary. Love was tiring.

When we returned, Heinrich and Monica were dressed and leaning against the car. Heinrich was cleaning his nails with his keys, holding his fingers up to the sun for inspection.

"Come," he said smiling, giving me a wink. "We late."

Kathrin and I crammed ourselves into the back seat. For some reason, I didn't feel like sitting so close to her. I was confused. We loved each other, we both knew it. Why wasn't it enough? Did love only end in tears and complications? I had travelled to the other side of the world and met a girl I would never have met in Australia; girls like Kathrin don't exist there. I couldn't possibly just flash my passport at the border, walk back to West Berlin and forget her.

We drove back through Altenhof, but didn't turn onto the highway for East Berlin. Kathrin held my hand, but looked out the side window. We entered a large town, negotiated streets wide and narrow, pot-holed and cobblestoned, and pulled into the driveway of a grey house that looked like a concrete bunker. Only the curtains in the windows and the flowerpots in the sills gave you any idea it was a place of residence. We piled out of the car. Heinrich handed me a box to carry. It was full of wine bottles and cans of beer. Kathrin helped Monica with some other things. We followed Heinrich through a gate and around to the back of the house. The familiar smell of barbecue filled the air.

"Heinrich," shouted a large man who stood over a small barbecue. He had a can of beer in one hand and tongs in the other, and raised them both in the air in greeting. The other people, old and young, turned to greet us as we walked through the garden. Hands were shaken and names were given which I quickly forgot. I found myself standing with Heinrich and the other man at the barbecue. I'd learned that this was Heinrich's brother, Frank. He was older and had a round, jovial face. He wore the same thick-rimmed glasses as Heinrich and had the same round chest, but was taller and better proportioned. He couldn't speak English and spoke German to me as if I understood. I could only smile. Heinrich explained Frank worked as a production manager at the Schweinemastanlage, a pig abattoir, the biggest in Europe. Frank was proud.

Kathrin came out of the house with some plates and started helping an older woman set the table. Two small boys were kicking a football around, urging others to join them.

"I am Rüdiger," a man said, sidling up next to me. "But you can call me Rudi. My wife says you are from Australia."

He was shorter than me but better built, with small beady eyes that were so brown you couldn't see where the colour ended and the black pupils began. They gave nothing away, as if he had trained them to be blank. There was a darkness there I couldn't explain, and it scared me a little at first. But his voice was soft and his face handsome. He wore a sport shirt that accentuated the roundness of his shoulders and straightness of his back. The muscles in his arm flexed when he put the can of beer to his mouth. But despite his attractive and rugged appearance, he looked like someone who took chocolate from children.

"That's right," I said, avoiding his eyes and trying to be friendly.

"And you come here to visit Kathrin."

He somehow had the ability to make questions into statements, as if he knew the answer already, but just wanted to hear you say it.

"Yes, but also East Berlin. We were at some lake all day today, and it was really nice. It's a great place. Is this your house?"

The words spilled out of me. The darkness in his eyes wouldn't let up until I told him everything.

"No. My wife, Christine," he said, pointing at the woman who Kathrin was helping with the table, "is the daughter from Frank." She looked average, but had exaggeratedly wide hips and short legs. An excellent breeder, as my father would rather nastily say.

Frank heard his name and said something playful to Rudi. Heinrich made a joke and the three men laughed, Rudi in a short, restrained way. I looked down at my feet.

"And so you like East Germany," he continued.

"Oh, it's great. I mean, really different to where I'm from, but in a better way."

"Better? How so?"

"I don't know where to start." I was unsure what I should say. Rudi was a good listener; he looked me in the eyes and gave his full attention, as if we were completely alone. He concentrated on each word and had a thoughtful look on his face. "In Australia, it's all about money. If you have it great, but if you don't, you've got no chance."

"And you think here the people have money."

"They're not rich, but they have what they need, and in my opinion, that's better. The best thing is, it's not about money here, and that's why I like it. And the people are nice."

"Tell me," Rudi said, leaning closer, trying to draw me into a private conversation, "what do you learn about East Germany and history?"

I thought about Thomas and how he'd asked the same question in Hamburg. Why were they so interested in what the world thought about them?

"Not much," I said. "We learn about East and West Germany, that they are separate countries."

"Really? East Germany is on your map?"

"Of course. But we don't learn much about the country, or the way of life. Maybe they learn more at private schools and in year eleven and twelve. I left when I was fifteen."

"And the private schools learn more."

"I think so. Only the kids with money go there. I guess they get what they pay for."

"Interesting." He sipped his beer thoughtfully. "And don't the children all learn the same."

"I don't think so. I mean, I don't really know. The rich kids get a better education and can go to university."

"And you can't."

"Not unless I'm a genius," I said, laughing.

"I see. This is very unfair, but, how do you say, typical?" He smiled. "What is your profession?"

I paused, wondering if I would be dragged off to fix another car. "I'm a mechanic."

Rudi nodded. "My father is also mechanic, but he must work today."

"Are you a mechanic?" I asked, hoping we might find some

common ground. For some reason, I wanted him to like me. He wasn't impressive or cool, but he had a confidence and calm I envied.

"I went to the university," he explained. "Everyone has that opportunity. It is also free."

"And now?"

"And now I work in an office like everybody." He laughed awkwardly, but his tone made me leave it at that.

"Rudi, this may sound like a stupid question, but where are we?"

He smiled. He was very good looking when he smiled, exactly the type of guy all girls want to bring home to show their parents.

"Eberswalde," he said, and seeing that this meant nothing to me, added, "about sixty kilometres north of Berlin. The lake you were at is called Werbillensee."

I nodded. It was interesting how he said Berlin, the same way all the border guards left off East.

"Do you live here, in this town?"

"No. I live in Berlin." He said this as if revealing a piece of personal information, the way someone speaks when saying they are a widower or divorced. The tone prevented you from asking further questions.

We watched Heinrich and Frank lining up sausages on the barbecue. When they had finished, I poured some of my beer over the top and the flames jumped briefly. The three men were hypnotised by the flames, then eyed me curiously.

"It's what we do in Australia," I explained. "It's tradition."

Rudi translated for the two men and they laughed.

"They think you try to finish the barbecue," Rudi said.

"Just gets it going a bit more, that's all. Everyone does it, and it cooks the sausages faster."

Rudi translated again. Frank took a step back from the barbecue and poured beer over the top. But he gave too much and the flames jumped over the sausages, igniting with a loud whoosh. The children gathered around to watch and Frank told them to stand back. This time, Heinrich tried, but he was too tentative and did not give the flames enough beer. Everyone laughed at the one pathetic flame that crept over the grill.

"You make it," he said to me.

I used the bottom of my can and gave the line of sausages of slight push. They rolled together, showing the black lines of the grill. I poured beer over the top and the sausages were lost in a whoosh of yellow and orange flames. The smell and sizzle of burning fat made me drool. I was seven years old again.

"Profi," Frank said.

"Frank thinks you are a professional sausage griller," Rudi explained.

I laughed. "No, but I am a professional sausage eater. These look great."

Rudi translated and everyone, including the children, laughed. Kathrin looked over from where she sat with her feet in a small wading pool and smiled at me. She attended a young girl who sat naked in the pool. I had the strange feeling that Kathrin wanted to sit naked in the pool as well.

I have only good memories of barbecues. The smell of burning fat and the heat of standing too close to the grill on hot summer's days always make me feel content. It was these times that had made childhood memorable. The way the men huddled around the barbecue, throwing back beers, advising each other the best way to cook a sausage, talking about football and cars, and laughing at the silliest things, shelving reality for the afternoon. The way the kids of different ages organised themselves into games with the minimum of equipment. One child would always end up crying and would run to the group of mothers. But more than anything, I remember the abundance, the wealth acquired from working together and pooling resources. Those barbecues were feasts, where we ate so much we felt sick afterwards. Us kids drowned our sausages in too much sauce and drank too much lemonade. The sugar made us hyper, but we were too full to move. Dogs licked the abandoned plates and hung around the tables for scraps. Adults got drunk and forgot about their dire situations: the bills left unpaid, the car that every week needed a new part, the boss who treated them like shit, the pathetic education their children were getting at the local, under-funded public school, and the retirement age that seemed so far in the future but didn't promise riches or a better life, only relief. The women drank casket wine and forgot about the cheap dresses they sewed themselves, the difficulty of feeding three kids with limited money, and the lives they lived in quiet struggle: not complaining when hit by their men, not hitting the roof when the kids went out at night and stole cars in an attempt to enjoy their youth. And us kids forgot that we were poor. We ate our fill and them some more, enjoying such abundance all the more because we spent our lives being deprived of it.

Such was the atmosphere at the barbecue in Eberswalde. There was too much of everything, and it seemed each person ate and drank and laughed more than they normally did. The kids had mustard on their cheeks and held out their plates for another long, thick Bratwurst which they wouldn't be able to finish, and would feed again to Frank's dog, Felix.

Everyone made room for the cakes that Monica and Frank's wife brought out. They were rich and sweet and made me feel sick, but I had two more pieces. Kathrin sat to my right, translating for me and keeping me in the conversation. She wiped sauce from my mouth and drank as much beer as I did. Heinrich sat to my left, smoking, drinking, eating and laughing, and talking all the time. More than once he put his arm around me and clinked his can against mine. The house, which had earlier loomed like an ugly war bunker, stood tall and bright in the evening sun. Speakers were positioned in the frames of open windows and boomed out old-fashioned songs which everyone knew the words to and sang along with when one took up the lead.

I was an outsider. I understood almost nothing, but felt as included as I had been as a kid at the barbecues in Maddington. I wished that my parents were here. More, I wished that I had been born here.

And all through the evening, I felt Rudi's dark eyes on me.

\*\*\*

Sunday passed in a blur. Heavy rain gave the day an out of focus look. I woke late and staggered to the border. Immigration was a breeze; already a routine, the time more of a hassle. I changed the twenty-five Marks and found Kathrin waiting on the corner where Monica had dropped me last night. Kathrin had slept in my arms on the way back from Eberswalde. Heinrich had snored in the passenger seat and farted without restraint. Monica had driven with her window down.

I spent the day with Kathrin. Her parents had gone to their garden house outside of East Berlin like they did every Sunday. Kathrin was furious in her love making, attempting to give everything only to finish with nothing. She had no time for me next week. It wasn't worth to cross the border and change all that money just for the evenings. There were youth meetings, swim training and other commitments. And I had to get back to London to catch my flight home.

Sunday was a bad dream. I moped around confused, wanting to speak, to say all that was in my head and heart, but Kathrin didn't want to talk or listen. She carried herself with a grim sadness and the day passed with both of us watching the clock.

Near the checkpoint, I gave her the twenty-five Marks.

"I can't take it back," I said when she refused it.

All at once, her suppressed sadness manifested itself in a stream of tears. She held me tight and wouldn't let me go.

"Kathrin," I said, looking deep into her sad eyes, "I love you. I'll be back. I promise."

Something in her eyes told me she believed me, but the expression on her face didn't change.

"Give me six months. If I'm not back here by then, well, then, give me another six months."

She laughed sadly.

"And I'll write to you every week, to give you the exact date I'm coming."

"Don't write anything bad about the government," she said.

"What are you talking about?"

"Only write good things about East Germany."

"What bad things could I possibly say?"

"Just trust me."

"Okay."

"I love you, Michael."

"I love you."

Kathrin let me go and walked quickly away. I watched her. She didn't stop or turn around and dissolved into the darkness. I walked under the humming lights of Checkpoint Charlie, past the faceless guards in the first white hut, through the immigration building and past the faceless guards in the white hut on the west side of the border line. And I knew I would be back.

# Perth

A long driveway cuts through the middle of a large lot. From here, the lot stretches down both sides of the road about fifty metres each way. There are no trees. The lot is full of cars: new, slightly used and used. All models, all makes. Whatever they can sell. There is a small showroom with an office attached. Here, the latest cars are shown, brightly polished and shining; you could comb your hair in the reflection of a fender. The salesmen occupy the office, with a small gaggle of secretaries. Seldom do I have any contact with these people. The office is air-conditioned and they only visit the workshop when absolutely necessary. Most of the time, they phone, asking after the progress of a certain client's car. The workshop is a long building behind the office. It has a separate entrance from a side road so the main driveway is not used to take the cars out to test. The workshop is kept tucked away and its occupants shunned by the rest of the dealership.

It was inside this steel fortress, stinking hot in summer, freezing on cold winter mornings, that I had toiled with greasy hands since I was fifteen. Still, I had always liked the workshop, because the workers were good men and this was my refuge from school. I would always think positively about this place because it took me away from the one institution I'd hated the most.

Mum had to wake me that morning, in the bed I'd slept in for twenty years. And like so many school days before, she had to pull me up by the hand and force me out of bed. I lay in bed thinking about the workshop. I was never a morning person, but on this particular Monday morning I was more ragged than normal. I'd slept almost twelve hours after failing to find sleep on Saturday night, arriving late from London. There was too much to think about, and the distance I had put between myself and the world I wanted was now so great, that that world seemed beyond my reach. I'd tossed and turned trying to figure things out. It would be easier just to forget Kathrin and East Germany, and live here. I had a job and a car. Soon, I would meet a girl and start a family of my own. It was that simple.

But I didn't want another girl. I wanted Kathrin, and I knew there were no girls like her in Perth. Kathrin took me for who I was. I had to get back to East Berlin. But it seemed so difficult. Home was here, in this bed, with these people, sweating in that workshop.

Narelle had said I was crazy, that Australia was the only country worth living in, Perth its only good city. Ashley said the Germans had no sense of humour, that they were dull and cold, and couldn't be trusted because they only wanted to start war.

"Only a matter a time before anuvva Hitler comes along," he'd said. He explained he'd been to Munich for a soccer match where his team was badly beaten. Ashley and several hundred other supporters had trashed a Bierhaus in the centre of Munich. Ashley spoke about this with intense pride, like a soldier recalling a victorious battle where all the odds had been stacked against them by a ruthless enemy. I didn't argue with him; it wasn't worth it, and arguing with him meant hearing his voice. I felt sorry for Natalie and for the baby that now bulged her stomach and made her change her standard wardrobe.

Dad echoed Ashley's words when I told him about my time in East and West Germany, but it was hard to interrupt him while he was watching TV. I wasn't interested in television anymore. It was loud and intrusive, and flashy advertisements invaded our home every seven minutes. I wasn't surprised that dad felt the same as Ashley. It was learned prejudice. It seemed the minute you said the word German to people, they were taken straight back to the Second World War, and acted like their father had been killed on the western front in cold blood. They thought all Germans, past and present, were Nazis. The Germans couldn't shake off this historical legacy, even though two generations had passed. Why should they be held responsible for the mistakes of the previous generation? And wasn't it the same in every country? Australia's history was covered in blood and haunted by racism, but no one was standing up to take responsibility for the actions of our fathers and grandfathers. We just wanted to forget and for the rest of the world to remain ignorant. The German people were victims of a horrible stereotype; that a child born today in Munich would one day be thought of as a Nazi by a foreigner. But the world thought Americans were great even though they'd wiped out most of Japan with a couple of cowardly bombs, an explosion that killed many more civilians than military. If you're going to hold one generation accountable for history, then you should hold all generations and all people accountable. It wasn't fair to point the finger only at Germans. Every country has had their tyrant.

I didn't tell dad about Kathrin. If he knew that a girl was responsible for my positive experiences in East and West Germany, he would say my judgement was clouded by hormones, that I'd been screwed over to the other side. But on my first Sunday back, when dad had gone to the footy and I'd said I was too tired, I told mum everything. She listened quietly, poured tea and offered the biscuits I liked so much that she had baked for my return. I tried to explain everything, but was still confused. I didn't have the ability to say the things the way I wanted. Mum didn't offer advice or use any throwaway lines from the Mother's Handbook. She never said things like It's just a phase, or Don't talk with your mouth full, or You'll grow out of it. She had her own way of speaking, in a plain, simple way that made you feel the words were for you and no one else.

"Sounds like love," mum had said, sipping her tea.

"Not just the girl, mum, but with the country as well. I mean, women have all the same opportunities as men. Get paid the same, too."

"Yes, I know. It's also made a difference for women in western countries. Nobody says that, of course, but it's true. But do you really want to live there?"

"I don't know. What do you think?"

"It's not a decision I have to make." She smiled. "You're old enough. You've got to decide what's best for you. But I suggest you think very hard about it. If you go, you might not ever be able to come back. Could you handle that?"

I shrugged my shoulders.

"Look, your dad's working nightshift tomorrow. We can talk more then. Just remember, you have time. You're young. There'll be lots of other girls. Be careful before you give your heart away."

Her eyes became distant as she sipped her tea, and she looked through the dirty kitchen window. So many things lost and forgotten, a young girl's dreams put aside because life gets in the way; her knight in shining armour just a dressed up peasant. I wondered if she was thinking the same as me, that if she had been born in East Germany, what opportunities she could have had, what things she could have accomplished.

"Thanks, mum. The bikkies are still great."

***

114

The old Ford roared to life. It seemed the size of a boat compared to the Trabant I'd squeezed into with Kathrin and her parents. It was such small recollections which were already starting to feel like old memories. A distant time in a distant land. I had to hold onto them.

Decaying houses and run down shopping centres passed the windows as I drove to the workshop. Small kids walked with older brothers and sisters to school; their parents unable to walk with them because of morning jobs, nightshifts or drug habits. Younger kids walked with shoes too big for their feet, in shirts that were windows to another era; hand-me-downs from older siblings or bought from the Salvation Army store. The kids shuffled along reluctantly towards their poorly-funded school: with its mean teachers waiting impatiently for transfers to better schools, not caring about the kids, knowing that educating them is pointless because they would simply leave at fifteen to do apprenticeships or take poorly paid jobs. Women waited at bus stops. They wore the uniforms of shop assistants, supermarket workers and factory liners. The only pleasure they get is from each other's company. And the men driving the Fords and Holdens in front and behind me, en route to plumbing contracts, construction sites, factories, workshops and then the pub afterwards. This was my future. I would have a house like that one, or that one, and in ten years there would be too many kids to feed and not enough space or money. And I would slink off every night to lose myself in alcohol, and then take out my anger on whatever poor woman had become my wife.

I pulled the car into the side entrance and parked behind the workshop. I loved that old Ford. The first day I'd driven it to the workshop was the first time I felt I was going to make it as a man. Until that day, I'd ridden my bicycle and the others had thought of me as a kid. But the car made me a man like them.

It was the only thing I owned.

As I walked in, they were all there, already with grease on their hands, fresh marks on their overalls and slashes of black grease on their faces. Stevo, Bazza, Col and Lurch. They wiped their hands on the fronts of their overalls, shook my hand, tousled my hair and called me Junior and Rookie, my old nicknames. But it was different. None of these guys had ever been to Europe. They were somewhat in awe.

"Our world traveller is back," said Bazza, who was short and had once been a football star, but had a bad injury and had since grown fat and idle. When he spoke about football, he never failed to mention his injury and ponder what might have been. He coached his son in the local junior league and gave a play-by-play account every Monday morning.

"Give him room boys," said Stevo, short like Bazza but wiry, and the oldest of all the mechanics, creeping slowly towards retirement. He spent every Friday night at the trots and Saturday at the races. "I heard he had tea and scones with the Queen."

"Quick, roll out the red carpet," shouted Col. He was thirty and the brother of Lurch. Two people couldn't be more different.

Lurch, tall and spindly, got down on one knee, which made him about the same height as the rest of us, and said, "Your Majesty," and took my hand to kiss, but I yanked it away. Our laughter echoed in the workshop.

"Come on, Mick," said Stevo. "You can gis a hand changing the radiator on this old bird."

I found a pair of dirty overalls and pulled them on. They smelled of oil and petrol and sweat.

They day passed quickly. I didn't think about Kathrin or leaving Perth. Because engines are great company. If you do the right thing, tickle them in the right spot, they reward you and purr with pleasure. But when things are wrong, they scream in agony, shouting fix me, please, fix me. If only people could be so simple.

That evening, I brought home barbecued chicken and chips. Mum was thankful not to have to cook. She questioned me if I'd made any progress with my decision. I had, but I couldn't tell her. There weren't the words to say I wanted to reject the life she had chosen with my father. I didn't want to live in a house like this, in a place where I was nobody, where my children had no chance, and where I had no chance. It wasn't fair that my destiny was outlined for me because of my geographical situation. And I loved Kathrin and wanted only to be with her. But I told my mother none of this.

"Well, just give it more time," she said. "The right answer will come to you when you least expect it."

I nodded, and hoped that time would give me the courage to be honest.

***

I stopped watching television. It was a chronic time waster, and watching it meant sitting in the living room with dad and listening to his inane comments and prejudices. I gave it up, read more books and wrote a long letter to Kathrin every week. I explained I was saving money and hoped to be there before Christmas. Replies took a long time to arrive, the date at the top of her page sometimes three or four weeks old. Her words were straightforward and plain, with simple news about her daily life. She didn't declare undying love or express hope for the future, but there was something intimate about her words; she wrote like she talked. I could hear her voice whispering in my ear when I read the letters. The envelopes were sometimes sealed with sticky tape, and other times Kathrin would refer to something written in another letter that I had never received.

When a small package arrived with the postage I recognised as West Berlin, I guessed it was from Thomas. It was a book, *The GDR: 300 Questions, 300 Answers*, and with it was a short note, written in block letters, without a single blemish or mistake:

"Dear Michael, I am informed that you are interested to come to the DDR. Here is a book that can give you some information about the country. If you want to come, I can help you get status as a 'Guest Worker of the DDR'. There is my address at the bottom of the page. Greetings, Rudi."

I had a brief vision of my letters to Kathrin being passed around to all members of the family. They would gather together to hear the poetic words of this closet romantic, with laughter all round. I knew it wasn't like that, but still felt that some personal border had been crossed. Perhaps Kathrin had told Rudi how serious I was about returning. Rudi hadn't said what he did, only that he worked in an office. But he offered help and this might have meant he worked in a government office or had friends who did. I hadn't thought about how I would go to East Germany, whether I had to apply for a visa or get special permission to work. My only concern was saving money.

I read the book several times. It outlined, in the form of questions and answers, East Germany's political, economic and social systems. I learned that control belonged to the workers and farmers: "All power derives from the people; plan together, work together, govern together." It was people like me who could make a difference. Everyone, from doctor to factory worker, was part of the process. The book described what sounded like the perfect society: "A socialist person is one who works, can realise own potential in work, leads a culturally-full life, and is devoted to the working class." I wanted to be this person, working hard for the collective goal, a major part of the community, reaping the rewards of group effort. The book explained how culture enhanced individuals, culture that had previously been in the control of the elite. I could afford, and be accepted at, the opera. I could take weekend art classes, be a regular at the theatre. The kinds of things that were out of my reach in Perth, and not just economically, but socially as well; the guys in the workshop would never take me seriously if I went every Friday to the opera and not the trots. I could get involved in sport and take evening classes to further my education. Perhaps one day I could be an engineer or an architect.

Everything was possible in communism, and as I read the book to the end for the fifth time, I wondered why the whole world wasn't communist. The system was perfect: equality, affordable basic needs, full employment, no poverty, health care for all. Why was the world full of haves and have-nots when this system provided for all? In a socialist world, there would be no people living on the streets, no crime, no arrogance and superiority that comes from wealth and status, and no places like Maddington.

But the question remained, why had communism always been represented as evil? In movies, in television shows, in newspapers, in books, it was always the mighty Americans, all good and shouting freedom and peace, up against the ruthless, cold, robotic Soviet enemy. James Bond saved the world from them, and politicians had always warned us to beware of the Red Threat. The Cold War was started by the Soviets: they built the Berlin Wall, divided Europe with the Iron Curtain, and constantly pushed the world to the brink of nuclear war. But the book Rudi sent me told the complete opposite, that the western powers were responsible for all these things. Who was right? Both sides talked about freedom and said they were working only for peace while the other was trying to start war. Who should we believe?

All in knew was that I lived in a western country and didn't feel I had unlimited freedom. Moreover, I felt completely enclosed in the world I was born into, that I had no opportunities beyond that world, and that the system only sought to keep me there. It was a system of inequality and discrimination. Why should I believe in a system that would never let me be more than a low-paid mechanic? Communism, on the other hand, offered me – offered everybody – so much more. This was a system that gave everyone a chance. And they stood up to the Americans, who held peace flags in one hand and loaded guns with the other. It was the Americans who wanted to dominate, who created weapons that could wipe out the world in ten seconds. They invaded Vietnam and tried to overpower other communist countries which were only interested in providing for their people. The Americans tried to take all of this away using the Cold War. Why couldn't they just leave them alone? Or, why didn't they see the benefits of the system and use it themselves? It was like the poor telling the rich how to live and what to do. The rich would never open their arrogant ears to the words of the inferior. I couldn't change the world, and I didn't want to. All I wanted was the best life for me, and after reading that book, it was clear that the best life was in East Germany.

I wrote on emotional letter to Kathrin, telling her what no one in Perth could understand. And something made me believe that everyone harboured a prejudice towards German people. Let them, I thought, and they could continue to suffer in this limiting society. I was heading for paradise.

It was a strange time. I withdrew, saw few of my friends, and had rather wild mood swings. The world around me frustrated me no end, and the idea that I would soon leave it all behind for something much better wasn't always a comforting consolation. I said little at work, didn't return telephone calls and lost interest in all the things that had sustained me before. I had already rejected this world and could only focus on the future.

Rudi replied quickly to my letter. He said it hadn't been easy, but he'd made it possible for me to come to East Germany as a Guest Worker, and that I should be very thankful. People from the west were seldom granted such permission. Something in his words told me he had done me a huge favour, and more, that I had to remember this.

So, it was set. I wrote to Kathrin and Rudi saying I would arrive in the first week of January, allowing me to spend Christmas with my parents. I still hadn't told them I was leaving, which was cowardly because I'd already bought my ticket. The time never seemed right to break the news. Christmas was my deadline.

It was at the start of that hot December that the burning light of hope began to shine in my eyes. I was leaving, escaping, breaking out and heading for a better place, and everyone else would remain here and suffer through miserable lives. I gave notice at the dealership, where all my work hours had profited managers I'd never met and satisfied customers whose gratitude I'd never received. The last day before the Christmas break was my last. I told the other guys that I was going to work for a friend of my father's, at a small private workshop. They chipped in some money and bought me a watch. It was then that my arrogance faded and the scope of what I was about to do became clear. I was leaving Australia, everything I had ever known, for a completely foreign world. I sold my beloved car. There was no turning back now.

On Christmas Day, my father asked me what kind of car I was planning to buy. We were having a quiet day. We'd spent Christmas Eve with relatives in the neighbouring suburb of Kelmscott and now had today to ourselves. We sat in the cool shadows on the veranda drinking beers. I missed German beer. Australian beer was watered down and thin by comparison. The afternoon was hot and still. The afternoon sea breeze wouldn't hit us until sunset because we were so far inland. Mum sat with us, quietly doing a crossword, humming the answers to herself all the while, her reading glasses low on her nose.

The time had come.

"Well," I started, "I'm not exactly going to buy another car, dad. And that's what I've been wanting to talk to you both about."

"Don't go crazy and get a motorbike," mum barked, her eyes peering above the glasses, making her look like a questioning professor. "I don't want to scrape you off the road."

Dad laughed. "Maybe you can buy yourself one of them tractor mowers and keep this grass under control," he said, gesturing with his beer at the overgrown grass we called our lawn.

"Look, this isn't so easy to say, so I think it's better you just let me speak, and then say what you think at the end."

Dad looked at me blankly. He didn't like being told what to do, least of all in his own home. Mum's look was different; she knew what was coming.

"Um, I don't really know how to start. But you have to remember this is a choice I've made and it's not against you or Australia or anything like that." I turned to dad. "When I was in Hamburg, I met a girl."

He smirked. His smile mocked me, but I wouldn't be intimidated. The man I had respected as my father had disappeared long ago.

"It's not what you think, dad. But I did go to visit her, in East Berlin. And what I saw there was really unbelievable."

"Yeah, a bunch of Nazi robots, I bet."

"Look, if you're not gonna listen, then I'll stop right now."

There's a moment in every son's life when he realises he has not only outgrown his parents but left them behind. It was exactly at that point that I knew I had for a long time been a better man than my father. I wondered if this was because I had developed or because he had declined.

"Let him speak, Gary," my mother said, reaching out and laying a calming hand on his shoulder.

"It's a different world," I said. "People are equal, everyone has a chance and everyone has what they need. I could be a doctor there. You could run the country. Christ, mum could run the country. Everything is possible."

I don't know why, but I found myself trying to convince them, to make them understand just what a great system it was, and how it meant that people like us went from the bottom of society to the top. Us workers were running the show.

"You know," my father said, chuckling, "thirty years ago they would've thrown you in prison for talk like that." And he became surprisingly melancholic. "I wish the world was like that, but it's not. Don't look at me like that. I know what you're on about. I'm not as stupid as you think I am. The worker's state. It's a good theory, but it can't work in practice."

"But it does, and has for a long time," I said. It was my turn to mock.

"Yeah, but come on, Mick, can you imagine me running the country? I wouldn't know the first thing about it. And neither do you. I'm not a smart arse, but I know my limits."

"Mike, the people are like prisoners there," mum said. "They can't leave, and the Russians have been trying for years to conquer the world."

"I don't trust those Germans," dad added spitefully. "Whether they're commies or not."

"But you've never been there," I said. "How can you say you know these places and these people if you've never been there. You ever meet a German, dad?"

"If I did, I'd smack him in the mouth." He crunched his beer can in his hand and threw it towards a scattering of others near the door. When my mother didn't move, he stood up and went into the house for another beer.

I shook my head.

"When are you leaving?" mum asked softly.

I couldn't look at her. I felt so sorry for her, almost as much as she did for herself. I looked down at the old wooden veranda. The wood was cracked and splintered, and there were holes big enough for mice to crawl out of to hunt for scraps of food.

"Fifth Jan."

She nodded, pushed her glasses up onto her nose and went back to her crossword. From inside the house, I heard the sound of the television; American accents and gun shots, and then loud advertisements for the latest car or for property deals and low interest bank loans. They shouted at you from inside the little box, urging you to buy things you didn't need and dream of the things you could never afford, the life you could never have. The television dictated what kind of life to aspire to, which system to believe.

I got up from the veranda and left the backyard through the side gate. The sun was hot and the only wind was a dry easterly which blew off the desert. It was the kind of wind that made your snot brown and your teeth grind with small grains of grit and dirt.

There were children everywhere, playing in the dead gardens in front of their houses. They tested new toys, kicked new footballs and formed small games of cricket using new equipment. Mums and dads and grandparents sat on fold-out chairs under the trees, drank alcohol and yelled encouragement. You could see in their manner how much had been sacrificed for the gifts. A child wasn't allowed to throw a new cricket bat to the ground, or treat a toy car badly. The kids had the zest of youth but the pasty coloured skin and limp hair the world identifies with poverty. Their round bellies stuck out over shorts several sizes too small, and their arms and legs were like sticks. They seemed so fragile, as if the world could crush them with one swift round of job cuts and a rise in inflation.

I could feel no happiness as I walked the streets. Each house told a story of pain and suffering. There were no winners here and there never would be. Maybe one youngster could rise above it to become a sporting hero, or a genius could be conceived in the back seat of an old Ford, but for the most part, these people would get nowhere. Their lives were planned out for them from the day they were born. They could hope and dream as kids, only to become bitter and resentful with each passing year as reality set in. There had to be more than this.

# Transit

Below, no man's land was brightly lit and snaked its way through the middle of the city. There was snow on the ground and the powerful searchlights turned it golden.

The plane veered over East Berlin to make its approach to Tempelhof Airport. The two cities show their contrasts at night, and it's most striking from the air. West Berlin is bright, with many cars on the road and colourful lights advertising businesses, hotels and restaurants. The whole city is on show, constantly attempting to invade your private world with images and glitter. The mood in East Berlin is more subdued. The city is enshrouded in darkness, compared to its neon neighbour, and is quiet and peaceful. As the plane crossed from west to east and back to west, I felt I knew both cities intimately and that I would always choose one over the other. West Berlin was too much like Perth. I wanted the quiet community of East Berlin.

In the arrivals terminal, Thomas stood alone in the crowd. He wore a suit of navy blue with a white shirt and red tie, looking like a business-style version of the American flag. He made me feel exceedingly common in my faded jeans and knitted pullover, but he rushed forward and hugged me, pressing his body against mine in a feminine way. The sweet smell of strong cologne mixed with sweat was overpowering and made me pull back slightly.

"If I'd known it was going to be formal," I said when he released me, "I would've dressed up."

"This?" he said, pulling at the lapel of the coat, treating the suit as if it was nothing but rags. "It's nothing. I have a half-time job now, working in the bank with Uncle Thorsten."

"Great."

"I must've forgotten to mention it in my last letter." Thomas laughed awkwardly. "What are you doing here? I mean, I didn't expect you to come back so soon."

"Yeah, it was bit of a rushed decision. Just had enough of Australia, I guess."

We moved quickly out of the airport. Thomas carried one of my bags. Outside, a thin layer of snow made the late afternoon seem brighter than it was. I stopped next to a low wall and scooped up a handful. It was light and surprisingly dry.

"Come on, Michael," Thomas shouted from the boot of his BMW. "It's freezing out here."

I made the snow into a ball and threw it at a tree. It whacked against the trunk and made a round area of white like a slash of paint. I joined Thomas at the boot and put in my bag.

"Amazing," I said. "I've never seen snow before."

Thomas laughed. I remembered his girly inhaled giggles; they certainly didn't match the suit.

"The fun doesn't last so long," he said, "and you can't ski here."

"Just to see it is incredible."

Thomas got into the car.

"Hey, what time is it?" I asked looking at my watch as I got in as well. I felt upside down, spun around, that my arse was watching the road and I was sitting on my face.

"Half past five."

"It's so dark."

"Yes. It's winter."

"But the days were so long in the summer."

"And it's the opposite in winter," Thomas said, making me feel stupid.

We lapsed into silence. It wasn't far from Tempelhof to Winterfeldtplatz. The traffic was heavy, but it moved along swiftly. There was much sounding of horns, lowering of windows to yell at passing drivers, flashing of lights and raising of middle fingers. It wouldn't have surprised me if Thomas had pulled out a gun and started firing it at people who made driving errors or took too long reacting to a green light. The aggression was fierce.

"So, what brings you back?" Thomas asked. "You didn't say much in your letter." He looked at me out of the corners of his eyes. A sneaky gesture.

"Well, I'm going to live in East Berlin."

Thomas almost collided with the car in front of us. He stopped just in time. The tires shrieked and we bounced in our seats slightly. Horns sounded.

"What do you mean?"

I had expected this. "It's all planned," I explained calmly. "I've got a visa to work, and honestly, I can't wait to get over there."

"Man, you're completely crazy."

Thomas began to drive more aggressively, letting out his frustration and confusion on the road. He said nothing until we were at the apartment. He got lucky, finding a parking place right in front of the building. Once out of the car, he looked at the space lovingly, making me wonder if he would ever move the car again.

The apartment was empty. Thomas explained that Joachim spent every January on some Greek island, and that Hans was still at work. It was when we were settled in the living room with beers in our hands – lemons again – that he started once more about my plans.

"Michael, you must think about this," he said. "I don't think you know what you get into."

"Well," I said, determined not to let him sway me, "it's too late now. The decision's made. Kathrin's waiting. Rudi says there is a job for me, and an apartment. Everything's set."

"How long do you stay?" His English worsened the more frustrated he became.

I shrugged. "I'll see what happens. I want to be with Kathrin, but I'm trying to keep things open."

"Nothing is open there," Thomas exclaimed. "That's the whole problem. You be a prisoner like them."

"I guess if I don't like it I can always leave, but I don't think that'll happen." I kept my voice calm and soft. Thomas could rant all he wanted; I wouldn't be influenced.

"Are you going tomorrow?" he asked, and he laughed sarcastically. The world didn't make sense to him.

"No. Day after. Sunday. Rudi said it would be easier then."

"Who is Rudi?" Thomas asked spitefully, as if this person was responsible for the whole mess.

"He married one of your cousins. I forget her name, the daughter of Frank."

"Christine." He stared at his beer bottle, pulling at the label with his fingernails, then drank from it. His shoulders slumped in a sad way and the suit began to wrinkle.

"You trust not Rüdiger," he said after a brief silence. "He's involved with their government."

"Yeah, I guessed that when he wrote to me saying he could help."

Thomas shook his head and drank some more.

Sitting there, the alcohol collided with my jetlag and sent a wave of fatigue through my body. I could've stretched out on the couch and slept with a live band playing in the room. I excused myself and went to Joachim's room. The double bed smelled of flowers. The cover was bright yellow, and there were three enormous pillows of the same colour. I unrolled my sleeping bag and slept on top of the bed. I didn't hear the shouts or the blaring of car horns coming from the street below. I slept the dreamless sleep of the innocent.

\*\*\*

I woke with my left arm throbbing and dead. It was under my body and in my deep sleep I had been unable to subconsciously move it. I rolled onto my back and stared at the ceiling, the blood pumping into my arm, pins and needles in my fingers. The darkness betrayed the time and made it difficult for me to become aware of my surroundings.

The bed was up against the double windows. Ice had collected at the corners of the window frames in the night. Through it I could see the stalls and vans of a market setting up on Winterfeldtplatz. The red church behind it loomed high, its bells tolling the hour. Eight gongs. It was eight o'clock. Saturday. West Berlin. Australia not only seemed like far away, but it also felt like a long time ago. I was here, about to move to East Germany and become a new Michael Smith.

I looked out the window. The grey sky didn't stop people from milling around the market place, carrying white canvas bags or wheeling personal shopping trolleys, the ones with two wheels you only see old people with back home.

Eight in the morning here meant it was three in the afternoon in Perth. Mum would be sitting in an armchair doing a crossword, and watching the cricket with one eye. Dad would be lying on the sofa, engrossed in the little white men on the flickering screen, offering a running commentary that conflicted with the announcers, and lining up empty beer cans on the rickety coffee table. It was an image so pure in its normality and predictability that I wanted to be there: to scoff like my father at the simple mistakes the players made, and to play cricket in the backyard with dad while mum prepared dinner. But it was only like that when I was young, when dad was a bricklayer. Life had been good then. It's a shame that things must change. We spend our whole lives getting to the point of perfection, and once there, it quickly passes, and we spend the rest of our lives trying to get back.

I gave my head a shake, wondering where such pathetic musings had come from.

The time in Australia was over, for now. I was here, on the brink of entering East Germany and on my own journey towards perfection. I was still young enough to dream. My words fell on deaf ears in Perth. The listeners had long ago forgotten their dreams and given in to reality. They didn't question the world around them, and believed everything they were told.

Before I left Perth, I gave the book Rudi had sent me to my father. But I didn't think he would read it; he was too stubborn. He barely spoke to me that last week. I was forced to play out many conversations with him in my head, saying the things in my imagination I could never say to him in real life. The truth is sometimes too hard to say, and you're scared of the impact it will have. So you tell the truth to yourself in a hope it may ease the strain. And then as time passes, you wonder if you actually had the conversation with the person or had only played it out in your mind.

I gave my head another shake and stumbled towards the bathroom. The door opened just as I reached the handle. I was too dopey to be taken by surprise, and stopped in mid-action. Steam came out with the person.

"Morgen," he said, smiling. "You must be Michael."

Hans wore a thick white robe and had a red towel wrapped around his hair the way a woman does. It made him look taller than he was. His face was smoothly shaven and glistened with moisturiser.

"Hi," I said dreamily, before stepping out of the doorway to let him past. "I'm not really awake yet," I added. "Gimme a minute."

Hans pranced past me, down the hall to his room. He didn't seem to use his heels when walking, staying on the balls of his feet. He was very short, even when walking in what looked like a practised way. From behind, with the red towel on his head and his rather large bottom, he could have been mistaken for a woman.

I had what I thought was a quick shower, but as I was getting dressed, the faint sound of bells ringing made me realise it was now nine. I was hungry. Airline food never sticks to your sides. You can fill your stomach with it and your body absorbs nothing. It just comes straight out the other end, looking as much like food as it did going in.

Thomas and Hans were in the kitchen. Hans still wore his bathrobe and sat cross-legged at a small table which was covered with a broadsheet newspaper. He was hidden by the section he was holding, and lowered it to smile at me when I entered. His face still glistened, but he had chocolate at the corners of his mouth. His face was round and soft, and with the chocolate, when he smiled he looked like a child who had eaten a whole cake. He organised some of the paper to give me room at the table. I sat down.

"Coffee or hot chocolate?" Thomas asked. He stood over the oven and looked to be boiling eggs. He wore tight jeans, a floppy sweater several sizes too big and ugly grandpa slippers. His hair was slicked back and shiny.

"Coffee, thanks," I said.

The kitchen was small. Too small for three people living separate lives, I thought. It seemed so crowded with the three of us, but there was also a large refrigerator, a double sink, several cupboards, and a washing machine; for clothes, not dishes. I was scared to move, and hunched my body in on itself. The window was closed and the air was thick and warm. The smells of coffee and toasted bread fought for supremacy in the stuffiness, but Hans's cologne was winning.

Thomas said something to Hans in German and again he lowered his paper to look at me. But he didn't force a smile this time, and his round face looked heavy and confused.

"Why do you want to go there?" he asked.

I wondered for a second how many times I was going to have to explain my decision.

"I'm in love with Thomas's sister Kathrin," I said flatly. It was not worth outlining the virtues of communism to these two. They would only mock me like my father had done; like Thomas had last night.

Hans looked at Thomas and the two exchanged a shrug and smile. "She is very nice girl," Hans said, "but is she so good you give up freedom?"

"I'm not giving up freedom. East Germany is just as free as anywhere else."

Hans laughed uncontrollably. A few drops of hot chocolate came out of his nose and splattered on the newspaper. He turned red with embarrassment, lifted the paper up slightly to hide his face and muttered to himself in German.

"Don't worry, Hans," Thomas said, looking at me. "He's not going forever."

There was assurance in his voice I didn't like. I would stay just to prove him wrong. I never liked it when people made assumptions about my own life and how things would be for me. They only ever thought about how it would be for them, and then believed it would be the same for everyone else. It was an extremely single-minded and arrogant way of thinking. Just because he hated it, didn't mean that I would.

Thomas put a boiled egg with two slices of dark bread in front of me. He did the same for Hans, who said "Danke" from behind the broadsheet. The table wasn't big enough for the three of us, so Thomas ate standing, leaning on the counter next to the sink. He drank several cups of coffee, taking big gulps and swallowing loudly. I noticed how much his Adam's apple stuck out. We ate in silence, with Hans occasionally commenting on something he read in the paper.

When finished, Thomas asked, "What are your plans today?"

He took my empty plate and placed it in the sink.

"No plans," I said. "I thought maybe you and I could hang out a bit. I mean, it's good to see you, Thomas."

He smiled warmly. I guess up to that point I had been a little cold, focusing only on the next day and also defending myself against his questions. Seldom are you warm to a person who pushes you against a wall.

"Well, I was hoping you can help us today," Thomas said. "My uncle and aunt are moving. Can you give a hand?"

It was the hopeful look on his face and the flat tone of his voice that made me realise I'd been the victim of sinister planning; that I was staying in Thomas's apartment and wouldn't be able to refuse. Thorsten had decided to move on this day because he knew I would have to help. And between the three of us, he wouldn't have to pay anyone. I never had any problems helping people, but I didn't like being suckered into it like this.

"Of course," I said. "But don't expect me to drive a truck or anything. It's all backward here."

Thomas laughed. "Don't worry about that. And I don't think it takes so long."

"Maybe you prefer to ride a kangaroo," Hans said, laughing. When we didn't laugh with him, he raised his paper once more and hid himself.

"If you're ready," Thomas said, "we can start."

Outside, Thomas roared the BMW to life and pulled reluctantly out of the prime parking place. He didn't bother to warm the car up, but simply started the engine and pulled away. The car lurched and sputtered. I wanted to say something, but thought better of it. Our breath fogged up the windscreen. Thomas didn't switch the heat to defrost it, and simply wiped the fog with the sleeve of his jacket. The heat came straight at us through the vents and smelled faintly of petrol.

The day was grey and grim, with the moisture frozen by the below zero night, making everything look shiny and slick, like Thomas's hair. I was surprised to see so many people out and about, braving the cold. Shopping, walking dogs. One man was even washing his car, using hot water that quickly steamed off. The whole city was up early and life was busily underway.

As we drove, I was reminded of West Berlin's streets: the wide main thoroughfares lined with shops and apartment buildings, and which cornered with train and underground stations; the narrow lanes and alleys that were tree-lined and leafy, and so full of parked cars traffic could only go in one direction at a time. But more, I was reminded of how crowded the streets are. So many cars, buses, trucks and bicycles, and smaller streets that had kids trying to play in the middle. There just wasn't enough space to accommodate everyone. Never is this more compounded than on a Saturday, especially one in January, when the people brace themselves against the bitter cold and walk with their heads down, their faces grim and sour.

In West Berlin, the traffic never flows; it jostles, in an endless competition of getting ahead, gaining advantage and leaving the small and weak behind. Thomas accelerated around slow cars on single lane roads, floored it to beat orange lights and forced his way into the traffic when entering a main road. He did all of this with a bored expression on his face, like the whole thing was a game which was no longer fun.

We reached the crowded intersection of a large shopping area and had to wait. There were several big department stores, lots of banks and small shops, and a large bus stop that unloaded and loaded money-laden shoppers. The scene was chaotic, with parents pulling back excited kids from crossing the road, and old people waiting patiently and muttering about the young people ducking between fast cars to get across while the lights were red. Every person was striding with purpose. Men in red aprons sold sausages from vans wheeled up

130

onto the pavement. Steam came out of hungry mouths as sausages went in. Shoppers carried large bags full of new clothes and expensive products and spoke loudly with each other. A man with a microphone stood in front of a shoe shop and told the world about the big sale happening inside, his voice loud and muffled by the amplifier. I was glad when we turned away from this scene of excess and waste, and headed down a side street.

Thorsten and Antje lived in a canary yellow building in a suburb Thomas called Friedenau. A large white van was parked out front. The back doors were open but the van was empty. They were waiting for us.

Thomas parked and led the way inside. I was happy when he stopped on the second floor and rang the bell; the building was five stories high. Antje opened the door and smiled thinly. The funniest joke in the world couldn't raise even a murmur from her throat. She wore tight black leggings that didn't disguise the meatiness of her legs as intended, while her long pullover only brought more attention to her large, round bottom instead of hiding it. For some reason, I felt sorry for her. There was something pathetic and pitiful about her, and worst of all, it didn't seem to be her fault. She was the perennial victim.

We shook hands and exchanged pleasantries. She thanked me for offering to help. I decided not to say I'd been coaxed.

Everything was packed in boxes, which were labelled in black pen so we knew beforehand what was inside and where it had to go. Very organised, but there were so many boxes. I could only hope there was no piano or canopy bed.

We found Thorsten in the living room. He wore sparkling blue overalls over a thick flannel shirt, as if he had just stepped out of a handyman fashion catalogue. A tool belt was slung around his waist, and was more than just a prop. He was in the process of dismantling a large sofa that was too big for the doorway.

"Morning, men," he said. "I hope you're ready to work hard today. Thanks for coming, Michael."

We watched him try to release a tight screw that held the sofa's arms to the base. The tendons in his neck strained. His comb-over titled the wrong way, hanging off his head like an open book. The screw wouldn't budge, and his attempt to move it using the force of his body was comical. I covered my mouth to hide my laughter. When Thorsten had failed, Thomas bent over to have a try, but had no success. They stood back from the sofa, staring at the screw, discussing the problem like expert carpenters. I held out my hand to Thomas and he put the screwdriver in it. I gave the arm a swift kick and then shook it with my hands. The screw came out easily and the arm fell to the floor. I handed the screwdriver back to Thorsten and he put it in his tool belt. He flicked what hair he had from his face, pressed it down on the side of his head and forced a smile. He clearly didn't like that I had so easily succeeded where he had failed. His smile told me that he was glad I could help, but don't take charge; he was the boss.

We set to work. The dust made my throat dry. The floor was laminated and dust had collected under everything. We stirred it up by moving furniture and soon we were all coughing. And yet, all the windows remained closed because of the cold. Thorsten stayed in the van conducting its loading while Thomas, myself and sometimes Antje, brought down the boxes and pieces of furniture.

"Looks like we need two trips," Thorsten said to me when I placed a box in the doorway of the full van. It was poorly packed, but it would've been a waste of time to repack. "Tell Thomas and Antje to stop."

I trudged up the stairs and did what I was told. Both were relieved to have a break.

Thomas drove the BMW to pick up Hilde and take her to the new house. The feisty old bird was going help with the unpacking and then cook us up a treat.

I went with Thorsten. He manoeuvred the van slowly, as if it were a ten ton truck. I think he even tried to double clutch, but only succeeded in grinding the gears and making the van lurch and shudder by being in the wrong gear. He stalled it at a set of traffic lights, and the resounding chorus of horns made him red with embarrassment. Antje sat between us. Her odour was strange; not bad, and not sweet, as if she smelt like nothing, or of something unidentifiable and unpleasant. She stared straight ahead and said nothing. The two seemed so mismatched.

Thorsten explained they were moving to a suburb called Grünewald, on the edge of a large forest. He was immensely happy about it, as if the forest was a unique and wonderful place. He was getting towards that stage in life when he could have everything he wanted; money could buy security and his idea of happiness.

We pulled – Thorsten chose not to reverse – into the driveway of a small two-storey house. It was grey concrete with a brown tile roof and matching brown windowsills and doors. It was ugly, smaller than the house I'd grown up in. There was a small patch of limp lawn out front halved by a narrow path that led from the door to the front gate. As I stood waiting for Thorsten to open the van's back door and bark orders, I heard the rumble of a train. It became louder and louder, the clickity-clack on the rails clear and rhythmic. I saw the train through the trees behind the house, a blur of colour, rusted wheels and dirty windows.

Thomas parked on the street and then helped Hilde out of the car. She saw me and smiled, and came over to shake my hand. She seemed shorter than before, and I noticed she was wearing white tennis shoes that had surely never seen a tennis court.

"You are nice man to help today," she said smiling, her little hand lost in mine but gripping hard.

There was no guilt from anyone that this day had been specifically planned because I was there to help.

Thorsten stayed in the van and moved things to the back doors where Thomas and I picked them up and carried them into the house. I learned words like Küche, Badezimmer, Wohnzimmer and Schlafzimmer from what was written on the boxes and with help from Thomas. Antje and Hilde worked in the house unpacking boxes and organising cups of coffee and other refreshments. Hilde had a strong work ethic, with nimble hands, and I rarely saw her stopping to catch her breath. I mentioned this to Thomas while we stood at the back of the van waiting for Thorsten to move boxes into place.

"She was one of the Trümmerfrauen after the war," Thomas said, leaning against the van door. He looked exhausted. His pink cheeks were slashed with dirt marks and his shoulders slumped forward. "They cleared up the rubble from all the destroyed buildings."

"Why didn't the men do it?"

Thomas looked at me incredulously. "All the men were dead, or had left Berlin to hide in the countryside."

I nodded trying to understand, but it was just so hard to imagine.

A loud crash from inside the van made us both look. Thorsten lay on the floor with a lamp in his hands.

"It's okay," he stammered. "I caught it." He stood up and brushed the dirt from his clean overalls.

Thomas and I looked at each other and laughed.

With the van unloaded, we left Hilde and Antje at the house and drove back to Friedenau. An argument ensued in German between Thomas and Thorsten. At one point, Thorsten pointed at the clock on the dashboard, but Thomas didn't give up. We detoured down a wide street called Clayallee. The trees were like skeletons, completely devoid of leaves. At any other time of year, it would have been a very green area, but in January it was dead, cold, grey and miserable. I missed the Perth summer.

We turned left onto another wide street. On the corner was a large collection of buildings surrounded by a high wall topped with barbed wire. It was like a small fortress. Thorsten pulled over to the side of the road, left the van running and we looked at the high front gate. Two soldiers stood guard. There was a small hut with a red and white barrier that could be raised to let cars through.

"Is that some kind of prison?" I asked.

"It's the Kommandatura," Thomas explained. "Where the Allied government is."

"Allied?"

"You know, America, England and France. From the war."

One of the guards looked at us and Thorsten immediately put the van in gear and drove away.

"But why are they still here? I mean, the war was years ago."

"Berlin is technically still under four power control," Thorsten said flatly, not hiding his distaste. "It's so Germany doesn't rise again as a superpower." He changed gears emphatically and accelerated hard. But he got the wrong the gear and the van shuddered.

"Try third," Thomas suggested.

"The allies want to keep Germany down," Thorsten continued, after correcting his mistake. "They are afraid of us. Because our little country has the power to do great things."

Thomas smiled sarcastically, shook his head and swallowed what he had wanted to say. I wondered if the two had clashed before on this subject.

"They have no business here," Thorsten added. "They only want to steal our technology and ideas."

He was angry and bitter, as I would've been if a foreign country had occupied my land for so long. The garrison, and the presence of the allies, was a constant reminder that Germany had lost the war, and had also made a big mistake by starting it. But why did the allies have to rub it in? The war was almost forty years ago. Two generations had passed. Why was there still a fear about Germany rising? None of the Germans I'd met, East or West, were militaristic or aggressive, and they weren't really so nationalistic either. They were just people, who liked to drink and laugh like any others. Why couldn't they just be left alone? The presence of the allies perpetuated the myth about Germans, that they were all Nazis and needed to be controlled. If the Americans took their guns and soldiers home, it would make it easier for the Germans to accept their history and move on, and maybe then the world would alter its prejudice towards them in the process.

I wanted to say all of this, but instead sat in silence.

"Come on," Thomas said to his uncle. "They're not scared of us. They're scared of the Soviets. They only stay here because this is the front line to the eastern bloc."

Thorsten nodded and seemed to agree, but wouldn't be shouted down so easily.

"All Germany has is its people," he continued. "We don't have great wealth in the land. We only have ourselves. The Americans know this. They understand we are better at making things than they are. We have better ideas and a stronger work ethic. They stay here, say they protect us from the Soviets, but only want to take our ideas without having to ask for them. The Americans only interfere in the world when they have something to gain. They don't want to save us, but they understand how they can use us."

"What about the airlift?" Thomas countered. "They gave a lot for that, just for the West Berliners."

"Ah, but you see they only wanted a, how do you say, foot in the door. West Berlin made a great place to spy on the enemy, and they also wanted to make us feel dependent, that we couldn't survive without them."

I leaned towards Thomas. "What airlift?"

"In 1948, the Russians cut off West Berlin," he explained. "Nothing could get in or out. The allies brought everything in by plane."

"Wow. I didn't know that."

"Yes, but even then it was because of the help of our best engineers in Frankfurt and Hamburg," Thorsten said. "But you never read that in the American history books. And it was Turkish labourers and old German men who built the airport in Tegel for the French. Americans have the habit of writing their own history without including anyone else."

"But it's always like that," Thomas said. "History is written by those who control it. The Russians are just as bad."

"This is true," Thorsten said. His concession surprised me. He seemed such a close-minded and arrogant man who seemed to feel his opinion stood above all others. "But it's funny that the Germans have the same role in both histories."

The two men laughed. I joined them, and realised that through the whole discussion the atmosphere had been relaxed and open. They couldn't change the situation, so they laughed at it.

Thorsten helped carrying boxes down from the apartment this time. His desire to take charge had diminished with his numerous failures. He was humbled by them but didn't seem to care. His overalls got dirty and he started to sweat a little, and he made a comment about how rewarding labour could be. I started to like him.

But he had so much stuff. With the apartment finally empty, I stood next to the van and stretched my sore back. But Thorsten called me back inside and led us to the top floor. The attic was dusty and sub-divided into wooden cells like a prison from an old western movie. Each cell had a small lock on the door. Thorsten's compartment was full. I looked at Thomas and we groaned together. Not only more carrying, but five flights of stairs as well. Thorsten clapped his hands together.

"Let's get started," he said. "The sooner we finish, the sooner we can drink beer."

It sounded like something my father would've said, and I wondered if manual labour reduced all men to the same level: hard work, cold beer, a few laughs and the simple life.

My tired legs stumbled up and down the stairs. We worked in sections: Thorsten carrying things from the attic down one flight of stairs, me carrying it three more flights, and then Thomas taking the last flight of stairs and loading the van. Everything was dusty and dirty and my throat became dry. I longed for a cold beer and just to stop. But we still had to unload at the house in Grünewald.

Finally, Thorsten followed me down the stairs. He took a last look in the apartment, then we drove to the new house, too tired to talk.

After another hour, we were done.

We took showers and sat down to dinner straight away. And it was spectacular. Thomas said it was a traditional German meal, Roulade, Thorsten's favourite. It was a long loaf of meat, with a delicious stuffing

136

inside. The beef was succulent and tender and melted in my mouth. It was topped off with round balls of mashed potato, sweet red cabbage and gravy. We all ate with the appetite that comes from hard work, and drank too much wine after drinking too much beer.

The house was still in disarray, but Antje had connected the stereo. We listened to opera. Bach, Hilde said. It was nice, but it didn't drown out the intermittent sounds of passing trains. Thomas and I wore old clothes from Thorsten. They were tight fitting and itchy. It felt good to be clean, and to be filling my stomach with such tasty food.

We didn't stay late. Everyone was very tired. We dropped Hilde at her apartment in Charlottenburg; Thomas double parked on the narrow street with cars from both directions honking horns and flashing lights to make us hurry. Thomas seemed to take a little bit of pleasure in making them all wait, helping Hilde out of the car and then taking his time saying goodbye. I shook her hand and jumped in the front.

"You were a star today," Thomas said as we got moving again. "After the first hour I was finished."

I shrugged my shoulders. "My dad was a labourer. I guess I wear his genes."

Thomas paused for a moment, then laughed. "Well, it was because of you that we did it all today."

I smiled, trying to forget the conspiracy that had me helping in the first place. Best not to dwell.

"No problem. It was worth it for the dinner."

"Grandma is a great cook."

"And so is your mother," I added.

"Well, she doesn't have such good ingredients, but she can make great things from nothing."

"Why don't you come over tomorrow?"

"I'd like to, but it's not really so easy. I can't just go like you. I have to apply for permission and that normally takes two or three days."

"Oh, okay."

"But I try to come next weekend. Call me. I think you want me to bring some things."

"Like what?"

Thomas grinned. He'd resigned himself to humour my intention of living in East Berlin, but he thought I wouldn't last very long.

"You never know," he said. "Call me from my parents' house if you want something. They actually have a phone."

137

"Okay."

I didn't really understand what he was talking about. Everything I needed was available in East Berlin. But then I remembered the man at Checkpoint Charlie who had been caught with magazines stuffed in his pantyhose, and the warning from Thomas not to take anything to read. And then the fact that Rudi had come out of nowhere to help me find a way into a country Kathrin had said was extremely difficult to enter. Did I know what I was getting myself into? I'd come this far. I had to try.

\*\*\*

The sky was a blue so clear and pale that it hurt the eyes. The sun was bright and low on the horizon. From the warm confines of my sleeping bag, it looked like a glorious summer day outside. But the minute I jumped out of bed and my feet hit the cold floor, the reality of winter set back in.

The procedure was for me to phone Rudi when I was ready to start. Then, we would rendezvous at the border crossing one hour later. I assumed it would be at Checkpoint Charlie, but Rudi told me on the phone to meet him at Glienicker Brücke.

"It is easier," he said. "Just wait for me there. Do not speak to anyone."

Then he hung up.

When I said Glienicker Brücke, Thomas looked at me strangely. He narrowed his eyes and seemed to have a hundred questions he could never ask.

"Where is it?" I asked, uncomfortable with his suspicious, questioning look.

"In the south," he said, still eyeing me carefully. "On the road to Potsdam."

"Kathrin told me about Potsdam. Said there were castles there or something."

"That's right. Sanssouci."

"I wonder why we have to meet at this Brücke place and not at Checkpoint Charlie."

Thomas titled his head. "Glienicker is very special."

"Why? Is it only for people going to live in East Germany?"

"In a way. It is where they swap spies."

"What do you mean?"

"When we catch one of their spies, we arrange a swap for one of our spies."

"Really? Sounds like a movie."

"Yes. It does." He paused. "Are you the star today?"

"You mean am I a spy?" I exclaimed laughing. "You've got to be joking."

Thomas forced a chuckle. "Well, we shall know if a man comes from the other side and I have to drive him back to West Berlin."

"You don't have to take me. It's all right."

"It's not so easy to get there," he said. "And I want to see what happens. And I'm also interested to see how Rüdiger looks now."

I wondered about his relationship with the girl Christine. Had they once been lovers? They were cousins. Was that frowned upon in German culture?

As we left the apartment, bells rang all over the city, calling people to church. We drove out of the city along a straight freeway, doing twenty kilometres over the speed limit. We passed no one; every car was doing the same or going faster.

"This used to be a race track in Hitler's time," Thomas said, after we had passed an old grandstand.

"Looks like it still is."

Thomas laughed.

He pulled off the freeway at the Wannsee exit. We drove through a forest until a large lake spread out before us in both directions. It was frozen and covered with a sprinkling of snow. Kids skated and pulled each other in toboggans. Near the edge, a group of men were playing ice hockey. Boats which hadn't been prepared for the winter were either frozen in the lake or had been pushed up and now lay on the ice on their sides. In the small village we entered, families braved the cold, wheeling babies in prams and helping small kids on bicycles, while the older members walked with canes and struggled behind. Everyone was well dressed.

It was such a beautiful day.

We left the town behind and were once more surrounded by trees.

As we approached the bridge, Thomas said, "This is your last chance. You can stay here, live and work in West Berlin, and visit Kathrin that way."

The fear in my stomach heard him and listened. It was the easier way, but I'd come here with a plan, and couldn't turn back now. Living in West Berlin would be as frustrating and disappointing as all my years in Perth had been. And I wanted to be with Kathrin all the time, not for thirty days a year.

"Thanks, Thomas," I said. "But I really think it's gonna work out."

He sighed, accepting that he couldn't make me change my mind. I was just like my father, stubborn and resolute.

Rudi stood just behind the first vehicle pole. He wore a dark brown trenchcoat, a leather cap and dark glasses, and stood ramrod straight like a soldier. His hands were in the pockets of the coat and he looked directly at us as we drove towards him. He pulled out a gloved hand and raised it to make us stop ten metres short of the pole. The gloves were the same colour as the cap. He smiled. It was Sunday, but his face was clean shaven.

"I hope you're not changing places with him," Thomas said. I couldn't tell if he was serious or not.

Rudi motioned with his hands for me to get out of the car. When he saw Thomas getting out as well, he held up his hands and pointed. Thomas sat back down.

"This is what you're getting into," he said. "Last chance."

"I'll see you in a couple of days," I said, throwing out my hand. He shook it limply. "We'll have a real party then."

"Good luck. And greetings to my family." He grimaced and looked at Rudi. "If you see them."

A guard joined me at the back of the car and helped me with my bags. He was young and his cheeks were bright red against his pale face. Under his saucer shaped helmet, I could see his ears were also pink from the cold.

"Danke," I said to him. He smiled and walked quickly to the other side of the pole, then to a black car parked at the other end of the bridge.

I shook Rudi's gloved hand. He seemed taller in the trenchcoat, and heavier, more powerful. He took off his glasses to look at me. But it made no difference whether he wore them or not; his dark eyes gave nothing away. Up close, he smelt of pine; not from cologne but from cleaning liquid.

"I am happy you are here," he said. "Welcome to the Deutsche Demokratische Republik."

"Good to see you, Rudi," I said, my voice stuttering with the cold.

"Come," he said, putting a hand on my shoulder and turning me towards the black car, which I recognised as a Wartburg. "It is cold here."

I turned back to wave to Thomas, but he was already driving away. The blue BMW turned the first corner and was gone.

# German Democratic Republic

The apartment blocks looked like they had been dropped from the sky. They were tall, white and uniform, with light-coloured tiles and decorations to make them look more attractive. I was amazed at how long they were, that one apartment house could stretch the length of a street some two hundred metres long. Other houses were at right angles to the street, with lawns, clothes lines and parking places between them. It was all very orderly, organised and symmetrical. Everyone had an equal amount of space.

These were the pre-fabricated tenements built after the war that I had read about in the book Rudi had sent me. Pre-set concrete, uniform floor plans for each apartment, central heating, modern facilities, the showcase of the quick success of communism; that the system catered for everyone equally. But from the outside, they looked like giant school dormitories.

Rudi introduced me to the Hausmeister, Herr Wolfmann, who lived on the ground floor and was responsible for all the tenants in the building. The two seemed to know each other but remained aloof. I heard them using the informal du when addressing each other. Wolfmann was short and stocky, with beady eyes, a suspicious look on his face and a mouth that was almost naturally formed into a snarl. He looked as if he would be more at home wielding a cane in a school principal's office than changing light bulbs and taking rent. He watched me closely as I signed his yellowed ledger, giving my home address in Australia and the date of my arrival. He handed me two keys and announced something.

"The rent is sixty-three Mark," Rudi translated.

I did a quick calculation in my head. I hadn't even seen the apartment, but had the feeling I wasn't in the position to choose. Rudi had organised this. I couldn't say no.

"Okay, but I only have D-Marks." I produced the same amount of money from my wallet. Wolfmann's eyes lit up. Rudi took the money, then paid for me with his own.

"You can change your money tomorrow," he said, "at the Reisebüro on Alexanderplatz. I will take you there."

I nodded. "Please tell him I'll pay him next week," I said to Rudi.

"That is not necessary," he said flatly.

"No really, I want to pay my own way."

"Of course," said Rudi a little bemused. "You can pay next month."

I followed Rudi up the stairs as my head tried to comprehend that sixty-three Mark was for the whole month and not for a week. It was like living for free. It empowered me. I was doing the right thing.

The apartment was on the third floor and was one room about the size of the bedroom I had grown up in. The walls were dull white. The floor was a worn laminate, thin and a little sticky in places. The only furniture was a low bed with an old mattress on top. It was very warm in the room. The main heating pipe ran through the room to service all the other apartments, and because the room was so small and the solitary window closed, it was like an oven. There was a small kitchenette that had two hot plates for cooking and a narrow counter. There were two cupboards that were the same dull white as the walls. Between the cupboard and the counter there was a picture of a man tacked to the wall. He had a large round face, slicked back hair, a big nose, a bushy moustache underneath it and an arrogant smirk of a smile. Rudi saw the picture and quickly took it from the wall. He wrote something on the back of it, folded it carefully and put it in his pocket.

There was no fridge, no television, no light and no life. It felt as if someone had died in there.

I dropped my bags in the centre of the room. "It's great," I offered, unsure of anything appropriate to say.

"Yes," Rudi said seriously. "Apartment like this very hard to get. People normally must wait a long time."

It was difficult to believe that such a hovel wouldn't be easy to find, but the tone in Rudi's voice told me I had one more favour to be appreciative of. I looked around the room and tried to comprehend that this little dog box was now my home. It cost sixty-three Mark and I wondered if I was getting ripped off.

"Zo, I leave you to become organised," Rudi said, making for the door.

"Thanks for the ride," I said. "And for the apartment and everything."

"It is nothing." He smiled and waved me off. "Perhaps one day you can help me with something."

It sounded off-hand but I knew these favours would be called in, one day. Rudi struck me as a man who rarely did something for nothing.

"Absolutely."

"I come tomorrow and take you to your job, okay?"

There was no end to his good deeds. I shook his hand hard, trying to seem grateful.

"When I am home," Rudi said in the doorway, "I call Kathrin and say you are here."

I looked around the room; there was no phone. "Great. Thanks."

I closed the door behind him. It opened again and Rudi pointed at the keys that still hung from the keyhole. But he hadn't knocked. He'd just opened the door like it was a room in his house. Rudi smiled one last time and was finally gone. I heard his shoes clicking on the concrete steps and echoing in the stairwell.

I sat down on the pathetic mattress. The bed was hard, and I wondered, given the bareness of the room, if I was lucky even to have that. Still, I had an apartment, my own space, and that was something.

I opened the window to let in some fresh air. The heat was so stifling. From my single window, I looked down on a low, grey concrete building shaped like a long rectangle. Next to it was a small playground. A lone child struggled to build a snowman with the remaining snow that was frozen.

Wanting to embrace my new surroundings, I began to explore. The cupboards were empty and had a thin layer of dust. A door just behind the front door opened into a small cubicle. I had not seen this door before because when the front door was open, this door was hidden behind it. By a feat of incredible engineering, a shower, toilet and small wash basin had been crammed into two square metres. There was no window. The room had a single light bulb positioned next to a small mirror that was above the sink. Even more incredible was that the door opened into the room. It was a squeeze to get past the sink to sit down on the toilet.

I turned the mattress over. There was a small round hole all the way through, but not wide enough for any of the stuffing to spill out. I fingered the hole; there were black burn marks where the material had melted. I looked under the bed, the space barely wide enough to fit my head. It was dark and dusty, and I was just about to pull my head out when something caught my eye. I moved further up the bed, to the end closest to the wall. I coughed dust. There was a list of initials carved into the wood. B.S. 10/68, W.A 2/72, R.T 9/77, D.S 8/81. The last resident had only been there for about four months, but the other three had lived there for long times. Perhaps D.S. had hated the apartment from the beginning and spent all his time trying to find a better place. But there was something symbolic about the carvings, that each person had explored the room like me, gone so far as to look under the bed, and then added their name to the list. I searched through one of my bags and found the army knife my mother had given me for Christmas. I carved my initials at the bottom of the list – M.S. 1/82 – and wondered how long it would be until another name was underneath mine.

For something to do, I started unpacking. I had no drawers to fill or shelves to put things on. So I emptied my bags, flattened them on the floor and piled my clothes on top. I lay my sleeping bag on the bed and thought about arranging some clothes into a makeshift pillow, but decided against it. I had several books with me, including a German language book I was struggling through, and made these into a neat stack next to the bed.

A loud knock on the door startled me. The sound echoed in the bare room. Just as I reached the door, the person started to knock again and, as the door opened, she fell forward into my arms. A whiff of apples went straight up my nose and strong arms clutched my waist. Kathrin looked up at me with tears in her gleaming eyes. Both of us were without words. I had held so strongly to the image of her, but it had become blurred with memory, so that I couldn't really form a clear picture of her in my mind. Seeing her again, her beauty became clear and I remembered just what a stunning girl she was. And seeing her made all the old memories clear in my head, as if my brain had only needed reminding.

Kathrin closed the door behind her and kissed me hard, forcing her mouth onto mine. Her lips were dry and cracked, but her tongue was warm and wet, and as we kissed some more, our kisses became softer and softer, until my mouth was melting into hers. She led me to the bed and we made love passionately and quickly. Suddenly, the room was full of light and life. Kathrin closed the window and the stuffy heat of the room and the physicality of our gyrations caused us to sweat. It was only when this release was over that we found words.

"Hi," Kathrin sighed, looking deep into my eyes.

"Hi."

"I can't believe you're here."

"Touch me," I said. "I'm real."

She lay on top of me. Kathrin still had a thick blue headband covering her ears. Her sweet smell filled the small room.

"You took your time," she said, mocking anger. "You said six months."

"Hey, there were lots of girls to say goodbye to."

Kathrin's body went rigid, her face pale. She looked on the verge of hitting me, or crying.

"I'm just joking," I said. "I dreamed of you all day and all night."

It took a few moments for her to relax. She didn't seem to find the joke so funny.

"You have a nice apartment," she said at last, looking around. "It normally takes a long time to find a place like this."

"Yeah. Rudi said that. I think he organised it."

"I'm sure of it," Kathrin said, her eyes distant and blank. "Be careful what you say to him."

"Why? The guy's done so much for me."

"Just be careful, okay?" She stared at me, her scarred eyebrow raised, a worried look on her face.

"All right. I will."

She kissed me, then started nibbling one of my earlobes. It was a signal I remembered from the summer. We made love again and lay in the dark afterward. The window must have faced east because it was dark in the room very early.

"Grandma said you were very good yesterday," Kathrin said, breaking the silence, "helping Thorsten and Antje move house." Her voice echoed in the dark room. If she hadn't been lying next to me, the voice could have come from anywhere.

"It was fun. I think Thorsten's not such a bad guy after all. He just needs to lighten up a bit."

"Lighten up? You mean relax?"

I nodded.

"I think he works very hard," Kathrin said.

"Everyone in West Berlin needs to lighten up. They're all so stressed. I much prefer it here, with you. Shit, it is so good to be with you again. I mean, I dreamed of this so many times, and now here we are."

Kathrin leaned on her elbow and stroked my face with her free hand. "It is like a dream," she said. "I hope you like it here."

146

"Well, it's started off pretty good."

Kathrin got me moving. It turned out she lived only ten minutes walk away. A light snow was falling as she led me there. It was magical, white and fluffy, like feathers drifting slowly to the ground. There was something pure about snow, so white and clean, and it took its time, as if nature understood its magic and let it fall ever so softly to the ground. I looked up at a streetlight; it made the snow golden. The snow clung to trees, covered cars, fell into my eyes and made me feel like I was a small child witnessing a miracle.

"Wow," I sighed, looking at the winter wonderland I had left the summer heat for. No bushfires and dry desert winds here.

Kathrin smiled. "Come on," she said, pulling me by the hand. "Dinner waits for us."

But she could not make me walk faster. She didn't understand I was experiencing for the first time something she'd had her whole life. The snow clung to my jacket, but was so dry I could just brush it off. When I shook my head, snow scattered from my hat, as if I had bad dandruff. Cars struggled along the road, slipping and sliding, churning the snow into brown slush. People walked under umbrellas with large wool hats on their heads. They smiled and talked, and the snow made everything bright and fresh. The day had started out sunny and clear, and was finishing with snow, the way I'd imagined winter here would be.

"We make a trip to the mountains," Kathrin said on the steps to her building.

Someone had already swept the snow, pushing it to the sides and into small mounds at the bottom of the steps. On the front grass, a fresh snowman smiled at me. You could see the grass from where the kids had rolled the snow together, picking it up from the ground.

"Fantastic. Is it far?"

"No, not really," she said, opening the door. "We can go to Thüringer Wald for the weekend."

It all sounded so exotic and exciting. Everything was possible in my new home. Kathrin brushed the snow from my jacket before we entered the building. It was the kind of motherly gesture I liked, that someone cared about me and was making sure I was all right.

Walking up the stairs, it struck me: I had a girlfriend, an apartment and a job. I'd walked into a ready-made life. For the first time, I breathed easy. I had gone from the limiting world of Perth, with its barriers of wealth and status, to the inclusive community of East Berlin. Here, I was someone. I had my place, and I could take my life in any direction I wanted. I felt a warmth inside I hadn't felt since I was very young. I was content.

\*\*\*

I woke to the sounds of children. It was still completely dark. The sky was heavy and the sun was having a sick day. Outside, I could see children filing towards their school, with bags on their backs or slung over their shoulders. They shouted and waved to their parents and ran to their friends. They all seemed pretty relaxed about going to school. The sight made me recall how I'd trudged along reluctantly from my first day until my last. The kids here seemed to be happy the weekend was over and they could be back at school again. Already, they were working together building snowmen, or starting snowball fights that were quickly stopped by parents and teachers. But there was no telling-off or scolding; the teachers didn't have to impose themselves and the children did as they were told. It was all very orderly and mature.

Watching the scene from my window, I liked the way the teachers were with the kids, involved in building snowmen, and making sure the kids had gloves and warm hats on. But better was the way the kids responded to the teacher. There was no malice or cheek, they looked up to the teachers and seemed to even like them. It was a far cry from Mr Bradford, my year five teacher who had held a thick forty centimetre ruler in his hands and had taken great enjoyment from slapping you with it. Or Mrs Foster, year three, who had wild hair, a vicious shriek for a voice and never wore the same dress twice. Foster made us sit in order from best student to worst, with bad kids at the front where she could keep an eye on them and make fools of them. She took as much enjoyment from humiliation as Bradford did with the ruler. And the other teachers were just doing their time and waiting for transfers. So much for the best years of our lives.

I showered and dressed. Once downstairs, I asked for directions and found my way to the workshop. Rudi's father was out in front, waiting for me.

"Michael," he shouted, greeting me like a long-lost son. "Me Dieter."

Dieter was over sixty and completely bald. He took his wool hat off to shake my hand and his head was so shiny, you wanted to rub it and make a wish. But more strange was that he had no eyebrows. When he raised his eyes, his forehead became of mess of deep lines, and I imagined that his eyebrows had once fallen into one of those lines and never come back. But with the wool hat hard on his head, he looked normal. He had a short hooked nose and sallow cheeks which made you wonder if at some point in his life he had almost starved to death. But his smile was warm, and it motivated me to do good things for him just to get that smile.

He spoke almost no English, but we managed to communicate using the language of mechanics and with mime. He put me to work and the day passed quickly, with Dieter talking more with customers than fixing cars. The other mechanic, a thin, quiet man simply known as Jo, came late, left early and did almost no work. I wondered if he was Dieter's son, or another friend of Rudi's, but he didn't act like that. He remained aloof and said not two words to me or Dieter. Jo kept looking at his watch, and simply moved tools from one car to another or drearily moved a broom back and forth over the clean floor. He stopped for cigarettes, working his way through a packet before lunch, and was gone for two hours in the afternoon under the pretence of buying another packet.

At the end of the day, Dieter and I had a beer. The workshop was closed. People banged on the door, but Dieter ignored them. He smiled at me and held out his hand for the dictionary I had in my pocket. Kathrin had given it to me the previous evening, and I was due to have my first German lesson with Monica after work.

Dieter's greasy fingers left prints on the pages. He didn't seem to notice or care. "Work du goot," he said proudly.

"Danke."

He wrote something on a piece of paper and handed it to me smiling, his forehead all wrinkled in expectation. "570 M/Monat," it read. He pointed from himself to me. I guessed this was to be my wage, and nodded. This satisfied Dieter and we lapsed into silence. It wasn't as much as I'd earned in Perth, but the rent was so low, I would put more in my pocket. I also liked Dieter and looked forward to the time when we could communicate in German.

I used the dictionary. "Wann Morgen?"

He held up eight fingers, then bent one thumb to indicate a half.

"Okay."

We shook hands and he let me out the back door, because people were still at the front banging on the roller door and shouting.

***

I settled into life quickly. Rudi helped me with a lot of paperwork: opening a bank account, registering at the local police station, becoming a legal worker at the finance office. I could never have done any of it without his help. I became used to hearing my name pronounced Mikhail Smit.

"Your middle name is Charles," Rudi said, checking my bank account application form while we waited.

"Yes, it was the name of my grandfather's brother," I said. "He died at Gallipoli."

Rudi didn't seem to know where or what Gallipoli was. "In Spanish the name is Carlos. I like to call you this name. Is this okay for you?"

I'd had nicknames before: Mic the stick, because I was a skinny kid, Flapper, because my ears stuck out until I was a teenager and I let my hair grow over them, and Noddy, because when I tried to run fast as a small kid, I nodded my head up and down. But I'd never liked any of those, mainly because they were less than flattering. Carlos sounded exotic and dashing.

"Yep, sure."

Rudi smiled. "It can be our secret. Only you and I will know it."

Rudi liked this. He seemed to want to keep things secret, and there was so much about him I didn't know. I wondered why he was giving up so much of his time to help me get settled in East Berlin.

***

By the end of the first week, I was completely settled. Monica and Heinrich helped me furnish my apartment with some old furniture they had in their basement. I also had a pot and a pan, and some assorted cutlery and dishes. I needed to save money for a refrigerator because it was rather expensive, but it wasn't so necessary. Snacks were cheap and I ate almost every night with Kathrin and her parents. My lovely girlfriend also showed me how to hang things like milk and butter out the window. By the summer I would have enough money.

Heinrich said I could take an interest-free loan from the bank, but I wanted to stay debt free.

Kathrin's parents were so good to me that first month. Monica laboured over teaching me German for two hours every night, and I was never allowed to speak English with her or Heinrich. Kathrin's father was in good health. He seemed to like the cold freshness of winter, and he fixed up an old bicycle for me. This meant the twenty minute walk to the workshop in Friedrichshain was now a five minute ride. The bike was rusted, had one gear and a metal rack on the back for carrying bags or boxes. When I hit a bump, the bike made an assortment of rattles. But the crafty engineer had it running smoothly, and I came to love that bike. Cars were expensive and Kathrin told me you had to wait more than ten years for one. It didn't matter. Public transport was cheap and effective, and I biked everywhere. It was a great way to get to know the city. The streets were wide and drivers looked out for me. The bike improved with consistent use, and I felt fitter for it.

***

The days and weeks began to pass quickly. Life was easy and never dull.

One weekend in March, Kathrin took me to Oberhof in the Thüringer Wald. We stayed in a small hotel that bordered a large forest. It was just beautiful. Snow weighed down the branches of the trees, was piled high on the sides of the roads, and was even higher on the roofs of the houses and buildings. Oberhof was a small town, but it was full that weekend; with all manner of ski enthusiasts in brightly coloured clothing.

We borrowed some cross-country skis from the hotel and headed into the forest. On the tracks were all sorts of animal footprints, and we saw deer scampering between the trees and away from us. I had no sense of balance and kept falling forward or to the side. Kathrin laughed and I laughed too. Others on skis laughed with us and shouted encouragement. Some stopped to talk or share hot wine from their thermos. That was such a nice day. Other skiers joined us for parts of the way. At one point, we were almost ten people, a long line of skiers using each others' tracks and chatting away. We were from all over East Germany and had no qualms about communicating or sharing the path.

In the evening, I recognised many faces in the dining hall, and Kathrin and I were invited to join a large group of people. There was much eating and drinking and laughing. It was unlike any holiday I'd ever experienced. In Perth, people in hotels and resorts keep to themselves. The only time I'd felt some kind of community was camping, but my father hated that. Here, I felt immediately as part of the group.

The next day, Kathrin took me ice skating on a frozen lake. I was as hopeless on skates as I was on skis, but I felt that rush of energy you get when doing things you never thought you would. I had the strongest realisation of just how alive I was; that I was being rewarded for taking a chance. The most beautiful girl in the country was on my arm, there was money in the bank, I had ice skates on my feet and a dusting of snow on my hat. It's times like these that you get the feeling that life is only a dream, and that you will wake up and have to force yourself down the road to school, or into a pair of dirty overalls to slave over someone else's expensive car. But then you are hit but the realisation that this is real, that this glorious moment is life and you are lucky to have it. Time was short. The body grows old quickly, and all the things you had planned can be quickly forgotten. But I had taken life by the scruff of the neck, given up everything to live in East Germany. And skating around the lake, my hand gripping Kathrin's hard so I wouldn't fall over again and hurt my already aching bum, I felt a complete awareness that I was Mikhail Smit.

\*\*\*

German proved difficult for me to learn. The vocabulary wasn't the problem – many words are the same or similar – and the alphabet is not so different. It was the grammar that I found impossible. Each noun has an article that can be either masculine, feminine or neutral, but the article changes with each tense and meaning. So, whenever I used the wrong article, the rest of my grammar would be completely wrong. My inability to grasp this frustrated Monica to no end. She would constantly correct me, becoming more impatient each time. If we were at the dinner table, Heinrich would laugh loudly, his face turning red as he made jokes about how I'd called one thing a woman and another a man, and so on. The end result was that I would say nothing, because I was too scared to make mistakes.

152

I seemed to learn more German with Dieter at the workshop. Once I had the vocabulary, the words came easily because I spoke the language of mechanics. And Dieter didn't care if I made mistakes with grammar. All that mattered was that we were able to converse with each other.

***

In May and June, the days became longer and the trees bloomed wildly in an explosion of growth the likes of which I'd never seen in a Perth spring. Kathrin had finished her course and was now working in a government building on Otto Grotewohl Strasse in Mitte. Sometimes, she would take a long lunch break, ride the train to the workshop and we would have lunch together in Volkspark Friedrichshain, sitting atop a small hill that was the remains of a concrete tower from the war. Some of its corners still jutted out and wild plants tried to grow over them. The days were long and sunny, and sometimes the thunder crashed in the evenings when storms rolled in from the west.

Some weekends, we borrowed Heinrich's older Trabant, this one champagne grey with a dull white roof, and drove out of Berlin to one of the lakes. Or when the weather was really warm we went to the Baltic Sea and camped on the beach. Kathrin called this Trabi the Plastik Panzer, the plastic tank, because of its colour and because it was made of fibreglass. If you had an accident, you simply took off the whole body and replaced it with a new one.

I'd learned in the last few months that the Trabi was a practical car, but not so great mechanically. Parts were difficult to get, and people were always lined up in front of our workshop to make appointments to have their cars fixed. The waiting lists were long and Dieter had to tell our customers that their appointments were in two or three months. This sparked conversations involving small bribes of West money or hard to get goods.

A conversation might go like this:

Trabi driver: When can you fix my car?

Dieter: (If it was June) October 20, bring your car then.

TD: But I need my car this weekend to transport a side of pork to my father's house.

D: Okay, then we can do it tomorrow.

TD: And I will give you three kilos of sausages.

Or whatever the customer could offer to make Dieter offer an earlier appointment. But it wasn't as if we were inundated with work. Each car had a set time for repair, normally too long, and when this time was over, it wasn't necessary to move on to the next car. Dieter often did side repairs late at night. It was private enterprise and I knew that was frowned upon by the government. Rudi didn't like it, but Dieter offered many of the things his customers gave him to his son, as well as to me. Nothing made me happier than bringing presents for Kathrin and her parents. I considered it a small repayment for all the wonderful things they had done for me.

Heinrich and I became good friends. I often helped him with repair jobs around his apartment, and together we painted his garden house, which was in Rahnsdorf near the Müggelsee. After that day of painting, we had a big barbecue with the neighbours. Anyone walking past the house was invited in for a sausage and a beer.

Heinrich was a good man in the way my father had once been. He liked to laugh, work hard and drink, but he also put great value in honesty and comradeship. You knew that if ever you were in a bad position, Heinrich would be there to help you out of it. He wasn't protective of Kathrin. If anything, he pushed us more together, even broaching the subject of marriage. I'd never thought about it. Kathrin had mentioned it once, when I'd talked about us living together. She'd said it was difficult to find a big apartment unless we were married and we'd left it at that. There was time.

And how much time there was. The workday finished early and as soon as I rode away from the workshop, I forgot all about being a mechanic. The work was easy, never stressful, and Dieter was a good boss. Jo had left, so it was only Dieter and I, and we preferred it that way. But there was always so much time. There was never a need to rush. Kathrin and I went often to the theatre and the cinema. Tickets were cheap and nothing was exclusive. We sat at the opera alongside metalworkers and doctors, people who spoke together at intermission and didn't scoff at each others' clothes or social position. We spent many evenings lying in the sun and drinking beer in the Volkspark. The days were slow and pleasant. And all the people around us did the same. They took their time; they didn't push onto the buses or drive their cars madly, and just enjoyed the lazy summer days. There were outdoor concerts, festivals, parades, fireworks, and it seemed every weekend we were invited to a barbecue or a party. I got to know some of Kathrin's friends. She knew a lot of people, but seemed only to have two close friends. I liked this discerning quality. One of her friends, a tall, big boned girl called Birgit, was about five years older and married. Her husband, Andreas, was also big boned and lumpy, but had a joviality and spirit that made you think every December he left for the North Pole for his yearly gig as Santa Claus. We became friends, mainly because we were often thrust together by our girls who wanted to see each other while not neglecting their men. But Andreas and I found many things in common. Most importantly, we both liked to laugh. He thought that everything in life was a joke, and nothing made him laugh more than the East German government. He called them Betonköpfe.

"And not just because they have thick, concrete heads," he explained, "but because their vision of the perfect socialist city is one made entirely of concrete."

Andreas always spoke slowly and clearly, because he knew my German wasn't very good. He was from Dresden and said everyone laughed at his Saxon accent. But he used the accent as a source of humour, not of humiliation, and had the habit of finding a good side to everything.

Andreas was the first person I met who was a member of the SED, the Communist Party. We had known each other for two months before he told me. I believed in communism, but Kathrin had warned me not to get involved with the party. We were having dinner at their apartment in Prenzlauer Berg, as we seemed to do every weekend. They lived in a beautiful old building that had somehow escaped the bombs of the Anglo-American raids. The ceilings were high, with intricately designed cornices. I'd supplied us with thick venison steaks acquired after a late night at the workshop, and we were topping this off with a second bottle of wine. Andreas and I sat on the balcony. The sun was finally setting after a long summer's day that had included a swim in the Müggelsee with Rudi and his family, a game of makeshift cricket with his two young sons until Rudi took me aside and told me to stop, and an afternoon sleep in the Volkspark.

"Oh, don't look at me like that, Smit," Andreas said. For some reason, from the first time we met, he had always called me by my last name. "I'm just a Beet Communist."

"Beet?"

"You know, like the vegetable," he said laughing. "Red only on the outside."

We laughed together. Andreas had a booming laugh that shook his whole body and made birds fly from the trees.

"Because of your family?" I asked.

"No, although my father is a huge fan of Modrow, the big wheel in Dresden. But to be in the party means you get a little bit of a head start. Our society is equal, but the party members are more equal."

Andreas was a dentist like his father. He had appalling teeth, the way the son of a banker is terrible with money, and the way Rudi was an awful driver.

"How are they favoured?"

Andreas smiled. He sometimes forgot that I had only lived in East Germany for a short time. I wondered sometimes whether he actually believed I was from Australia. He couldn't understand why someone from the west would choose to come here while everyone else was dying to get out.

"Cars, apartments, jobs, holidays, things like that. Not much, but it makes a difference here."

I nodded.

"But it also means I must go to meetings and speeches and other tedious things, and I also have no chance to emigrate."

"Why's that?"

"Because I'm a dentist, and that's a rather specialist job. The country needs me. They will not let me leave."

"Do you want to?"

"Why did you come here?" he asked, firing a question straight back at me.

"Because it's better. I told you this before. There are more chances here, more equality."

"Yes, but we can't go anywhere."

"That doesn't matter when the life here is good. I have no desire to go back."

"Ah," Andreas said, raising a finger in the air to make his point, "but you have seen what is on the other side. And you can make a judgement. But we haven't seen it, and because we are denied, we want to see it even more."

"Hear me," I said smiling. "This is the good side."

Andreas laughed. "Say it more, Smit, and hopefully I'll start to believe you. Boy, you would make a great party man."

It was Andreas who took me to my first meeting. He told me it would look good on my record if I attended a few. The speeches were hard to understand at first, but became easier for they were rather repetitive: impassioned cries for sacrifice and for the workers to give their labour willingly for the benefit of all. The west was responsible for wars and economic crises but the workers' state would survive for the greater good of mankind and one day all the world will look toward their communist brothers to free them from capitalist enslavement. Each speech had the same idea, but with slightly different words. Andreas listened with a look of intent concentration on his face. He told me later over beers in the nearest Kneipe that he was trying to keep himself from laughing. The beers were fifty Pfennig and we drank more than we should have.

"They are all so earnest," Andreas said. "But it's just an act."

"I don't know," I said smiling. I always seemed to smile when I spoke with Andreas. "They're only politicians, and politicians are all the same."

"Ah, but no, Smit, they are not," he said, mimicking the speakers and raising his voice. "They are workers and farmers from the glorious socialist state. They speak from their hearts. And together with our Soviet comrades we shall conquer the world, and then every person will have bread and work and a Trabant."

His Saxon accent and powerful voice drew mocking cheers from the crowded bar. They laughed with him and raised their glasses to each other.

"You should be up there," I said, when the cheering and laughing had died down.

"Yes, but then I would have to get my teeth fixed to be beautiful for the camera, and that we would mean a trip to the dentist."

We both laughed. Andreas was easily the best friend I'd ever had. He had the same shining qualities of loyalty and honesty that Heinrich had, and that my father once had, but with a sense of humour and a vitality that was contagious.

\*\*\*

Weeks passed, months, seasons. The letters I had written to my parents and sister diligently every month became every two months, then three, as did their replies. Sometimes the envelopes were taped shut and dated weeks before. And other times my parents made references to events I had absolutely no clue about. I didn't read the paper. I didn't have a television. I was practically cut off from the world and didn't care. All I knew was that life was easy and good, better than I could ever have hoped, and I had no desire to return home.

I changed.

I'd spent my life wanting all the things I could never have. I grew up watching black and white television wishing we could have a set in colour, and when we had that, I wanted one with a bigger screen. My entire life had been spent riding the rollercoaster of desire. The system always offered up new things: better technologies, new designs, tempting products, and made you feel you just had to have them. Advertising invaded your home. People were able to show off by having one thing better than their neighbour.

But it wasn't like that in East Berlin. I lost my great desire for all things new and fancy. I lived without a television and life was all the better for it. I read a book every week, worked on my German, took in all types of different culture, went to discos and took weekend trips. Life was rewarding, full and slow. Without the burning desire for new things, I had no holes in my life. I didn't need a television to make me happy because I was happy, and I didn't need it to entertain me because I was never bored. But this was also by design, for in East Germany there was a substantial lack of consumer goods. It was easy not to want what you couldn't have anyway. When Thomas or Antje came to visit, they would always smuggle in something that was lacking in the GDR. Antje would wear three or four layers of pantyhose, or two pairs of jeans, or carry in her purse extra make-up. Thomas wrapped simple presents in posters of singers and bands which Kathrin would then use to barter for records or clothes with other young adults at discos or at Albert's Cafe. It seemed everyone wanted a little bit of the west in their lives while I had completely rejected it all outright. Kids paid enormous amounts of money for a clothing label which they could then sew onto their jeans or jacket. But more than anything, the people dreamed of going west. Andreas said it was because they couldn't, that by being denied it, they only wanted it more. He was convinced that if they opened the border, all East Germans would go and visit and then come back with the knowledge that life was better here. But because they only saw the west on television, that was their only means of comparison.

"Yes, but television doesn't show the crime, the poor people and the inequality," I once said to Andreas.

"This is correct, but until they see that for themselves, they won't know about it and will want only to go there because they think the streets are made of gold."

***

Kathrin and I got married on 20 May, 1983. Andreas was best man, and the only people missing from that wonderful occasion were my parents and Narelle. I was unable to send them many photos because most were taken at the church and the reception, in public places. The reception was held in the courtyard of Kathrin's building. Everyone was invited. Some brought instruments and an impromptu band was formed. Traditional songs were played and everybody danced. It was such a wonderful time. Between dances, Rudi took me aside. He carried a bottle of Sekt and refilled his glass as quickly as he finished it. His body staggered, but his eyes were clear, and they'd lost none of their darkness. We sat down, toasted glasses and he congratulated me.

"Thanks, Rudi," I said, the alcohol and the dancing starting to take its toll. "But I have to say, we wouldn't be sitting here if not for you. Thank you."

"Ah, it is nothing, Carlos. You are my friend."

The word surprised and sobered me. I had never considered Rudi my friend. Kathrin had always warned me to be careful with him, to keep my distance and watch what I say.

"Your man Andreas is quite a character," Rudi slurred, throwing down more sparkling wine. "How do you know him?"

I realised then how little I had seen of Rudi the last year. He sometimes came to the shop, but then there would be no sign of him for weeks.

"He's the husband of Kathrin's friend, Birgit."

"Ah, big Gitte," he said laughing. But I found his joke distasteful and stared into my drink, unsure what to say.

"He's in the party, you know," Rudi continued, slowly turning his clear eyes on me.

I nodded.

"Tell me, Carlos. He is a good comrade?"

"Yes. Sure. He sometimes takes me to his meetings."

"Good, good. And he speaks well of Honecker and the other members of the party."

"Not so much," I said, sipping my drink and wondering that it was a strange question to ask. Seldom did anyone in Kathrin's family talk about politics, except to use the government as a punch line. "He calls them Betonköpfe."

Rudi laughed slightly. "Maybe it is because of their teeth," he said. "He is a dentist to many in the party, I believe."

I nodded again and we fell into silence. Rudi watched the dancers, but I felt his eyes on me. His oldest daughter, Tina, came skipping over and asked him to dance. Rudi smiled at me.

"She's her mother's daughter," he said, letting himself be pulled towards the revelry.

I saw Andreas dancing with Birgit, their larger bodies creating a little more space around them. There were such a well-matched couple, made for each other, and they seemed to know it more than anyone else.

My bride saw me sitting alone and waved for me to dance with her. She dumped Heinrich in a chair and grabbed my hand.

As we headed for the centre of the circle, Heinrich wiped the sweat from his red face and shouted, "She's too much woman for me, boy. You wear her out."

We twisted and twirled in amongst the crowd. Monica danced with Dieter, Frank with his daughter Christine, Thomas with Antje and Hilde, the three dancing together swinging arms. Everyone sang, Andreas's bellowing tenor the loudest of them all. People arrived, others left, and then they came back again. The party went well into the night. Dancers fell asleep on the grass surrounded by empty bottles and beer cans. Tenants in the building brought down blankets and mattresses. The band fell asleep with their instruments in their hands. The night was warm. One man I didn't recognise used a Sekt bottle for a pillow. They slept on the grass like fallen trees in a forest.

Kathrin and I slept in each other's arms in her bed. She smelled pleasantly of expensive perfume mixed with the sweet smell that was her sweat.

In the morning, the tenants put on breakfast for all those who still remained. And they all cheered as Kathrin and I drove our wedding present, Heinrich's old Trabant – it had a new sky blue shell, but was still the same car – away from the building and north towards the island of Usedom.

***

When we came back, Monica said that Birgit had been trying to contact us all day. Distraught and crying over the phone, Birgit said Andreas had disappeared. We went straight to her apartment.

"He's tried to escape, I know it," she said, opening the door. Her face was swollen and her eyes red from crying. "To go west."

"No he hasn't," I said. "Andreas would never do that."

"How long has he been gone?" Kathrin asked.

"I haven't heard from him since he went to work yesterday."

"Maybe he had some kind of accident or something," Kathrin offered.

"I called the hospitals. There's no sign of him." Birgit blew her nose loudly. "He's gone, I know it. He always wanted to go to the west, and now he's done it and left me here alone. The Stasi will give me hell now."

Stasi was short for Staatssicherheit, the Ministry for State Security. I didn't know much about them except that they were hated, rarely spoken about and had an enormous office in Lichtenberg that was guarded like a fortress. Kathrin had once told me that the Stasi made life very difficult for those who wanted to emigrate or escape, and for those who were opposed to the government. She also said that you never spoke about them with anyone.

"Come on," Kathrin said, putting her arm around Birgit. "He probably just bumped his head and forgot who he is. Or maybe he drank too much and fell asleep in the park. You saw how much he drank at the wedding, and then he slept right through breakfast."

Birgit nodded, wiping away her tears and trying to be strong. I had come to greatly admire the strength and resilience of East German women.

The awkward silence was only tempered by the sound of Birgit's sniffing and blowing of her nose. I didn't know what to do. Kathrin had her arm around Birgit so I couldn't do that. I went into the kitchen to make some coffee. We all turned as we heard a key sliding into door and then ran together to the doorway.

Andreas stumbled in. He had a black eye and a deep bruise on the side of his swollen face. He forced a smile.

"Sorry I didn't call," he said as Birgit enveloped him. "Couldn't find a phone."

He looked incredibly tired, as if he hadn't slept at all. His shoulders slumped forward wearily, and his hair was a mess, enough for the first signs of grey and baldness to show. He looked suddenly old and worn.

"Where have you been?" Birgit cried.

Andreas looked at Kathrin and me, and chose to keep it private. "I had a small accident," he said. "Give me a hot a shower and a bed and I'll be new in the morning."

He left the door open, with his keys still in the lock, and staggered past us, walking with a slight limp. Kathrin hugged Birgit and we left.

A few days later, Andreas, Birgit, Heinrich and Monica helped us move. It was a Friday and we were all given the day off. Being married, and with Kathrin pregnant, we had been able to apply for a large three-room apartment. We were a young married couple and were thus given precedence. But in the end we got lucky; I was able to swap my apartment with a young man who had just got divorced. His ex-wife moved back with her parents, and we took their three-room apartment on Leninallee in Friedrichshain. The balcony looked down on the Volkspark we loved so much. The street was loud, with a tramline running down the middle, but that didn't matter. We were young, making a life for ourselves and Kathrin was ecstatic to be finally out of her parents' apartment.

It was more a party than a move. Andreas brought two cases of beer with him.

In the evening, Birgit and Kathrin sat in the kitchen while Andreas and I sat on the balcony. We drank beers and listened to the cars motor past, enjoying the heady waft of the fumes mixed with the lush smell of summer rain.

"We've known each other for almost a year now, Smit," Andreas said. "But there are many things we don't know about each other."

"There's time. I like the fact I don't know everything."

"Yes, but there are some people who know more about me, and have no problem saying it to others." He leaned closer and lowered his voice. "The other night, the Stasi grabbed me after work. That was my...accident."

"But why? You're in the party and everything. And you don't want to leave. At least, you don't apply to."

"That's right. I think there's an informer at my practice." He said the word informer with a hate I had never seen in him before. "It doesn't surprise me because many of my patients are from the party."

"What happened?"

"I resisted, and that's when they hit me."

162

"How did you know they were Stasi?"

"Before I became unconscious, I noticed they drove a Lada. They always have Ladas."

"And?"

"They questioned me, made some threats. They didn't let me sleep. They knew everything about me, and Birgit. I answered their questions, but they weren't the answers they wanted. I'll have to be very careful from now on."

I was speechless. It was always other people who had experiences with the Stasi. Dissidents and artists who criticised the government and wanted only to go to the west. I didn't think my friends would ever be involved.

"Please don't say anything to Birgit," Andreas said softly.

"You have my word."

\*\*\*

Kathrin and I spent a lot of time having fun arguments about names. She wanted something traditional while I wanted something more cross-cultural. We decided on Markus for a boy and Jennifer for a girl. Kathrin became huge, and had an appetite for foods that weren't so easy to get. The meat and potatoes diet didn't satisfy her. I was forced to make more trips to the market and sometimes to the Delikat shop on Unter den Linden for special requests. Dieter had been in hospital for most of the summer and I'd been running the workshop myself, building up a small supply of D-Marks which allowed me to buy the special coupons for shopping at the Delikat.

Dieter's health was a real worry. Rudi came to the shop often to give me updates and to negotiate with customers while I fixed the cars. There was no way I could run the workshop alone. One evening towards the end of summer, Rudi stayed late to help me with an old Wartburg. He drank beer from a can and handed me the tools I asked for. The owner was a carpenter who had offered to make Rudi a nice table if the car was fixed immediately.

"You're a very good mechanic," Rudi said. "It's no wonder my father likes you so much."

"Thanks. I had a good teacher."

When visiting like this, Rudi had the habit of lurking in the workshop. He wouldn't stand in the one place. He moved around, and you felt him pass behind you, or heard his voice coming from a different place as before. It was very disconcerting.

"Yes, but my father is old," Rudi said, this time from the other side of the car. "He'll be sixty-five before Christmas."

"We should throw him a party."

"His health is bad. He suffered in the war." Rudi moved to the back of the car. "His mother was a Polish Jew. He will retire soon."

"Good for him," I said grunting. A spark plug was stuck and wouldn't budge. "He deserves it. What's his plan?"

"I think he and my mother will spend more time at their garden house in Oranienburg."

"That's great." The plug came free, and I sighed with relief, only to realise I had broken it off. The other half still remained. "Mensch."

"And what will happen with you?" Rudi asked, now standing behind me. "Unfortunately, you are not yet old enough to manage a workshop like this. Another mechanic, older and more experienced, will be sent here to take over."

I looked up at Rudi. Like any worker, I feared a change of boss, especially because Dieter had been so great to work for.

"I'm happy just to be working," I said. "I have nothing to complain about."

I felt Rudi pass behind me again. He stopped and leaned over the engine, his elbows resting on the front of the car. It creaked with the new weight.

"I have a proposition," he said, almost in a whisper. "Our world here is changing. The people of the DDR are always trying to improve themselves. That is the nature of the socialist worker, to always strive for a better life for all."

I stopped my work to listen to him. Something in his tone cued me to pay attention. I almost hit my head on the bonnet when I straightened up.

"Do you know that in school children learn Russian from the fifth class?"

I shook my head. I knew little about the school system except from what Monica had told me: that every child all over East Germany learned the same things at the same time. For that reason, I thought it was a brilliant system. There were no private schools. All kids got exactly the same education, and it was free.

"Well, they do, and they also have the chance to learn other languages. French, Italian, Spanish or English." He let the last word trail off and raised his eyebrows at me.

"Come on, Rudi. I wouldn't know the first thing about being a teacher. I'm just a mechanic."

"Yes, but the children are becoming more interested in English, and our connection with the Soviets is beginning to dwindle. They sit on their hands while East Germany keeps the Warsaw states powerful. Soon, they will look to us to hold them together. East Germany will be at the forefront with the west. We are no longer an isolated, unrecognised country. Honecker has done many things to improve our world standing."

It was quite a speech, and it made me wonder if Rudi ever took centre stage at party meetings or at workers' motivational sessions. He had a forceful speaking style, using strong language and emphasis to gain attention and sway opinion.

"So, we must start with the children," he continued, "and we don't have many English teachers, especially not with English as their mother language."

I was taken aback by his political delivery. But the idea of me being a teacher was completely far-fetched.

"I'm not sure I'd make such a good teacher," I said, returning to the Wartburg. "I hated school, and I left when I was fifteen. I didn't go to university or anything like that."

Rudi moved to the other side of the open bonnet. "Carlos, I don't think you are stupid. If you had been a child here, you could have become a doctor or an engineer, if given the chance. It is your system that is stupid. It suppresses the workers, keeps them down, stops them from taking control in a way that should happen with the course of history."

I couldn't argue with him. I had been in the GDR for over eighteen months and I hadn't regretted my decision for one second. Life was much better here, and now I had a wife and soon a child, and that child would have all the opportunities I didn't. My veins pumped with gold I was so happy.

"So, what happens? Do I just leave the workshop and start teaching tomorrow?" I asked.

Rudi chuckled. "No, it's not that easy. You must go to the Pedagogical College in Potsdam. It normally takes three years, but I think I can get you past the first year because you are an English speaker."

"You mean go to university?" I said, so dumfounded I almost dropped a heavy wrench on my foot.

Rudi nodded. "Everyone has the chance to realise their potential in communism." He handed me a piece of paper with a name and an address. "Go tomorrow afternoon and see this man. I'll tell him you're coming."

Rudi had once again organised everything without asking. He knew that I would accept his offer and had arranged all the necessary things beforehand. He was a crafty character.

"So, it is settled," he said.

"Thanks, Rudi." I always seemed to be thanking him.

I worked in silence. Rudi picked up tools and examined them. He grabbed a long pipe and swished it in the air like a sword. It was childish behaviour.

"So, how is your friend Andreas," he said, breaking the silence with a rather loud voice. "He helped you move, I believe."

I looked up and nodded. Rudi had taken off his jacket. It was warm in the workshop, but not that warm. I noticed in his pocket was a large pen, dark brown against his tan shirt.

"What a good friend. Does he say much about his work?"

"Sometimes his patients talk so much he can't look into their mouths," I said.

Rudi's laugh echoed in the workshop. "Politicians are full of air."

"I don't know. I don't pay much attention to politics. Andreas says their dirty words rot their teeth, but I'm happy with the way things are. I have no reason to complain."

"That's correct, and now you are going to be a university man."

I didn't want to give Rudi the satisfaction of seeing me so ecstatic about going to university. There was nothing worse than people who did you favours and then spent the rest of the time reminding you they had done them. It was as if I had to show Rudi gratitude for the rest of my life.

"Is Kathrin interested in politics?" Rudi asked.

"No, not really. She works in a government office, as you know, but she never brings work home with her. That's the great thing about working in this country. Once the day is over, you forget about it and can do other things. Shit, even at the dealership in Perth I found myself taking paperwork home."

"So, Kathrin likes the government."

166

"Do you?"

In all my conversations with Rudi, I'd discovered the best way to combat his questioning statements was to respond with a direct question. This always caught him off guard.

"The government is not as important as the system. They are only representatives. Anyone can sit in the Politbüro or the People's Chamber."

"And that is another reason why the system is great," I said, pointing at Rudi with a screwdriver. "I could be party secretary, and so could you. I like the fact that my child is going to grow up in this world and not in Australia."

Rudi smiled and patted me on the shoulder.

"You will see the professor tomorrow?" he asked, putting on his coat.

"Yes. Thanks again."

"We're family now, Carlos," he said, forcing a big smile that didn't suit his face. "Perhaps you will call your son Rüdiger." He laughed at this.

"Kathrin is convinced we're having a girl," I countered.

"And she will be beautiful like her mother."

He slapped me hard on the shoulder, then left through the back door. I was glad he was gone. I smiled at the Wartburg engine, spoke to it in English, using the language I hadn't spoken in over eighteen months. I was headed for university, to become an English teacher.

I missed my language. Teaching it would give me the opportunity to use it again. I could probably still work as a mechanic on the weekend, make D-Marks and get other things on the side. Lost in my daydreaming, the stubborn spark plug popped free. I finished the job quickly, and while washing my hands with the chemicals that stung anytime I had raw skin, I told myself I wouldn't have to wash grease from my hands for much longer. I was moving up.

***

Jennifer was born two months after I started at the Pedagogical College. We used our one thousand Mark child bonus to buy a cot and other necessary bits of furniture. Kathrin was home the whole time – she had six months paid maternity leave – and took meticulous care of our beautiful baby. Jennifer was a peach. She had white hair,

167

the round face of her grandfather, the aqua eyes of Kathrin, but was burdened with the sticking out ears of her father. She was just gorgeous. Everyone said so. But it wasn't how she looked, it was the way she looked: opening her eyes wide to the world around her, mouth open in wonder, with everything going into the mouth for testing. She wanted to know everything, and the only time she ever cried was when we took things from her that interested her. Kathrin was beautiful with the baby in her arms, and she loved to take care of her. I was a self-conscious father, not so good at goo-gooing or discipline.

I resolved to speak English with Jennifer from day one so that the child would grow up with both languages. Kathrin liked this idea. We each had a language with our child.

But as much as Kathrin thrived being a mother, she also made plans for the future by applying for night courses to further her own education. I think she was a little jealous that I was at university. Her plan was to become a legal secretary. The law interested her, and both she and Monica were consistent Eingabe writers. This was a written petition a citizen could make to the responsible authorities. For example, Heinrich had broad feet, and when the shoe stores didn't have his size, Monica would write to the shoe manufacturer, explain the situation, and sometimes get results: either a reply, or a pair of correctly fitting shoes. Kathrin continued this family tradition. She had a way with words and almost always got at least a reply. She kept her petitions non-political, wanting only the simple things she had been denied. As a legal secretary, she wanted to help citizens use this right as a way of bringing about reform, change, and improvement. She thought the country was stagnating.

The fact I was at university was an endless source of humour for Andreas. He and Birgit were the godparents of Jennifer, and given that they seemed unable to have a child of their own, they came often to our apartment, or minded Jennifer while Kathrin and I went to the theatre or out for dinner.

"Only in communism could a mechanic became a teacher," Andreas said, "and a roofer our blessed leader."

Poor Andreas was really starting to get fat. He had such a large frame that he had no problem carrying extra weight, and he also had an appetite for rich food and alcohol. But he lost none of his joviality. If anything, he was heading further towards the stereotype of the jolly fat man. His increasing run-ins with the Stasi didn't get him down.

He was convinced the dental practice was bugged, because the Stasi wanted to know what party members had to say about the system and each other. The Stasi spoke with Andreas only for confirmation; that a certain patient had been in his practice on a certain day. They were always the same, Andreas said, and he got to know them and often invited them into his office for a vodka or two. He wanted to be on good terms with them, because he was still shaken by his abduction, though he never said as much. He also enjoyed telling me funny stories of what some of the party members said in the chair, how with mouths wide open and stuffed full of cotton, they were still unable to be quiet.

\*\*\*

On Peace Day in 1984, Andreas dragged me along to hear Honecker's speech. For a peace celebration, I thought there was a strong representation of the armed forces. The People's Army, Border Troops, People's Police, Transport Police and even the armed militia of the working class were all well-represented in full uniform and standing in orderly groups. We were surrounded by flags, both GDR and communist red, and people held placards of Honecker aloft. Groups of young people carried large banners that said which section of the Free German Youth they represented. They wore their blue shirts with pride and held their banners high. Younger kids had their Ernst Thalmann Pioneers uniforms on and were being supervised by older members of the Free German Youth.

Andreas was able to get close to the podium, and there was a loud roar as Honecker went up to the microphone. The photographs lie, I thought. The one staple picture you saw of Honecker in all the newspapers, in classrooms and in workshops, was out of date. In it, he looked middle-aged and serious, with a stern look of determination on his face. In reality, he was an old man, with thinning grey hair combed back from his face, thick brown-rimmed glasses and skin the colour of day old scrambled eggs. There was no purpose in his manner. His shoulders were slumped and his hands shook. He looked small and frail. The old freedom fighter was dying.

"They're propping him up from behind," Andreas whispered to me. "Krenz is holding a big stick behind him. Look, see how he's leaning back."

I laughed, too loudly, and several people turned to look in my direction. They wore sunglasses, were dressed in brown suits and had hard faces.

Honecker's brittle voice crackled through the speakers: "The German Democratic Republic has over the past thirty-five years developed successfully as a state of peace and socialism, as an effective factor of stability and security on the European continent. Rising from a heap of rubble and setting out for the future, the country has followed a path rich in work and struggles. The achievements recorded have been for the people's benefit and have made it possible to meet international obligations."

There was a brief silence between the end of this sentence and the recognition by the crowd that it was their cue to shout and applaud. Andreas clapped and whooped, but was smiling.

"Any minute now, he's going to fall over," he said, his jovial face bright with hope.

"Our state is irrevocably anchored in the world of socialism," belted Honecker, "a world of freedom, democracy and human dignity."

Andreas pretended to blow his nose to cover his laughing face. "I'll tell you all about the democracy later."

Honecker listed economic figures and increased production levels, and bragged about the improvements in the standard of living. I stopped listening. It was a speech the same as all the rest. It could have been May 8, Liberation Day, or October 7, Republic Day, or the third Sunday in February, Day of the Commerce Workers, or March 1, Day of the People's Army, or July 1, Day of the People's Police, or December 11, Day of Public Health, or the Pfingsttreffen Youth Festival in mid May, or any time there was an election or a visiting diplomat.

Honecker waited for the cheers to die down. "The US administration..."

"Here we go," Andreas whispered sarcastically. "Save us from war, Hony."

"...Which is pursuing a policy of confrontation and arms building and a crusade against the socialist countries, is making concealed war plans. With the consent of some of its NATO allies, first strike nuclear weapons have been deployed in a number of west European countries, including West Germany."

Substantial booing and jeering from the crowd.

"Do you believe that?" I asked Andreas.

He shook his head and smiled. "The best way to win a war is to start an imaginary one yourself."

Honecker's face was flushed and his voice was losing its substance and power. "The peoples of the world can always count on the first socialist workers and farmers' state on German soil in the struggle for securing peace, for the strengthening of socialism, for progress and a happy life."

The speech ended poorly, but the crowd still cheered as Honecker shuffled off the stage, his hands high in triumph.

"He's just happy he finished the speech without falling over," Andreas said.

Suddenly, a hand grabbed my shoulder. I jumped and turned to see Rudi standing behind me. He wore dark glasses and an ill-fitting suit.

"It's good to see you here, Michael, and you Andreas."

He shook both our hands. Andreas and Rudi stared at each other for what seemed like a long moment. The colour drained from Andreas's face and his cheeks sagged.

"The speech was good, no," Rudi added.

"Very good," Andreas said shortly. "Come on, Smit, we'll be late for dinner with our wives."

"Of course," Rudi said. "Greetings to them both, and to little Jenny."

Andreas moved quickly through the crowd. For such a big man, he was surprisingly light on his feet.

"Everything all right?" I asked, when we were away from the crowd.

"I know that man," he said quietly. "That voice."

"Sure, that's Rudi. He was at the wedding."

Andreas stopped. His eyes went wide, and he smiled. "That's right." He sighed loudly. "I guess he just looks like someone else. Or sounds like it. Come on, I think a cold beer is in order."

We sat alone in a Biergarten. The sun was hidden behind the trees and when the wind picked up, it was chilly outside, but Andreas didn't think it was safe to sit in the crowded bar.

"What Hony said about democracy is a joke," Andreas said, looking around to be sure we were alone. "We have basically only one political party. All the parties were brought together under the National Front back in 1949. The Front decides the candidates for the People's Chamber and local assemblies. Everyone must vote, but it's the lack of choice that results in no democracy. And it's the People's Chamber that does all the important electing. They elect the Council of State and the Council of Ministers. It's these two councils that are responsible for running the country."

"Maybe the other parties just want to be communist," I said. "They know it's the better way."

"Smit, you sound like a party member. Just because you believe in God doesn't mean I do. You see, the problem isn't that we have no democracy, it's the hypocrisy. We have no democracy, everyone knows it, and yet the government always shouts about it. The same with our so called freedom. The result is no one believes anything the government says. Even the party faithful laugh at the hypocritical speeches when they're in the privacy of their own homes. I tell you, it can't go on like this forever. Something will give. The people will one day wake up and realise that the GDR is a country based on lies. I hope I'm still around when that day comes."

"But why will the people react against a government, against a system, that gives them everything? It doesn't make sense to me."

"Germans like truth," Andreas said, draining his beer. "But more than anything, they always want what others have. All the comrades want the west. If it's west, it's good. Hony can shout all he wants about the standard of living here. Sure, we're better off than all the other socialist countries, but West Germany is our benchmark. The comrades will want what they can't have."

His words scared me. I was resigned to the world the way it was. I didn't want things to change. I had left the west behind. There was no dignity in that society. Why didn't everyone understand that?

\*\*\*

Jennifer grew quickly. She started at day care when she was four months old. I took care of her in the evenings when Kathrin had her night courses. To look at Jennifer, to see small bits of myself, a person that I'd had a hand in creating, amazed me. I couldn't believe it. She was like me, like Kathrin, but she was also her own distinct person. She took the good traits of both of us and added them to her unique personality.

I was sent to the Reinhold Huhn Oberschule in Prenzlauer Berg. I found being an English teacher wasn't so different from being a mechanic. Everything would be fine as long as I was prepared and had a plan. And for some reason, the children liked me. They were very disciplined. It wasn't the way I remembered school to be. The parents participated in after school programmes and with discipline. Kids who showed aptitude in certain subjects were encouraged to fulfil their potential in these areas with extra programmes and studies. But being a teacher was also a metaphor for life in the GDR: generally good and rewarding, but with a few drawbacks. The school programme was heavily regulated and controlled, and this was fair, but it also resulted in a complete lack of spontaneity and creativity, from teachers and students. After teaching the same lessons a couple of times, the teacher could simply become a robot. Herr Lemke, the principal, called me into his office several times to discuss the occasional swaying from routine that I brought into my classes. One of the kids must have told him, or at least kept him constantly informed about my teaching practices, or there was a camera in the classroom, because he knew everything, even quoting in English things I'd said. Lemke was short and weedy, like a nasty principal should be, and was also head of the local Young Pioneers, the youth group that all children up to the age of fourteen had to join.

Aside from these minor difficulties, I found teaching to be a highly rewarding occupation. I'd noticed when Jennifer was a baby how I could give her some information or teach her something and then one day she would show me what she had learned. She knew how to do a certain thing because I'd taught her. It was like listening to an engine purr after I'd fixed it. The rewards for effort were there.

It was interesting how so many of my life's events transpired to entrench me deeper in East Germany: married, a father, a better job, friends and so on. However, there were some things I missed about Perth. More than anything, I missed being able to walk into any store and, if I had the money, buy what I need. Such a thing in the GDR was a complete novelty, even though it was well known that East Berlin had a wider range of products and services than anywhere in the country. The people in the small villages and towns had nothing by comparison. But it wasn't just quantity limitations; production times also greatly affected our lives in small and pathetic ways. A toilet brush would be made for three months only in red, then the next three months only in green. Colour coordination in the bathroom was impossible, unless you bought everything you needed and then swapped it with others until you had a matching bathroom.

The coffee was awful; the tea was weak. The Trabant was a shit heap and the subject of endless ridicule, yet people got out on Sunday mornings to wash their beloved plastic tank, and stocked up on accessories and spare parts. And because buyers had to wait fifteen years for one, a second hand Trabi was more expensive than a new one. Monica and Heinrich had a system that every five years one of them would apply for a new Trabant, depending on whose turn it was. Thus, they always had two cars, one new and one five years older.

Telephones were scarce. We had one, but it was sometimes difficult to call or to be called because the whole building shared the one line. Andreas joked that it was easier for the Stasi to tap the phones that way. It was more common that if people wanted to communicate they visited each other. Andreas and Birgit were always popping around, as were Heinrich and Monica. There was always time for that.

But the lack of goods had a positive effect. The people shared, swapped and helped each other. They understood that individually they had little, but collectively they had everything. It was just a matter of knowing the right person, making the right connection and sometimes offering the right bribe. This sharing brought complete strangers together. And it was through this that I met a great many good people who were always willing to offer up what few precious things they had and help out when you had a problem. Nobody was rich, nobody was complete, but this was compensated with great loyalty and strong friendships. The communist system forced people to come together, and I thought this was the system's most endearing quality.

The media was all but useless. The daily paper, *Neues Deutschland*, was highly censored and full of pictures of Honecker. People read it not for information but for signs; something was wrong when certain events weren't reported, like bad election results in other communist countries, or successful uprisings. There were two radio stations, one for entertainment and the other for culture and education. But we were able to pick up stations transmitting from West Berlin, including RIAS, Radio in the American Sector, which played American and British music. However, it wasn't allowed to listen to west radio in public places. It was the same with television. The GDR had two stations, but most people could also pick up two stations from West Germany. This meant that many citizens crossed the border at eight in the evening by switching on their televisions. This wasn't a factor in our apartment because we had no television, but for everyone else, it was an intricate part of their day, and they built their fantasies of the west based on the programmes they watched. Televisions were expensive, but almost every apartment had one. Kathrin was an outdoors girl, and Jennifer was growing up to be the same. We always went to the lakes and parks in summer, and to Thüringer Wald in winter. Kathrin took Jennifer to her local swimming club twice a week, and they would come home stinking of chlorine, eyes red and have a long bath together.

Not being such a sporty type, I still got around on the bicycle Heinrich had given me. Andreas called me Der Fahrrad Lehrer. Our old Trabi wasn't very reliable and was saved for weekend trips to the Baltic Sea or to the mountains in the south. I didn't have the time to keep fixing it.

I missed Australian sport more than anything else. Cricket and Australian rules football. Rudi sometimes took me to soccer matches, but I found them boring and unsatisfying. Two hours for no result, and too much play-acting and not enough aggression. His team, BFC Dynamo, was the best in the league and always won. Even though the games were dull, I liked standing in a large crowd of men at a sporting event, drinking and cheering and enjoying the camaraderie. It reminded me of going to football games with my father. Rudi asked a lot of casual questions at these games, but never took his eyes from the field. He always wanted to know how my friends were doing, what they thought of this recent event, or that military parade. He often talked about my school, asking about teachers who I only knew by name, even if I couldn't vouch for their opinions. This was Rudi's only form of conversation, and because he had done so much for me, I humoured it. He loved it that Andreas had dubbed me Der Fahrrad Lehrer. He asked a lot of questions about Andreas.

I also missed my parents. Kathrin sometimes didn't understand that it's not always easy being in a foreign country and so far away from family and home. I had my own family here, but occasionally wished I could sit down with mum over a cup of tea, and tell her everything that weighed heavy on my heart.

I did the best I could and spoke little of what I missed.

We began to see more of Thomas. A new negotiation between East and West Germany had made it possible for him to now visit forty-five days in a year. Poor Thomas was out of shape and prematurely bald. His lack of hair for some reason made his nose look bigger. We didn't have much to talk about; he couldn't understand why I liked East Berlin so much. He thought it dull, ugly and boring. But I knew he looked at it through tainted western eyes. He didn't think he suffered in his capitalist society, because he had a good job and made lots of money. But what he didn't realise was that he was a slave to his own desires, like I'd once been. And he had no appreciation for small things because he was able to have everything all the time. In the GDR, we only had fruits and vegetables when they were in season. It meant everyone looked forward to melons in summer, mushroom picking in autumn, wildberry jam in September and oranges at Christmas. When you only had things for a certain time, you appreciated them more. But Thomas was only interested in satisfying his immediate desires, and resented the idea that he could be denied things.

Years passed in a blink.

Jennifer could switch from English to German as if the languages were the same.

Gorbachev came to power in the Soviet Union. His lack of coverage in *Neues Duetschland* meant that something was wrong. We learned through western media that Gorbachev was a reformer, attempting to modernise communism in Russia. He introduced Glasnost, and later Perestroika, and opened up the economy, promoting competition and a free market. Andreas was convinced that the East German government was scared these reforms were a threat to their own regime. Honecker wanted very little to do with Glasnost, and he and other leaders avoided the word reform like the plague, using instead words like perfections or improvements. It was becoming clear the leaders were old, that the country had stagnated and had failed to change with the times. People were unhappy, and hoped that Gorbachev might have a positive influence on the GDR; people could use him as an example in their campaign for change. But the SED hierarchy turned their back on Gorby, much in the same way the statues of Marx and Engels had their backs turned to the Palace of the Republic. At this time, there was a wave of escape attempts. But few people had sympathy for those who tried to escape; they knew the danger and accepted it, and so got little pity if they were shot or thrown in jail. The real danger of escaping wasn't the threat of death, but the end of your existence in society and that of everyone in your family too. A person convicted of Republikflucht, and the members of his family, were branded Asoziale and had little chance getting jobs or apartments or any of the things that were automatically granted to all citizens. This was the risk of trying to escape, and all members of the family suffered, not just the escapee. Kathrin knew people who had tried to escape, and after their escape attempt, she no longer associated with them. It was safer that way.

Hilde turned seventy in March 1987. Monica, Kathrin and Jennifer went to West Berlin for the party. Their visa application took six months to process. The whole time, Kathrin was convinced they would be denied, because so many were that year, and the previous Christmas as well. The Stasi were clamping down and the mood in the country was turning sour. As Gorbachev continued his reforms, which included a widening foreign policy and an end to the Cold War, the GDR seemed to constrict on itself, tightening emigration restrictions, widening security and increasing the presence of soldiers on the streets.

Kathrin and Jennifer returned happy to be back in East Germany. I asked Jennifer what she thought of West Berlin.

"It's colourful," she said flatly.

She was mature beyond her years. She'd never sucked a thumb, or carried a toy with her everywhere. She didn't speak with imaginary people, and she had an astute understanding of very adult matters.

"They have bananas," she added, "but I don't like them so much."

"It's just awful," Kathrin said. "I hate it when they look down their noses at us. Especially when Thomas does it."

I laughed. Kathrin was funny when she was angry. Her forehead scrunched into a maze of intersecting lines, and she set her teeth firm so that her face shook a little. I never argued with her, because I don't like to argue with anyone about anything. I don't think it's worth it. But sometimes she pushed me just to rile me up, because Kathrin liked a good argument. She thought it was healthy. She and Jennifer sometimes screamed at each other, only to be hugging and laughing the next minute.

"They have nothing to be superior about," I said.

Kathrin scoffed.

I turned to Jennifer. "Mr. Lankowski put water in the little lake outside and it froze overnight. Shall we go skating?"

Jennifer squealed and ran to get her skates.

Kathrin looked at me and smiled. "You're just a big kid, Michael. I sometimes wish I could be as light-hearted as you."

177

I took my darling wife in my arms. She still looked young and I loved her more than ever. The fixed routine of our lives had never dampened our feelings for each other. We had full lives and sometimes I wouldn't see her until we climbed into bed, too tired to talk. It meant that I could miss her for a couple of days and long to have her back again.

"And I wish I could be as passionate about things as you are," I said.

"Together, we are light-hearted and passionate," she said kissing me. Jennifer groaned as she saw us embracing. But I knew she liked it; it was better than parents who only shouted at each other.

\*\*\*

From my arrival, seven years passed. The time flew by, yet those years were full and satisfying. It was the best time in my life. Never had I felt more happy and complete. But more than that, I felt I'd transcended the meagre world I'd been born into and had given myself the opportunity to realise my potential. The communist world, which I'd grown up believing was evil and had been taught to hate, was my world. I was respected, influential and loved. I'd found my place. The GDR supplied me with all the things that were lacking in my own society.

Of course, there is that horrible moment in everyone's life when they have spent so many years trying to ascend the mountain, only to stand on top of it and realise that it was the journey that had mattered and not the final result. The person then has a choice: to sit on the top for as long as they can, or to go in search of a new mountain and a new journey. But in some cases, the mountain can be swept from right under your feet.

Such a thing happened when on 2 May, 1989, Hungary dismantled its border fortifications to Austria. The iron curtain was breached. In July, citizens of the GDR watched the television – the West German channel – dumfounded as hundreds of their holidaying comrades streamed through this hole in the border and into the west.

I knew then that my world was coming to an end.

# Summer 1989

Ever since returning from Hilde's seventieth birthday party, Monica had started to talk more and more about moving back to West Berlin. She pestered Heinrich, who countered saying it was too risky to try to emigrate. He said his Volkseigener Betrieb, People's Own Factory, was inundated with Stasis and it was hard enough keeping them off his back because his wife was originally from West Berlin. She threatened to go on her own, but she also feared the Stasi and what would happen to Heinrich if she left him behind. The Stasi were giving would-be immigrants a terrible time, using all sorts of methods to persuade people to stay. They infiltrated offices, workshops and sports clubs, and even the protesters groups that met in the churches. The Stasi were everywhere, so the people said, but I was sure they had not invaded my world.

That changed when Lemke was suddenly replaced as principal of my school. Margot Honecker, education minister and wife of Erich Honecker, was tightening things up in the schools, under the belief that the children held the key to the security and future of the state. Lemke's replacement was a bitter old woman called Frau Professorin Siegrid Preller, who requested that all teachers and students address her as Frau Professorin. She was tall, thin and matronly, like an unmarried aunt descending ungracefully into aged spinsterhood: bitter, resentful and spiteful, but given to outbursts of generosity and joviality that made you all the more suspicious and wary. The Frau Professorin spent most of her time walking the corridors and sitting in other teachers' classrooms. It was very disconcerting having her stride into my classroom in the middle of a lesson and sit down. I called her Prowler, but only to myself.

The atmosphere at school turned quickly sombre. Teachers were dismissed without explanation and children were threatened to the point of complete subjugation. Lemke and I had clashed in the past, but had reached a certain understanding developed over a long working relationship. I had never liked him, but he seemed like an old softie compared to Preller. She had it in for me from day one, and always narrowed her eyes when speaking to me, a suspicious look on her face. She knew I was from Australia, and this was her main source of distrust. I tried to avoid her.

When telling Kathrin about my work days, she laughed at how Preller probably thought I was a spy; me of all people. I'm glad Kathrin thought it was funny. It was because of the Frau Professorin that the teachers had more contact with the Stasi, including me.

The first visit I got was in early April, 1989. I sat in my classroom after school marking tests, like I did most days; testing was done on a weekly basis. Two men entered the room without knocking while another stood in the doorway. They were all the same and could well have been brothers: tall, blank faced, athletic, broad-shouldered and squeezed into ill-fitting suits. The older of the three, who did all the talking, said they were from the Department of Education and wanted to speak to me about a student named Stefan. I had several Stefans in different classes, so I asked for the surname. The man wouldn't give it, and instead described the boy. It was Stefan Gross. He was tall and thin in a gangly way that inspired other kids to tease him and resulted in him slouching forward to not appear so tall. He was extremely quiet. Getting him to speak in English was impossible, yet his tests had him near the top of the class.

I saw in attendance that he had for the last three days been absent.

"Is everything okay?" I asked.

At that point, I believed these men were from the department and so also believed they had a genuine interest in Stefan's well-being.

"We are interested in his work," the man said. He idly spun the globe that sat on my desk. It squeaked. "Tell me, he is a good student in English."

"Yes, one of the best," I said, putting my pen down and leaning back in my chair. It also squeaked. I felt the presence of the other man behind me, but didn't turn to him. "His speaking needs work, but his written grasp of the language is excellent."

The man behind me joined the elder and the two spoke close together. They held up their hands to cover their mouths the way small girls do when talking about boys or sharing secrets. I didn't like this childish behaviour.

"Has he done something wrong? I can vouch for him if necessary."

The older man turned to me slowly and raised his eyebrows, annoyed I had interrupted. He had a thick scar on the point of his double chin. The features of his face were soft, but the scar lent a certain violence to his look; an old menace subdued, but one which could come quickly to the surface if called upon.

"That is not necessary," he said, forcing a smile. He handed me a business card that had only a phone number on it. "If he comes to class, please call this number and do not let the boy leave."

The men left abruptly.

Stefan never appeared in class again, or at the school. Kids sometimes changed schools without warning. I had learned not to question these, or any other, changes. Some men came to collect his records.

The second visit came a few days after Hungary had opened the border to Austria. I had encouraged the kids in my tenth class to discuss the issue, because I was curious as to how they felt about it and wanted to talk about my feelings as well. The class went well and though reluctant to speak at first, by the end of the lesson, the kids were feeling better about the situation from discussing it. After school, three men charged into my classroom and surrounded my desk.

"You must come with us for a ride," the leader said, the same scarred man who had done all the talking previously.

Like an animal threatened, I became defensive.

"But I have these tests to finish marking. Tomorrow is a better time, or perhaps you would like to wait." I held out my hand and offered them seats. My hand shook a little.

A signal was given, an ever so slight nod. The two men next to me picked me up by the arms and escorted me to a waiting car: a black Lada. I decided to say nothing. Andreas had warned me never to give the Stasi more than they asked for. They were very suspicious, even of each other.

We drove east, out of Prenzlauer Berg, then along the wide expanse of Karl Marx Allee, which had been completely rebuilt after World War II as the show piece of socialism. The facades of buildings were crumbling, the colours had faded and metal pipes had corroded; everything had been built too quickly. The men said nothing in the car. We turned left on Rusche Strasse, the same direction Rudi took on our way to watch BFC Dynamo play.

The walls were high and made of red brick. The parking lot was full of Ladas, with the odd Volvo parked close to the main building. The sign on the door we entered said "Oskar Ziethen Krankenhaus Polyklinik". It was like walking into on office from the late sixties: the colours were brown, yellow and tan, with chipboard furniture, heavy carpets and thick brown curtains. Even the heaters were dark brown.

The Stasi man opened the door to a small office and let me enter it first. He sat behind the desk and when I remained standing, offered me the single chair in front of the desk. It wobbled slightly. On the wall was a picture of Lenin and the staple photograph of Honecker. Both had that stern look of determination that all the old politicians had. The battle had long been won. Why did Honecker continue to present himself as a fighter? The office was clean and bare; the artificial pine smell of floor cleaner lingered in the air. On the desk sat a dial telephone and a small lamp, nothing else. On a shelf was a radio, with thick white strips of tape on the dial to indicate GDR radio. I assumed this was a room where people waited or were interviewed, and not any single employee's office, let alone this fieldman's.

He got straight to the point. "You are a guest in our country," he said, clearing his throat and beginning what sounded like was going to be a long speech: a talking down. I found it interesting how he used the informal du. I decided to stick to the formal Sie. "Your record here is very good. You have served the GDR well. That's why we find it interesting that you're willing to throw all this away by promoting propaganda hostile to the state. Under paragraph one zero six, this is a crime in our country."

"No hostility was meant," I said.

"It's bad for the future of the GDR for our children to be pushed by our teachers to speak poorly of the state. You have the responsibility to guide our young comrades to be the leaders of the future. Frau Professorin Preller was sent to the school because Herr Lemke failed in this regard."

There was no question. I said nothing, but many things had become clear.

"But you have done good work for us, and this cannot be ignored. We feel it's just necessary to prevent any possible damage to yourself or your family."

"My family has nothing to do with how I conduct my classes," I said. "But I'll refrain from such discussions in the future if that's what's expected of me. I wasn't aware that free discussion was frowned upon in this democracy."

He rightly detected sarcasm in my voice and reacted against it. I'd tried to sound sincere, but the hypocrisy that Andreas had once tried to explain to me had all of a sudden become very clear. Preller was, if not a Stasi agent, then an important informer. I had to be more careful in the future and stick to the book.

"It's unwise to play games," the man said. "You have a family here and I do not need to remind you that you are a guest. You're here because it serves our purposes. And you should be careful of the company you keep."

Was he referring to Andreas or to someone else? Were Kathrin's minor petitions for dresses that fit and different coloured toilet brushes causing a stir?

"This is an important time for the GDR," he continued, knowing that my family was my weak point, and smiling arrogantly because of this knowledge. "We need to be sure who are our friends and who are our enemies. If you are not our friend, you are our enemy."

"I can assure you that I have always been faithful to the GDR," I said, trying to keep my voice even. "I came here because I thought life would be better and it is. Mine is not the faith that must be tested."

The man smiled and nodded.

"You aren't scared of us, are you?" he said, slightly confused.

"Are you scared of me?"

He shook his head.

"Then why should I fear you?" Small droplets of sweat trickled from under my arms and down the sides of my chest. It was hot and stuffy in the room. The short leg of the chair clicked against the floor and sounded like a gunshot. "We're equal here. I respect you because you maintain the society I believe in, but you should respect me because I educate the sons and daughters who will inherit this society."

The man set his jaw firm and nodded. "You speak good words, but it takes more than words to control a people."

He stood and we shook hands. Two men escorted me out of the building and to the main gate. They said nothing.

I took the train home. Hundreds got on with me at the Magdalenen Strasse station, all carbon copies of each other: the men with brown suits, clean shaven and blank faces, and athletic builds; the women dressed like well-paid secretaries, but distinguished by their plain, conservative hairstyles and makeup. I wondered how many people worked for the Stasi.

"Where have you been?" Kathrin asked, meeting me at the doorway. "You were supposed to be home hours ago."

"The Frau Professorin cornered me for a short interrogation."

I took off my coat. Kathrin laughed when she saw the dark wet patches around my armpits.

"Only an East German woman could make a man sweat like that," she said.

***

May and June had the longest days of the year. And because they marked the end of winter and the beginning of summer, the people surged outdoors as if woken from long sleeps. Legs were white, and sometimes unshaven, while men showed their pale winter chests to the new sun. Hair became blonder and spirits lifted. The smell of grilled sausages hung over the parks as people gathered for barbecues. Soccer players came out for impromptu matches with pullovers for goalposts. Bicycles were dusted off and the Trabis headed north for the Baltic Sea, or for garden houses in the outer districts.

It was my favourite time of year.

The winters were long and dark, but it made everyone explode into spring, as if each person was a flower waiting for nature's permission to blossom. The smells were rich, the trees burst to life, faces showed some colour and dark eyes disappeared. I looked forward to afternoon swims in the Müggelsee, camping trips to the Baltic and quiet evenings drinking beer in the park. Each summer promised new things: a fresh start, longer days, more time.

But the summer of 1989 started poorly. The winter hung on, casting dark rain clouds over East Berlin and keeping the temperatures low. The mood in the city was sour. The spring was bringing no hope with it. There had been clashes with police near Brandenburg Gate after youths had tried to listen to concerts being given on the west side. Others were clambering towards Hungary in the hope of sneaking through the hole in the iron curtain. Russia was liberalising and Poland had rediscovered its solidarity voice, but none of these changes reached the GDR hierarchy. Andreas had been right. The GDR, in an attempt to secure its government, had closed in on itself and was bound to self-destruct.

At this time, Kathrin was working as a legal secretary for a lawyer named Jörn Weise. He had a small office in Pankow and specialised in representing people persecuted by the state, but did so using the law. This meant he had some success, but was also hounded by the Stasi. He helped protestors get released from jail and others to emigrate. His picture was sometimes in the paper, but he was never described in a

184

positive way. He was a good looking man, but the pictures were never flattering.

I liked Jörn. He and his wife, Tatjana, a Ukrainian, often came to dinner. They had a son who was a couple of years older than Jennifer and the two seemed to get along. Jörn was short, but he had the face of an old Hollywood leading man: that big square jaw, with a large mouth, deep set eyes and wavy hair greying at the sides and in streaks. Unfortunately, this marvellous head looked somewhat out of place on such a small and slight frame. Sitting, he was very handsome, but the minute he walked around, he looked so out of proportion you couldn't help but stare. It was almost comical.

Jörn encouraged Kathrin and I to join him and some others at meetings in Prenzlauer Berg. They met at a church because this was the one area of public life that the government had limited control over. Kathrin pushed me to go until I finally agreed. I respected Jörn and valued his opinion.

The meetings turned out to be something akin to a hippy sit-in. Most of the participants were artists and writers; people who had suffered at the hands of the government. Good ideas were thrown around, grievances aired, but the meetings lacked order and the people couldn't seem to agree on things. They wanted reform and change, but all had different ideas of how to go about it. They could only think of their own situations, wanting to change the country so that it suited their needs better. Some of the participants were strapping young men. Jörn said these men were Stasi spies, but it didn't matter because the Stasi would find a way to listen in even if they didn't have spies in the group. He said they had a refrigerated truck parked out front which was an observation unit; the one with "Milch" or "Obst" written on the side. Anyway, Jörn claimed he wanted the Stasi to hear them. Kathrin continued to attend the meetings, even after I stopped, sometimes coming home very late and tired. I found the meetings time consuming, boring and somewhat useless. In every country there are people who think they know the right way to change the world, but never get the chance. They are people of words, false promises and weak loyalty. But Kathrin found in these meetings an outlet for the dissatisfaction she was starting to feel towards the state; she thought control was too tight. But more than anything, she wanted to travel, to see the worlds she had been denied her whole life. She started to speak about living in Australia, broaching the subject awkwardly at first, but somehow making me

185

think about it by reminding me of all the things I had once told her I missed. I followed Heinrich's thinking, that to apply to emigrate was not worth the potential risk. Life was good for us, and not being able to see parts of the world was a small concession to make for the life we had.

\*\*\*

Hungary and Poland followed Russia's lead by opening the market and trying a free economy, while also encouraging the development of opposition political parties. It was what many people thought was needed in the GDR. Having this change around us fuelled the fires of the growing number of protesters. Kathrin would come home from her meetings with Jörn's group riled up and passionate.

"There's no need to change the whole system," she said one evening after coming home late and waking me up to talk. "All we need are a few improvements. The right to travel, real elections, free speech. Simple things that could change the country. But the Politbüro are too old. They're stuck in the ways of the past."

Kathrin had told me that the general elections held in May had been rigged by the government, that her group had proved that many people hadn't voted; the 98% turnout had been falsified.

"I don't see how being able to take pictures of the Eiffel Tower will change the country," I said, my voice slow and tired.

"I agree, but don't you see, it's the simple fact that we can't go that makes us angry. That we are nothing more than inmates in a giant prison. And worse, the state doesn't trust its people to return. This is why they've become distant and disconnected from the people, and hiding in their mansions in Wandlitz."

The SED hierarchy lived in a walled community in Wandlitz, north of East Berlin, and it was rumoured they had all manner of luxuries and western products. People called it Volvograd.

I sat up in bed. "Kathrin, be careful. I don't want you getting in any trouble. You've seen how dissidents are dealt with."

She laughed. "Maybe I'll be deported and we can leave this mess."

"I thought you loved this country."

She slipped off her dress and climbed into bed. Her feet and hands were cold and they ventured over to my side to steal my warmth. I flinched.

"You know I do, but I'm just sick of being kept here. I'm tired of making do with what we have. I want a dishwasher, a BMW that goes like the wind, dresses that fit my body and not the body of Miss Average Comrade."

"Well, it's not easy to make dresses for you because you have the sexiest body in the world."

She snuggled up to me, lay her head on my chest, but there would be no nibbling of earlobes.

"I don't know how you do it," Kathrin said softly, her breath warm and ticklish against my chest.

"Do what?"

"Stay here. I want you here, I couldn't live without you, but life must be so much better in Australia. The sun, the beach. We could have a house and go swimming before breakfast. Jennifer would love it. We could start from the beginning again."

"You make it sound like paradise, but I guarantee that after two weeks you would hate it."

"Maybe, but I'd sure like to try."

I kissed her forehead. "I'm here because of you and because I believe that this is a better place. I've accomplished things here I would never have done in Perth."

"I know, but I have the terrible feeling that things will only get worse unless we do something."

We fell silent until the sound of Kathrin snoring softly against my chest started to fill the air spasmodically. Her snoring sometimes kept me awake because it had no rhythm; I found myself laying awake waiting for the next snore to come, hanging on it, and then the next, hoping to learn the rhythm and then fall asleep. She only snored when worried. I wished she would stop going to the meetings. She snored so much lately.

When I arrived home from school the next day, Rudi was leaning against a tree across the road from my building. A light rain was falling, which sometimes dampened otherwise wonderful Julys in Berlin, and my pants were wet from cycling through puddles. After we made eye contact, Rudi started to cross the street. I leaned my bike against the wall of the alleyway.

Rudi took off his sunglasses and reach out his hand. Even after all this time, we still shook hands formally every time we met.

"Der Fahrrad Lehrer," he said grandly. "Not even the weather can stop you."

"How are you, Rudi?" I asked flatly. Over the years, I had slowly started to dislike him. I didn't like the way he just appeared, unannounced, coming out of the shadows as if he'd been lurking there all the time, watching and waiting for the right moment. I also didn't like the way he did me favours without asking, as if trying to buy my friendship.

Rudi nodded that he was fine. "Christine is pregnant again."

"Congratulations," I said. "Five more and you've got yourself a football team."

Rudi laughed. "Perhaps you can be the goalkeeper, Carlos."

Rudi wasn't a good father. Even though his children loved him and competed for his affection, he seemed to feel no real love towards them, that they were the product of his existence the way a shoemaker produces shoes. Christine had confided to Kathrin that Rudi was often absent from home, sometimes for several weeks, and would then walk into the house as if he had only gone out for a beer. It was possible he wanted children for financial gain, because the state rewarded big families with child bonuses and allowances. Parents with more than two children could take free days, with full pay, if one of their children was ill. Having more children was a sign that the system was working, that people wanted to have their sons and daughters inherit this world. Schools were good and there was a fixed standard of one teacher for every twenty students. Parents could put babies in day care when they were three months old. Schools took care of kids for the whole day if necessary, and also gave them a hot meal. Mothers were encouraged to resume working after their maternity leave. Christine still worked as a secretary at a VEB.

"You want to come in? Have a beer or something?" I asked. I didn't want him to come up, but had to offer.

"Thank you, no. I would prefer if you and I took a short walk through the park."

I left the bicycle against the wall. Rudi watched me curiously as I walked away from my unlocked bike.

"Hallo, Michael," called out my neighbour, Thilo, a jovial character who lived with his wife and three boys in the apartment below ours. He was hunched over his beloved motorbike, still wearing his metalworker's overalls.

"Will you take the beast out for a burn this weekend?" I asked him.

Thilo squinted his eyes to the grey clouds above and frowned.

"When the weather is better, and the wife lets me, then maybe." He laughed, then looked past me at Rudi and nodded hello.

"Sorry, Thilo," I said. "This is Rudi, my…" I paused. The husband of my wife's cousin was such a mouthful. "He's a friend of mine."

They shook hands, forearms flexing.

"Nice bike," Rudi said, leaning in for a closer look.

Thilo smiled proudly and quickly reeled off the technical specifications. Rudi nodded knowingly, and described the bike he had when he was younger. Thilo was impressed.

"I hope you have good weather this weekend," Rudi said, motioning for us to go. "This bike deserves a good hammering."

Thilo smiled, and went back to vigorously polishing the metal. I liked Thilo, and admired his work ethic and parenting ability. His sons were polite and well-behaved. With both of us young fathers, we often swapped advice. He was just a simple worker, with a limited education, and not such an intellectual, but he gave simple and clear advice. He loved to break everything down to analogies of metalwork, like my father had with bricklaying. Thilo was a happy guy, and had reason to be. His wife, Bea, was a lovely girl from Rostock. She and Kathrin sometimes went shopping together. Thilo's job was secure, he made good money and his boys had the opportunity to go to university. No metalworker in Australia or America had it as good as Thilo. The GDR catered for everybody, and Thilo lived the life my father had been denied.

Rudi and I crossed the road and walked under the shelter of overhanging trees. A few drops of rain seeped through, and there were shallow puddles on the path that we had to walk around. Joggers ran past, some even raised a hand in greeting; locals who recognised me as they huffed past. Dogs ran loose and chased after tennis balls or sticks, tongues flapping from their mouths happily. They wagged their tails and barked for another ball to fetch. Rudi said nothing. The silence was fine for me because I had been speaking and listening all day. We climbed the Grosse Bunkerberg, the small hill that resulted after one of the patrol towers from the war had been destroyed and left here as a pile of rubble. Concrete corners jutted out as we followed the path around to the top. The lookout was encircled by a low wall. It was empty, and raining harder here, with no trees for shelter. Rudi stopped and leaned on the wall, looking west towards Mitte and the television tower rising high in the distance, the view partly obscured by trees. The sun was shining through the clouds in West Berlin. I looked hard, hoping to see the golden angel in the distance, but couldn't.

"How's Dieter?" I asked.

Dieter was in hospital, recovering from heart surgery. Nobody had thought he would survive. I'd visited him two weeks ago and felt bad that I hadn't been back since.

"Getting better," Rudi said flatly. "The doctors say he must change his diet. No alcohol, no meat and no smoking either."

"Poor Dieter, but I'm glad to hear he's well."

"The doctor said he also must see the dentist. My father never went, you know." Rudi turned to me. "How is your friend the dentist?"

"Andreas? He could use a change of diet as well. I keep telling him to lay off the heavy food but he won't listen."

Rudi laughed the fake laugh I hated. I imagined him sitting in a class with twenty other men learning to laugh, all of them chanting together the same mirthless ha.

"What's your secret, Rudi? You never seem to get fat."

I said this because I too was starting to see an increase in the size of my stomach. I hoped I was just filling out in the way I remembered my father had at the same age. But this was fat, not muscle. I needed to do more than just cycle to work.

At that moment, a jogger puffed up the steps, stopped, and leaned on his hands and knees, trying to catch his breath. It was too warm for the tight leggings he wore, and I wondered if this was his first day jogging. He had that grim determination of someone who had been forced out here.

Rudi said nothing and stared at the view until the jogger left the lookout, walking back down.

"I run, but not like him," he said, jerking a thumb in the direction of the departing jogger. "Perhaps Andreas should do the same."

"I'd like to see that. The earth would shake with every step."

Rudi offered that same laugh again. "Ha. Perhaps he would like to run all the way to Hungary."

"Andreas is not interested in leaving," I said, somewhat offended. "But he was disappointed with the last elections."

Rudi eyed me curiously. "In what way?"

"He would have liked Modrow to have got a place in the government. He's from Dresden after all."

Rudi shook his head. "Modrow is too liberal. He would ruin the GDR the same way Gorbachev is ruining the Soviet Union."

"Is that why you brought me up here, to talk politics?" I was growing impatient and it was raining harder now, yet the sun still shone to the west.

"I have something to ask you. It's very important to me." Rudi paused. "We have known each other a long time, Carlos, shared many experiences." He cleared his throat. "I would like you to be the godfather of my next child, with Kathrin as godmother, of course."

It was the kind of request you couldn't refuse. "We would be delighted," I said.

Rudi smiled, genuinely, and not in that fake way when his smile became too big for his face and his neck muscles strained.

We started to walk back down the hill. The rain had stopped and the clouds were beginning to dissipate.

"And how is Kathrin?" Rudi asked. "Will Jennifer soon have someone to play with?"

"That would be nice. But she's working quite hard at the moment, focusing on that and not on having another child."

The sun burst through the clouds, glistening on fresh puddles and wet grass. Joggers looked to the sun and felt renewed, jogging faster with greater purpose and losing their grim focus for the enjoyment of a summer run through the park. Dogs barked and lapped at fresh puddles between retrieving sticks. Ten young boys had started a soccer match, with one small dog chasing after the ball. One boy wore long pants and kept having to pull them up because they were wet and heavy at the bottom.

"A friend told me he saw Kathrin at one of Jörn Weise's church meetings. This is true?"

"Yes. I was there once or twice as well, but it's a bit of a waste of time. Just a lot of talk."

"But Kathrin keeps going."

We were almost out of the park now and Rudi had slowed his walk to a stroll.

"I think she just likes to talk about some of the country's problems, that's all, and she almost always feels better afterward. Talking can be therapeutic."

"What kind of problems do they talk about?"

"Oh, you know, what everyone complains about. No chance to

travel, no free speech, wanting the same reforms as Gorbachev, the opening in Hungary, people camping at the West German embassies in Prague and Budapest."

"Kathrin talks about leaving?"

"Sometimes, but this is her home and she loves it. I think she wants to stay and make it better, and not run away from it like others do."

At the road, the sound of the traffic was loud. Trams rumbled past and Trabis and Wartburgs took Leninallee out of the city to the outer suburbs of Lichtenberg, Hohenschönhausen, and Marzahn. They drove quickly, wanting to be out of the city and away from the factories and offices. The evening was turning pleasant and they wanted to get home to enjoy it.

I waited for a break in the traffic and then started to cross the road. Rudi grabbed my arm and held me back. His eyes were black as he stared at me.

"If I were you, I wouldn't want my wife going to these meetings," he said. "Those people are troublemakers, Carlos. They want to destroy the state."

I shook my arm free. "Come on, Rudi. It's just a bunch of artists letting off steam and talking shit. There's no way they're going to start a revolution."

"It would be unfortunate to have our own Tiananmen Square," Rudi said, as if warning me.

"That was in China. This is East Germany. The people here will never turn on the government or on each other."

Rudi smiled grimly. "I always thought you should've been a politician, Carlos. When you speak like that, even I believe you." He turned and walked back into the park, disappearing into the shadows of the trees.

\*\*\*

Kathrin continued attending the meetings. In early September, she returned home clutching a single piece of paper in her hand. She burst through the door and slammed the piece of paper onto the desk where I sat reading. Behind me, Jennifer lay sprawled on the floor, sleeping face down with her head in a book. She didn't stir.

"Read this," Kathrin whispered excitedly. She stood next to me, waiting, expectant, full of hope.

"'We are forming a political arena for the entire GDR,'" I read. "'In it, citizens from all walks of life, occupations, parties and groups will be able to participate in the discussion of this country's most vital social problems. To identify this general initiative, we have chosen the name New Forum. We call upon all citizens of the GDR who want to collaborate in the alteration of our society to become members of New Forum.'"

I put the piece of paper back on the desk.

"Well?" Kathrin asked loudly, forgetting that Jennifer lay asleep behind us. "What do you think? Say something?"

"Sounds like organised petitioning," I whispered, motioning with my hands towards Jennifer, "which is what you do at work. And it sounds like you have a place where people can come to discuss things, which you already have with the meetings. So what's different?"

"The difference is," Kathrin whispered intently, "that we're going to publish this and apply for authorisation."

"Okay, now that means something. When's the next meeting?"

"Tomorrow night," Kathrin said smiling, happy that I was on her side and supportive. "Jörn's very excited about it. Everyone's excited about it. If we get enough people interested, we can force dialogue and change. They're rising in Leipzig and Dresden as well. It's not just here."

"Careful," I said, pulling her close. "You'll wake Jenny."

Kathrin nibbled my ear. "Let's put her to bed," she whispered, her breath warm against my ears.

As we tumbled and struggled, I felt I was back by the lake, so many years ago, when we had laid on the grass naked like two lost animals who had found each other in the forest.

\*\*\*

New Forum's application for authorisation was denied because of a "lack of social necessity". The group was disappointed, but Jörn remained positive and upbeat.

"Don't you see?" he said at the first meeting after the rejection. Kathrin sat next to him – rather close, I thought – diligently taking notes. "They know who we are now. They don't recognise us, but they know our name. It is only a matter of time before the social necessity arises."

"From the ruins," a voice mumbled.

193

A few people laughed. The GDR anthem was called *Arisen from the Ruins*. It was never sung, only played, because of its reference to the German Fatherland, which was a little too close to what Hitler used to say.

Jörn sat in his chair cross-legged and relaxed, his big Hollywood head looking more prepared to deliver a Shakespearean monologue than to lift this small band of misfits.

"This is just the beginning," he said. "The Monday demonstrations in Leipzig get bigger every week. They will spread to other cities and the state will be forced to make a decision. Crush the demonstrations or open a dialogue. I don't believe that German will fight with German the way it happened in China. The order to shoot at the border has been suspended, the people are crowding the embassies in Prague and Budapest, and more and more people are learning the power of their voice. Be patient, for when the changes come they will be swift. The government is old. They can't live forever. They will all go at once."

Jörn was referring to Schiessbefehlt, the order to shoot those trying to escape. It was when someone was shot at the wall that people were reminded quite clearly the wall was there and what purpose it served. People thought the suspension of this order was a signal for reform.

"We can make a protest on the seventh of October," Jörn continued. "A peaceful protest against the anniversary celebrations. But we must not protest against the government. We only want reform. Nothing makes me angrier than the people who go to Hungary and to Prague to get out. They are weak and make it harder for us to engage in dialogue with the SED."

One man, young and athletic, stood up from his chair and left. Nobody watched him go.

"You say that German will not fight with German, but this has already happened in Dresden and here."

This was Ute, a writer and a member of the initiative Women for Peace. She was middle-aged and rather ugly, with stringy hair and a heavily lined and pale face. She liked to speak, but it was sometimes difficult to concentrate because you couldn't really look at her. She had a penchant for wearing singlets, which only brought more attention to her withered chest and hairy underarms.

"That's true," Jörn said.

"And remember that the government applauded Tiananmen Square," she continued. "Krenz even went there to shake their hands."

She laughed incredulously, a high pitched cackle that echoed in the church.

"Our weight of numbers will win," Jörn said quietly.

"Or they'll be our downfall," Ute countered. "As more people gather in Leipzig, the more I become scared that we'll have our own massacre. A hundred people walking with paper banners is nothing compared to fifty thousand. The state will respond. The Stasi will break their heads."

"They can't just put fifty thousand people in prison," Jörn said. "And they can't go out and mow them all down with guns. Germans won't do that to each other, and the government won't allow it anyway."

Ute scoffed, and folded her arms defiantly.

"And I think it's a shame that you think so poorly about your fellow people, Ute," Jörn continued. "They're like you and me. Some have had different upbringings, were raised to believe in different things, but inside they are the same as us."

"Perhaps Hony will join us in the march, and carry a big picture of himself."

I laughed, as did Jörn and the few others there who had a sense of humour. I had asked Andreas to come because I wanted to know what he thought of the group. He stated proudly at the beginning that he was a member of the SED and had fielded many questions, grievances and insults because some had decided he represented the government. Andreas took it all in good humour and was too smart for all of them.

"And what do you think, comrade?" Ute asked spitefully. "Will your friends squash us if our meagre voice becomes a slight squeal?"

Ute had been at Andreas's neck the whole meeting. Andreas was enjoying it immensely.

"By the sounds of things," he said calmly, "you won't be there at the front line to see exactly what happens. You can't drive a car from the backseat, Ute. Not even a Trabant." To stop her from responding, Andreas turned to Jörn. "But I have to admit, I don't think having a protest on the seventh of October is a good idea. Why not just start having Monday demonstrations like the ones in Leipzig?"

Jörn liked this idea, as did many others in the group, but felt that the anniversary celebrations were the perfect time to put the spotlight on protest. West German television was bound to broadcast something about it and this would help get New Forum, and other protest groups, into every home in the GDR.

"If everybody shouts, the government will have no choice but to listen," Jörn said as the meeting broke up. He looked tired and his handsome face drooped. "I'll tell my associates of our plans and try to get them coordinated."

I shook his hand before we left. He gave me a weak smile and thanked me for bringing Andreas.

"It was nice to have one more voice of reason," he said. "Try to get him to come again. He could one day become a very important cog in our country's wheel."

Andreas's apartment was only a few streets away. Kathrin and I walked on either side of our large and beaming friend.

"Who knew a group of lousy dissidents could be so much fun," he said, his voice loud on the empty street, his strides long and purposeful.

"All they want is to make things better," Kathrin said. I found it interesting she said they and not we. "It's because of these groups that the government will be forced to make changes."

"Oh, I have no doubt," Andreas said happily. "But it's interesting that Weise is trying to organise a group that is half Stasi."

Kathrin and I both stopped walking. Andreas walked a few extra paces before realising we weren't with him. He turned around and walked back. His stomach was large and hung over the belt of his trousers. His legs and arms were thick, and even his hands were chubby.

"Didn't you know that?" Andreas asked, chuckling. "Why, I bet that witch Ute is an informer as well."

"Now that I can't believe," Kathrin said, putting her hands girlishly on her hips.

"Ah, but you see, the best informer is the one you least suspect." He turned and started walking again. "Come on, if we don't get home soon, Jenny will love Birgit more than she loves you." He laughed and started to whistle as he walked.

We caught up with him, and walked in silence except for Andreas's tune. Then, Kathrin started to sing. It was an old communist battle song they had learned as children in the Young Pioneers. Sometimes, a person walking in the opposite direction or on the other side of the street would sing a line or two as they passed. The song was sombre and sad and fitted the brisk autumn evening.

\*\*\*

196

Every apartment in East Berlin has a flag holder, sometimes two. Ours was on the balcony. On special days, we would slide the East German flag and the red communist flag into the holders. Every building's Hausmeister would check who had their flags up and who didn't. Whether you were patriotic or not, you put the flags up.

The seventh of October, 1989, was the fortieth anniversary of the German Democratic Republic. It seemed like such a short time, but the event was planned to be of fantastic grandeur. Only last year, I had received letters from my mother and sister, who was now divorced from Ashley Pritchard and back home in Perth with her son, about the celebrations for Australia's bicentenary. Two hundred years was reason to celebrate, not forty. But the GDR was using the event as an excuse to arouse old nationalist feelings, and to reaffirm the government's position.

The parade went down Karl Marx Allee, a street that was designed for such an event. It was always best not to be in your apartment during a parade, so we took Jennifer to see the tanks and the guns and the marching soldiers. She was heavy on my shoulders. We ran into Thilo and his family. Thilo proudly wore his hat from his metalwork VEB, and each of his boys sported similar hats.

"Lovely day for a parade," I said.

Thilo slapped me on the shoulder. In his hand was a can of beer, and I could see several more jammed in the pockets of his overalls. His breath stank of beer, but he was in excellent spirits.

"Forty years," he shouted. "A big reason to celebrate, but every day is worth celebrating, because we live in the best country in the world."

He drained the beer, scrunched up the can and dropped it to the ground. His two younger boys grabbed an arm each and started dragging him away, closer to the street.

"Have a good day," I yelled out, but they got lost in the crowd.

We stood not far from the main podium where Honecker sat next to Gorbachev, practically ignoring him. The other leaders of the party all sat with that grim look of stern determination that I identified as the communist pose. Gorbachev looked bored, as if he'd rather be swigging vodka in his own backyard and teaching his grandkids the Cossack dance. The soldiers marched past, kicking their polished boots high in the air, their uniforms spick and span. But their faces told another story: their cheeks were sallow, their eyes sad. Every man was forced into the army for eighteen months, longer if they wanted

197

to go on to university, and you could see in their eyes they hated it. Even Andreas had served his time. He had driven a water cannon, and when inebriated, he sometimes bragged that he had been very good, able to fire water through hoops and accurately at targets.

The lines of soldiers never seemed to end. I wondered why such an army was necessary when all the leaders ever talked about was peace and security. The soldiers didn't wear metals of honour earned in battle. Their uniforms were dull green and void of any sign of conflict. And they were just boys, with pink cheeks and small black scabs on their faces, and others with red blood marks from where they had cut themselves with blunt razors, and a few still with puppy fat faces. To watch them march past, and not look at their faces, was to see an army of robots, or clones, the army training reducing all of them to the same level. I was glad I had been spared national service; Rudi had organised that.

We left the parade to join the protestors gathering on Alexanderplatz. The group was mainly young people. We couldn't find Jörn or his New Forum band, or any of the other protest groups. The mob was disorderly, with a small collection of right wing extremists and punks looking to cause trouble. The atmosphere was tense and the police moved in to force the group away from Alex. We went with the flow of people headed for Prenzlauer Berg and the safety of the churches, but the group was large and disorderly. Fear welled in my stomach.

"I'm taking Jenny home," I shouted to Kathrin. We were being separated by a rush of people trying to escape the blast of a water cannon. The police were becoming brutal, hitting people with clubs and dragging them into police vans. There were grunts of pain, pleads for mercy and shouts of defiance. Kathrin said something, but her voice was lost in the throng and she was carried away. Jennifer was crying. I picked her up and carried her down a side street. I kept looking behind to see if Kathrin was coming, but she didn't follow. I could hear the noise of the crowd shouting and the wail of police sirens and wanted to get myself and my daughter as far away from it as possible. We walked all the way home. Away from the scene, the streets were deserted, but some people looked out the windows of their apartments in the direction the noise was coming from. All the flags still fluttered from the balconies.

At home, I gave Jennifer a warm glass of milk and she fell quickly asleep. I sat on the balcony with a beer, waiting for Kathrin to walk out of the park or from further down the street, and debating whether I should leave Jennifer asleep and search for her. I decided to wait. Kathrin was the strongest woman I had ever known. I knew she would be all right.

The loud shrill of the phone startled me. It was Jörn. He was breathless and spoke in short bursts. Kathrin had been taken to the Charité after being crushed in the crowd.

I threw Jennifer into the Trabant. The car wouldn't start and I banged the steering wheel angrily. Jennifer, too tired to understand what was happening, began to cry. I ignored her, and so she cried louder. Finally, the car started and the sound of her crying was drowned out by the loud engine.

I drove to my in-laws.

"Michael? What's going on?" Monica asked bleary eyed. "There's been sirens all night."

"Kathrin's at the hospital. I'm sorry to wake you like this, but I don't want to take Jenny there, just in case."

"Is she all right?"

"I don't know."

Monica nodded and whisked the crying Jennifer into her arms. I kissed my daughter, but I think at that point she hated me, and buried her face into her grandmother's chest.

"I'll let you know what happens," I said, rushing down the stairs.

I had left the Trabi running and thankfully it was still there. The streets in Mitte were a mess. Large groups of people were running around, seeking refuge from the police, while others drank in small groups, oblivious to the happenings around them, with some sleeping soundly as wailing police cars went straight past them.

In the Charité, people were holding white cloths stained red to their faces, while others had cuts that dripped dark blood straight onto the floor. Still more people were searching for others, shouting names over the crowd in a vague hope their loved one had only a cut on the head.

A frazzled nurse at first ignored me, but I persisted and she helped me locate Kathrin. I found her lying on a bed, a man in a white coat leaning over her, putting stitches in one of her eyebrows. She tried to sit up when she saw me, but the doctor ordered her not to move. At the other end of the bed, her left foot was raised by a pillow and was bruised black, blue and purple. I rushed to her and grabbed her hand. She smiled, and then grimaced in pain. I started to talk, but she shushed me.

When the stitches were done, the doctor left, saying he would return soon to talk about her foot. He needed to look at the x-rays.

"Is it broken?" I asked, pulling a chair next to the bed.

Kathrin nodded. She seemed unable to speak, hurt by pain and still in shock.

I looked at her stitches. "Now you have a matching set. Both eyebrows are scarred."

She laughed, grimacing again, then mouthed the word "Jennifer."

"She's okay. I took her to your parents after Jörn called. But I don't think she likes me anymore." Kathrin looked at me quizzically. "I pulled her out of bed. You know how she hates that."

Kathrin leaned back on the pillow and smiled. Her face had small cuts, and a few bruises were starting to shine, but she still looked beautiful.

"What happened?"

"Later," she whispered, and her eyes told me to give her time. She would tell me when she was ready.

"You're very lucky," the doctor said as he came back in. "The ankle isn't broken, only sprained. We'll strap it up and send you home. I'm afraid there are others with more pressing injuries who need the bed more than you."

Kathrin looked relieved, not so much about her foot, but because she could go home. She hated hospitals. On the way home, we picked up Jennifer and she didn't stir from the moment she left one bed to when she was in her own. Both of the women in my life had had terrible days and I resolved to pamper them for the next few days.

\*\*\*

"Has she said anything?" Andreas asked.

I shook my head. "Jörn told me enough to get an idea what happened."

"And?" Heinrich's once strong voice had become throaty and weak, and his face was sallow and grey. The body was the same, but Monica had said to Kathrin a few weeks ago that he had lost almost ten kilos in the last year; losing weight from the inside. His health was deteriorating, and I worried for the father-in-law I considered a great friend.

The three of us were sitting on the balcony, cans of beer in our hands, and trying not to show that the stiff breeze made us feel chilly. Monica and Birgit were preparing dinner while Jennifer played at the foot of the sofa on which Kathrin lay. With all the people that loved her in close proximity, she was in high spirits, but she still refused to talk about last night.

"There were just so many people," I said quietly, "and it was almost like they were dogs let off the leash. There have been protests before in East Berlin, and you remember the damage those west concerts caused two years ago, when they pointed the speakers towards the east. But that was nothing compared to this."

"The Stasi are not music lovers," Andreas said.

Heinrich wheezed a laugh and then tried to calm the coughing that followed.

"They had a couple of water cannons and there were a lot of police," I continued. "All the people had no choice but to go with the flow, which was towards Prenzelberg and the churches. But they were already full, so one crowd of people slammed against another. And all the time sirens were screaming and the police were hitting people and dragging them into vans. It was absolute chaos."

"Why did you leave Kathrin?" Heinrich asked.

"Believe me, I didn't want that, but we got separated by the crowd and I still had Jenny with me. I had to get her out of there."

Heinrich considered this and drank his beer thoughtfully. "You did the right thing."

"Thanks, Heinrich. But everyone's more concerned about what's going to happen tomorrow in Leipzig. Jörn said a lot of people are converging there. If the police fight with them, try to put down the protest, we could have a small massacre on our hands."

The two men nodded and became sombre.

Sunday had been a quiet day in the wake of last night's chaos. Reports were coming in from all over the country of protests and clashes with the police and Stasi. Hundreds were in jail and many others were nursing wounds as Kathrin was. Nobody was in the mood to celebrate. The tension was too high. The people were realising the power of protest and collective voice while at the same time harbouring deep fears about state reaction. Nobody wanted to go to prison, nor did they want to become an Asoziale.

"It was just a matter of time before the people got themselves together," Heinrich said. "Fifty-three was a long time ago, but many have not forgotten. The Russians won't come this time to stop any protest or uprising. Gorbachev has deserted us."

"We have deserted Gorbachev," Andreas countered. "We had the chance to follow his lead, but the party leaders rejected this. And that mistake will bring about their ruin. Communism can't survive without the support of the people."

"And so we just throw away everything that we've worked for," Heinrich said passionately. "The country we've lived in and a system that gave us everything we needed after the Nazis and the war took everything away. You underestimate the people here. You're talking about the destruction of our identity."

"I don't mean that the country will be finished," Andreas said, holding his hands up in apology. "What I'm saying is that the chance to make changes passes with each day. The situation gets worse, and the party leaders get older and more out of touch. I am a communist, Heinrich. I believe in the system, but what we have isn't communism."

"What do we have?" I asked.

"A dictatorship. The government controls everything, and they have nurtured a people scared to sneeze in a politically incorrect way. And worse, they have developed us into a submissive society. You were never a Young Pioneer or in the Free German Youth, Smit, so you don't know what kind of ideological tampering is done to the kids."

"I see it at school," I said, "and it's no different to what I had growing up in Perth, only that the words and ideas are a little bit different. Every ruler knows the best way to secure his rule is by controlling the next generation, and that happens in every society. I grew up being told that the Russians, and all communists, were the most ruthless, heartless, evil people in the world, and that the Americans were the good guys fighting for freedom, truth and justice."

Heinrich and Andreas both laughed.

"I don't think a child is born with an ideological belief," I continued. "The same with racism and prejudice. The child learns what he's taught."

"And we were taught to worship the production quotas," Andreas said, laughing softly. He found even the most fervent political discussion funny.

"Progress, progress," sang Heinrich.

"Ah, Smit, you have become a smart man in our country. The system here has succeeded in turning a mechanic into an intellectual."

"He was such a green frog when he first came," Heinrich said. "Like a boy from the country marvelling at traffic lights and tall buildings."

"How much did you get for the pig, Smit?" Andreas asked seriously. "Was it enough to buy a new sickle?"

Heinrich roared with laughter.

"Oh, I could never sell the pig," I said. "It was my dowry."

The three of us laughed so loud that Kathrin called from the living room wanting to know what was so funny. Monica appeared behind us, smiling broadly, and announced dinner was ready. I looked at Heinrich and Andreas and wondered why I'd had to travel to the other side of the world to make such great friends. At that moment, the whole country could have collapsed. I was happy just to sit and have dinner with the people closest to me. The state could never control the small world that existed inside my apartment.

\*\*\*

Ute held the floor for almost the entire two hours at the next New Forum meeting. She had been in Leipzig and gave a detailed account of the Monday demonstration. There had been no clashes with police, even though they were there in strength. Someone had ordered them back, and in doing so, had prevented a large scale conflict and also opened the door for more demonstrating. The people in Leipzig could now march without fear and this feeling was sure to spread through the country. Candles were appearing in windows as signs of solidarity, and there was an overwhelming feeling that change was very close.

But when it came, it was so quick and abrupt, that if you blinked, you missed it. After eighteen years in power, Honecker resigned with a whimper as Secretary General of the SED on the seventeenth of October. With him went Günther Mittag, responsible for the economy, and Joachim Hermann, responsible for media. These three were part of the old guard, and their departure gave hope to reforms and changes. But these hopes were dashed by the election of Egon Krenz, former head of the Free German Youth and groomed over the last few years as Honecker's successor. Andreas was bitterly disappointed that Günter Schabowski wasn't elected as Secretary General, because he saw him as a German Gorbachev: liberal, ambitious and reform minded, and also a native Berliner. Krenz was just another of the old guard, but in a younger body. It was also he who had travelled to China to congratulate the Chinese leaders on their handling of Tiananmen Square. Nobody trusted him, and after his first television address, many people realised that reforms wouldn't be forthcoming, that Krenz was not the man to usher in a new era. He missed the chance to ask for time and patience, that reforms would come if the people had faith in the leadership. Instead, it was the same old song, as if he was reading an address the former leader Walter Ulbricht might have given thirty years ago.

If Krenz had given the people what they wanted, then things may have turned out a lot differently. But he accepted power in the mediocre and pathetic fashion that fitted the man.

New Forum continued to meet, as did the other groups such as Democratic Awakening, the Initiative for Peace and Human Rights, Women for Peace, and the Peace Circle. And not just in East Berlin and Leipzig; protestors were gathering all over the country, becoming more organised, and realising the power of their collective voice.

On the twenty-first of October, a large group formed a human chain demanding the release of prisoners arrested at the protests two weeks earlier. Three days later, twelve thousand people gathered outside the Council of State building to protest the election of Krenz. They lit candles and placed them in front of the building.

A significant event happened on the twenty-sixth of October, when GDR TV telecast a round table discussion that included former Stasi General and now writer and advocate for liberal reform, Markus Wolf, novelist Christoph Hein, writer Stefan Heym, whom the west had dubbed the leader of the revolution, and Bärbel Bohley, founder of Women for Peace. Kathrin and I watched the telecast with Andreas and Birgit. None of us could believe that such a show was on GDR television.

"It's because Hermann's gone," Andreas said, referring to the resignation of the former media minister. "That old fart would never have allowed this. He wanted to burn Bohley at the stake."

Birgit and Kathrin scoffed at Wolf, the ex-Stasi man, and criticised everything he said. He wanted a real form of socialism where everyone could speak.

"This from the man who wanted to hear what all of us had to say and only made us talk less," Birgit said, making Andreas laugh.

Wolf was like a double agent who had walked off the set of an old spy film. He had shifty eyes, never focusing on anything, and he looked uncomfortable on camera.

Heym and Hein were the voices of reason, with both extremely eloquent in their delivery. Heym, the crafty old writer who had published books in the west that were banned in East Germany, asked if only three people were responsible for the mess that was East Germany. It was up to each citizen to take responsibility for the situation and work to improve it. Hein dreamed of a socialism where the people didn't want to leave. I agreed with him. The system was worth keeping, but had to be improved and altered so that people could leave the country and always want to return. Bohley said her dream had been realised, that she was able to speak freely; this was all she had ever wanted.

But like so many New Forum meetings and probably countless others of protest groups, the members of the round table couldn't agree on how to improve the situation. After such fruitful discussion, the telecast left us with an empty feeling.

"It's one thing for a bunch of intellectuals to sit around and discuss hypotheticals over red wine and it's another for someone to stand up and lead us," Andreas said. "What's a revolution without some charismatic fighter to lead the march?"

We looked at Andreas hopefully. He threw up his hands and smiled.

"Don't look at me. I'm just a dentist. I'm more than happy to give the leader big white dentures to help him with his smile, but revolution's not my game."

"But you've got a point," Kathrin said. "Jörn got New Forum going, but he never wanted it to be a political party or an underground movement. And he's no Lenin."

"Do we really want another Lenin?" Birgit asked. "I'm so tired of seeing his face everywhere."

"What we need, or what we should have had," Andreas said emphatically, "is Modrow. We wouldn't have any of these problems if Modrow had been elected. And his accent would have made everyone laugh as well. But I'm afraid he's missed his chance. He could've done great things for this country."

"Ah, you're always going on about Modrow," Birgit said. "He's just an old comrade like the rest."

"Sure, but look at how he has handled that mess in Dresden, with all the people being shipped back from the Prague embassy. And remember," Andreas said laying on his accent thicker, "we don't get west TV down there. Sometimes we don't know what is happening in the real world."

We all laughed. If only Andreas's life had at some point taken a different turn, he could well have been the one to lead our small revolution.

\*\*\*

Three days later, Schabowski engaged in an open debate with a large crowd outside city hall. The discussion was supposed to be inside, but there were too many people. Schabowski and other politicians fielded questions from the crowd, who called for an end to the Stasi and for a new, less restrictive travel law. The debate was orderly and the crowd silent as questions were raised and answers given. Andreas and I stood at the back of the crowd. Schabowski seemed to be enjoying himself.

"You're not close enough to the microphone to ask a question."

I turned around. Rudi was behind me. He wore a light brown trench coat drawn tight at the middle by a belt of the same colour. I shook his hand.

"Rudi, nice to see you. How's Christine?"

"Getting bigger every day," he said smiling. He looked tired. "Your godchild is going to be a big one."

"The biggest are always the best," Andreas said, shaking Rudi's hand. "More to go around."

Rudi smiled weakly. He looked like a soccer player who had run hard the whole game, only for his team to be losing badly and there were only a few minutes left. His spirit and desire to fight were almost gone.

"But what a world to be born into," he said. "So much chaos and protest. We're losing everything that makes this country great."

"A little bit of discussion never hurt anyone," I said.

"That's easy for you to say. You were born into a world like that."

The debate was ending. People left the square while others lingered and discussed the results. Once again, people looked empty and confused, as more constructive talk had resulted in nothing.

"Rudi, why don't you scoop up that lovely wife of yours and come over for dinner next week?" I asked.

He smiled. "Thanks, but I have really too much work this week. Maybe after the birth." He started to move away.

"Okay."

"I must go," Rudi said, his eyes scanning the crowd. "Greetings to Kathrin and Jennifer. I hope her foot is better."

He disappeared into the crowd. Andreas glanced down at me, his face blank and pale. At that moment, he looked so old, and I wondered if I looked the same.

\*\*\*

The following evening, Kathrin and I were back at Andreas's apartment to watch the Leipzig demonstration broadcast live on TV. There were so many people. They walked close together, some with linked arms, and they carried banners that said "We are the People". It was encouraging to see such an outpouring of support and togetherness. I had always loved the East German sense of community. Even in protest they gathered together in large numbers and supported each other. And it was orderly and non-violent.

"I hope our demonstration is like this," Kathrin said quietly.

\*\*\*

The fourth of November, 1989, broke bright and beautiful, cold and clear. Kathrin was beside herself with nerves and excitement. Leipzig had grabbed all the attention with the Monday demonstrations, but today would be East Berlin's day. The people of Leipzig couldn't change the country, but the people of East Berlin could, if enough of them came out.

We gathered at the bottom of Schönhauser Allee. Jennifer kept playing with her green and yellow slash. It said "No Violence", but she wore it as if it said Miss East Germany. We all had them; Andreas's stretched tight over his broad chest and stomach. Spirits were high, but there was still some apprehension in the air, especially from those who had taken part in the last demonstrations on the seventh of October. Kathrin was nervous, but trying not to show it. Jörn had told us earlier that the police would be at the demonstration, but that a deal had been made with them and there would be no confrontation. Everyone spoke too fast and a little too loudly; nerves and anxiety manifesting themselves in boisterous speech. Only Heinrich was solemn and quiet. He was a survivor of the uprising on the seventeenth of June, 1953, which had been crushed by the Soviets. He had been shot in the arm; you could still see the scars, how the bullet had passed through his forearm and amazingly missed the bones. Even now, his left forearm was clearly thinner than the right. He liked to scare children by stubbing out lit cigarettes on his scar, claiming with a smile and a wink that it was magic.

The crowd began to walk towards Karl Liebknecht Strasse. They walked slowly and chattered about this and that; a motley crew of all ages and from all walks of life. Some wore the uniforms of their trade, proud to show they were butchers or carpenters or which VEB they worked for. Parents carried children who were too big to be carried. People gathered in small groups not so unlike ours: family members, friends, colleagues. Some recognised each other from a distance and waved.

It was such a warm atmosphere; a real sense of community.

This large group of people, individual and yet wholly together, was drawing power from its unity. Its collective strength grew with each step and with each person who joined the march. Banners were held aloft.

"Stay in the street and don't ease up."

"An end to SED dictatorship."

"Stasi be put to work in factories."

"We are the people."

Some banners were left at the steps of the Palace of the Republic, while candles and signs were placed in front of the Council of State building. The people had found their voice, their unity, their socialism. Andreas had been right. East Germany had never had real socialism; it was too tightly controlled and restrictive. Now, the people were walking without fear in collective protest, hopeful for the future and believing in the good qualities of mankind. This was the essence of socialism.

Andreas was beaming. He looked around at the happy faces of the crowd, talked to complete strangers, and laughed with old ladies who had lived through Nazism, Russian occupation and SED dominance, and who now had hope for a better future. Finally, they were going to get the society they had waited their whole lives for.

Alexanderplatz was full. We stood near the world clock because Monica hated crowds and Kathrin was apprehensive about going back into the centre of such a large group. We watched with concern as a small number of right wing extremists approached the crowd, but they soon dispersed and were lost in the throng. Nearby, I saw Heinrich and Andreas engaged in an animated conversation with three policemen. Heinrich lit a cigarette for one of them and they all laughed at something Andreas said.

The speeches began.

Markus Wolf was jeered down by the crowd. The ex-Stasi had good ideas and spoke plainly, but had no chance to reach the people because of his background. He represented the one institution the crowd wanted disbanded the soonest.

Schabowski was also jeered and whistled at. Kathrin told me he had reverted to the Berliner dialect halfway through his speech, tossing aside his notes and trying to reach the people with local language. He had limited success, but seemed to enjoy himself.

There were so many speeches. One after the other, writers and leaders of protests groups took the microphone to raise the call for reforms and liberalisation.

"Our society has little to do with socialism," said Christoph Hein. "Rather, it's a society marked by bureaucracy, demagogy, spying, illegal use of power, infantalisation of the population, and criminality."

"We want a socialism," cried Stefan Heym, "not a Stalinist one, but the right one, which we can finally build for our use, and for the use of all Germany. This socialism is unthinkable without democracy."

Heym received the loudest cheers. He was one of the few dissidents who had refused to emigrate, wanting instead to stay and try to change things. But he was now in his mid-seventies. If he had been younger, he could have been the leader the movement craved.

Jörn Weise reluctantly stepped to the podium. He looked the part with his handsome face and winning smile, but as always, he didn't want to occupy centre stage.

"Our rights are everything," he said, trying to sound sincere. "We must stand together and use our rights in front of our bosses and colleagues, in front of everyone, and stand with the person who uses these rights, and not step back and let them stand alone. Socialism is about the power of the people, to band together for common goals and to help each other. We have long been denied this and now have the chance to move towards real socialism. It is up to each and every one of us to make this happen."

The crowd cheered, but Jörn lacked the delivery and charisma required of a leader. Another speaker took his place and his words were lost in the jumble of prophetic phrases and calls for solidarity.

By early afternoon, it was all over. We walked as a group, still wearing our "No Violence" sashes, towards Monica and Heinrich's apartment; it was the closest.

"So, Mr. Party Man," I said to Andreas. "What do you think of that? Are we on the right road?"

Andreas nodded solemnly. "Smit, I never thought I'd live to see such a thing. We have just witnessed the socialism that Marx envisioned, and that all the leaders that followed him have preached but never delivered. All power belongs to the working class, but Stalin took that away, and made all other leaders do the same, so that the workers were just as oppressed as in any country. But now they're taking the power that's always been kept from them. The only problem is, half a million people can't govern. We need a leader."

"What about de Maiziere, Böhme, or Schnur?" Birgit asked. "We need a free election and then the people can decide who the leader shall be."

"Yes, but Andreas is right," Heinrich said, solemnly puffing a cigarette stub. "These men are politicians, but they aren't the socialists we need."

"And they come from the other political parties," Andreas explained. "The CDU and SPD, and they've been part of the National Front for forty years. How will these men be different from Krenz or Honecker?"

We didn't have an answer, and that same feeling of emptiness returned. There had been no question of the solidarity of the group on Alex but now, as a much smaller group, our doubts returned, and I wondered if the same was happening all over the city as people left the crowd and the strength of its unity behind. As individuals, they had been trained not to think beyond the standard ideology, and that they would be punished if they did. Now, it wasn't so simple to reject everything they had learned: the system which had removed the stigma of Nazism and replaced it with a new identity, a system which had nurtured their existence and given them almost everything they had needed. But the truth was always concealed, the society too tightly contained and restrictive. Two generations had been reared to be fully submissive, moulded by ideological training in the Young

Pioneers and Free German Youth, and constricted in adult life by the Stasi and by the collective fear of being forcibly excluded from society – an Asoziale.

How many generations would it take to undo this damage?

But we forgot our doubts as we popped the corks of Sekt bottles and toasted the future of the country. There was no going back now. Everyone was hopeful that a real socialism would come one day because the people believed in it strongly and there was a large enough movement campaigning consistently for its cause.

"To a socialist East Germany," Andreas said, lifting his glass. "And may all those party bastards rot in hell."

# Bornholmer Strasse

On Monday, people went to work like it was a normal day. They smiled to each other, didn't crowd to get on buses or trains, didn't honk the horns of their cars, and stopped to let children cross the street. It was a normal day, like any other I'd witnessed in my last eight years. The only difference was that the people were really shining. Their eyes were filled with hope for the future. Things were changing, and that change could be slow as long as it happened. Nobody rushed in the GDR; it was something I'd always liked. The people were prepared to wait patiently, as they did for products and car parts, for the changes to come. A revolution wasn't necessary. There would be no storming of the Palace of the Republic, no beheading of Krenz. This was peaceful, socialist change, and it would come about in time because everybody wanted it.

But Frau Professorin Preller was gone. I didn't know whether to rejoice or be concerned. Such a change in the faculty never happened without long explanations and also an immediate replacement. But nobody came to fill the drawers of Preller's empty desk. Even the students were concerned. This wasn't normal.

"Something is coming," Andreas said to me that evening.

We were jogging through Volkspark Friedrichshain, on his doctor's orders. Andreas wore a new red jogging suit that jiggled and bounced with every step because it was, quite amazingly, several sizes too big. He must have written an Eingabe to get that.

"I had a Politbüro member in the chair today," he continued. "He told me that things are really grim, economically, and also environmentally. The country is going under."

"Really? Preller wasn't at school today," I said between short breaths. It felt like my chest was going to explode. Nine years of bike riding hadn't made me fit.

"The Stasi witch?"

"Her desk was cleared out. She's gone."

"I thought you'd be happy about that. Maybe she's just gone shopping with Lady Honecker in Paris." Andreas stopped and doubled over, hands on knees, wheezing loudly. "Let's rest a minute, Smit," he breathed.

I grabbed him by the arm. The forearms were still firm. "We can rest at the top."

Reluctantly, he staggered after me and we climbed the Grosse Bunkerberg. Darkness was falling and heavy clouds were rolling in from the west. The faint shadow of distant rain could be seen over West Berlin and that meant it would rain here in half an hour.

At the top, Andreas collapsed against the wall. Steam rose from behind his neck and from where the jogging suit was open at the front.

"I don't know what the doctor was thinking," he said. "This is definitely bad for my health."

I laughed. "If it hurts, it must be healthy."

We stood in silence, catching our breath. The stitch in my side slowly began to fade.

"What do you mean about the country going under?" I asked. "All I ever hear is that East Germany is one of the world's top industrial countries."

Andreas smiled. His cheeks were bright red, and he already had small white flecks of dried salt on his eyebrows and in lines down the sides of his face.

"Smit," he said, "the party would've loved you. Don't believe everything you read. The economy is in the toilet. We've been taking loans from the west for years. It was the only thing that kept us going, the west money. Our currency is worthless. We can't import anything."

"So what does it mean? It sounds like we can't go on like this forever."

"You're right. The government will be forced to open the market and encourage some competition. But if you want my opinion, I think the government is going to implode. And," he looked up at the sky, "I also think it's going to rain."

"Right. Let's get moving." I started jogging on the spot. The mind was willing, but the body was struggling.

"There's never a taxi when you need one," Andreas said.

We jogged down the hill and into the darkness of the park, separating at the Brothers Grimm fountain.

\*\*\*

As in October, the changes came so fast, if you blinked you missed them. On Wednesday, the Council of Ministers resigned. The following day, the whole Politbüro resigned and the SED central committee began new elections. Nobody knew whether to celebrate or panic. All people knew how to do was to get up in the morning and go to work. They had no experience handling such radical change. But there were others who only wanted out, who flocked to the embassy in Prague hoping for the West German passport that would be granted to them once they were in that building, and others who headed for Hungary and the open border with Austria. The government was gone, people were trying to leave in droves, and those who remained didn't know what to make of it all. The solidarity and unity of November 4 seemed like a lost dream.

On Thursday, Andreas called me.

"Come over quick," he said. "You've got to see this."

We drove over to Prenzlauer Berg, and walked in just as the writer Christa Wolf appeared on the TV screen. There wasn't time for greetings.

"Dear fellow citizens, men and women," she began. "We are deeply disturbed. We see that daily thousands are leaving our land. We know that their mistrust in the renewal of our social well-being has been reinforced by a politics that has failed us right up to the last few days. We are aware of the impotence of our words compared with mass movements, but we have no other means than our words. Those who are now leaving deflate our hope. We ask you to remain in your homeland, stay here by us."

I felt Andreas's arm around my shoulder.

"What can we promise you? Nothing easy, but a useful life. No quick prosperity but participation in great changes. We want to work with democratisation, free elections, legal security and freedom of action. One cannot overlook the fact that decade old encrustations cannot be done away with in weeks. We stand now at the beginning of fundamental changes in our society. Help us to construct a truly democratic society, which also preserves the vision of a democratic socialism. We need you. Pull yourself together and come to us, to those of us who want to remain here. Trust."

Kathrin and Birgit wiped a few tears from their eyes. Andreas was also clearly moved. He stared at the screen from where this message of hope and solidarity had come. If only the people would listen and stay here, and not run to the west. It was so cowardly and selfish to run away from all our problems.

"I'm hungry," Jennifer said, pulling at her mother's pants.

We stayed for dinner. The mood was sombre, the conversation stilted. If we didn't trust our fellow people, who could we trust? Why did they keep leaving, aiming for whatever gap existed to get out of the country, to leave the mess to those who stayed? Socialism was about believing in the positive qualities of man, the strength of collective effort, the power of community, and yet these people left a sinking ship with no thought for those they left behind.

Bereft of things to say, we began to reminisce. Birgit told the story of how she and Andreas had met at a Free German Youth camp when they were only fourteen.

"Andreas had just had his Jugendweihe," Birgit said, "and he was feeling pretty good about himself."

The Jugendweihe was the traditional ceremony when society marks the transition from child to adult.

"I thought she was part of the process," Andreas said innocently. He turned to me and said loud enough for everyone to hear, "She made a man of me that summer."

Birgit laughed and turned scarlet. She retaliated with stories of the disaster that was Andreas on skis. We had once gone together to Thüringer Wald and all laughed remembering Andreas barrelling down the mountain, shouting with enjoyment, leaving a trail of frightened kids in his wake, only to crash into tree or a bush to stop himself.

Or the time we went together to the Baltic Sea and Andreas and I had taken Jennifer out in a small sailboat, only for the wind to die after an hour.

"We had to paddle all the way back with our hands," Andreas said, laughing and slapping me on the shoulder.

"I don't remember that," said Jennifer.

"You were too young," Kathrin said softly.

"But I remember Uncle Andy falling through the ice on the Müggelsee," Jennifer said proudly.

We were skating a few weeks after Christmas. Andreas was finally getting the hang of it. He tried a small spin in the air and landed it successfully, throwing his arms out like a professional. But as he hit the ice there was a loud crack. His look of triumph turned to worry. He looked down at his feet and then disappeared into the water.

"I have never been so cold in my whole life," Andreas said.

"It took three men to pull you out," Birgit said. "You were completely blue."

"The stupid thing was that the jump was great. Who knew what jumps I could've made if the ice hadn't destroyed my confidence? I could have given up dentistry for a career as a professional ice dancer."

Our laughter was interrupted by the telephone. Birgit got up to answer it.

"It's Monica," she called to Kathrin.

What followed could only be described as the most animated and excited of phone calls.

"Come on," Kathrin said. She hung up the phone and threw on her jacket. Her eyes were wide with excitement and disbelief.

"Where are you going?" I asked.

"We've got to get to Bornholmer Strasse." Her hands shook as she fastened the zip of her jacket. Her face was pale, but her mouth was formed in a smile of expectation. "The checkpoint is open."

We rushed downstairs, pulling on jackets as we ran. The five of us squeezed into Andreas's Wartburg. Jennifer sat on my lap; her hair smelled of apples.

None of us could talk.

We didn't make it all the way to the checkpoint because the streets were too full. We abandoned the car in the traffic and joined the others converging on the bottleneck crossing, walking up the hill to the bridge. In this part of the city, the railway line divided east and west.

"What happened?" I asked Kathrin. "What did your mother say?"

"It was on the news, our news, but she didn't believe it until she watched the west news," Kathrin said breathlessly, almost too excited to talk. "There's a new travel law. Schabowski read it out. We can go to West Berlin. We can get passports. We can go anywhere we want."

"We're not the only ones," Andreas said. He was tall enough to see over the crowd that had gathered at the Bornholmer Strasse checkpoint. People were talking to each other, asking complete strangers if it was true, and shouting towards the checkpoint to raise the barrier. Kathrin scanned the crowd for her parents.

"The border's closed," Andreas said. "But the Grepos aren't pushing anyone back. If they don't do something soon, they could have a big problem on their hands."

"Let's pull back," Birgit said. "Get out of this crowd."

More people arrived behind us and the crowd started to squeeze together in a bid to get closer to the crossing. It was a tense atmosphere, one that could quickly turn dangerous if the people were denied.

"No," Kathrin said firmly. "We have to stay. They can't turn us back now."

Suddenly, the crowd started to move forward, then it surged. Shouts of delight carried over the crowd. People were pouring across the bridge and through the open checkpoint. A few guards were trying to move a concrete barrier out of the way to allow faster passage. People passed them, ignoring their requests for help, interested only in getting west. Andreas and I stopped to help. Together, we pushed the barrier aside, and shook hands with the Grepos. They were young and didn't seem to comprehend what was happening.

What was happening? We suddenly found ourselves in West Berlin. Two men next to us popped a cork and poured Sekt into plastic cups, spilling most of it on the ground or pouring too fast so that it fizzed out of the cup and onto our cold fingers.

"Welcome to West Berlin," one of them shouted raising his cup.

We cheered, but the two men turned to give Sekt to the next people. All around was the sound of popping corks and cheers. The warmth of the crowd heated the cold night.

A man came rushing up next to me, grabbed my shoulder and shouted, "Where's the Ku'damm?"

I shrugged my shoulders and he went to ask the next person, in the hope of finding a West Berliner.

More people poured across the bridge and converged on the checkpoint. Trabis forced their ways through the crowd. People cheered and clapped. Some got in the cars while others sat on the front and back. Complete strangers embraced. People once divided mixed tears with Sekt and said over and over words like crazy and unbelievable, and shook their heads with disbelief.

A man leaned out the window of his Trabant and said to a photographer, "I'm taking the old crank straight to Kurfürstendamm."

And still more poured through the checkpoint, pushing us further into the west.

Behind me, I heard one West Berliner say to another, "My God, they look so poor."

I held Jennifer's hand, which was lost in my big gloves; she had forgotten hers in the rush to leave the apartment.

"This is just incredible," Andreas shouted, looking over the crowd. He held Birgit close to him as they walked. Tears streamed down her cheeks. "Never thought I'd live to see this. Where are we, Smit?"

"Wedding."

The streets were dirty and littered with scraps of paper, broken glass and scrunched up beer cans. At a nearby bus stop, a rubbish bin had been turned upside down and rummaged through, and the glass of the bus stop had been smashed and lay in a mess on the ground. The buildings were concrete and decrepit, and they reminded me of the decaying neighbourhood around the Reeperbahn in Hamburg.

My senses were inundated with neon lights, brightly lit shop windows and pictures telling me to drink Coca-Cola, smoke Malboro and wear Levis.

The West Berliners were there in as great a number as us, and they came out with bottles of Sekt and arrogant faces. A few enterprising people were selling alcohol from the boots of cars, while others were leaning out the windows of their apartment buildings and shouting. But there was something mocking and superior in their manner, the way priests welcome sinners to a church. They were ready to rescue us and forgive all that we'd done wrong if we admitted our mistakes and accepted their way. I could see in Kathrin's expression that she was seeing this as well. But the majority didn't see the negative side. They marched through the checkpoint with wide, greedy eyes, ready to make true all the visions they had harboured about the west; those myths generated by television and fantasy. They didn't see the crime hidden in the dark and narrow side streets, the drug addicts and drunks cowering in doorways, their hands open for scraps of loose change, or the people that capitalist society ate up and spat out every day. They came through with hungry, expectant eyes, pressed their faces up to the shop windows, marvelled at the bright lights and drooled on the VWs and BMWs parked in long lines down both sides of the street. Greeted by bottles of Sekt and rich Wessis, they firmly believed these streets were paved with gold.

"It would've been better to have crossed at a nicer part of the city," Kathrin said quietly to me.

She looked around the crowd with disdain and I wondered if she was thinking all the same thoughts as me: that these people were crossing the border, not with surprise or disbelief, but with a look of intent that said they didn't want to go back.

I had sudden visions of people camping on the lawn in front of the West German Embassy in Prague, climbing the walls to get inside, fighting and pushing to be first; and others who rushed to the Austria-Hungary border intent on getting west. They left their posts at factories, walked out of classrooms in the middle of lessons and abandoned their beloved Trabis on the side of the road. They left behind young children, distressed wives and confused families, all because they held so fast to an ideal that was built on fantasy.

I saw the crowd on Alexanderplatz just last Saturday, united in protest, solidarity and socialism, hopeful for a brighter future, realising the power of their collective voice and believing that things would get better, that we could have a real socialism. It was up to us to make it happen, not the politicians. That was what socialism was all about. And now, those same people pushed and shoved in a desperate hope to get out before the border, which had just magically opened, closed just as quickly.

Everyone was talking about the new travel law Schabowski had read out on television. East Germans could apply for passports and travel to the west. And yet here stood thousands in the west all without passports. The wall was now redundant, and I thought then that the state policy of travel restrictions may have been the right policy after all. Could the GDR have succeeded as a country without the wall?

"Daddy, I'm tired," Jennifer said, rubbing her wet nose with one of my big gloves. Her cheeks were flushed red from the cold, for she had also forgotten her warm hat. None of us were prepared. "Can we go home now?"

Kathrin and I exchanged a look and a secret code that came from being together so long. We had seen enough. People were getting drunk fast, the crowd was continuing to build, and the situation could quickly turn from reverie to danger. But more than anything, the people, my comrades, disgusted me; because they had so quickly changed teams, all to satisfy their own selfish desires. There would be no real socialism because these weren't the people who could achieve it.

"We're going to take Jennifer home," Kathrin said to Birgit and Andreas. "She's really tired."

"But you can't leave now," Birgit shouted. "We're in the middle of history."

"Don't worry," I said. "This is only the beginning."

Andreas eyed me slyly. His smile turned to a frown and I felt he was reading my thoughts. All around us were the voices and shouts of celebrating people.

"You look like you carry the world on your shoulders, Smit," he said while Birgit and Kathrin had a long hug. "You think the people won't return. Sure, I'm thinking the same, but you have to remember that most of these people didn't think they would live to see the west at all."

"Seeing it is one thing, worshipping it is another."

"I would have thought that by now you would understand the Germans better," he said smiling. "We have Wanderlust, the desire to travel, to see new places and experience new things. The GDR took that away, forcing us to take holidays to Bulgaria and Romania with limited currency, and succeeded in locking up our adventurous spirit. But it's free now and the people will venture down new streets and into new lands."

"But what about our country," I said angrily. "How can they be so willing just to leave it behind, especially after what's happened the last few weeks. The people can see it, sure, but do they have the ability to be critical of it. They only know the west from television."

"True," Andreas said nodding. "But you must remember that Berlin suffered the most from the division of Germany, the way a man does when he loses his legs in a car accident, and then tries to live without them. This is what happened to Berlin. The wall cut us in half. And now we have woken up with our legs again and just want to run and run."

"Yeah, they'll run right to the west and never come back."

Andreas put a large arm around me. "Smit, have faith in the people. A man who gets his legs back loses the novelty of having them again. Even the most amazing things become less amazing with time."

I wanted to believe him, but couldn't. We left Andreas and Birgit behind. I turned to look at them one last time and perhaps wave, but they were busy buying beer from the back of a Volkswagen. As we fought against the crowd still pouring through the checkpoint, I felt I was swimming against the tide. My whole world was under threat. My life was here. The past few weeks had renewed my passion for the country, its system and its people. But as they shoved through the checkpoint, pushing me and my family aside, eyes filled with the desire not for travel but for blue jeans, expensive cars, unlimited supply, bananas, coffee, and all the wealth that was before only a thirty-metre death strip away, it felt as though my world was about to come crashing down.

I gripped the hands of my family and led them through the burgeoning crowd, each face more eager and greedy than the last.

Beyond Bornholmer Strasse, the streets were deserted, except for all the cars that had been abandoned. It seemed the whole city was drinking west Sekt and pressing their noses against shop windows. But what would happen tomorrow? Would people pile their possessions onto carts and push them out of East Berlin and into the west, refugees from the Cold War? Would there be anyone left to drive the trains and buses, to add up the groceries in the supermarkets and deliver the mail?

There were too many uncertainties.

We got home and went to bed. I lay awake staring at the dull grey ceiling wondering what the next days would bring. Kathrin snored. Outside, there was silence. Cars normally chugged along Leninallee at all hours. The silence was eerie, and I lay there longing for the familiar putter of a Trabant, knowing this simple sound would put me to sleep. But it didn't come, and I lay there for hours, watching my nine years in the GDR play like a movie in my head. There was a sinking feeling that everything was slipping away, like a movie fading to darkness, and then the credits rolled.

\*\*\*

The next day was Friday. Most people went to work, but there were still long lines at the checkpoints. Half of my classes were empty. The remaining children could only talk about going to West Berlin tomorrow.

Kathrin and Jennifer spent that Saturday in the deserted Volkspark. But I joined Andreas and Birgit and ventured into West Berlin. Thomas said on the phone he would meet me under the ruined tower of the Gedächtniskirche at eleven, to have brunch together. The train was packed. There was an atmosphere of excited children on a day trip to Disneyland. People laughed too loudly, spoke too quickly, took short, jumpy steps to get on and off trains, and were swept away by the collective euphoria. They came from all over the GDR to experience West Berlin. Kurfürstendamm was so full it had been turned into a pedestrian mall. Long lines of people stretched out of the banks as the

Ossis queued for the one hundred D-Mark Welcome Money that the West German government had promised. We joined the back of the line. The people stood patiently, making jokes that it was just another Wartekollektiv; because you often had to wait in line for things in the GDR.

People came out of the bank clutching their precious west money, holding the notes to the sun to see if they were real, admiring their colour, strength and value, and imagining all the wonderful things they could buy. They didn't understand that a hundred didn't go as far in the west as it did in the east. By the time we reached the front of the line, the bank tellers had turned from polite to disgruntled and were sure to be surly by the end of the day. The people just kept coming, throwing out their hands for the free money, further cementing the idea that this was the richest place on earth, where they could afford just to give money away. But the look on the teller's face when she gave me the crisp notes was take it and get out.

We stood outside the bank, wondering where to go and how to spend the money.

"Pretty smart," Andreas said, looking at the money. "They welcome us with their money and then we pump it back into their economy."

Once in the moving throng, we were forced to go with the flow and ended up inside the famous department store, KaDeWe, the Kaufhaus des Westens. The East Germans looked like foreigners in a distant land. Their look, manner and behaviour were completely different to that of their West German brothers. But in amongst the happiness and joy, there was suppressed contempt, a scepticism and suspicion. The West Berliners were looking down at the visitors, and it was clear from the beginning that shoppers were only interested in looking and trying, and not in buying. They wouldn't part so quickly with their west money, knowing what they could buy with that money in East Berlin. They picked up expensive items, fondled them in their hands and gasped at the incredible array of foods, especially the chocolates. They tried on designer clothes, laughed at themselves in the mirror, and didn't listen to the shop assistants who asked them not to touch expensive jewellery or to test every kind of perfume. Free chocolate samples were gone within the minute, and laughter rang through this huge department store, for they were sure at some point there would be an announcement ordering them to leave, calling the joke's end, and they would trudge back to East Berlin. It was all too unreal and fantastic. But price tags brought people back to reality, and they pushed that precious money deeper into their pockets.

I left Andreas and Birgit in the fashion section of KaDeWe. They were marvelling at the range of fashionable clothes in their sizes. GDR clothes, while cheap and strong, were never very flattering, nor did they come in a wide range of sizes. Birgit always had a tough time buying clothes. She looked forlornly at herself in the mirror, dressed in black slacks that accentuated the length of her legs, and not their width. My departure was barely recognised.

I found Thomas on the steps of the ruined church tower, his face turned to the sun. He wore leather gloves, a thick scarf and a look of contempt. I came from behind him so he didn't know I was there until I was right next to him. I followed his gaze down the Ku'damm. It looked like Hay Street Mall on a Saturday in Perth. Row upon row of slightly bobbing heads. I wondered how it was possible for so many people to walk in such a small space without constantly bumping into each other.

"Don't worry," I said, making him jump. "They won't stay forever."

He turned with a start, running a nervous hand through what was left of his hair and then embraced me awkwardly. We had last seen each other in the summer last year, when Thomas had stayed the night at our apartment. A new law passed that year had made such a visit possible. He'd left on a rather sour note, arguing with Kathrin that Jennifer looked so dowdy in her cheap dresses; that she was such a pretty little girl, western clothes would do her much more justice. Kathrin had taken this as a personal insult, thinking that Thomas was referring to her and only using Jennifer as cover.

"I was just looking for you in the crowd," he stammered, forcing a weak smile and, as always, standing too close.

"Don't we all look the same?" I asked. Thomas had said such a thing before my first venture into East Berlin.

"You'll always be different, Michael," he said, trying to laugh. "You were never like them."

I looked over the crowded street. People waved and shouted, called to people they recognised, and showed other family members the things they had bought. The smell of Trabi exhaust pervaded the air.

"You're right. I'm not like them. It takes more than free money to make me change my allegiance."

223

Thomas frowned as he looked back over the crowd. There were so many people.

"Don't pity them," I said. "And don't look down on them. They're the result of their system just like you are."

"Come on, Michael," Thomas said, our shoulders touching. "Let's not fight. Let's enjoy the time here. You never know. This may not happen again."

I nodded. "It won't happen like this. The people will still come, but not like this."

I felt sad, and all of a sudden, old, as if the last nine years hadn't registered in my mind or body, and had just caught up because I'd come back to the starting point, allowing reflection. Being in West Berlin was a step backward. Levis and BMWs and McDonalds for a day weren't going to fix the problems in the GDR. They would only compound them. The strict control of the GDR state had succeeded in a rearing a generation of capitalists, whose main characteristic was desire. In denying the people travel and goods, they only grew to want them more. Like anything unattainable, you dreamed harder to have it, desired it more, made it seem that life would only be complete when you had what you were denied. The East Germans would trade their new Trabis for a used Mercedes in a minute, and give up their system for another one simply to satisfy their built up desires.

"I know a good place to have brunch close by," Thomas said, walking down a few steps to get me moving.

"Just get me away from here."

My bitterness and anger surprised me. I had no faith in the people after all. Andreas had told me to believe in them, Christa Wolf had urged everyone to trust, but the reality was completely different. This was no day trip to Disneyland. This was the future. Once they'd had a taste of the things available on these golden streets, the East Germans would never be able to go back to the way things were. And socialism couldn't offer, or compete with, such abundance and over supply; such glamour.

Two corners away from Ku'damm and we were practically alone. We sat in an empty cafe at Los Angeles Platz. Thomas knew one of the waiters. They were friendly with each other. The waiter seemed always to have a hand placed lightly on Thomas's shoulder, and at one point, he sat down to drink a cup of coffee and smoke a cigarette. They acted like a couple. Christoph was thin with slicked back hair and a pencil neck. He complemented me on my German, but looked at my clothes with distaste. I was an Ossi and the minute he had identified me as such, started to become snobbish and superior. He had been to Australia and was flabbergasted that I'd moved to East Germany when I'd been born in paradise. He had a high pitched whine of a voice that went up an octave when he spoke with disbelief.

"It is the most astonishing thing I've ever heard," he said. Thomas put a hand on his shoulder and tried to calm him, but Christoph wouldn't let up. "You have no idea how lucky you are to be from Australia. What I would give to live there."

"Well, the next time you're there, I hope you meet my father," I said, keeping my voice even and calm. "He doesn't like Germans so much. But I'm sure he'd make you feel welcome."

Christoph formed his mouth into a round circle of shock. His eyebrows almost reached his hairline; he looked like animal about to be hit by a car at night.

"So, don't look down your nose at me," I said. "Everywhere in the world there are good people and bad, and just because their clothes aren't as good as yours or because they don't have as much money in their pockets doesn't make them any less human than you."

"Come on, Michael," Thomas said softly. "Let's just enjoy our brunch." His quiet voice made me realise I had shouted. Christoph look startled and defenceless.

But I didn't like the breakfast. The potatoes were like paper and too salty, and I felt like I gained a kilo with every small amount of butter I smeared on my bread.

"Don't you get it, Thomas?" I said. "Things will never be the same again. How are all of these people going to go back to their old lives after today?"

"Their lives are being enhanced," Christoph said grandly.

"What, with crime, drugs, poverty, selfishness and greed? Are these the positive qualities of man?"

"It's also like that in East Berlin," Thomas said. He didn't like the discussion. He moved uneasily in his chair, leaning back as if threatened.

"No it isn't, and I'll tell you why. Because we never had anything to fight over. People have what they need. Why go and steal the same thing from someone else? West society makes people want what others have, with everything always just out of reach for most people."

Thomas and Christoph looked at each other, sharing the intimate communication of an old couple.

"I'm sorry," I said. "It's just that this time last week, I stood on Alexanderplatz and I really felt that the people would prevail, that life would be changed for the better. But I can't see that happening now. The west has bananas and that means the life here is better."

Thomas and Christoph laughed, but I didn't. I heard Christoph mumble "Banana Republic" and watched him try to suppress his giggles. I wanted to hit him. Instead, I stood up and placed the hundred Mark on the table.

"I think you can use this more than me. Maybe you can buy yourself a new personality," I said to Christoph. "I don't need your money. I have enough."

I walked out of the cafe and through the suburb of Schöneberg, negotiating streets I hadn't seen for such a long time. Cars were newer, the odd building renovated, but nothing much had changed. I got lost, but didn't ask for directions. Everyone looked at me. They spoke to each other in whispers while pointing at me. My clothes gave me away. I was an Ossi. I walked without rushing, spoke slowly, took my time with everything. I was poor, looked unhealthy, grey, dull, stupid, useless, desperate for bananas. Like the East Germans entering the west with stereotypes, so too did the West Berliners see what they wanted to see. After forty years of separation, they were happy to discover they were still superior.

Checkpoint Charlie was crowded with tourist buses, border crossers and journalists. History was being made and duly recorded for prosperity. But what will history say about this day, about Thursday night, when the wall was breached? "Victory for the west in the Cold War." "The Russians are defeated and evil communism can be swept away." "Coca-Cola trucks can drive safely to Moscow, McDonalds can build restaurants in Prague, and East Berlin can be sold to its rich brothers."

We had come so close. After forty years, the GDR got just one day of real socialism. I turned away from Checkpoint Charlie.

Further down, at the Heinrich Heine Strasse border crossing, the people carried large shopping bags full to the brim with all the things they could never buy in East Berlin. The bags were plastic, brightly coloured and showed where the products had been bought. Others carried big boxes: televisions, computers, stereos. The border guards laughed and joked, looking forward to their days off when they too could venture west and spend their free money.

But the people spoke little with each other, and clutched their bags tighter if they saw someone looking at their purchases or in their direction. For the first time, people feared each other. Having spent their whole lives in fear of the state and the Stasi, they had never had to fear their neighbour. Now, people walked with priceless goods and felt insecure and threatened by those who watched them. They ducked into their apartment buildings and closed the door behind them.

I walked with my head down, avoiding eye contact and suspicious looks. I came out of the west empty handed. What valuable item was I concealing? The future held crime-filled streets.

I crossed Jannowitzbrücke and walked under the over-ground train line towards the tall, white, pre-set concrete apartment blocks that loomed over Alexander Strasse and Holzmarkt. Strausberger Platz, that glorious three-lane roundabout that was built along with Karl Marx Allee as a visible demonstration of the success of communism, was in decay. Tiles had fallen from the facades. Windows that had been smashed but never replaced were sealed with plastic and tape. And one lone old man sat on his narrow balcony drinking vodka straight from the bottle, small steam clouds accompanying each swig. Further along, Lenin, carved from red stone, looked over the square of his own name, that stern look of determination on his face. But today, he looked more sombre than usual, almost placid, as if he knew the comrades had given up and the revolution was over. The red defiance was gone. The progression of capitalism to communism to socialism had somehow been derailed and we were regressing back to where we had started. Poverty, unemployment, crime, insecurity, hunger and class division would all come to East Germany. I wondered if a single red tear might trickle down Lenin's face should the Eastern Bloc completely crumble like it was threatening to do.

Jennifer and Kathrin were on the swings in the deserted Volkspark playground. They climbed higher and higher until their heads were level with the cross bar. I heard Kathrin tell Jennifer to be careful, but she too kept trying to swing higher, that perhaps together they could fly off the earth, if they went high enough. I sat on a bench behind them and watched. They both wore headbands to cover their ears, but their hair was loose at the back, and it rose and fell with each swing. They could have been sisters; Kathrin still looked so young.

She remained one of the top swimmers in her club, while Jennifer had taken to the pool like a fish. How they both loved the water, like a pair of mermaids wasting time on land until they could once more be wet.

Jennifer started to sing an Australian song I had taught her, one I had learned long ago at primary school. She used the swing for rhythm. Kathrin knew the words too and joined in with the first chorus:

"Click go the shears boys, click, click, click, wide is his blow but his hands move quick."

I moved around in front of them and took up the next verse, clapping time with my hands. They smiled and then all three of us sang the chorus. At the end, Jennifer leapt from the swing and hugged me, her thin arms strong around my legs. Kathrin followed and kissed me on the cheek.

"How was it?" she asked, seeing the sadness in my eyes.

I sighed, and looked from my wife down to my daughter. They looked so similar, especially now that Jennifer's hair was long enough to cover the sticking out ears she had inherited from me.

"It's much better here," I said.

"And Thomas?"

"I've got some news for you. Thomas is gay. I met his boyfriend."

"I know. I met Christoph before we went to Hilde's party." She smiled, thinking the whole thing rather funny. "But you always knew." She showed me her crossed over teeth in a sly smile.

"I had a feeling, but I would never have said such a thing until I was sure. Why didn't you say something?"

"Well, with you being a real man's man, I wasn't sure if you could handle it."

"You're probably right. It's not exactly a common thing where I'm from."

"Daddy, what does gay mean?" Jennifer asked.

"You want to field that one?" I asked Kathrin. She shook her head. I turned to Jennifer, getting down on one knee. "Well, sometimes, boys only want to play with boys, and not with girls."

"It's like that at kindergarten."

"I'm glad to hear to that," I said, knowing one day my little girl was going to be a heartbreaker like her mother.

Kathrin laughed. "Come on. Let's go home and have something to eat. It's cold out here." She turned to Jennifer. "Maybe later we can go to the pool."

Jennifer cheered and skipped ahead as Kathrin and I followed arm in arm. It was so quiet in the park you could hear the chirps of birds in the trees and the rustle of rabbits in the bushes. There was peace here, comfort and security, and I wished then that time could have stopped. The winter sun went behind a cloud and a cold wind rushed down the wind tunnel made by the row of trees on either side of the path. It prickled my skin and found its way up my pants and down the back of my shirt. The wind blew from the west, and it chilled me and made me shudder.

At our building, I saw Thilo doubled over his motorbike in the small car park. He pumped the accelerator, but the engine sputtered and stalled.

"What's the problem?" I asked.

He wiped his hands on his overalls and sighed. He looked sad and tired, like an overworked and underpaid labourer, an old coal miner staggering out of the mine after pulling a double shift.

"I'm still waiting for a new part," he said. "I was down at the shop today, but they didn't have what I needed."

He sighed again and stared at his bike, but with frustration and not the usual love.

"You could go over to West Berlin and buy what you need."

"I don't want any west products." He spat the word west. His negative demeanour didn't suit him, and it was a side of his character I'd never seen.

"Well, you'll just have to wait then," I said.

"The bike is like our country," he said softly, "beautifully made and wonderful when it works, but with one or two vital things missing that make the difference between a bike that runs well and one that doesn't. And no matter how much work you do, the bike will never work without those missing parts."

"I guess that's the thing about life. You do the best you can with what you have."

"Yes, but what we have now is not what we'll have next week, next month, or next year. Our world is changing. The Wessis are going to overrun us now the wall is open."

I agreed with him, but something in the conversation had cast me in the role of offering reassurance, that Thilo was looking at me to tell him that everything was going to be all right; that his job was safe and the world wouldn't change as dramatically as he feared. I opened my mouth to speak, to offer words of encouragement and security, but nothing came out. Thilo sighed and bent back over his motorbike. He could polish the metal as much as he wanted, but that wouldn't make up for the missing parts.

# Wende

Erich Mielke was the head of the Stasi. Like Honecker, Hermann, Mittag and ex-Prime Minister Willi Stoph, he was part of the old guard, over eighty. Before the war he had been a young member of the communist party which had attempted to share power with Hitler after the failure of the Weimar Republic, so Andreas once told me. However, the Nazis decided to purge the Reichstag of its enemies and Mielke was forced to leave Germany and travel to Russia. At the same time, Honecker was put in prison and stayed there until the end of the war; he had never been shy about saying he had been a political prisoner.

With the resignation of the Politbüro and the Council of Ministers, Mielke was the last of the old guard remaining. He was a fossil of a man, in looks and manner. He also acted old, out of date, and his final speeches showed his senility. In his last address on the thirteenth of November to the People's Chamber, he shouted, "I love, I love everyone." He was laughed out of the building and out of the Stasi. He was the one responsible for the hate the people had for the Stasi, how lives had been invaded and destroyed for the benefit of national security. It was said that there were informers in every household, and in every office, school and factory. And it was towards the Stasi that people directed their hate, their desire for change and for the re-privatisation of their lives. The people claimed they were happy to continue with socialism as long as the Stasi were gone. People wanted to be able to speak freely, and not have to worry about whether their neighbour was informing on them.

Not disbanding the Stasi was Modrow's biggest mistake.

When Andreas phoned me to say Hans Modrow had been elected as interim Prime Minister, he was breathless with excitement.

"They took their time about it," he said, "but we've got him now and he'll take us in the right direction."

"I hope so."

I wanted to believe it, but I didn't think the people would be interested in Modrow. He was, after all, an old SED leader, and the public had lost faith in the party. The opposition movements were gathering force. The traditional parties, the Christian Democrats, Social Democrats and Liberals, were emerging from under the umbrella of the National Front and campaigning for their own cause, which wasn't socialism. The protest groups, like New Forum, had only wanted to instigate change and wouldn't be successful as political parties. They were artists, lawyers and writers, and not politicians.

In his inaugural speech, Modrow announced that the Stasi would be converted into the Office for National Security, headed by Major General Wolfgang Schwanitz, who had been Deputy Minister of the Stasi. The public recognised immediately that changing the name didn't change the function and this greatly affected Modrow's popularity.

But, under Modrow, things did begin to change for the better. A roundtable was set up to discuss the future of the GDR, and on the first of December, the People's Chamber voted out the SED's monopoly of power. Mielke was arrested and imprisoned. At the same time, people occupied the former Stasi district offices with the help of public prosecutors, as there was the fear that important documents would be destroyed. On the fifth of December, the staff of the Office for National Security stepped down. Things were really changing. The SED leaders were under house arrest in Wandlitz, and people still took to the streets in protest, calling for free elections and prosecution of SED leaders and Stasis.

The numbers venturing to West Berlin diminished with each passing week. It was so easy to spend money there, with the black market exchange rate fluctuating greatly, to the East Germans' disadvantage. But you couldn't be in West Berlin without hard currency. People took their children hoping to get another hundred Mark from the bank, or they used different identity cards. Worse, it was clear that the East Germans were houseguests who had worn out their welcome. What had been an incredible achievement of humanity was now being clouded by reality. The West Berliners looked down on their neighbours, and got tired of seeing them in the streets with their dull clothes and strange manner. After thirty years of separation, two very different cultures had emerged. Now, they were attempting to come together and it wasn't working. The East Germans were shy and quiet, keeping their children close to them and the family unit secure, taking strength from solid friendships and displaying great loyalty and community. These were characteristics foreign to West Berliners, and they kept themselves distant from the visitors, looking down their noses at them with scornful, insulting eyes.

The East Germans knew the west would only save them if they surrendered completely.

Kathrin and Jennifer weren't interested in seeing West Berlin. They visited Hilde once or twice with Monica, but stayed away from the temptations of shop windows. Kathrin had long ago seen the west and rejected it. Andreas on the other hand, was over there almost every second day. Sometimes, I went with him and we stood in a narrow street off the Ku'damm so Andreas to could change some money. The black market handlers were sly characters, wearing long, dark coats with hats low on their eyes. They always had a few friends lurking in the shadows. With the money, Andreas bought presents for Birgit, shopped for cars and looked at apartments. He knew that as a dentist, he could make a successful living in West Berlin. He could have a Mercedes and all the other valuable things the westerners had. His eyes were wide and eager with greed.

We started to drift apart and I went with him less. The jolly fat Andreas I had known for almost nine years was being replaced by a money-focused greed machine. The things we had always laughed about were no longer funny. He gave up on Modrow, left the party and looked west for salvation and satisfaction. I started to feel that he thought himself superior to me; with him a dentist and me just a lowly English teacher, and before that a simple mechanic. West society lent him a higher standing and he carried this back to East Berlin.

Letters from my family arrived. My father even wrote, in a brittle, broken English loaded with grammar and spelling mistakes. They all spoke about the images they saw on television of the wall coming down, the end of the Cold War, the triumph of capitalism and freedom over communism and oppression. Mum hinted that this event might even bring me home, that because communism was over, I had no reason to stay. But I had a family, friends, and a job, and I couldn't just abandon all of that. But these were petty excuses. In truth, a small part of me held onto the idea that socialism would prevail, that it was the better way and that after seeing the west and knowing they were no longer welcome there, the people would realise this.

The only problem was Modrow. He was likeable enough, a petit bourgeois, a member of the working class. But he did not have the charisma or the strength to rally the country behind him. He was an interim leader, a good man in the wrong situation, and he didn't seek power. His only ambition was to take East Germany to free elections. Then, he would step back and let the elected leader run the show.

233

His character was clearest on the twenty-second of December, when Andreas and I stood in freezing rain at Brandenburger Tor. West German Chancellor Helmet Kohl took centre stage while Modrow stood behind him looking like a secretary or aide. When he took the podium, his speech lacked delivery. The words were good, but he was no inspirational speaker. Kohl was more powerful, pushing the case for unification, and relishing this historic moment of opening the Brandenburg Gate. The crowd cheered for Kohl, heard his dream for a united Germany, and Modrow slinked into the background.

"I like Kohl," Andreas said clapping. "He knows what to do."

I looked at Andreas and then at Kohl. They could have been father and son, both fat men with big floppy faces, booming voices and dollar signs in their eyes. I swallowed the words I wanted to say, knowing they would fall on deaf ears. Kohl had western currency, promised financial aid, would rescue us, but only if we submitted and let ourselves be bought.

"The people like him as well," I said, my hands still deep in the pockets of my jacket.

Kohl raised his hands to the cheering public and was enveloped in the flashes of cameras. The crowd seemed to be made entirely of press and media, all here to record this victory of west over east. The fall of the wall, the one physical representation of east-west division, marked the end of the fight. The Americans had prevailed, and the cries of the red stone Lenin could be heard from Leninplatz all over eastern Europe and into the Soviet Union. The world that so many people had known, lived and died in, loved and laughed in, was soon to be gone, pushed into the propaganda-laden pages of history books and eventually forgotten.

The East Germans would give up their sovereignty for unlimited products, new cars, higher wages, promises and myths. The fall of the wall dashed our hopes for a real socialism. The world was changing, too fast, especially because for East Germans, change had always been predictable and slow. We were suddenly thrust into a world of insecurity, fear and change. It was all happening too fast. It was a slight shifting of snow on a peak that becomes an avalanche the further it slides down the mountain.

\*\*\*

Visa restrictions and minimum currency were lifted that Christmas. It meant that as many people went east as they did west. It was a unique Christmas, with some families seeing each other for the first time, meeting relatives they only knew by name or photograph.

Hilde came with Anjte, Thorsten and Thomas, and we had a large dinner at Monica and Heinrich's apartment. They brought lavish presents, expensive wines, rich chocolates and real coffee. We could not match them, and I saw in Monica's eyes envy towards her younger, uglier sister. Thorsten was now bald and had substituted his glasses for contacts. They seemed to magnify his eyes and made him look like a rabbit, because he also had long front teeth. Antje was overweight and trying to disguise it with dark clothes. Her skin had the orange tinge you could only get from artificial sun, and her hair was bleached. She looked sad and empty. Sometimes, her eyes became lazy and she locked onto an object and stared at it, seemingly oblivious to the world around her. Hilde was going strong, and had the same zest for life that Monica, Kathrin, and now Jennifer had. She spent almost all of her time that evening with her great granddaughter, as if trying to make up for lost time. Her eyes gleamed as she saw little bits of herself that had survived three generations: aqua blue eyes, tumbling hair and the using of a spoon with the left hand; small things that almost brought tears to her eyes.

All this was good, except that Heinrich wasn't well. This was clear to all of us, but he put on a good show for Christmas dinner. He had nothing in common with Thorsten and the two kept away from each other, yet competed for the role of leading male figure in the family. He drank too much and started to reminisce about the war, a subject that was seldom broached. He had been a teenager during the Battle of Berlin. He said that the street fighting had raged around his apartment building on Schönhauser Allee, and he'd helped his mother carry dead people off the road so that the tanks could move unhindered. His mother had been shot while she tried to help a boy trapped in the rubble. Heinrich wasn't sure if the shots had come from the Germans or from the Russians. She took the war bullet and became a statistic. Then, he was given a rifle and told to join the battle. Boys his age were collected into makeshift brigades, given baggy uniforms and heavy rifles, and sent out to keep the Russians at bay until the mighty weapons Hitler had promised would be ready. These weapons would end the war with the Nazis as victors. Drunk on expensive wine, Heinrich

235

forgot about Hilde's own past and delved into the concealed historical world of the Russian victory: the rape and pillaging, the stealing of machines, precious furniture and goods as war reparations, the mass graves of German soldiers near Oranienburg, and the thousands of German prisoners captured in Russia after Stalingrad. In his telling, the war had no winners; everyone was a victim.

Nobody spoke. They looked into their glasses or at the table to avoid eye contact with Heinrich. He had long ago told me all these stories one drunken night at his garden house in Rahnsdorf, when Kathrin and Monica had both fallen asleep. I was the only one who could look him in the eye. I had no guilt.

Heinrich continued, not caring whether anyone was listening or not, talking because these were things he had wanted his whole life to say.

"The Russians were an evil lot," he said, "but they helped us. They got what they wanted and as repayment gave bread and coal. I know you all think the wall was a mistake, but without it, East Germany would have crumbled. So many people were leaving every day. You could be waiting for the bus to work, but it wouldn't come because the driver had gone west before his shift had started. But worse, we lost the intellectuals of society, the ones who knew they could make it big in the west, but would be equal with factory workers if they'd stayed. If they'd been strong and stayed, then things would be very different today."

"We were happy only to see a wall," Hilde said. Everyone turned to her as she spoke. "There were always rumours that the Russians would invade. There wasn't anywhere near enough troops to defend the city. We lived with this threat every day. The wall made us relax, that we could live without guns under our pillows."

Heinrich smiled at Hilde, and the two shared a moment of having lived through one of the hardest times in Germany's history. They got comfort from each other.

Monica turned to Thomas in an attempt to ease the tense atmosphere. "Do you remember Christmas a couple of years after the wall went up?" she asked. "You were just a toddler. There were special visas that year. I waited at Oberbaumbrücke with a friend of mine and you went running to her screaming 'mummy, mummy', and wrapped your arms around her."

Thomas blushed as everyone laughed. Even Antje chuckled.

"I don't remember that," he said.

"Selective memory," Kathrin said.

"The sixties were good," Heinrich said wistfully. "Things improved so quickly. Everybody worked hard, drank together in the bars and helped each other. Everyone believed in the system. There was equality like never before."

"So what went wrong?" Thorsten asked.

Heinrich stared at Thorsten for a moment. The two men represented both the positive and negative qualities of each of the societies that had reared them.

"I'd say for most of the people, it wasn't enough. It was too limiting. They became obsessed with the idea of travel. And socialism caters for the every-man, and not for those who are more intelligent or motivated."

"The government was always too old," Monica added. "They had no new ideas, and they also lived in Wandlitz, distanced from the rest of the population."

"Things will get better now the wall's open," Thomas said. "The influence of the west will change East Germany for the better. And eventually the country will be one again. Kohl will make that happen."

"Don't be so sure, Thomas," Hilde said. "Europe fears a united Germany."

"Come on, Oma, that's years ago. Germany wouldn't start another war."

Thomas's words hung in the air, with no one wanting to agree or disagree, or even to comment. I didn't want a united Germany. East Germany had to stay sovereign and socialist, but this was a dream.

Heinrich excused himself and rose wearily from the table. Five minutes later he could be heard snoring on the couch. Hilde took the conversation in a lighter direction, asking questions of Kathrin, who was pregnant again. She wanted another girl, but I was keen for a son. Jennifer squirmed in her chair, uneasy about the coming sibling.

"And what about you, Thomas," Hilde said. "When are you going to bring home a nice young girl and add some great grandchildren to the mix?"

Thorsten smiled, Antje looked more grim and Thomas giggled.

"I'm working on it, Oma," he said. "I'll only give myself away to the right person."

"Yes, love comes around only once or twice," Hilde said, staring blankly at the table.

I knew her story from Monica. She had remained unmarried since her husband had been killed in the war. She and her sister Gertie had both lost their husbands. The images they preserved were their men in full Nazi uniform, bright eyed and handsome, and off to die for someone else's cause. At that moment, I felt very sorry for Hilde. She looked so sad and lonely, her life overshadowed and ruined for another's glory.

They left early. This was family, but you could see in their eyes they didn't like being in East Berlin. Thorsten mumbled something about wanting to beat the traffic and this was their cue. They wanted the safety and comfort of their own homes. Jennifer slept in a chair, her soft snore barely audible over Heinrich's wheeze. Kathrin and I sat with Monica at the small kitchen table drinking the real coffee that Thomas had brought. It was so strong, I thought it would keep me awake all night.

"How quickly the time passes," Monica said. "Thomas is almost thirty and he still hasn't told Hilde. And I don't think he ever will."

"Why don't you tell her?" Kathrin suggested.

"Thomas has to fend for himself." She paused, then said more forlornly, "I was never there for Thomas anyway, so I can't go fighting his battles for him now."

"It's a sign of weakness. He doesn't have the courage to tell her. He didn't even tell Michael. He guessed."

Monica looked at me and I nodded.

"I met his boyfriend back in November," I said. "What a slimy character."

"I'm not so interested in meeting him," Monica said spitefully. "I'm glad we don't have so many of those people here. Sure, we have them, but they keep themselves private. They flaunt it in West Berlin. It's disgusting."

Jennifer came into the kitchen rubbing her eyes, one half of her hair flattened from where she had rested it against the arm of a chair.

"Something's wrong with grandpa," she said slowly. "He's not snoring and his face is all red."

We leapt from our chairs and rushed into the living room. Heinrich lay on the couch, with his eyes closed, but his face was crimson and he was grimacing, as if holding his breath. Monica shook him and called his name, but he didn't stir. I checked his pulse and it fluttered weak and inconsistent.

"Come on," I said, throwing the heavy man over my shoulders. "We've got to get him to the hospital."

Monica went ahead to start the Trabant. They had a new one, the result of a joint project between Trabant and Volkswagen. You didn't have to open the bonnet to put petrol in this one, and it always started straight away.

It was cold outside and none of us had jackets or gloves. We put Heinrich in the front, and Kathrin, Jennifer and I huddled together on the back seat for warmth. Monica drove like a maniac. The whole way, Heinrich didn't stir, and his face was turning from red to purple. A white drool dribbled out of his mouth.

We stopped in front of the emergency section of Charité. Monica rushed inside while I bent over to pick up Heinrich. His face no longer held a grimace, and he was even smiling slightly. As I removed his seatbelt, he opened his eyes. They were bloodshot and heavy, but still clear. I thought I could see his soul, that in that one look he gave me all of his life's memories. I saw the ruined streets of Berlin, the long lines of heavy-jacketed Russian soldiers marching into the city with their red flags held high. I saw the protesters eight years later, the Russian tanks encircling them and firing without mercy. I saw barbed wire strewn along the ground marking the first divide of East and West Berlin. I saw the garden house at Rahnsdorf that Heinrich loved so much, with the wide expanse of the Müggelsee stretching into the distance, and the sailboats swaying and tipping in the wind. I saw myself, an old man struggling for breath and dying without dignity in a world I hated, longing only for the world of the past, for the youth I had taken for granted. I saw all the loose ends untied, business left unfinished, dreams forgotten.

Heinrich blinked slowly and forced his eyes open again.

"I'm tired," he murmured.

"Don't worry," I said. "We're at the hospital. You'll be alright. Just hang on."

He held me with his eyes. "Don't be so hard on Monica," he said. "She did what was best."

I picked him up and carried him into the hospital. He felt lighter than before. Inside, I dropped him on a gurney and two doctors went immediately to work. Monica tried to stay beside the gurney, but the nurses dragged her back. She wailed after Heinrich until Kathrin took her into a hard embrace and tried to calm her.

We sat for hours in the waiting room. Jennifer was asleep, using my thigh for a pillow. A nurse had brought her a blanket. It was grey and itchy, like a prison blanket.

I knew that Heinrich was dead, and I thought the delay in informing us caused only more pain and frustration. But I couldn't say this to Kathrin or Monica. So, like them, I maintained false hope, offered words of encouragement and played out my role as the supportive male.

The doctor was tall and young. He had a full beard that was supposed to make him look older, but only removed him from this time. He looked more like a doctor from a century ago, when all men wore beards and smoked pipes.

With one look at his face, Monica fell into Kathrin's arms, and they cried and rocked together. Jennifer woke up and joined them. I shook the doctor's hand.

"I'm sorry," he said. "He fought really hard, but if it wasn't today, then it wouldn't have been much longer."

"Thank you," I said. "Merry Christmas," I added, trying to smile.

The doctor nodded and smiled grimly. "Our last one, I think."

He shook my hand again and then left. I sat down, buried my face in my hands and started to cry.

\*\*\*

The sky was overcast, with heavy grey clouds that promised neither rain nor snow, only darkness. We gathered at the small cemetery in Eberswalde. Heinrich's brother Frank was there with his family. His daughter Christine was heavily pregnant with my godchild and with her were her five children of assorted ages, shapes and sizes. The children looked at the coffin with bemusement, each trying to comprehend the nature of death, dealing with their first confrontation with their own mortality. Rudi's absence was clearly visible as Christine struggled to keep her younger kids under control.

Heinrich lay next to his mother's grave. On her headstone were the details of Werner König, Heinrich's father, killed at Stalingrad in 1942.

The funeral was brief. After, a small collection of us went to Frank's house for coffee and cake. It was a quiet gathering until each told a story, a memory, which signified Heinrich for them. I went first.

"We were driving on a forest road out near Fürstenwalde," I began,

240

my voice dry and croaked. "An old man was on the side of the road with the bonnet of his Trabi open. Heinrich pulled over and joined the man at the front of the car. Heinrich knew cars so I went behind a tree to relieve myself. When I came back the man was shaking Heinrich's hand, then he got into his car and drove off. I asked Heinrich what the problem was. 'Broken fan belt,' he said. 'You had a spare?' I asked him incredulously. He shook his head and smiled. I looked under the open bonnet and saw that he had taken the fan belt from his own car and given it to the man. That was Heinrich. Knowing him made me a better man."

The others around me shared their stories, and we all felt better for them. Monica was the only one too distressed to talk, but I knew she got comfort from the memories.

\*\*\*

Monica spent New Year in West Berlin with Hilde. Kathrin and I decided to decline Andreas and Birgit's invitation to join them at Brandenburg Gate. We didn't feel like celebrating just yet. Kathrin was completely shocked by her father's death. As a family, we withdrew from the world and spent several quiet days just with each other.

It turned out to be a good decision. The historic new year's celebration got completely out of control, with many people injured in the crush around Brandenburg Gate.

Andreas told me the next day things had started very well, with people from both sides of the wall mixing together and celebrating. The GDR flag was taken down from the gate, the emblem removed, then raised again, looking like the German flag. Everyone cheered and the atmosphere was warm and friendly. Then the European Union flag went up, followed by the Canadian flag, which confused everybody, Andreas said. People climbed onto the gate using nearby scaffolding. The scaffolding collapsed and many were injured and some killed. Because there were so many people, it was hard to get the injured out of the scene. Andreas confessed that he had never felt more scared or threatened. This drunken mob, out of control, without law, like vicious animals let off the leash. He said they'd been lucky to get out unhurt.

It was a sobering event for all. Such a thing never would have happened in the GDR. It was because of the west that things had got so out of hand.

The days passed. Life started to get back to something like normal. The hole that Heinrich left slowly got smaller.

When school started again, we still had no replacement for Preller. One of the senior teachers had temporarily taken over the position until a new principal arrived. Half the teachers were missing. Those who remained had to pick up the slack. Classes increased in size and nobody was happy about it.

One day, Andreas visited me at the school. With fewer teachers, the days were long and hard, and worse was to come. I felt drained, doing the work of three people. Tomorrow, the thirteenth of January, was the last shopping day before the prices in East Germany were to be set to West Germany levels. The GDR was dying a slow and miserable death. The roundtable discussions were steering us closer to unification.

I sat at my desk. Andreas sat at the first table in front of the desk, squeezing himself onto the small chair. In his hand he held a small piece of paper.

"You know about this?" he asked, waving it in the air. I shook my head. "They're going to try to occupy the Stasi headquarters in Lichtenberg. Like what's been done in all the other cities."

"I guess it was just a matter of time. Are you going?"

"Of course," he said loudly. "I want my file."

"What are you talking about?"

"The Stasi has a file on everyone, and I want mine. I thought maybe you would want to come and get yours as well."

"Why would I have a file?"

"Maybe Preller had some things to say about you, and Lemke. And remember, you were involved in New Forum from the beginning. Kathrin is sure to have a file. And Monica too, because she's originally from West Berlin."

We were silent for a moment. Then, I asked, "What's in the file?"

"I'm not sure really," Andreas said, shrugging his massive bulk. "Reports, information. Hopefully, I can find out who it was that informed on me."

"Do you really want to know that? What if it turns out to be someone close to you, or someone you care about or respect?"

"Well, Smit, that was the society we lived in. But I know what you mean. That's why the files have to be protected and not made public, so that each person can deal with theirs on their own."

"I don't know, Andreas," I said. "If I have a file, I'm not sure I want to see what's in it."

"Better you than someone else."

He heaved himself from the chair and placed the piece of paper on the edge of my desk. We exchanged a glance where we both asked each other what had gone wrong with our friendship. How had we gone from being great friends to passing acquaintances? I knew the answer, but didn't have the courage to say it.

"Think about it," he said. "And tell Kathrin, though I'm sure she knows."

\*\*\*

On the fifteen of January, the government made an appeal on the radio in an attempt to prevent a violent demonstration at the Stasi headquarters.

"The democracy that is just beginning to develop is in great danger. The government of the GDR appeals to all citizens in this critical hour to stay calm and collected."

Kathrin and Monica went with Andreas and Birgit while I stayed home with Jennifer. We played language games to pass the time. I would say a word in German and she had to translate it. When it was her turn, she had to describe something in English, until I gave her the German word. Her English was better than kids twice her age, and her German was better than mine. I still made terrible mistakes with the articles. These always made Jennifer laugh. She believed I did it on purpose, that it was a joke.

They arrived at the apartment in early evening, all pale and shocked, each wanting to describe what had happened, interrupting and talking too fast. I gave everyone a glass of vodka to calm them down.

"Everything was fine at the beginning," Kathrin said, declining the vodka. "But then this large group arrived and stormed the building, and everyone followed."

"I think they were right-wing extremists," Birgit said. "They were so violent."

"Anybody hurt?" I asked.

"We left when it started to get dangerous," Andreas said. "A file isn't worth dying for."

243

"They were like an army the way they went in," Monica said. "So organised. They're occupying the building as we speak."

"I guess that means all the documents are safe," I said.

Andreas nodded. "Or at least destroyed."

Once they had calmed downed, we enjoyed a quiet dinner together. Andreas and Birgit left early while Monica stayed the night. Since Heinrich's death, she had avoided her apartment, spending more and more time in West Berlin.

That night, Kathrin and I lay in bed reading. The buzz of the doorbell startled us. We looked at each other, confirming that we both had heard it and didn't want to get up to answer it. But then it buzzed again. I hauled myself out of bed, went out to the balcony and saw Rudi standing in the shadows of the front doorway, stamping his feet for warmth. He looked over his shoulder and reached out to press the bell again. I pulled on a jacket and went downstairs.

"Evening, Rudi," I said. "It's a little late, but still nice to see you. Where have you been? You weren't at Heinrich's funeral."

Rudi nodded. He looked old and worn. "Sorry. The last few months have been terrible, work-wise."

He paused, then reached inside his trench coat, pulling out a large brown envelope.

"What's this?" I asked as he handed it to me. I started to open it.

"No. Not here," he whispered harshly, looking around quickly. "Do it somewhere private, where no one else can watch you."

"Okay."

Rudi nodded again. "And destroy it if you want. In fact, I recommend it."

He looked past me through the open doorway, making sure no one was there. I turned around to see if anyone was there and when I turned back, Rudi was walking away.

"Rudi," I called out, but he kept walking, crossing the street quickly. He pulled up the collars of his coat and disappeared into the darkness of the Volkspark Friedrichshain.

I looked at the envelope as I climbed the stairs. It was heavy, full of paper, and I could feel some kind of metal clip that bound it all together. I slid it into my briefcase and climbed back into bed.

"Who was it?" Kathrin asked.

"Rudi."

"You're joking? What did he want? Where has he been?"

"He was just passing by and wanted to say hello and see how we're doing."

"Why wasn't he at the funeral?"

"Had to work."

"I never liked him," she said, closing her book with a snap.

We kissed and turned off our lights.

Kathrin spoke in the darkness. "I always thought he was a Stasi."

\*\*\*

The next day, when the last class had finished, I closed the door and sat down at my desk, staring at the brown envelope. All day I had thought about it. Was it my file or Kathrin's, or maybe the file of Andreas? Rudi had always asked about him.

I took out the file. It was dirty yellow and bound tight by a metal clip. In the centre, written in black pen, was "Carlos, the Bicycle Teacher." I stared at the file, debating whether I wanted to see what was inside or if I should just walk away from it. But the curiosity was overpowering, and I turned the cardboard cover.

There was a copy of the front page of my passport, copies of forms I'd filled out when I'd first passed through Checkpoint Charlie. There was also a photograph stapled to these forms of me standing at the immigration counter inside the building. I knew by my pants that it was taken on my third day in East Berlin; the day after I'd met Rudi at the barbecue. There was a long profile that clearly outlined my personality, likes and dislikes, right down to the question mark about my sexuality because of my connection to Thomas. Had they watched me in West Berlin as well? There was a separate file of letters: copies of ones I had written to Kathrin, letters she had written to me, and others my family had sent, or tried to send. Paragraphs were marked, sentences underlined and comments written in the margins. There were transcripts of recorded conversations with Rudi, and sometimes with Andreas or Kathrin, represented as A and K. And so many photographs, as if this was the personal history of my life in the GDR. There was a picture of me crossing at Glienicker Brücke, sitting in a meeting of New Forum, teaching a class, skating on Müggelsee, running through the park with Andreas, and countless others. They had watched me the whole time. My private world had

245

been completely invaded. I was the informant who had tormented Andreas. How many other lives had I affected?

There was a picture of Kathrin with Jörn Weise. The light was bad, it was late at night, but I could make out the front door of the building that housed Jörn's office. They held hands going up the front steps.

I slid the file back into the envelope and left the school. The wind was cold against my face as I rode home. Anger and confusion swirled around me and I didn't concentrate on the road. Horns sounded and brakes squealed, but I paid no attention, thinking maybe I was better off ground into the tarmac by a passing car. I detoured into the Volkspark and walked the bike up the Grosse Bunkerberg. I stood admiring the view, waiting for the jogger, who was stretching at the top, to leave and continue his run. I used the concrete wall as a windbreak and set fire to the envelope. It burned slowly and it would have been quicker to burn each piece of paper separately, but I didn't want to open the file again. But the fire did it for me, burning away each layer, exposing each document in turn and photographs that melted and sent chemicals up my nose.

I felt invaded and used.

Rudi had taken advantage of my ignorance, and in exchange had helped me further myself in society. As his final act of generosity, he had brought me this file, giving me the chance to see the truth and destroy it. Slowly, the documents turned to ash and were scattered by the wind. A dog came up next to me and rubbed its cold nose against my foot. He wanted the warmth of the fire. I patted the dog. His coat was damp, cold and slimy. The minute I touched it I wanted to wipe my hands on my jacket. I heard the owner call to his dog and I turned around. He had stopped at the bottom of the last steps, just enough to see the top and the location of his dog. But he didn't look at me, and had eyes only for his dog. The dog ran to him and he turned, his head disappearing down the rise.

I kept lighting the fire until every piece of paper had turned to thin black ash. My hands were cold and I kept putting them into the pockets of my jacket for warmth, but once hands are cold, it's very difficult to make them warm again without hot water. As I rode back down the small hill, I promised myself two things: not to mention my file to anyone, and never to speak to Rudi again.

Down on the street, Lenin frowned at me, his grim face and hollow eyes ordering me to stay in the GDR. How easy it would be just to pack up and go, leave all the lies, secrets, pain and disappointment behind. I stared back at the old communist, searching his carved face for answers. With his pointy beard and chin, he looked more like a pirate, sailing the high seas, stealing and killing, and searching for a land of lawlessness where he could assert his own rule. Is that what I gave up my own country for, a pirate who had hoisted his blood red Jolly Rodger over Russia and Eastern Europe? And now, how quickly were the pirates being swept away by the colonists, with their big guns, heavy treasure chests, and endless promises. And how happy the peasants were that the pirates were one by one being made to walk the plank. Having cheered and supported them for years, they were now laughing heartily and drinking American rum as each comrade fell into the shark invested waters. Pirates, colonists, imperialists, soldiers, priests, communists, capitalists. What did it matter? The people were still dominated, still told how to live, what to wear, what to like and hate, who to worship, what to fight and die for.

"I didn't come here for you," I said to Lenin, my words quickly enveloped by the cold wind. The old pirate ignored me. "I always said it was because of you and your system, but that's a lie. It was the girl."

A crow landed on Lenin's shoulder.

The system was good, I thought, but in the end the people were just like crows. They were scavengers, circling, waiting to pick on the weak and defenceless, but cowering when larger birds were in their midst. The crow will take advantage of you, attack your weaknesses and ignore your cries for help. He will deceive you, take your small bread offering and then squawk and cry that the bread was too dry, too old or not enough. Then, the crow will fly away before you have a chance to respond, and will look for another feeder to deceive.

It was Kathrin, not communism. We tell ourselves lies to make the things we do sound better than they are. How pathetic it was to give up Australia for just a girl. I needed more, my own cause to fight for, the adventurous spirit necessary to jump a pirate ship and sail the uncharted waters. Even in lying, communism made me more than I was.

But the girl was deceptive, taking my meagre offering of bread and soul, then looking elsewhere when what I offered wasn't enough. I remembered her squawks and moans, the lies in the night, screams I believed as real, but which had an emptiness I was too deaf to hear. What fancy bread did Jörn offer? Did he seek her out? Is Kathrin the devil or the victim? The crow that killed the mouse, or the one invited

247

to join the feast? Does it matter? A lie is a lie no matter how it is perpetrated.

Modrow's round table debated this fervently: what to do with the Stasi files? What secrets they hold and how dangerous those secrets could be. Imagine if everyone in my family had been able to see my file? My secrets, my lies. Our lies. They wouldn't believe my plea of ignorance, that I hadn't known. Secret service, spying, surveillance photographs, recorded conversations? This was the stuff of movies, of cheap crime novels sold at airports. It wasn't life.

But the file was gone, my secrets up in smoke and reduced to black ash; my lies cremated and scattered over East Berlin as a memorial to the pain and suffering they had caused. I alone held the truth. I had to decide what to do with it.

Vladimir Lenin, communist hero, in red stone on Leninplatz, at the bottom of Leninallee, my street, in East Berlin, my city. Vlad the Pirate, Vlad the Red, Vlad the forgotten revolutionary. Jump your boat and sail the high seas before the mob cuts off your red stone head and drags it around the city. Escape now. The crows are circling, waiting to pick at your remains, until all trace of your existence disappears.

I stood opposite my apartment, my home, waiting for the traffic light to turn green. Cars rumbled past, trams also, but the smell was different. Potent Trabi exhaust was mixing with the clean exhaust of VWs and BMWs. The brisk winter winds blew clean air from the Baltic Sea and purified everything.

The don't walk man is a soldier. Eight years in this town and I only just noticed. He's a stick figure with a saucer helmet, like all the soldiers and border guards wear. He turned from red to green and I crossed the street. Breaks squealed. A truck stopped just short of me. I looked left and all I saw was the Mercedes star, in gleaming silver and wedged on a radiator grill, inches from branding me.

I heard the driver shout: "What a stupid place for a traffic light."

He glared at me like it was my fault. The driver was stressed. Time was invading East Berlin: use it, make money with it, for God's sake don't waste it. The soldier turned back to red, but I still stood in front of the truck. Its loud and abusive horn sounded and a chorus followed. Cars pulled around the truck and sped down the second lane. Trabis, Wartburgs, Ladas, Beetles, the drivers staring at me as they passed. The truck driver started to get out of his cabin. The soldier turned green and I continued across the road.

"Bloody Ossis," the trucker yelled as he slammed his door and drove through the red light. He didn't even have enough time to argue or fight with me. And there were no police left to ticket him for running a red light.

Upstairs, life was normal. I waited, patiently and quietly, silent through dinner. I was circling, biding my time until Jennifer went to bed. Too many nights I'd stayed awake listening to my parents argue: the drunken slurs of my father, the weak protests of my mother, the abuse, the crying, the occasional hitting, the bruises covered by makeup in the morning, the pathetic remorse of my hungover father as he attempted to make amends. And me? What about me? Didn't they care how it made me feel? My father never waited until I was in bed and safely asleep. He just went for it.

But my sombre mood created a tense atmosphere. I was never very good at being fake. I avoided Kathrin's eyes, turned to stone when she kissed or touched me, and answered her questions like a robot. It was the eye of my cyclone. Savage winds had blown and would blow again after this lull, after the house was secured and its occupants safe from potential harm.

I kept thinking about the ball of life inside Kathrin's stomach; if it would jump out with Jörn's big Hollywood head, look at me with his grey eyes and wonder who the hell I was. It made me sick to think about it. Kathrin wasn't working anymore, as she's due in a couple of weeks. I wanted to smash Jörn's head into a brick wall and leave it for the crows. But I wanted the truth first. I gave this woman my life, gave up everything for her. It couldn't be for nothing.

I closed the door to Jennifer's room. I'd read her a story and waited patiently for her to fall asleep. She slept with her mouth open, on her stomach, like me. The tangled mess of hair and broad shoulders were Kathrin's. She let her hair grow over my floppy ears. My daughter. So peaceful and quiet and innocent. What kind of world will you inherit? You will be old enough to remember, and I hope you don't forget. Hold on to those years that we are now leaving behind, for the world will do its best to erase the memory. Communism will be buried, the people with it, if the west has its way.

"What's with you tonight?" Kathrin asked as I fell into the sofa next to her. She was reading a newspaper Monica had brought over from West Berlin. The pages rustled as she folded it away. "Bad day at school?"

A dilemma: to tell her I know the truth begs the question as to how

I know the truth. Who told me? I would have to lie, say a friend of a colleague saw them together once, or something like that. Perhaps the origin of truth wouldn't be necessary.

"Don't tell me Preller is back?" Kathrin pushed.

I turned to her. Pregnant, nearing thirty, beautiful, my wife, a stranger. I spoke softly, calmly.

"I know about you and Jörn."

Kathrin feigned shock. "What are you talking about?" she stuttered.

I looked at her, wanting to look mean and angry, but I'm sure I only looked sad and pathetic; a wounded dog.

"How did it happen?" I asked, my tone still soft. I wouldn't get angry. I wouldn't yell and wake up Jennifer. "Did he come after you or did you go after him?"

She bit her lower lip. Her cheeks turned red, and tears flowed like a river breaking a dam.

"Is this his baby?"

She shook her head violently. It was a forceful action and I wanted to believe her, but couldn't.

"What happened?"

She sniffed, wiped her eyes with her shirt, and said, "Tatjana was always away, visiting her family in Kiev. Jörn was lonely."

"And you? Were you lonely?"

"No," she said loudly.

I held up my hands to make her stay quiet.

"It was just with New Forum, and everyone respected Jörn so much, and it was exciting, and we believed we could change things." Her voice began to rise. "And you were never there. You thought it was stupid. You never supported what I believed in. And that meant you didn't believe in me. Marriage is about support and helping each other."

"It's also about trust and honesty, and commitment."

"Oh grow up, Michael. Everybody did it. Sex is a form of excitement here. It always has been."

"You don't get it, do you? I gave up everything for you. I haven't seen my family for nearly a decade. I gave up my home to be here with you. And now you throw all that back in my face because you're bored?"

"Don't blame me if things haven't worked out the way you wanted them to. Life is unpredictable. In a couple of months, there'll be no

East Germany. What will you do then? What about Jennifer? Now that you've suffered here, does that mean you'll run away from these problems like you did in Australia? Don't look at me like that. I know your story. You haven't seen your family, so what. All you ever talk about is how much an arsehole your father is. Don't tell me you miss him. And don't make me the reason for your screwed up life. You made all your decisions on your own."

I stood up, threw on my jacket and walked out. Kathrin called after me, but I didn't turn back.

The truth hurts. Kathrin was right. I had run away from Australia, and I had done it willingly. I had made my own bed, my own choices.

I walked the streets. East Berlin was changing. The lights were on, the flags gone. The wall was being torn down and sold to the highest bidder, and the streets hummed with new traffic, new hopes, new lies.

What happened?

Not long ago, I had felt so complete and happy. When did the world go wrong? When did I become a deceived husband? Life used to be so good, and we were young and free, and there was always so much time. No stress, nothing to worry about. A carefree life. What happened to that? My marriage was in ruins, and so was my country. Run away. Forget the problems, the lies, the truth. Leave it all on this side of the planet and hope they stay there. But this wasn't the answer. After leaving Australia, all my problems had come with me. I sought out friendships with Heinrich and Dieter to fill the void left by my own father. I could prove to them I was a good man in ways I could never have done to my own father; all our problems and differences got in the way. Stay. Face it. Make it better. There were more people than just me connected to this mess. People make mistakes.

I crawled back to the apartment. Kathrin was in bed. I climbed in, smelling of cigarettes and beer from the bar I'd wasted some of the evening hours in. Kathrin ignored the smell and took me in her arms.

"It was over a long time ago," she whispered in the darkness. "It was nothing."

No words, just sleep. Tomorrow, life begins again.

\*\*\*

The eighteenth of March was the date for the first free election. Modrow reluctantly accepted nomination for the PDS, which was the new name of the SED. It had been changed to remove the old stigma. Gregor Gysi was elected Chairman of the Party and also had ambitions to win the election, but nobody trusted him or the communists.

It was the Wende, and this meant change, a turn around.

New Forum had lost popularity, mainly because they had successfully achieved everything they had wanted – free elections, travel, disbanding of the Stasi – and now had nothing left to campaign for. The attention was shifting towards the traditional parties, the CDU and SPD. But every party was plagued by allegations of their leaders' involvement with the Stasi. The popular leader of Democratic Awakening, Wolfgang Schnur, was the first big casualty, and his party suffered as a result. Ibrahim Böhme, charismatic leader of the SPD, was forced into resignation by Stasi allegations which were never proven. Whether the accusations were correct or not, the impact was the same. Much to my quiet satisfaction, Jörn Weise was in disgrace. It was proven that he had informed on his own group and other protest groups. The search for informers turned into a witch hunt, and had everyone second-guessing each other. The Stasi files had to be kept secure so that they could be rifled through in the search for truth. But what of the impact of this truth on society? I was glad my file no longer existed. Several teachers from the school had already left because they were known informants.

Lothar de Maiziére was the leader of the CDU. With his main rival party, the SPD, ruined by Stasi accusations and the PDS haunted by its past, he had a clear run to win the election. He was aided by the support of Helmut Kohl. They had the biggest campaign, funded by the west, and the move towards unification became stronger. The GDR was being bought.

De Maiziére was a weedy, button-faced man. He seemed to hold his mouth together firmly and blow out his cheeks slightly, to make his face look bigger and stronger. Standing with Kohl, it was clear who was the big brother and who was the little. The west was powerful and would solve all of our problems with money. The East Germans went for this. At the last Monday demonstration in Leipzig, the banners no longer claimed, "We are the people", but said "We are one people". With the CDU in power, a united Germany would be only a matter of time.

Andreas was now a member of the CDU. He and Birgit had moved to West Berlin.

Monica was living with Hilde and trying to come to terms with her loss.

Jennifer was in strange mood, at once excited about the baby, but also scared as to how it would change our family; she would no longer get all of the attention. She also knew that something had happened in January, when Kathrin and I had attempted to patch up our faltering marriage. Kids aren't stupid.

Kathrin and I slowly put the pieces back together.

Rudi tried to call, but I wouldn't speak with him. Christine had given birth to a boy and I had refused to be the godfather. My explanation to Kathrin was that Rudi and I were no longer friends, that we never had been, and we left it at that.

In the week leading up to the election, there was fervent campaigning. The CDU, well financed and popular, were going all out for total victory. The step from East Germany to Germany didn't seem so far if the leading political parties were the same. Kohl was pushing for unification. He had money, and the west would save us. I tried not to think about the future. Communism was over, and whatever the new system was, changes would have to be made.

On election day, we drove back from the polling station and then detoured to the hospital as Kathrin went into labour. She struggled and thrashed, pushed and screamed, and I silently prayed she wasn't forcing a Jörn-sized head through the eye of needle. The doctor handed me the baby boy. I took it nervously.

Poor kid. Big, floppy ears again. I handed Heinrich to Kathrin and she smiled at me.

"Come on," she whispered. "There was never any doubt."

I slept in the chair next to Kathrin, who slept soundly. A nurse woke me to say the PDS had won East Berlin, but the Alliance for Germany, led by the CDU, had won the election. The GDR had voted itself out of existence.

# Berlin

Money. It had always been something few in the GDR had cared about. The currency was flimsy, and you always got your pay check whether you worked hard or not. With currency reform, the dissolution of the East German Mark, set for the first of July, people were starting to panic. The GDR money was worthless; all of our savings would amount to nothing. East German goods were sold at huge discounts in the weeks and months leading up to the reform. In May, you could buy a Trabant on the spot, but no one wanted one. The market was for used Mercedes, BMWs and VWs, and makeshift used car lots were set up in the old checkpoint car parks. People took all their money from the bank and tried to work the black market exchange in West Berlin, which was ballooning out of control.

I opened an account for my son and deposited two thousand Mark, the limit I would get exchanged one for one in the currency reform. I did the same for Jennifer, moving money from my account to hers. Of the money we had saved, we had three thousand five hundred in my account and the same in Kathrin's, because adults got one for one up to four thousand, while each of our kids had the two thousand limit. This money they would keep, and we could use it for clothes and other things, if need be. We had to be prepared because prices were so high. I thought our savings would evaporate in months, especially because East Germans were only going to earn 65% of the West wage. Older people needed the younger members of their family to explain what was happening, to help them comprehend the changes that were coming swift and fast.

New environmental laws shut down a lot of factories, leaving many without work. Unemployment rose as the desire for GDR goods diminished, closing down many production facilities, and also because it was easy to lean on the west for a handout. They gave you money for doing absolutely nothing. People couldn't believe it.

Everything changed so quickly. The community we had was gone. People locked their doors, counted their change and kept their wallets and purses securely stashed away. They worried about rising rents and unemployment, the closing of day-care centres and the reduction of child support. In this new world, you had to pay for everything, and it was clear that the East Germans would bring nothing to a united Germany other than their own poor selves. They needed to be retrained and re-educated. The westerners thought they were slack workers, unmotivated and lazy.

I couldn't handle it.

The euphoria of unification on the third of October was undermined by all the walls within. East was still east and west still west, and the two wouldn't come together for a long time. When before we had been subject to the SED, now we were subject to the west, to those who controlled the banks and the industry in a monopoly that was similar to how the GDR economy had been. Everything was private now instead of public, but still monopolised. The West Germans were only interested in establishing their way. Everything east was rejected.

With all the changes, nothing really had changed; we just had different leaders.

The old security was gone, replaced with a society circumscribed by fear, with the people constantly subjected to an onslaught of change. The East Germans had trouble adapting, and they looked at each other and wondered how the peaceful revolution had got lost along the way. The reality wasn't what they had envisioned. And they all knew who was going to survive in this new society and who wasn't.

Honecker had resigned on the eighteenth of October, 1989. A year later, the GDR was no more. But there was no time for crying, because time is money, and if you sit down and think for too long, someone else will beat you to the prize.

The two German cultures were very different. The Berlin Wall was gone, but the wall in the head remained. Many East Germans moved west hopeful of high paying jobs and a better life, but were often disappointed. East workers were discriminated against, worked harder but were paid less, and felt the wrath of prejudice. Many gave up and went on welfare. The Wessis held fast to the idea that the Ossis had nothing to offer society. All the old systems were rejected and replaced. Nothing from the GDR made it into the new Germany.

But the people of East Germany had engineered their own fate. The chance for socialism had existed, but it had been given up in exchange for the West German Mark.

I got up every morning and went to work because I didn't know what else to do. Kathrin stayed home to look after Heinrich because there were no places in the limited day-care facilities, Many of the previously state-run centres had closed down, and the places that were still operating had become too expensive. She would have to stay home until he was old enough to go to kindergarten.

Jennifer didn't like her brother at first, but the difference in age meant that two babies weren't in competition. She quickly started to like him, and even helped take care of him.

Kathrin and I had come through our dark patch. I had forgiven her, but I wouldn't forget.

I sometimes saw Andreas. He lived in a house in Zehlendorf and drove a Mercedes. He had lost weight, thanks to visits to an exclusive fitness club, but he wasn't happy. He worked long hours, and the West Berliners frustrated him, always complaining about service and not paying their bills. I would listen to him whine and look at my watch, wondering how much longer I had to sit with him, and calculating how much my time was worth. I missed the old Andreas who had been my best man, who had fallen into the frozen Müggelsee and come out laughing.

Teaching frustrated me. The kids had no discipline, and they were divided by fashion and wealth. I lost interest in my job, going through the old routine with no enthusiasm.

"Give it time," Kathrin said. "We all just have to make a few changes. Take my mother, she's thriving."

Monica was teaching at a school in Wedding and had a boyfriend who I had met several times and didn't like. No one could ever replace Heinrich, and it bothered me that Monica tried to find someone who could. I was still haunted by that last look he had given me in the car outside the Charité and by the things he'd said.

Thilo and his family had moved out to Marzahn, where the rents were cheaper. His metal works VEB had been closed down for environmental reasons and he was having difficulty finding a new job. The last time I saw him was when they moved. He looked depressed. This new capitalist society would make him and his family suffer. The good times were over. He was now just a useless labourer, poorly educated, simple minded and destined to become a welfare leech, and his sons had the same existence to look forward to.

***

Ten years passed in the blink of an eye. The previous ten years had crawled along, each day full and slow. There had always been so much free time in the GDR. Now, I found myself marking tests in the evenings and planning classes on Sundays. In this society, you lived with the constant threat of being without a job. If you had no job, you had no money, and this meant the end of your existence. If you weren't good at your job, you would be fired. Stress and pressure followed you into your sleep, and into arguments with your children and wives. You ignored your neighbours and turned down invitations for dinner, because there just wasn't enough time. There were too many other things to think about.

The government moved to Berlin. The SPD, lead by Gerhard Schröder, was in power now. New buildings were being built, old ones torn down, and the city was being transformed into a capital worthy of Europe's dominant economic power. The wall remained in small sections, but most of it had been chipped away, collected and sold to the highest bidder. It no longer cut across streets or divided families. Large tracks of no man's land remained throughout the city as court cases raged to decide who owned the land. Everything was being rebuilt and renovated. Many old apartment houses in Mitte were painted, standing out now in garish colours of burnt orange and lime green, as if the renovators decided the grey Ossis needed a little extra colour in their lives.

The tourists came in droves. Berlin, once the closed, walled-in city was now the open city. Everything Ossi became kitsch, with our old products and oddities on sale at special stores. The Wessis now wanted little bits of the retro east in their lives, when twenty years ago it had been the opposite.

Pockets of Berlin remained East, still voting for the PDS and trying to live life as before, drinking the old East German beer and buying Ostbrötchen from the bakeries that advertised it. They were clinging to a forgotten time, but became increasingly lost in the great mass that was Berlin. The GDR was a punch line for jokes, an excuse for failed lives.

Everyone longed for the days of before. The Wessis complained about rising rents, the influx of foreigners, the loss of tax exemptions and subsidies, and the useless Ossis. They too had lost their security. Their little island was now part of the big land.

The city remained divided.

"He's an Ossi," people would say. He's not to be trusted, a bad worker, looking for a handout, give him a banana and he'll be your friend.

"He's a Wessi," others would say. He's looking for your weak points, insulting your clothes, buying out your factory, reclaiming his property.

If only the process had been slower, with the people given the chance to explore their new identity. But the East Germans were thrust into a society of kill or be killed, and many of them succumbed to poverty. The simple worker in the GDR had been well off. His job was secure, he had money in the bank, and he had the same opportunities as everyone else. In the new Germany, he was nothing.

A lot of East Germans became Ostalgic, longing for their previous lives: the security, the slow life, the community, the equality. I suffered from this, wishing the clock would go back to the time in the eighties when I thought life couldn't get any better. Now, life had stagnated in the never-ending game of get, use and throw away.

I sat down with my family and we talked about making some changes. It was Heinrich who suggested going to Australia. He wanted to see real kangaroos.

\*\*\*

On the morning of the second of October, 2000, the day before the ten year anniversary of unification, I rode through the city I had called my home for almost twenty years. I rode past buildings I knew and others I didn't recognise, down Mühlen Strasse and past the longest remaining section of the wall. It's painted, signed and chipped, with tourists having no qualms about hacking off a souvenir. I rode over Oberbaumbrücke, with its two medieval towers, towards Treptower Park and past a lone observation tower. Then through the Soviet War Memorial, with its grand statue of the Soviet soldier carrying a small girl while crushing the Swastika with his boot. Quotes from Stalin adorn sculptures portraying the triumphs of socialism. So much fighting, so much death, so much talk, and all for nothing. Quickly through the decrepit suburb of Neukölln, with its dirty streets, cheap shops and thousands of Turkish immigrants. I like to ride here because it is a good reminder of how the west really is; for every dentist in his house in Zehlendorf, there were hundreds of people crammed into decaying one and two room flats in places like Neukölln; families living on welfare with little hope of their lives improving. Down the wide street of Columbiadamm, past an old plane used during the Berlin Airlift, a Rosinen Bomber. Behind the plane, within the fence of Tempelhof Airport, are two abandoned baseball fields. The scoreboards are rusted, the grass overgrown, but on sunny days, you can imagine American troops thirty years ago organising themselves into makeshift teams for want of nothing else to do; because there would be no war, cold or not, it was all just a lot of talk. Up Mehringdamm with its honking cars and crowded streets. Onto what is now called Wilhelm Strasse, then left at Niederkirchner Strasse, where another section of the wall remains.

Familiar territory.

I locked the bike, my new trekking bike with front shocks and more gears than I can count, or need. It was no faster than the bike Heinrich had given me twenty years ago.

This small piece of the wall was suffering from the attacks of tourists. It would soon be chipped away, with only the steel support bars left. I searched the wall, trying to remember where it was, if it was here and not on the other side of the street, where the wall was now marked by a double line of cobblestones in the road.

No, it was here, somewhere.

Perhaps it had been hacked away. A tourist had pocketed the small fleck that has my name on it.

I looked higher, and then I saw it, faded but still clear: Michael Smith 12/6/81. I took my pen and added, to 2/10/00.

# Perth

The afternoon was clear as the plane took off from Tegel Airport bound for London. Berlin stretched out below. The snake was still there, but had been cut and removed in places. Some sections of the former death strip had been left, and were now overgrown with weeds and a dumping ground for old refrigerators and broken sofas. A place to exercise dogs with no guilt as to where they took their shits. This area was still clear from above. The divide between the city remained, even though the physical wall had long been torn down.

The plane rose above the clouds to where the sky was pale blue. We headed west, towards the setting sun, from one home en route to another. I sat alone, drinking vodka from small plastic bottles with screw top lids. Each bottle held barely enough for one glass, so I kept ringing the bell for the toothy stewardess. I lined up the empty bottles like soldiers, the fold down tray my parade ground. I marched them around, ordered their goose-stepping, their boots thumping on the hard plastic. The man in the aisle seat watched me closely.

I kept drinking.

The stewardess appeared, teeth shining, and explained we were preparing to land. She scooped up my soldiers and folded away my parade ground. A swift, decisive movement, the bottles thrown into a plastic garbage bag.

There was a metaphor in there somewhere, but I was too drunk to recognise it.

Heathrow depressed me as I moved through the terminal. It was too bright, too stuffed with stores selling expensive goods. Men in suits pulled small overnight cases and talked loudly into mobile phones. Bleary-eyed tourists read books and moved their boarding cards from one pocket to another in their jackets of a thousand pockets. Children screamed with excitement or cried because they felt tired but couldn't understand why. Lovers were left crying, luggage was lost, visas denied, all manner of strange languages spoken, and all kinds of clothing worn.

I was on auto-pilot.

On the next flight, I didn't line up vodka soldiers. I drank lemonade, sometimes mixed with orange juice. Movies played, but I refused the headset and stared blankly ahead. If I had been in private, I would have buried my head in my hands and cried.

I was thirty-nine. My hair was grey and receding. In a few years, it would all be gone. I had the round softness of a flabby stomach, a body like a milk bottle. Black hairs had appeared on my shoulders. I had to wear glasses when driving a car. Kathrin said they made me look more intelligent, more like a professor. Small comfort for recognisable ageing.

Memories blurred with dreams until the line couldn't be separated.

When had I become so old? In the eighties, we were young and thought we would have that feeling forever. Even when Jennifer was born, I didn't feel so much like an adult. The years passed slowly and I didn't feel them because I was too happy and content. Only in sadness and depression does the time affect you.

Jennifer was about to finish high school, was going to attend Curtain University in Perth, and had grown into a beautiful young woman, the way her mother had been in the beginning; naked by the lake, pure and angelic. Kathrin was now old like me. It was as if we woke up one day and looked at each other wondering who that stranger was, and had to get to know each other all over again, and forget the past, good and bad. She had crow's feet at the corners of her eyes, and when she smiled, her face became heavily lined, the way Monica's had when I'd first met her in Hamburg. Her hair had started to thin until she cut it short in the way businesswomen did. She resembled her mother, and I remembered Monica's naked body by the lake, handsome in its maturity but also sad in its ageing, for it had once been something of great beauty.

At Tegel, Kathrin had told me that before the wall fell, Monica had for many years conducted an affair with a businessman from West Berlin. He had given her D-mark and other presents, and Heinrich had known about it. This was the man Monica had married a few years after Heinrich died. That was what he had meant in the car in front of Charité. He had asked me to be fair, but I didn't know if I could.

But this was already old news, with me the last to know. Monica and Jürgen, will someday visit us in Australia or we may visit them in Berlin. I don't like Jürgen. He's a typical Wessi. At some point, he had enticed Monica with money and west products; buying her love like it was a car in a showroom.

Thomas said he would come, with a new boyfriend no doubt. He was still handsome, but no longer hid his sexuality. Hilde had died five years ago. I found it awkward being around Thomas because he was now so openly homosexual. I couldn't deal with it.

Rudi and Christine were divorced, and had been for almost ten years. Most of Rudi's pay check went to Christine as child support. The new Germany hadn't accepted Rudi so well into society because of his career with the Stasi. A taxi driver was the best he could do. That was a joke in Berlin, that most of the Stasis had become taxi drivers; you only had to tell them your name and they knew where to take you.

Andreas suffered a severe heart attack two years ago. It was a sobering experience and forced him to rethink all his priorities in life. It also made us friends again. He now lives on the Spanish island of Majorca, making a good living from the large numbers of German tourists and residents. Both he and Birgit love the beach life. I miss them dearly and hope they come one day to Australia. Maybe they will retire there.

Retire. God, I feel so old.

And now I sit on a plane, bound for Perth. Almost two decades later. A lifetime.

Heinrich is terribly excited. All he can talk about is surfing and kangaroos and how jealous all his friends are. I hope he adjusts to the life. It won't be easy for him to leave the only world he has known at such a young age.

Kathrin is also keen for the new start. She's been telling me for years to forget the GDR, but I can't. I hold on to that time the way an athlete holds on to the years when he was at the top of his sport. It was the best time in my life, and I need to tell myself this to be sure that I haven't wasted my life, that going to the GDR in the first place was the right decision.

I had come so close. At one point, I'd embraced happiness, surrounded by family and friends and a community where everyone was included. And I'd found something that I believed in with all my heart. My place.

Communism failed the people, this is what we are told to believe. But it's the opposite. The people failed communism. Assuming to have a belief in the positive qualities of man is the one mistake Marx and Engels made with their ideology.

Once, the East Germans were my people, but they anger me now, holding out their hands for government money, staying unemployed, and only complaining about the world when at one time we had banded together and tried to change it. The GDR was a used car. West Germany had bought it, scrapped it and used it for parts. Worse was how close we had come as a nation to a real socialism. That one day, the fourth of November, 1989, when we had gathered in solidarity, only to sell out to the west a week later. A carrot dangled in front of a lame donkey to make it walk.

Kathrin once said to me, a long time ago, that she liked the Berlin Wall, that it was like a security blanket. But even a child outgrows a security blanket, or has it ripped away by someone bigger and stronger, by someone who thinks they know what's best.

The seat next to me is free and I am happy about that. No one is asking me any questions, or looking into my sad eyes and wanting to make me feel better.

I'm scared.

Twenty years is a long time.

I'm different. My parents will be different. There's so much to talk about. They live in a retirement home in Rockingham, south of Perth.

I have a lot to do when I arrive: find a house near the coast, have my interview with the language school, buy a car, start this new life. My family will arrive at Christmas. That gives me four weeks. Kathrin is bubbling with excitement. She thinks Australia is paradise. I hope she is right. Maybe she's just excited about having a fresh start.

*\*\*\**

We land. It's morning and the sky is clear, not a cloud in sight. I put my hand to the small window and feel the warmth of the sun. My head is filled with blurred images of Perth summers: the odd trip to the beach, water restrictions and bushfires. Those sweltering nights when the air wouldn't move, and we would sleep on the back porch and wake up scratching fresh mosquito bites.

Through the window, I can see the grey and yellow smoke of a fire burning in the Swan Valley. I remember going with my father to his brother's house in Pickering Brook, helping move things out of the house while nearby a bushfire screamed and raged. A hot desert wind was blowing from the east. With the car full of the necessary things, the wind swung around and blew from the ocean, and the fire drifted away from the house, burning out in an hour after raging all day. I could still hear the crackle and whoosh of the fire, how it breathed and lived, inhaling dried-out trees, scaring animals from the bushes, and how it had died without a whimper once the wind had changed and blown from the west.

The terminal is air-conditioned. I feel its chill while I wait for my bags. Most of my things are still in Berlin. Kathrin will sell the BMW, sell everything, and we'll start from the beginning in Perth. A new life.

The bags spin around the carousel. People push and struggle, blocking each other's way, not giving space or helping lift heavier bags. They are animals. I stand back and wait. I'm in no rush. My sister's standing on the other side of this wall and I'm nervous about seeing her. She's now almost fifty, an old woman, her son fully-grown and working as an electrician. Is Darren here? What about Narelle's new husband Brian? I've only seen pictures of him. Will I recognise Narelle? We're different people now. What could we possibly have to say to each other?

The doors open and I walk through the barrier. I'd expected some kind of girlish rush, but Narelle simply walks towards me and we hug. She's crying, her lined face puffy and wet with tears. Her hair is more white than blond, and I wonder if she still colours it. She's wearing a dress. Her legs are thick with blue veins bulging around her white calves. The dress is belted in the middle. Her stomach is round. It's difficult to see where her breasts end and her stomach begins. But in this hug we are brother and sister, still children in each other's eyes. We hang on to those images from childhood when we knew that person better than the one we know now.

It's good to see her.

"Look at us," Narelle says smiling. "Aren't we old?"

"You look fine, sis." I have a thick lump in my throat. "You haven't changed a bit."

"Come on," she says, starting to walk for the door. "I'm parked in a five minute zone."

From the international airport, we drive through the industrial area around Kewdale and Welshpool. It's not the best introduction to a city, and I feel like a foreigner. The streets are wide and crowded with trucks and vans. Every second building is a petrol station. Large warehouses are surrounded by high fences with guarded gates.

This area hasn't changed.

I'm overdressed. Narelle's car is an old Toyota that has no air-conditioning. The seats are vinyl and I can feel the sweat collecting around my thighs, sticking my legs to the seat. The open window only lets in hot air.

Narelle and Brian live in a two-story townhouse in the fashionable suburb of Como. We get there by taking Mill Point Road, which runs along the south side of the river and offers a wonderful view of the skyline. The grass in the parks is lush green and the trees are tall and old. I'd forgotten what a beautiful city Perth is, or perhaps I'd only ever known another Perth, ugly and dry and poor, a place to leave and never return.

Narelle explains that she works as a secretary at a real estate office in Victoria Park. Brian has his own mobile landscaping company. She leaves me at her townhouse to sleep and goes to work. To live in this townhouse means they're doing well. A secretary and a gardener.

I sleep two hours, then have a shower.

It's lunch time.

With some help from the Transperth hotline, I figure out which bus to catch and where to catch it. The trip to Rockingham takes an hour.

I'm in a daze.

It's a long walk from the bus station to the retirement home. It's close to the beach and the smell of salt is carried on the cool afternoon breeze. Overhead, seagulls circle and squawk. The retirement home looks new and has a brick wall around it. I have to ring a bell at the gate to be let in.

I know my parents' apartment by the old Ford in the driveway. A different car, but same license plate.

I stare at the door. In front of it is a thick metal security screen. The windows have the same thick metal screens.

I ring the bell. My heart's in my mouth as a stooped old woman answers the door. Her face is tanned, with brown and white points from a lifetime spent in the sun. A smile reveals false teeth and she catches a single tear with a pink hankie. The lock on the screen door clicks. I pull the door open.

"Hi, mum."

I embrace her. She's thin and bony, light as a feather. I wonder if I hugged her too hard, I might crush her.

"Is that you, Mick?" a cracked voice calls out.

Mum sets her mouth firm to stop herself from crying. "Don't excite him," she says, grabbing me by the shoulders. Her hands are small and withered. "My God, I can't believe it's you."

She locks the screen door and the front door behind me. The locks have resounding clicks, like the slamming of a prison door. The apartment is warm and musty. An oscillating fan whirrs in the living room in front of the television. When the fan hits my father, it blows his shirt open a little so I can see his thin white chest. His hair comes out of his head in single strands. I can see large brown moles and white points on his scalp. His ears are large and sagging, like the rest of his face. The smile takes considerable effort. He tries to stand, but can't, so we shake hands with him still sitting.

"Jesus, Mick," he says. "Except for ya hair, ya haven't changed a bit."

"You either, dad."

"Bullshit. I'm better than ever."

I laugh, and so does he.

It's like waking from a long sleep, finding the world older, but not so different.

"It's good to see you both," I say after a short silence.

"We never thought you would come back," mum says. "What with your family there and all. Oh, I can't wait to meet Kathrin and Jennifer and Henry."

"They'll be here at Christmas. I think the weather'll be a bit of a shock, though. I'm gonna try to find a house out near the beach."

"Don't live here," dad says. "Nothing but bloody teenagers and drug addicts."

"I'll be looking up near Scarborough."

"Had enough of Maddington, eh?"

Dad was old, but his eyes were still sharp. His bottom lip quivered when he talked, and his hands shook when he wasn't gripping the arms of the chair, but the brain was still working. This weak old man could still find a way to hurt me.

"Kathrin wants to live near the beach," I say, with what I hope is conviction.

"And how's Berlin?" mum asks, trying to prevent an argument.

"Not what it used to be."

"Nothing is," dad says, and he stares at the spinning blades of the fan. "But I warned ya that the worker's state couldn't work."

He's right. I hate him for it.

***

Weeks pass. Christmas comes and goes. School starts. I still feel like I'm on auto-pilot.

One Saturday night, we arrive home from dinner at Narelle's townhouse. Darren was there with his wife Lisa. She's pregnant.

266

Kathrin and Darren had argued about how women are treated in Perth. Darren couldn't comprehend that a woman would even stand up to him. Lisa never did that, yet Kathrin was in his face, having grown up in a country where women were completely equal. I tried to explain to her on the drive home that Darren was a product of his society, like she was, with Lisa as much a victim of society as Darren. They can't be held fully responsible for the way they are, because men and women have different roles here. Kathrin tried to understand.

In just a few months, she has become increasingly frustrated with the people in Perth. The society is too old fashioned and traditional, she says. I explain to her that Perth suffers from its location. It doesn't have enough contact with other cultures and remains provincial. She compares it to isolated villages she had visited in the Soviet Union.

But how she loves the life by the beach. Henry has taken to surfing, and Jennifer is a member of the local surf lifesaving club. The boys line up to take her out. My family has blossomed here, though we don't have many friends. Our accents and manner are suspicious, and we still talk German together. The people here still hold a grudge with Germans. It's pathetic. They hear me speaking the language and hold me responsible for atrocities committed sixty years ago.

At home, I close the door to the garage and walk down the drive to close the gate. The wind rustles the trees and smells of salt. I hear the comforting lapping sound of the ocean, like a shell held permanently to my ear. The house has a high fence around it, the gate as tall as the fence. I lock the gate with a padlock. Through the iron bars, I see a dark car cruise past. The engine rumbles, and the alloy wheels shine in the streetlight. Four pairs of eyes look at me as the car slows to a crawl. Are they judging me or the strength of the gate? The car disappears down the street, the brake lights come on, and the car stops in front of the house two doors down. I know that family is away on holiday; I saw them drive away with their caravan yesterday, but I don't know their name. The neighbours here keep to themselves.

Four car doors slam.

I turn and walk inside my house. I switch off the front light, lock the screen door, lock and bolt the front door, and sit down in front of the television with my family. The news describes a bushfire that raged near the eastern suburbs only to be blown out by a fresh wind from the west. The soft wail of a house alarm can be heard through the closed windows. Kathrin speaks, but I don't hear her.

I'm standing on Alexanderplatz. The weather is cold, but the atmosphere is warm. Speakers take the podium and raise the call for free elections, unrestricted travel, East German sovereignty, and an end to the Stasi. The people have spoken. Socialism will win in the end, but only when the people have evolved enough to accept the compromises that result in everybody getting an equal share; when they have lost their selfishness, jealousy and greed. But I will never see this. I am not a communist. History has shown that the system cannot work. The people aren't worthy of it. That time has already been forgotten, though America still gloats; former President George Bush even planted a chunk of the Berlin Wall outside CIA Headquarters, like it was some kind of war trophy. Such arrogance. Never is a thought given to all those who lived in communist countries and had their identities and histories swiped away from them, swapped by politicians for Coca-Cola and McDonalds.

In a few years, my accent will become more Australian and people will stop asking questions. I'll forget the GDR just like everybody else.

But in my dreams, I ride my clanking bicycle home from school early in the afternoon. Kathrin and Jennifer are waiting for me at home. They smile as I come in, and tell me to hurry as I change clothes. With the working clothes off, I forget that I am a teacher. We pile into the Trabant and drive out to the Müggelsee. We stop to buy drinks. Andreas and Birgit are bringing the meat. Heinrich will man the barbecue, and Monica has made salads. It's a warm July day. The sun is high and won't go down until around ten. We will swim, eat, drink and lie in the sun. There will be others there, people we don't know who will join us, and we will offer them what we have and they will do the same. Someone will have a radio and we will listen to RIAS. The kids will dance on the sand. Adults will get drunk and fall asleep. Teenagers will sneak off into the bushes for some fun. The sun will go down and shimmer on the lake. Boats will cruise past and we will hear laughter and music. We'll wave if they see us. We'll make a fire and huddle around it wrapped in blankets, finishing the last of the alcohol, inviting anyone who passes to join us. Jennifer will sleep on my lap and I'll marvel at her angelic face which I'd had a part in creating. She was mine. Everything was mine. And after everyone has fallen asleep or gone home, I will sit and stoke the fire, watch the burning embers, and listen to the gentle lapping of the tiny waves on the sand.

# Travel Page (cont.)

Printed in Great Britain
by Amazon

39087949R00160